THE
BLACK SWAN
EVENT

— THE AMERICA, INC. SAGA —

MIKAEL CARLSON

WARRINGTON
PUBLISHING

Danbury, Connecticut

Novels by Mikael Carlson:

– The Michael Bennit Series –

The iCandidate

The iCongressman

The iSpeaker

The iAmerican

– Tierra Campos Thrillers –

Justifiable Deceit

Devious Measures

Vital Targets

Revealed Secrets

Decisive Endgame

– Watchtower Thrillers –

The Eyes of Others

The Eyes of Innocents

The Eyes of Victims

– America, Inc. Saga –

The Black Swan Event

Bounded Rationality

Boiling the Ocean

BLACK SWAN EVENT:

A random, unforeseen incident that has a profound influence and whose significance is only understood after it has happened. People in power then rationalize the occurrence, who claim it should have been predictable, although if the event could have been anticipated, it would have been.

The metaphor comes from the early belief that swans of that color did not exist. "Black swan" is thus representative of the prevailing attitude that events are foreseeable after studying the warning signals of them in hindsight. "Black" also denotes the negative consequences associated with most of these types of events.

For mom, the most loving and caring woman you will ever meet.

CHAPTER ONE

LIBERTEUM

Commercial District 2B5
Secaucus Municipal Corporation

The small box on the dashboard beeps, causing the five men in the utility van to jump. They nervously stare at the LED lights flickering on the unit as they enter the tunnel. Haven takes a deep breath. After years of planning this operation, it's terrifying to think that success or failure hinges on this black transponder.

"That thing had better work," Nyvar says from the driver's seat.

"It will," Haven says, far less sure than his voice sounds.

"We'll know soon enough if it doesn't," Jasper says from the back, a computer balancing on his lap. "If that thing isn't transmitting the correct code, we'll have a welcoming party waiting for us on the other side of the river."

Haven forces himself to relax. He's been on edge since they left their Hell's Kitchen motor pool. New York may have the most magnificent skyline on the planet, but he lives his life underground now. This tunnel is closer to home than anything else he'll experience on this mission.

"Here we go," Nyvar says, gripping the wheel tighter.

Everyone holds their breath. Scivix checks for the tenth time that a round is chambered in his rifle. All five men are armed, not that the pair of hackers will be of any value in a firefight. Adiz and Jasper would be nothing more than additional targets for Public Safety and Security to shoot at.

Traffic is light in the tunnel at this hour. There will be no warning if the transponder fails and the barrier is closed. Fortunately, nobody is waiting when they emerge back under the inky blanket of the night sky. Haven exhales as they clear the tunnel exit without incident.

"You know how to get there, right?" Haven asks his driver.

"You didn't bring me along for my looks."

"You need to slow down, Nyvar," Adiz whines from the far back. "I can't disable the cameras fast enough."

Nyvar glances over at Haven, who shakes his head. They are on a strict timetable. The whiny hacker will need to work faster.

"I'm serious. I can't disable them fast enough."

"Quit your bitchin', Adiz. You have one job to do. Do it," Haven commands.

Nyvar guides the van down an exit ramp off the main road. He turns left and heads past one of the countless data centers occupying this street. Haven checks his watch. They're less than five minutes from their target.

"Talk to me, Jasper."

"I looped the feeds of the three cameras covering the building. That's all I can do remotely. We need to be on-site to isolate their IP addresses and take control of the monitoring system. It will register as active, but I can suppress all reporting back to the PSS."

"Then don't waste time talking to us."

Jasper nods as Nyvar pulls the van into the office building parking area and guides it around back. Scivix follows the hacker out the back, his rifle at the ready.

"Give me the rundown, Scivix."

"Two guards on shift alternate going on rounds at the top and bottom of every hour. They take eleven minutes to complete. The second guard should return to the security desk in four minutes."

"No mistakes, Scivix. And zero body count."

He nods and closes the back door before Nyvar drives off. Their first target is less than a quarter-mile up the street. This part of Secaucus was a commercial area before the Great Collapse. It hasn't changed much, other than adding more data centers to house corporate information technology operations.

Nyvar pulls up to the intersection, and Haven checks up and down the thoroughfare. There are still no conveyances on the streets at this hour. The first hint of dawn on the horizon means they're about to lose the comfort that darkness provides.

"Adiz?"

"Street cameras within a half-mile radius of each junction are inoperative. They're blind."

"Good. Let's go, Nyvar. The clock's ticking."

The men make quick work of their first and second objectives, a half-mile apart from each other. With two-thirds of the mission accomplished, they circle back to the intersection.

"Last one. Let's go."

The two men exit the vehicle and hustle to the black roadside box that houses the underground communications utilities. They could target the power conduits a dozen feet away and blackout all of Secaucus from here, but that defeats the point of what Liberteum is trying to do.

Nyvar pops open the panel as Haven digs through his duffle bag. He activates the remote detonator for the brick of plastic explosives and sets it in the cabinet. It's the smallest of the three but will do the job.

Flashing blue strobes bathe the area in light. Haven curses under his breath. He never heard them pull up.

Nyvar reaches for his weapon, and Haven shakes his head. "Last resort only."

Haven turns to the PSS guardian, who greets him by shining a torchlight in his face.

"Lower it a bit, will ya?" he says, shielding his eyes. "Good morning. What can I do for you guys?"

"We have reports of cameras being out in this area. Do you know anything about that?"

"Yeah, we were dispatched here to fix them."

"I see. Playing a little fast and loose with the municipal corporate dress code, aren't you?"

Haven rubs his unkempt brown beard and looks down at his clothing. Liberteum managed to procure two sets of standard-issue utility coveralls and vests. He wasn't concerned about grooming since this was an early morning operation and didn't expect interruptions.

"I've been working long hours. We've been experiencing outages all over the grid the past couple of weeks."

"Mmhmm. Can I see your work order?" the guardian asks.

"Sure. The tablet is in the van."

One of the guardians keeps a watchful eye on Nyvar as his partner accompanies Haven over to the driver's side of the vehicle. He moves as slowly as he dares without looking like he's stalling for time. Adiz had better be doing his job.

Haven opens the door and pulls a tablet out of the center console. He turns and hands it to the guardian with a pleasant smile on his face.

"Here ya go."

The guardian taps the screen. Nothing happens. He cocks his head to the side to look for the power button. He glances up at Haven and finds himself staring down the barrel of a gun. Haven squeezes the trigger and sends the round through the guardian's forehead and out the back of his skull. Another shot from behind the van rings out. Haven moves quickly to peek around the back. Nyvar stares at him, standing over the body of the second guardian.

"We need to move fast. The PSS will respond in minutes once they notice that the biojacks aren't broadcasting," Adiz announces from inside the van.

"What do you want to do with the bodies?"

"Load them in their conveyance. The explosions will take care of them."

Haven climbs into the passenger seat and turns to face Adiz. The hacker tries to avoid eye contact.

"What the hell, man?" Haven asks.

"The guardians weren't broadcasting on the network. I had no way of knowing they were there until they triggered their lights."

"You almost got us killed."

"It wasn't my fault!" the hacker argues.

Nyvar climbs in and slams the door. He fires up the van and pulls a U-turn before flooring it. The three men share the hope that Scivix secures the building without incident. They'll be toast if he doesn't.

"Bring it around back to the loading dock," Haven commands after the driver veers into the parking lot and stops at the front door.

Haven jumps out and walks to the entrance of XQ Systems as Nyvar speeds away with Adiz. He is comforted by the cold steel of his rifle as he reaches the door. Their research indicated this is a seldom-used satellite office for the technology subsidiary. Security should be the only issue, and a new shift will arrive at noon. Haven hopes to be long gone by then.

"Building secure," Scivix says, wearing a security guard's uniform and sitting behind the desk in the foyer. "Jasper hacked the Maester system and suppressed alerting. The two guards are restrained in their office."

"Good. Help Adiz and Nyvar unload the gear."

Scivix does as instructed. Haven races up the three flights of stairs to the building's roof access. He climbs the ladder and pushes the hatch open when he reaches the top. It's dawn, and a stream of pulsing blue lights converges on the target area from three directions. Haven checks his watch and frowns. It's almost seven. Waiting any longer will jeopardize the mission.

He moves across the roof to the north, careful to stay close to the sizable solar panel array. There is a nice view of the New York skyline off his right shoulder. The sun is coming up from behind the skyscrapers, silhouetting them. Part of him misses seeing sunrises and sunsets. Even their beauty isn't worth living a life in a corporatist society.

"Here we go," Haven murmurs after fishing the detonator from his cargo pocket.

He flips up the guard and presses the button. A split-second later, three fireballs less than a mile away erupt and belch flames into the early morning sky. The farthest detonation is the brightest as the ruptured gas main sends a massive column of fire high into the air. The shockwave from the nearest explosion hits him first, followed by the rumble of the soundwave.

Haven closes his eyes and enjoys the sensation. His work is done for the time being. What happens next is up to Jasper and Adiz. His focus needs to shift to getting them back into Manhattan alive. That's easier said than done. Hundreds of guardians and Bureau of Corporate Security agents will be flooding into the area now.

CHAPTER
TWO

INTERCORPEX

Intercorpex Hall of History
Manhattan Financial District
ICX New York Exchange

Lyris checks his perfect blond hair and straightens his tunic one last time. He enters the security foyer and struggles to force a smile as the small group of eight passes through the virtual screening. Patricians, especially those who recently joined their ranks, are not known for their patience.

"Good morning, ladies and gentlemen, and welcome to Intercorpex. My name is Executive Director of Global Exchange Operations Lyris. I'll be giving you a tour of our New York facility and will answer any questions you might have about global trading."

Now that these newly minted patricians are permitted to use their family names for the first time in generations, they're all eager to introduce themselves. The reality of their situation won't dawn on them for a few more months. While they may have ascended into the ranks of the *gentez-minorez*, they're the small fish in that pond. The *gentez-majorez* call the shots within the ranks of the global elite.

"They're all cleared, sir," the uniformed ICX security guard says. At six feet tall and two hundred fifty pounds of pure muscle, he's the smallest of the three men working at the Wall Street visitors' entrance checkpoint.

"One quick administrative note before the tour begins," Lyris says, clamping his hands together. "This is a controlled-access facility. Please don't misplace your holographic badges or get separated from the group. You'll find the reaction to either occurrence less than accommodating. With that unpleasantness out of the way, please follow me."

Lyris hates doing tours. Specialized teams of trained employees handle most corporate visits to the facility. The administrator-general of Intercorpex feels that someone with a more impressive title should host patricians out of respect for their station. As the highest-ranking person in the building, that burden falls on Lyris.

The administrator-general doesn't care if Director Lyris thinks it's beneath his role. He's only responsible for the trading operations at the global stock exchange's three locations where billions of Bytecoin trade hands every day.

"Much of the Intercorpex Network Operations Center was built following the incorporation of the exchange in 2044," Lyris explains, passing through an arched entrance into a vast hall. "This facility encompasses two of the three buildings that used to hold the New York Stock Exchange, including Eleven Wall Street, with its recognizable façade. Of course, we made a significant number of modifications.

"This is History Hall. We start with the origin of world stock exchanges, beginning with the Buttonwood Agreement—signed under a buttonwood tree by twenty-six brokers in 1792, only a hundred yards from this very location. Before requiring more space, those early brokers operated out of the Tontine Coffee House for twenty-five years. In 1865, they moved into the building where you now stand."

The patricians are reasonably interested in the holographic images on the walls depicting the history of stock markets. One casualty of the global economic collapse was a collective understanding of world events. Now, corporations teach whatever they feel is pertinent for their future employees, or in some cases, little at all.

"The widespread use of the telegraph led to market consolidation and New York City's dominance over Philadelphia as a major economic hub. Buyers purchased shares of corporate stock via an auction format. For most of the twentieth century, it was a manual process with transactions printed out on a ticker tape machine like this one."

Lyris pauses at the pedestal with the ancient-looking device protected under a glass shroud.

"With the advent of television and computers, these machines were no longer necessary. Digital mediums relayed market information and executed orders far faster. Information flowed freely, and new ways of making money through high-frequency trading and dark pools became en vogue in the early part of this century."

Lyris reaches the end of the corridor and moves through another arch into a second large hall. Dim lighting reflects the gloomy mood of the space. The imagery of hopelessness and human suffering is depressing.

"The journey to get to where we are in March of 2088 wasn't an easy one. This is the Hall of Horrors. It showcases all the major crashes and economic events stock markets endured up through The Great Collapse. The first notable event is the Panic of 1907, where the stock market lost half its value."

The patricians amble down the curved hall, whose marble walls grow steadily darker in color until becoming pitch black at the far end. The architects who designed this museum knew how to get the point across.

"One of the worst events was when the stock market lost more than a quarter of its value in two days in 1929," Lyris continues. "That crash led to a ten-year Great Depression. The mini-crash of 1997 and the downturn after the terrorist attacks on the World Trade Center on September 11th, 2001 are other traumatic examples."

They pass holograms of planes hitting the two World Trade Center buildings and vivid imagery of their collapse. Lyris finds it hard to conceptualize that level of violence today. There are occasional minor attacks from societal outcasts in the corporate-controlled world, but only in the Middle East can anything comparable to the old world be found.

"All of those events pale compared to what would happen in 2039. After a half-century of governmental mismanagement, ballooning debt, and fiscal irresponsibility, the world economy could no longer shoulder the burden. On March 14th, after decades of rampant deficit spending, the United States of America defaulted on tens of trillions of dollars of debt, and the world plunged into chaos.

"What followed was the darkest period in human history. Politicians were dragged from their homes and executed in the streets during the Cleanse. Cities around the world burned to the ground. The United States government collapsed, and the rest of the world's governments fell in the following months. Hundreds of millions of people perished worldwide through violence and starvation. Everyone else survived any way they could.

"Governments were gone. Militaries and police forces were disbanded. Society descended into anarchy after services broke down. There was one small glimmer of hope in the darkness. Several large corporations jumped into action, if only on a small scale."

The darkness yields to the dancing flame from the struggling flicker of a holographic candle at the end of the corridor. If there is any part of the tour Lyris likes, it's this one. He turns sharply to the right and stops at a set of thick black monolithic doors with no handles or visible opening mechanisms.

"Corporations had the workforce, infrastructure, and leadership to fill the vacuum the collapse of nations created. First in the United Kingdom, then here in the United States, they began restoring order by providing basic human needs: food, shelter, and safety. Their intervention gave birth to a new age and brought light to an otherwise dark world."

The computer monitoring the tour acknowledges the phrase "dark world" and sends a command to the server that opens the massive doors. The brightest white light imaginable pours into the dark corridor from the room beyond.

"Ladies and gentlemen, welcome to Genesis Hall," Lyris says with outstretched arms as everyone's eyes adjust. "This great space is Intercorpex's tribute to the corporations that brought us into existence and whose shares trade on our exchange every day. Feel free to walk around."

Lyris watches the patricians marvel at the sight of holographic displays depicting the corporate takeover of governance, the rebuilding of infrastructure, and the restarting of the global economy. Five minutes later, he escorts them up a grand staircase to the mezzanine level and onto the balcony overlooking the NOC floor.

On the opposite wall are three massive super-nano LED displays streaming critical information about exchange operations for consumption by the staff below. Smaller ones below and on each side of the video wall stream various worldwide news channels. Below them are three long bank workstations where uniformed analysts monitor every aspect of exchange operations.

"Welcome to the Global Network Operations Center," Lyris announces with the enthusiasm of an AME TV game show host. "We call it the NOC, and it's the beating heart of Intercorpex. You may recognize the room below us as the trading floor of the old New York Stock Exchange. We preserved the original character of this historic room to the extent possible."

"Do the trades happen here?" one of the patricians asks.

"No, this may be the heart of the exchange, but our matching engines are its brain. Hundreds of millions of shares change hands through Intercorpex every day. Those orders pass through here but are matched and fulfilled at our ultra-secure data center across the river in Secaucus. The information is transferred back and forth via high-speed fiber optic cables."

"Do the other locations have setups like this?" a Japanese man asks.

"Not quite. The Frankfurt and Beijing centers monitor local exchange systems. The global NOC monitors everything. Intercorpex operates twenty-four hours a day, seven days a week, every single day of the year. Since our inception, we've always been available for trading, and we take great pride in that fact."

"Has there ever been an outage that ceased trading?"

"Intercorpex has never closed since it began trading on October 1st, 2045. It's a streak that will never be broken on my watch."

The patricians nod as they marvel at the sight before them. None of the people in this group will be active traders, and what trades they make will mainly be in the subsidiary market. The *gentez-majorez* has a near-monopoly on trading shares of parent companies.

That hasn't always been the case. Militaries no longer exist, so corporations draw their power from economic prosperity. Intercorpex's power comes from the authority to delist for noncompliance. If a parent or subsidiary corporation gets delisted for a transgression, it's a death sentence. Executives will no longer provide for their employees, and others will step in. The Patagonia Corporation came into existence because Intercorpex delisted its predecessor following a dispute with the Central American Corporation.

Bright white strobes set into the walls around the NOC begin flashing. It's an unmistakable signal to anyone in the room that something is amiss. Lyris turns in time to see Norilah materialize behind the group.

"I apologize, ladies and gentlemen," he says. "Some urgent business requires my immediate attention. It's my pleasure to introduce you to Manager Norilah. She will complete your tour this morning."

CHAPTER THREE

AMERICA, INC.

Chief Guardian Teman's Domicile
Upper West Side Geographic District
New York City Municipal Corporation

Chief Guardian Teman stares at the elevator's mirrored wall on the ride up to his floor. He's getting old. Lines appear in the corners of his eyes, and his dark hair shows signs of graying. Some of it is the stress of being the head of New York City's Public Safety and Security. The rest has to do with his rebellious son and inattentive wife.

The door opens into the small foyer. He would never rate the four thousand square foot space with a commanding panoramic view of the Hudson River if not for his lofty position. It's a life of privilege, but one he worked hard to secure.

"Good morning, Chief Guardian," the Maester system announces as he walks through the elevator's open double doors into his Upper West Side domicile.

Teman shakes his head. Maester is equal parts administrative assistant, home automation system, guard dog, and snitch. Every employee in America Incorporated despises the system because of its relentless nagging and dominion over everything they do. His distaste for the intrusive system is why he hasn't given it a nickname, as many employees do.

"I didn't expect you back home this morning," Ilaria observes, rising from the couch to give her husband a peck on the cheek.

"We had a problem up in the Bronx. It's been handled, so I thought I would stop in before heading back to One Guardian Plaza."

That's all Teman dares say. The Maester system does more than inform him when the refrigerator's water filter needs replacing. It's a live-in spy that reports on employee behavior – the higher a worker's position, the more stringent the controls. Transgressions considered by the software as subversive or treasonous get reported to the PSS before being forwarded to human resources. In extreme cases, the Bureau of Corporate Security is notified.

"Where's Rykos?" Teman asks, adjusting his tunic as he sits on the sofa.

"Dinsmore. Where else would he be?"

"His modules don't start for another hour. He's hanging out with Balin, isn't he?"

"They're best friends, Teman. It's not against any corporate rule to spend time together."

Teman frowns. "Ilaria, you're still responsible for him for a few more months. If he gets into trouble...."

He doesn't bother finishing the statement as she rises and moves into the kitchen area. Ilaria knows the deal. When employees have a child, one of the members must leave the workforce to assume a full-time parenting position. America pays a homemaker to raise the next generation of workers.

In most circumstances, the wife assumes that responsibility. Ilaria is responsible for the actions of their children until they come of age and either enter undergraduate training or become productive members of the workforce. The consequences of parental negligence are severe. Her relaxed attitude toward child-rearing worked fine with their daughter, Varella, but may end in disaster with their rebellious son.

"Put Rykos's location on the main screen," he commands the Maester system.

"Maester, disregard. Teman! What are you doing?" Ilaria demands, stomping back into the living area.

"Your job," he snaps.

"You are *not* checking his biojack."

"I most certainly am."

About thirty years ago, executives in Washington ordered every employee implanted with a subcutaneous transponder to reduce absenteeism and petty crime. Biojacks range from standard versions that transmit geographic location and facilitate financial transactions to advanced models that monitor health.

"My job is to raise our children," Ilaria protests. "Part of that is teaching them right from wrong and allowing them to make their own decisions. You have to trust Rykos to do that."

"I don't trust him and never will," the chief guardian says, shaking his head. "Maester, show me Rykos's location."

Ilaria moves between Teman and the main display in the living room. Despite her petite frame, she manages to block out two-thirds of the map. "Have you ever wondered why you have no relationship with your son? This is why."

"I'm sure it has nothing to do with him being a derelict who bends every rule."

"Were you any different at that age?" Ilaria asks, causing Teman to grimace and shake his head. "He's graduating in a couple of months. After that, he'll be heading to the Ivy League. He needs the freedom to make his own decisions, and you need to let him."

Teman stares at his wife. He was fortunate to end up with her. They first met at a meeting the CEO hosted at Corporate Hall. Her mysterious green eyes and long golden blonde hair captivated him from the moment he laid eyes on her. Ilaria was on the executive fast track in the municipal corporation, and he was a cocky, confident young guardian who stumbled through asking her out. Despite the clumsy overture, she accepted the date, and they've been together ever since.

"Maester, cancel my last command."

"Biojack display canceled," the Maester system informs him as the map behind Ilaria dissolves back into AME programming.

"I have the right to check up on my son just as all parents do," Teman argues. "It's why we have administrative rights to their biojacks."

"You're the chief guardian of New York. You can monitor anyone in the city, but you don't unless you have a reason to. Rykos hasn't given you one."

"Your faith in him isn't warranted," Teman says as Ilaria sits back down on the sofa. "He doesn't take his academics seriously. I pulled a thousand strings to get him and his sister into that Dinsmore Academy. I want my children to have—"

"A better life than we did. I know; you remind us all of that every day," Ilaria moans, flicking her hand in the air.

"Because it feels like everyone forgets. All I've ever asked is for Rykos and Varella to make the most of that opportunity I provided. One did. The other isn't."

"His grades are good," Ilaria argues.

"Not good enough to join Varella at Harvard."

Ilaria shakes her head. Rykos and Varella are oil and water. She followed the path Dinsmore laid out for her and never wavered. Rykos is the exact opposite. He challenges authority and wants to break every rule.

"Varella made her choices. Rykos will make his, even if you disapprove of them. What he does with his life is up to him, not you."

Teman is about to respond when the small tablet affixed to his arm chimes. Ilaria knows the tone from the Real-Time Crime Center when she hears it. She pats him on the leg and heads down the hall toward their bedroom.

"Teman," he says after tapping the display.

"Chief Guardian, we have a situation," the urgent voice on the other end of the VidLynk says. "We need you back here immediately."

CHAPTER
FOUR

REGISTRANT RYKOS

Corporate History Module 343-A-1
Dinsmore Executive Preparatory Academy
New York City Municipal Corporation

All registrants are taught to focus on multiple tasks in a hyper-threading process. While we receive our modules, I regularly check the display mounted in the corner where the Intercorpex Global Index and Global Corporate Subsidiary Index scroll current prices. As executives-in-training, we're conditioned to remain constantly aware of how America Incorporated is performing in the market.

The ticker is showing AME down over seven and falling. AME News isn't reporting anything happening, not that I find the suppression of information surprising. They don't report facts but instead manufacture and polish information for our consumption. I'm just not stupid enough to risk the ire of my instructor and certain disciplinary action by pointing that out.

Dinsmore Preparatory Academy occupies an old building on Manhattan's Upper East Side. With its elaborate stonework, vaulted ceilings, and art deco style, the whole place oozes the prestige that comes with being the New York City Municipal Corporation's premier preparatory school. It caters to registrants on the executive management track. Everyone's goal here is admittance to the Ivy League – the training ground for the highest levels of executives. From there, it's on to climbing the ladder in the world's most powerful corporation.

My classmates aren't friends so much as competitors, with Balin being the exception. Yale, Harvard, Princeton, and the other elite schools have only so many openings. Most major urban centers have preparatory academies filled with registrants running the gantlet to fill one. I'm the exception to the rule. Unlike my sister, I don't give a damn.

"Registrant Rykos?"

My attention snaps back to the front of the classroom. A wave of anxiety washes over me as I suffer Instructor Shaef's withering glare. I never heard his question.

"Yes?"

"Your answer is yes?" Shaef says, sarcasm dripping from his lips to the amusement of my peers. He knows that I'm not paying attention.

Instructors are presenters more than teachers. Their function is to execute blocks of instruction called "modules" using methods and timetables dictated by the corporation. Improvisation or diversions from those lessons is forbidden. It falls on a registrant to learn the material. Instructors evaluate that learning and assign it a measurable criterion that Human Resources uses to assess a registrant's talent and capability to contribute. That will determine a career path for us and ultimately, the rest of our lives.

"Executives are expected to multitask, Rykos. If you can't follow stock prices and focus on items that demand immediate attention, you're going to have a short executive career."

"Apologies, sir."

I don't mean it, but I will do whatever it takes to get Shaef to stop hassling me.

"Rewind the module thirty seconds," he commands Aristotle, the classroom control system. Powerful images captured during the Great Collapse of 2039 are shown on the four-by-eight-foot display that dominates the front of the room. Shaef paces in front of the screen as the images replay.

"Let's try this again. Registrant Rykos, if the people had turned to corporations to govern them sooner, would the crash still have happened? You did read last night's assignment, correct?"

I scanned it more than read it. Page after page of the text talked about how people viewed Carnegie, Vanderbilt, Ford, and other great twentieth-century industrialists and tycoons as "robber barons." It explained how the industrial might of the United States was what won the Second World War, and the government only took the credit. It ended with examples of how politicians demonized corporations for following the inept laws Congress passed early in the century. It was a one-sided portrayal, as most of our history modules are.

"Yes, sir, I did."

"Excellent, then stand and give the class your thoughts."

"The short answer is yes, sir, it still would have happened," I rise and say, to the shock of my classmates. Even Balin buries his head in his hands, and I know that he agrees with me.

Aristotle must be on high alert. The classroom management system does more than play modules—it also monitors for aberrant behavior. Answers given during modules deemed contrary to the corporation's interests are reviewed. The offending registrant becomes a target for closer examination or, in extreme cases, reeducation. Balin's gone through that twice here.

"I think you should explain yourself," Instructor Shaef warns.

I can't stomach having another conversation with my father about how much of an embarrassment I am. One call from Dinsmore will make that an unwelcome reality. I choose my words carefully.

"We cannot exclude the human element. Employees understand the benevolence of America Incorporated because we live under this system. Before the collapse, the democratic government conjured an illusion that the people controlled their leaders. Politicians portrayed corporations as evil monoliths disinterested in the public good. As a result, corporations couldn't ascend to their rightful place without a catastrophic precursor."

Balin smirks, knowing I didn't mean a single word of that. After all the late-night conversations in Central Park, he'd bet his monthly stipend that those words would never slip from my mouth. I don't despise America Incorporated. I only refuse to believe it's as noble as the books or my instructors say.

"Interesting answer, Registrant Rykos. See me after class," Shaef commands before returning to the module. I settle in for a long explanation about the reasons behind the demise of democracy and the superiority of corporatism.

I look back to the corner at the display that got me in trouble in the first place. AME is now down eight points, even on lower volume. I would love to know what's going on right now at Intercorpex's Wall Street operations center.

CHAPTER

FIVE

THE PATRICIANS

Keating Family of the Gentez-Majorez Estate
Greenwich Geographic District
Southern Connecticut Municipal Corporation

Denali takes his responsibilities as head of the Keating family very seriously. Most patricians are content living their privileged lives. They sleep late and preoccupy themselves with various social activities. Denali is an exception to that rule. He is intimately engaged in every family dealing and financial transaction.

He watches the Intercorpex ticker in his study. This is his favorite of all the rooms in this massive Greenwich mansion. It is decorated with his grandfather's finest antiques, and he's never dreamt of modernizing it. The only technology among the volumes of dusty books and ornate woodwork is the display he's staring at.

Denali's long-time butler and faithful confidant swings the study doors open and steps into the room. Abbot refills the china coffee cup from the silver service without a word.

"Do you remember the last time AME was down this much?" Denali asks, gesturing at the display.

"I cannot recall," Abbot says. "You still need to return the call from your financial operation. They're having issues with executing high-frequency trades and sound increasingly desperate."

"I will, Abbot, thank you."

"It's my pleasure, sir," Abbot says before a knock at the door pulls the butler away.

He admits Denali's security commander into the room and assumes a position along the wall. The man with the short haircut stands before his boss, waiting to be addressed.

"What is it, Commander Lacune?"

"There has been a series of explosions in New Jersey."

Denali presses his lips together to stop himself from cursing. If this is what he thinks it is, why didn't his son inform him?

"Confirmed or unconfirmed?"

"Confirmed, sir. We have a video feed from a drone near the area. If I may...."

The commander calls up the information on his tablet and sends it to the large display. The video feed is unmistakable. Emergency response is in place at all three smoldering sites. One of the blasts did a significant amount of damage to surrounding structures.

"Archimedes," Denali mumbles.

"Sir?"

"Nothing. If our data center was impacted, it would explain the high-frequency trading interruption. Has the BCS or Intercorpex contacted us?"

"No, sir."

"Thank you for the information, Commander Lacune. You may return to your duties."

The man nods and returns to Denali's command center on one of the mansion's sublevels. Denali stands and looks around the study. After the global collapse, his grandfather joined other great men in rebuilding society. Families like his, the Covingtons, and the Bettancourts were handsomely rewarded for their sacrifices and successes. Now times have changed, and people have forgotten. That ends now.

"Would you like me to contact the White House for you?" Abbot asks, moving alongside Denali.

"No. Have my helicopter prepped for immediate departure. Contact Shalius Covington and tell him to meet me in Manhattan. I will be spending the next couple of days in the city."

"Of course, sir. Anything else?"

"Yes. Have my son contact me."

"Sir, he's likely indisposed at the moment," Abbot warns as Denali rises from his leather upholstered chair.

"I have no doubt. Leave him a message. Tell him that it's urgent I speak to him."

"Consider it done, sir."

Abbot leaves to make the transportation arrangement and contact his wayward son. Denali looks around this magnificent room, reflecting on the decisions made here in the early days of the recovery. The world has come a long way since those dark days, but they've veered off the path. Now it is up to him to continue his grandfather's tradition.

CHAPTER

SIX

INTERCORPEX

Global Network Operations Center
Manhattan Financial District
ICX New York Exchange

Two workstations built on a raised platform below the balcony give a commanding view of the network operations floor. Each features curved glass displays and desktop space surrounding a captain's chair. Director of New York Operations Wyeth sits in one, staring at a digital timer. Director Lyris races up the metal stairs to the other.

"Forty-seven seconds. You're slipping, Director," Wyeth chides, noticing that his superior is a little winded.

"Damn patrician tour," Lyris grumbles. "What's going on?"

"We have a network outage. Engineering teams are filing their reports."

Catastrophic system failures within Intercorpex's infrastructure are exceedingly rare. Networks are resilient and built with multiple layers of redundancy. The has been no need to shift operations from Beijing, Frankfurt, or New York to the disaster recovery center in London for decades.

"On comms," Lyris states, signaling his surgically implanted communications device that he's ready to start receiving voice updates.

An intelligent information relay facilitates communications in the NOC while eliminating the chaos and heightened tension that shouting creates. Wyeth and Lyris have specially designed, voice-activated implants that integrate communications with NOC operations staff.

Lyris scans the workstations arranged between him and the video wall. Dozens of analysts, engineers, and support staff are engaged in troubleshooting. The network infrastructure is Intercorpex's central nervous system. Without adequate communications between their facilities, nothing runs efficiently. Time is of the essence.

"Wyeth, turn off that strobe light before I have a seizure. Talk to me, people," Lyris commands.

"Director, this is NetEng. We simultaneously lost connection to three data centers in Secaucus."

"Why didn't traffic automatically reroute to the secondary circuits?" Lyris asks as the strobes cease their blinking.

"Secondaries are down as well," another voice on that team relays.

"Is it our switches?"

Wyeth checks his console display and shakes his head. The Intercorpex network is exceptionally complicated, but until now, nobody could have fathomed both the primary and secondary circuits simultaneously going down. Lyris frowns. Something is very wrong.

"Diagnostics came back fine," a third voice relays, confirming Wyeth's conclusion. "They're in working order."

"Run full diagnostics on all systems. NetEng," Lyris barks, causing the communications system to route his comment directly to that team. "What you're saying doesn't make sense. How can there be failures on the primary *and* secondary circuits going to three data centers? They take different paths. It's not possible."

"Director, I would agree with you, but that's what's happening."

"Which three data centers are out?"

"Secaucus Two, Four, and Five, sir."

Wyeth inputs a couple of commands on his keyboard, and an overhead image comes up on the NOC's center display showing the behemoth buildings in red.

"Off comms," Wyeth directs as he leans over the divider. "Lyris, those data centers host most of our high-frequency traders."

Lyris rubs his chin. There were dozens of exchanges before the global economic apocalypse. In the United States, the NASDAQ, NYSE, and ICE were the largest. Each housed its systems outside the city to prevent disruption during a natural disaster or terrorist attack. After corporations chartered Intercorpex, technicians consolidated New York operations to Secaucus One and Three, a pair of redundant data centers just across the river.

Other nearby facilities hold special equipment for the *gentez-majorez*, who enhance their fortunes by conducting thousands of trades a day via computer algorithms. This high-frequency trading is reserved for the elite of the elite, raising the stakes of this outage.

"The *gentez-majorez* have just been frozen out of trading. I need a root cause, Wyeth, and I need it now. Go find it for me."

"You got it," he assures, disappearing down the stairs and rushing over to the network engineers.

Only patricians are entitled to trade stocks of the world's corporations. Three classes of elites have arisen through evolution more than decree. The highest is *prima*, encompassing patricians with controlling interests in parent corporations. They're more interested in increasing their shares and wielding their power than playing the highs and lows of the market.

Below them is the *gentez-majorez*. If patricians are the top three percent of the global society, then these patricians are the three percent of the three percent. They're wealthy beyond imagination and among the most demanding people on Earth.

The last is the *gentez-minorez*, like the men and women Lyris escorted on the tour. They're at the bottom of the elite ladder, making trades through the Intercorpex Trading and Quotation System. Right now, they're the only ones in a position to trade anything.

"Volume alert," an analyst informs the team as another warning sounds on the floor.

"Director, this is NetEng. The outage appears to be caused by breaks in the fiber optic circuits in Secaucus."

"Acknowledged."

"Director, this is Global Monitoring. Secaucus Public Safety and Security have reported three explosions across the river that matches the time our systems alerted."

"What kind of explosions?" Wyeth asks, sharing his boss's concern.

"We're not getting any further information. America Incorporated Public Affairs initiated an information blackout. The Secaucus PSS switched to a secure communication link and restricted access."

"Off comms," Lyris orders as Wyeth bounds up the stairs to his workstation.

"If America Incorporated is calling for a blackout, it's something they don't want intercorporational media getting a sniff of," he surmises.

"This isn't an accident," Lyris concludes. "It's starting to look like an attack."

Wyeth's brow crinkles. "From whom?"

"I don't know, but it's their problem, not ours. We can't restore operations if we don't know what we're up against."

"What do you want to do?"

Lyris shifts his eyes from the massive display to his subordinate.

"Get me a VidLynk to the White House."

CHAPTER
SEVEN

AMERICA, INC.

The White House
Corporate Governance District
Washington-Arlington Municipal Corporation

"Ma'am, you have an incoming VidLynk request from the Intercorpex Network Operations Center in New York. Do you wish to accept?" Fiolla's digital receptionist asks over the office speakers.

Calls that come into any America Incorporated executive office get filtered through access lists updated regularly by their intelligent communications system. As the perpetually swamped staff vice president of Corporate Affairs, most end up on her memo display. "Rosie" routed this direct request from Intercorpex through the system.

Fiolla glances over to the secure feed beamed onto the right-side display hanging on the wall. Market volume is down, and the NOC is looking for answers about what happened outside their data centers. She wants to decline, but that would only make matters worse.

"Accept."

"Thank you, Executive Fiolla. Audio or video?" the disembodied English-accented voice asks.

"Video. Put it on the main display, Rosie."

A reporter is prattling about one of their subsidiaries' efforts to build a playground for children in Detroit. The information blackout ensures AME News won't run any stories about the explosions. Fiolla can only hope Corporate Communications can keep global corporate news stations in the dark as well.

"Connecting."

Fiolla moves in front of her desk as the VidLynk is established. Director Lyris is a tall, handsome man with a muscular frame, short blond hair, and blue eyes you could get lost in for hours. She has only met him a handful of times, but each encounter made her insides tingle. Only Farron, her current beau, has ever made her feel like that.

"Good morning, Executive Director Lyris."

"Executive Fiolla, we both know that it *isn't* a good morning."

"You're referring to the minor incident outside New York?" she asks, trying to downplay the impact. From the look on his face, he isn't buying it.

Fiolla is charged with interfacing with the world's corporations, America Incorporated's subsidiaries, labor unions, and the Intercorporational Exchange on behalf of the White House. Most days, she handles mundane business unworthy of attention from other high-level executives or the CEO. Today, she's a shield against an angry exchange administrator.

"Do you always instigate an information blackout for 'minor incidents'?"

"Executive Director Lyris, you of all people understand that publicizing events without the benefit of facts doesn't serve anyone's interests. America Incorporated doesn't allow speculation about any incident before we understand it ourselves. The blackout was ordered for your protection as well as ours."

"Save the empty rhetoric, Fiolla. We're not one of your corporate interests and couldn't care less about your obsession over controlling the narrative for your employees. I'm not talking about the AME News blackout. I'm talking about the public safety one. They should be providing us with information critical to restoring our operations, not to mention reaffirming their responsibility for safeguarding our facilities."

"I wasn't aware that your operations were interrupted," Fiolla states, hoping he realizes that he hasn't shared any information with her.

"I think you know better than that."

Fiolla stalls for a few moments to collect her thoughts. "Lyris, I haven't received any reports of damage to your facilities. Secaucus Public Safety and Security reported three infrastructure failures. Am I missing something?"

"Eighty-seven percent of all high-frequency trading operations are down. Those *explosions* severed the primary and secondary connections to the data center where the majority of the *gentez-majorez* house their trading operations."

Fiolla tightens her jaw as her mind races. This crisis is much bigger than she thought. If the upper class of patricians is affected, Intercorpex will be under siege with complaints. They will, in turn, blame America Incorporated. If this is a terror attack, Chief Executive Valen will be blamed for failing to stop it.

"Director Lyris—"

"Don't embarrass yourself by pretending this was an accident. It was an attack, and we both know it was probably Liberteum."

Few things can ruin a person's day like mentioning that name. After the United States government collapsed, people's gratitude toward corporations for restoring order from anarchy waned. After America Incorporated announced its charter on July 4th, 2041, dissenters longing for the return of democracy organized resistance groups. Most of them were eradicated, but one that arose in New York City caused massive headaches. That band of misfits and miscreants calls itself "Liberteum."

"I know no such thing, and neither do you," Fiolla snaps.

Lyris presses his lips together and shakes his head. "You're smarter than that. The explosions happened within seconds of each other and severed fiber optic cables that run between data centers. It was well-planned and intentional. There's only one group in this part of the world capable of executing that."

"You're speculating."

"My job is to oversee exchange operations. All I care about is normalizing them. We've wasted valuable time having this conversation. Lift the information blackout to us, or I'll have Administrator-General Raimius explain America Incorporated's lack of cooperation in restoring our systems to the patricians."

Fiolla stares impassively at the display. If Lyris is right and this is an attack, Valen needs to be made aware. The longer she argues, the longer it takes for him to get that information. Fortunately, her position grants her the authority to override Corporate Communications and give Lyris what he needs.

"I will caution you to keep this event in perspective," Fiolla warns.

"The clock is ticking."

"The Bureau of Corporate Security will provide you with all relevant information. The media blackout will remain in place, and I trust nothing we provide you will leak to intercorporational news outlets."

"I understand discretion, Fiolla. Thank you. I'll be in touch if I need anything further," Director Lyris says before the image goes to black. The AME News feed returns to the display.

"Rosie?"

"Yes, Executive Fiolla."

"Contact Corporate Communications and have the information blackout to Intercorpex lifted."

"Request confirmed."

"Excellent. Now contact the BCS and tell them to release all information on the Secaucus explosions to Intercorpex Global Network Operations in New York."

"Request confirmed."

Fiolla leaves her office and walks down the hall past the entrance to the Oval Office that only the senior executives are entitled to use. She passes the vacant Charter Room where America Incorporated was born, and she veers into the CEO's administrative office.

"Is he free?" she asks his executive assistant. The Oval Office is one of the few places where a live human being answers that question.

"He's on a VidLynk with the CEO of Southern Europe trying to expand a trade deal. Valen's a sucker for Tuscan red wines."

Alcohol is illegal within the sphere of influence. Possession of intoxicating spirits or mind-altering drugs comes with severe consequences for most employees. High-level executives can indulge without fear of recrimination, including Chief Executive Valen.

"Is this important, Executive Fiolla?"

"Very."

The admin jumps on the line and interrupts the conversation. After a moment, she looks up at Fiolla and nods.

"You can go in," the admin informs her, pressing the button that automatically opens the door.

The Oval Office is an iconic room. It hasn't changed much from the pictures printed in history books. The décor is different, as is the breed of the man who currently occupies it. Valen has no constituents to answer to, at least in the historical sense. He is only accountable to the board of directors and patrician shareholders, both of whom are more problematic and demanding than the citizens of the United States were.

"This had better be good, Fiolla," Chief Executive Valen says. "I'm only halfway through these trade calls."

"We have a problem," she says, launching into a quick summary of the VidLynk with Intercorpex's Executive Director of Operations.

Valen admires the view of the Rose Garden out one of the windows as he listens. There's nothing more beautiful anywhere in the executive complex when it's in full bloom. Nothing is budding in early March, and spring is still a long way off.

"We haven't had a confirmed attack from Liberteum in a couple of years," he says, still facing the window.

"No, sir, but it doesn't mean that Lyris is wrong."

"Who's running the investigation?"

"Secaucus Public Safety and Security responded, but I'm sure that the BCS has assumed control. There's one more thing, sir. I lifted the information blackout and directed them to share information with Intercorpex."

"Chief Executive Valen," a voice interrupts. This disembodied woman's timbre sounds lusty, like a seductive eastern European vixen. "There is abnormal market trading activity on AME."

The curved display on the wall opposite his desk changes to show the stock's volume and activity. The CEO is held accountable for stock performance. AME, the stock ticker symbol for America Incorporated, is rarely down more than three points on any given day. Valen frowns at the sell orders driving the price down more than five. Key subsidiaries are also falling on the secondary market. A drop of this magnitude isn't good news.

"Could Liberteum be trying to manipulate our stock?"

"I don't see how that's possible, sir," Fiolla responds.

Patricians frequently try to influence the direction of stocks of subsidiary companies around the globe. Underground groups aren't brave, organized, or savvy enough to try something that bold.

"We need to get in front of this," Valen decrees. "Halie?"

He named his digital assistant Halie after HAL, the computer in a science fiction film made over a hundred years ago. Fiolla doubts she sounds anything like that computer did.

"What can I do for you, sir?"

"Get me the directors of Corporate Security, Treasury, and the CEO of New York City on a VidLynk immediately."

"Arranging it now."

"Do you need me here, sir?"

"No, Fiolla, I'll handle this. Contact as many sympathetic patricians as you can and urge them to place buy orders to increase our stock price. Under no circumstances should we close down more than five. Prima Bettancourt may be able to help if they push back."

"Right away, sir," Fiolla says, knowing Prima Bettancourt hates Valen and won't lift a finger. Regardless, she'll make the call. There's nothing like sticking her head in the lion's mouth first thing in the morning.

CHAPTER
EIGHT

Intercorpex Global Network Operations Center
Manhattan Financial District
ICX New York Exchange

An army of calm, efficient, and competent professionals is tasked to keep vigilance over Intercorpex's systems. Most days pass with nothing more than a simple failover to a redundant backup, at most. Today is different. The quiet buzz of the network operations center has morphed into a roar now that they are facing a problem they don't understand and cannot seem to fix.

"Sir, the Bureau of Corporate Security is insisting that this is a random event and not an attack," a member of the global monitoring team says over the communications system.

"They *can't* be serious! Simultaneous explosions within a mile of each other are random events? That's crap. What's the status of the repair team?"

"Crews are heading to the sites now," the infrastructure team reports. "Remediation time won't be known until they coordinate with the Secaucus Municipal Corporation to get in there and assess the damage."

"Assume it's bad," Wyeth says. "What's the worst-case scenario?"

"Fiber splicing is time-consuming. Even a temporary bypass will take hours. It's not going to be a quick fix, even under the best circumstances."

"I need a better option," Lyris moans.

"We can use the tertiary links," the network engineering team leader offers.

"We've never used the point-to-point, have we?" Wyeth asks, sounding apprehensive.

"Not for production, but the link is tested monthly. It's old technology but will work as designed. It's our only option, Director."

Lyris rubs his forehead. Intercorpex maintains a line-of-sight microwave transmission system between data centers in the event of a disaster scenario. Flooding is not uncommon in the low-lying marshes of Secaucus, so engineering implemented this backup system as a fail-safe.

"Executive Director Lyris, you have an incoming call from the administrator-general," the electronic voice in his ear announces.

"Connect us, my station only."

Lyris climbs the stairs to the platform and arrives as Administrator-General Raimius appears on the VidLynk. He's a slight man with short gray hair and a clean-shaven face that all Intercorpex employees must maintain. Lyris finds his piercing steel blue eyes the only thing physically impressive about Raimius. Right now, they are boring into him over the VidLynk.

"Lyris! What the hell is going on over there! I've been fielding inquiries from angry patricians for the past twenty minutes. Is this situation under control or not?"

Lyris takes a deep breath and gives him the rundown on the explosions, the discussion with Fiolla at the White House, and what they've learned from the BCS. He doesn't mention Liberteum. Raimius is paranoid enough. There's no benefit to feeding his legendary insecurity and distrust.

"Sir, three data centers used by the *gentez-majorez* are out of commission due to their primary and secondary circuits being severed. The ITQS is unaffected. Patricians can still process orders through—"

"Are you an idiot, Lyris? Do I have a complete moron running our global operations?"

"No, sir."

"Patricians pay billions of Bytecoin for high-frequency trading capabilities that are unavailable using our standard trade and quotation system. You are responsible for this network. Get those systems back online, or I'll come down there and do it myself."

"Yes, sir."

Lyris knows that's not an idle threat. Raimius can be here in fifteen minutes from their Forty-Second Street headquarters. The devious mind that catapulted him into the most powerful position in the world has no room for virtues like patience and understanding. He'll abuse the NOC staff until the problem is rectified, likely causing it to take even longer.

"I'll contact you in fifteen minutes. I'd better hear good news when I do," Raimius threatens before abruptly ending the VidLynk.

"I'm surprised he doesn't make you genuflect when he calls," Wyeth quips from his workstation.

"Don't give him any ideas. On comms. Infrastructure, what's the status on the repair team?"

The woman looks back at Lyris from across the room. "They're not being given access to the sites yet, Director."

"Acknowledged," he says, hanging his head.

"Lyris, they aren't going to be given access in the next fifteen minutes, let alone splice fiber in that time," Wyeth postulates. "The tertiary links are the only option left."

Lyris runs his hand through his short hair. "I know. The problem is security. Any fool with a roof antenna between the two points can intercept the signal."

"The data is encrypted, and who even uses antennas anymore? It's a reasonable risk given the alternatives."

Lyris can't argue with that. He would much rather cut over to the London disaster recovery site, but patricians removed their high-frequency trading presence there years ago due to its cost and infrequent use. It was a shortsighted decision considering the patricians' unrivaled wealth.

"Initiate tertiary connections."

"Attention in the NOC," Wyeth commands over the communications system, causing an immediate silence. "Prepare for initiation of microwave communications protocols. Begin network routing changes and report statuses."

The room jumps into action. The center display in the room shows a three-dimensional mock-up of the data centers and the red primary and secondary fiber links that connect them. A dish on each building moves from black to amber as they energize.

Lyris settles into his chair and watches the microwave dishes turn green when they're active. Ten seconds later, the lines connecting the data centers to Intercorpex's primary trading site turn the same color.

"This is going to work. Don't look so sullen," Wyeth advises, his head leaning over the short wall that divides their areas.

Lyris stands and tugs at the bottom of his black tunic. "Contact Commissioner-General Jurghen in Zurich. Brief him on the explosions and inform him that we're operating on an unsecured data link because of them. Restoring trading solves the immediate problem. Now I want to know why we had to in the first place."

CHAPTER NINE

LIBERTEUM

XQ Systems Office Building
Secaucus Municipal Corporation

Haven sits on the corner of the desk and stares at the two gagged security guards bound to a pair of old chairs. Neither is willing to look him in the eyes. Instead, they hang their heads and tremble in fear.

A puddle lies at the feet of one of the guards. Without his uniform, there was nothing to absorb the urine after his bladder let go. The woman is slightly more courageous than her counterpart. They're both weaklings, just like all the people who support this corrupt system.

Haven leaves the small office to escape the stench of urine and failure. He steps up to the security desk that Scivix is dutifully posted at. After a quick check of the video displays and noting nothing out of the ordinary, he pats his subordinate on the shoulder.

"I'm going to check on the progress."

"Tell them to hurry the hell up," Scivix demands without looking.

Haven rounds the corner and makes quick work of the three flights of stairs. He reaches the roof access to find Jasper and Adiz huddled over their computer. The two barely notice his presence, not that he would expect the pair of hackers to have any situational awareness at all.

"Do you have what you need?" Haven asks impatiently.

"I think so," Adiz says, not looking up.

"You think, or you know?"

"It's not that simple. The encryption is very complex, and we—"

"Make it simple. You have the data, or you don't. Every minute we stay here increases the chances that we'll have to fight our way out."

Adiz looks at Haven and presses his glasses back up on the bridge of his nose. "These messages are complicated. We need to ensure we have enough of them."

"How much data do you have?" Haven asks Jasper, no longer willing to suffer Adiz's whiny explanation.

"One-hundred and thirty terabytes."

Haven crosses his arms. That's more than enough for him. Michele and Quarren told him that they only need a fraction of that.

"Pack up the equipment and prepare to move out."

"But—"

Haven pulls out his weapon in one swift move and points the muzzle inches away from Adiz's forehead.

"I know you like it above ground, Adiz. You probably miss it. Another word, and I'll plant you below ground permanently. It wasn't a suggestion. Pack up the equipment. *Now.*"

Compliance is immediate. They used the solar array on the roof to conceal the antenna dish. Haven hopes they can disassemble it more quickly than they erected it.

He moves around the panels to the north side of the building. There has been a tremendous emergency response at the explosion sites. The PSS must have pulled in units from neighboring municipal corporations. Secaucus doesn't have this much manpower.

"We're done, Haven," Jasper relays after five minutes as Adiz heads down the ladder with the portable antenna.

"Good. Time to go."

Haven surveys the scene one last time before following the hackers back into the building and rendezvousing with his two soldiers at the security desk.

"There's no way we're getting the van outta here with all these streets blocked off. It'll get searched," Nyvar says.

"I know. Did you check the guards' conveyances?"

"They're in the employee lot," Scivix says, pointing at a display.

"Are the transponders coded to their biojacks?"

"Negative."

A new plan forms in Haven's head. Extraction was always going to be the trickiest part of this operation. The exfil plan is infeasible now, so he needs to improvise. Without returning the data the hackers collected to Manhattan, this mission is worthless.

"Pull one into the loading dock and load the equipment in the trunk. We will drive it back across the river and dump it near the rally point. Then we'll travel underground to the old subway station."

Jasper rubs the scruff on his chin. "It's risky."

"Would you rather swim across the river?" Haven asks, causing the hacker to shake his head.

"What about *them*?" Scivix asks, pointing a thumb over his shoulder at the office with the bound guards.

"Leave them to me."

"Michele said no body count," Adiz warns, earning a glare from Haven.

"I heard her."

Haven enters the small office while his team goes about their tasks. He pulls the gag off the male security guard. The weakling stretches his jaw before glancing at his captor with pure hatred.

"You will never get away with this, urch scum."

"That's a bold statement coming from a man who pissed himself." Haven leans in close. "I have already gotten away with it."

"The BCS will hunt you down, and when they find you, they'll kill you. I'll be the first to stand and applaud at your execution."

Haven stares at him impassively. The arrogance of corporate employees is astounding. They never believe that anything bad can happen to them. This one is about to get an education.

"That will be a neat trick for a dead man to pull off."

Shock registers on his face as Haven grins and pulls his weapon. He puts a neat hole in the man's forehead, sending his brains splattering on the wall behind him. The woman looks at him in horror. Haven doesn't flinch, knowing that the terror will be forever frozen on her face. He squeezes the trigger, sending her to the same fate.

Holstering his weapon, Haven takes one last look at the pathetic pair and turns out the light. Their biojacks will alert public safety within seconds, and there are dozens of units in the area available to investigate. The five men have only minutes to escape back through the tunnel to the relative safety of the Manhattan underground.

CHAPTER TEN

REGISTRANT RYKOS

Central Park
New York City Municipal Corporation

Dinsmore Preparatory Academy is located on Manhattan's Upper East Side, meaning I have to commute through Central Park each day to reach it. Most days, I make the journey with Balin at my side. Today is no different, except my gait is faster. After today's events, I want to put as much distance between myself and that building as possible.

"What did Shaef say after class?" Balin asks as we wander down the path.

"The same thing he always says. Watch what I say in case Aristotle perceives it as disloyalty."

He scoffs. "Hell, I get that speech every week. Is your dad going to get a call?"

"No, I don't think so." At least, I hope not.

"Shaef expects that behavior from me, but you're the son of the chief guardian. What had you so distracted?"

"Something was seriously wrong with the market today."

Balin shakes his head. "Who cares? We have the rest of our lives to worry about that. For a guy who runs his mouth about challenging the status quo, you spend a lot of time obsessing over it."

"I was curious. There was nothing on AME News about it."

"Is there ever?"

I look down at the ground as we walk. You can always count on AME News not to relay anything important. The media only reports what our executive overlords want us to see and hear.

"Balin, your distrust of the system is legendary. I'm only now beginning to realize mine."

"What's taking you so long? We sit in the same classes and get spoon-fed the same horseshit. You live a block away from me. Does what you see on the streets and what you're told ever match up?"

I don't bother responding. We pass a rock formation that we hang out at on Sundays when we're not at Dinsmore. The surveillance in the park isn't as prolific or intrusive as it is in the rest of the city. That makes it the perfect place to get a brief respite from prying eyes.

"All I know is what our instructors say under Aristotle's watchful eye," I finally say.

"The corporation controls that message. There is no reason for them to tell the truth, and millions not to. Are you dumb enough to believe anything they say?"

"I try not to think about it."

"I do. All the time."

"Why? You can't change it," I argue. "This is the system we live in. It's not perfect, but it's better than the alternative. They've given us a beautiful, safe city, guaranteed employment, first-rate healthcare, enough money to live on… It's more than any government ever provided its citizens. What more do you want?"

We fall silent as a pair of employees stroll by us on the path. This is the kind of conversation best not overheard by others. Balin stops walking and faces me once they're out of earshot.

"I want the one thing the corporation doesn't provide: the ability to make my own decisions. You fight with your father every day. Are you telling me you don't want that for yourself?"

"Of course I do. What choices my father doesn't make for me, the corporation will once I graduate from university. Some miserable soul in human resources will decide when I can take a vacation or attend a sporting event. They'll tell me what job I'll have and in what city. My whole life is predetermined. It's not right."

"Exactly! You're getting dangerously close to subversion, Rykos, and I like it," Balin says, an approving grin creasing his lips. "Since you're walking along the edge of the cliff, let me give you a push."

Balin reaches into his pocket and pulls two silver circles out. I study the two old coins pinched in his fingers. I've only seen them in photographs. One side of these has a picture of George Washington, the first president of the now-defunct United States. The other side has an eagle, which ironically is still prominent as the corporate logo of America Incorporated.

"Put those away before some camera or drone sees them," I demand, looking around at the buildings towering over the park. "Where did you get slugs?"

"I have connections."

"You know possessing old coinage is forbidden. Do you have any idea what will happen if you get caught with those?"

"All too well. They're not keepsakes. These, my friend, are our admission to an urch rave."

I fight a sudden bout of apprehension at the prospect of fulfilling a teenage dream. I've been pining to go to one of these since the moment an older classmate told us about what goes on at them. The risks have always been too great to consider making an appearance at one.

"Do you have any idea what my father will do to me if he finds out?"

"Then we don't get caught. Come on, Rykos. How many times have you told me that you'd risk everything to go to a rave? We're talking music, urch shine, and loose women with no morals itching to hook up with a man of a higher station. It's everything we dream about."

Possession of slugs would be a slap on the wrist compared to what would happen if my father found me at a rave. For starters, Balin and I would get charged with consorting with urches, imbibing illegal alcohol, attending an unsanctioned event of more than twenty people, trespassing, and entering a restricted zone. I'm sure there are a half-dozen municipal corporate policies that I'm missing.

"Let me think about it," I say, wondering how I can pull this off with a father who checks my biojack location whenever I'm not home.

"Okay, tell me tomorrow," Balin says, slapping me on the bicep. "I know you'll eventually make the right choice."

Balin and I part ways, and I head home. He has me worked up. There's truth in his words, but he doesn't understand the risks. I have a lot more to lose than he does.

My thoughts preoccupy me as I climb off the elevator and enter the doors to our domicile to find my father sitting on the couch, still dressed in his uniform. His eyes don't move from the main display when I enter the living room.

"Why did you stop in Central Park?"

"What?"

"Are you deaf, Rykos? I asked why you stopped in Central Park," he says, pointing at the display.

I move deeper into the room and turn to see what he's looking at. A map of Manhattan is up, and a bright red dot pulses the location of my biojack. He must have tracked me all the way home from Dinsmore.

"What the hell is this?" I shout.

"Teman!" my mother says, rushing out of the bedroom.

"Not now, Ilaria. What does it look like?"

"Why are you spying on me this time? I was walking home from Dinsmore."

"Constant supervision is the only way I can get you to care about your education and your future."

"I get it," I say, nodding defiantly. "You have a reputation to maintain."

"What I'm doing is fighting to maintain yours because I don't think you give a damn about what people think. You don't listen to a word I say anyway, so talking to you is pointless."

"Maybe that's because you don't talk *to* me; you talk *at* me. You treat me like one of your subordinates."

"No, my guardians command my respect. I treat you like a child because that's how you act. Answer my question. Why did you stop in the park with Balin?"

"We were talking. Is that a crime against the corporation now?"

"I hate being lied to, Rykos. Your sister—"

"Can we have one conversation where you don't compare me to Varella?" I ask, throwing my hands up in the air.

"I only bring her up when it's relevant," my father says, his voice even.

"Which it always is! Yes, I'm aware she walks on water."

"Watch yourself!"

"Or else what? I'm sorry I'm not living up to your expectations, but I'm never going to be my sister."

My father's face flushes red with anger. That comment hit home, and the truth hurts when you get smacked in the face with it.

"I'm not asking you to be. I worked hard to get you into Dinsmore. I wanted to provide you with an opportunity that I didn't have. You need to seize it."

"Opportunity for what? The one where I get to work as a minion for America Incorporated?"

"Hold your tongue, Rykos!" he says, standing and turning to face me.

"Why? Are you afraid the Maester will tattle on me and hurt my chances of going to the Ivy League? You know I'm not going anyway."

"So, you're going to throw away your chance at a better life?"

"A better life? Is that what working for the parent corporation is? I don't think it's living at all. It doesn't matter which corporate master I serve. I'm going to be enslaved, just like you."

The reaction is immediate. My father pulls his arm back and swings it forward, the back of his hand connecting on my face with a loud smacking sound. My head jerks to the right. I stumble but refuse to fall to the ground.

"You will not talk like that under this roof. Do you hear me?" my father asks through clenched teeth as I wipe the blood oozing from the corner of my mouth. "Do you?"

"Chief Guardian, your presence is requested at PSS headquarters immediately," the Maester system announces, shattering the tension. "Details are being downloaded to your wrist tablet."

My father glares at me with fire in his eyes. He forces himself to glance down at the tablet fastened to his left forearm. With his index finger, he brings up the display and swipes it a couple of times, scanning the information on the screen. He flashes a look of displeasure, then shifts his gaze back over to my mother.

"I have to get back downtown. We're dealing with some things."

"Are the guardians cracking down on jaywalking or something?" I ask under my breath.

"Teman! Don't!" my mother shouts as he raises his hand again. "Rykos, don't talk to your father that way!"

"Talk sense into him, will you? I have to get back to work." He doesn't make it to the elevator leading down to the lobby before stopping and turning his head. "I'm disappointed in you, Rykos."

He looks at my mother one final time before walking into the foyer and pressing the call button on the elevator. The high-speed lift arrives seconds later, and he steps in, turning and staring at me with ice-cold eyes as the doors close. My father left, but the tension in the room didn't follow him. My mother is fuming.

Before I have a chance to react, she crosses the living area and slaps me across my face hard enough to make my vision go starry for an instant. It didn't physically hurt as much as my father's. Only…she's never hit me before. My father has always administered my punishments. I touch my cheek tenderly, feeling the heat from the slap as silence grips the room.

"You hit me," I say, rubbing my cheek.

"You are out of line. Sit down, Rykos," she commands in a motherly voice. I comply.

"I'm not in the mood for another lecture."

"You're not going to get one." She sits next to me, placing her hand on my knee. "I've failed you."

"What?"

"I've been too easy on you. I play peacemaker instead of letting you and your father iron out your differences."

"It wouldn't matter," I whisper.

"It would. You both see the world differently, but he doesn't love you any less than your sister."

I let out a heavy sigh. "Say it all you want, mother, but you're only convincing yourself. We both know that isn't true. I have modules to prep for tomorrow."

I stand and retreat to my room, closing the door behind me. I don't want to argue with her. My mother has always been the family diplomat. There's nothing to be gained by upsetting her now that the relationship with my father has just gone from bad to worse.

CHAPTER ELEVEN

INTERCORPEX

Global Network Operations Center
Manhattan Financial District
ICX New York Exchange

Chief Inspector Zyree lets out a long sigh. Four hours ago, he was soaking up the sun on a charming Caribbean island under the guise of investigating violations of the Zurich Canon. Intercorpex takes accusations of corporate espionage seriously, and he thought he could milk the assignment for another month. He was wrong. Whatever prompted his reassignment to New York must have the brass in Zurich concerned.

At 4:59 p.m., a large numerical display on the center monitor of the NOC begins a countdown as technicians perform their final checks for handover. With ten seconds left, the bell rings, triggered by a delegation from one of the Asian corporations. A ceremonial gavel smashes down when the bell finishes sounding, marking the transfer of market operations from New York to Beijing.

"Chief Inspector Zyree?" an uptight admin holding a tablet asks as he approaches him.

"You already know I am."

"Yes, sir. Executive Director Lyris is expecting you. May I show you to his office?"

"He's right there," Zyree says, pointing at the raised platform. "Can't he show me himself?"

"I'm sorry, he's conducting the hand-off briefing with Beijing. It should only take ten minutes. You'll be more comfortable waiting in his office."

"I doubt that," Zyree says, gesturing for the lackey to lead the way.

Zyree was instructed to maintain a low profile. It's why he chose to wear the exchange operations uniform. The navy blue jacket with a diagonal opening from the right shoulder to the left hip is comfortable, but he misses his black Intercorpex Security attire.

The chief inspector glances at the left display in the NOC showing the closing prices. AME made a decent recovery following this morning's turmoil, losing only four at the New York close. The Far East exchange opens at New York's prices, and the Intercorpex Corporate Index immediately climbs into positive numbers.

Zyree follows his babysitter to a well-appointed corner office on the twenty-third floor and is offered a beverage. The ten minutes he was promised turns into a half-hour. The chief inspector's patience is about exhausted when Lyris finally bursts through the door.

"I'm sorry to keep you waiting, Chief Inspector Zyree. Today's been eventful."

"I'm sure it has, and I'm also sure you aren't the least bit sorry."

"Jurghen warned me about you," Lyris says, taking a seat on the opposite side of the large desk.

"Oh yeah? What did the commissioner-general tell you?"

"That you're one of the most capable inspectors in Intercorpex and harbor a healthy dose of resentment for authority."

"I follow the rules," Zyree offers as a lame defense.

"Really? I didn't realize our dress code authorized beards."

He reflexively rubs his hand over the scruff. Zyree has been in the room with Lyris for two minutes and already doesn't like him.

"I wouldn't know. I only follow the rules that matter."

"You were told to be inconspicuous and yet arrive with facial hair and wearing an unfastened operations tunic."

Zyree looks down at the open flap of his synthetic fiber coat. It's far more comfortable the way he's wearing it. "Maybe you can dress me tomorrow, Mommy."

Lyris gives him a hard stare. "I need you to find out who was behind this attack in Secaucus and eliminate them."

Zyree's handsome face scrunches at the bizarre request. "Uh, that isn't what I do."

"You do what the exchange needs you to, Chief Inspector. Right now, this is what we need," Lyris says.

"What *we* need, or what you need?"

"Is there a difference?" he asks, the corner of his mouth curving upwards.

"A big one, I would imagine. The Bureau of Corporate Security is responsible for protecting ICX assets in this sphere of influence. They take that job seriously. Why is exchange security involved?"

"They aren't involved. *You* are," Lyris says, smirking. "This operation is being conducted off the books."

Zyree would like to knock that smile off his face. ICX Security publicly maintains transparency, but they conduct a host of activities that corporations are never made aware of.

Intercorpex is the love child of the patricians and the corporations. Its purpose is to operate a marketplace for the elites to increase their already incalculable wealth. Under their current administrator-general, the exchange's power has grown. Some patricians have accepted that, while corporations are far less understanding. They'll do whatever is necessary to protect their places in the world order.

"You don't trust the BCS to do their jobs?"

"America Incorporated does what's in its best interests, and that's usually at odds with our wants and needs. They have a long history of failing to handle their urch problem. Underground movements have been allowed to fester, and they're more organized and aggressive than in the past. Now they're targeting us."

"Urch" is the slang term that became popular in North America and Europe when corporations came to power. The term is derived from "street urchin" and applies to those who have shunned the comforts the world's corporations provide their employees. These wayward souls have illegally fled society and now scratch out an existence while living underground.

There is no official count of urches, but there are rumored to be thousands in New York City alone. The larger the city, the more places there are to hide. Many of these derelicts find their way into resistance movements, and the one here is particularly troubling.

"You think this was the work of Liberteum?"

"That's why you're here, Zyree. We can't ignore the possibility of Liberteum's return."

"They've only targeted corporate assets in the past."

"Past performance is no guarantee of future results," Lyris responds, quoting an age-old financial adage. "The BCS is stonewalling us. If they confirm that Liberteum was behind this, we'll be the last to know. I need somebody to uncover the truth, and you're my man. You work alone, can operate in the shadows, and you get results when others can't."

Zyree sighs. "When do you want me to start?"

"The moment you get out of that chair."

Lyris waves his finger through the air, moving pages on his transparent display. He grasps one in his hand and throws it toward the wall. He makes a couple of other gestures with his finger.

"Neat trick," Zyree says. He resents reliance on technology. It makes lazy people overly dependent on it.

"We have all the best toys here. I just sent this information to your tablet."

Zyree blinks. "Okay, I received it."

"How do you know?" Lyris asks. "You don't even have your tablet on you."

"I do. You just don't see it," Zyree says, pointing to the augmented contact lenses in his eyes. "You're not the only one with cool toys, Executive Director."

The fifth-generation lenses Zyree wears are connected wirelessly to an implanted personal biological computer that maintains a permanent connection to Intercorpex Security. Data displays in his peripheral vision, providing him with valuable information about people, places, and events in real-time. It took months for Zyree to get used to the constant information he receives on his lenses and the headaches that accompany them.

"Right. Talk to no one about this assignment, especially anyone in America Incorporated. Report to me daily. You're dismissed."

Zyree wastes no time heading out of Lyris's office and the Wall Street NOC. He's surprised that Commissioner-General Jurghen agreed to this. Finding out why he did is another item to add to his to-do list. A message pops up in his peripheral vision that helps answer that question. He quickly scans it and stops walking.

"You've got to be kidding me."

CHAPTER TWELVE

AMERICA, INC.

The White House
Corporate Governance District
Washington-Arlington Municipal Corporation

The nine o'clock meeting in the Oval Office is taking longer than usual. The CEO's principal advisors pack the room to discuss yesterday's events outside New York. Those not physically present join via VidLynk on the large curved displays molded onto the walls. Every aspect of corporate governance has convened to update Valen on the explosions and reactions from Intercorpex and the patricians. The exercise was routine until the BCS poured gasoline in the room and lit a match by mentioning the possibility of Liberteum's involvement.

"Sir, the PSS has been unable to eliminate this threat," Director Virtari says. "How long are we going to be patient with their ineptitude?"

Valen frowns. Pushing fifty-five, with a terrible comb-over of rapidly thinning hair, Virtari is more ruthless than most chief executives. He enjoys bringing misery to others, which means he loves his job as director of the Bureau of Corporate Security.

"This is their first attack in years," Valen argues, "assuming it was Liberteum at all. Do you have proof that you're not sharing with us?"

"No, sir, but look at the facts. Two guardians in Secaucus are dead. Explosions crippled trading at Intercorpex. Two security officers at a nearby building were found murdered. This was a sophisticated attack, and the only group of urches in New York capable of that is Liberteum."

"That's speculation," Chief Executive Safmor says over the VidLynk.

It was a reflex. Safmor has been the efficient and effective chief executive officer of the New York City Municipal Corporation for more than a decade. Liberteum was largely eradicated on his watch, or so it was believed. He is competent and respected, if not by the belligerent head of the BCS.

"It's a reasonable conclusion," Virtari counters, glaring at the New York Municipal Corporation's CEO. "Chief Executive Valen, I believe we should round up the urches and make them talk. It's the quickest and easiest way to determine if Liberteum has resurfaced."

"If we start recriminating against urches, it could spark an uprising."

"We'll take care of that if it happens," Director Virtari reassures the group. As the man who runs the Bureau of Corporate Security with an iron fist, there's no doubt in anybody's mind about what that means.

"Chief Executive Valen, we can handle the urch problem ourselves. Intervention from the parent company is likely to inflame the situation. We have ways of getting the information you need without the spectacle the BCS will undoubtedly create."

Virtari takes the comment personally. "Yes, let's negotiate with urch terrorists. We can send Fiolla from Corporate Affairs to smooth things over by batting her eyelashes at them," Virtari says, mocking her. He gets a smattering of laughs from the others in the room.

Fiolla's beauty makes her an easy target for harassment. Even with her long red hair pulled back, she stands out in a room. Fiolla's mother always said her beauty would be more of an asset in climbing the corporate ladder than her brains. Men stare at her chest more than her eyes, so maybe her mother wasn't wrong after all.

"That's all, people," Valen says, rising from his desk and ending the meeting without any reprimand for his BCS director's behavior. "I will take your comments under advisement and issue my orders later today. You're dismissed. Fiolla, please stay for a moment, won't you?"

The office empties efficiently while she remains seated on the Oval Office sofa. When the door closes, she turns her attention to the CEO, who is looking out the window at the Rose Garden again.

"Sir, if this is about Virtari's comment, I can assure you—"

"It's a nice day. Let's go for a walk, shall we?" Valen says, opening the door leading out of the Oval Office with a smile.

Before the collapse, the Rose Garden was nothing more than a rectangular section of grass surrounded by flower beds and crabapple trees. The location was used for receptions, bill signings, and media events.

The third chief executive of America Incorporated had landscapers remove a large section of lawn and add more plantings so future CEOs could enjoy the serenity of beautiful flora. It provides another purpose – it's the one place in this complex where you can have a private conversation.

"It's been a crazy couple of days, hasn't it?" Valen asks, adjusting his glasses as the pair walk.

"We've been through worse."

"Of course. Unfortunately, I don't have the luxury of relying on best-case scenarios. Circumstances dictate that I plan for the worst case. Managing our position in the global corporate community is like tossing around a Ming Dynasty vase. Everything is fine when you catch it, but if it hits the ground and breaks, it's tragic."

"And you think we dropped and broke something irreplaceable because we failed to stop the attack on Intercorpex?"

"China and Russia will use this incident as propaganda to sour pending trade deals with several European corporations. Others will criticize Intercorpex, claiming they should have been better prepared to deal with the outage. Intercorpex, in turn, believes it's our fault for letting the attack happen at all."

"And the patricians?"

"They're doing what they do best – blaming everybody, including each other," Valen says.

"I understand the need to do damage control, sir, but what concerns you enough that we need to stroll through the Rose Garden?"

"The bigger picture."

Chief Executive Valen is a visionary who ascended to his position because the board of directors recognized his ability to prepare a response for market moves that nobody else saw coming. He's brilliant but also cryptic. Communication is not one of his strong suits.

"You need to help me with this one, sir?" Fiolla asks, having no idea what he meant by "the bigger picture."

"Singular anomalies don't carry much meaning. However, they expose flaws that must be addressed. It doesn't matter if Liberteum was behind the Secaucus explosions or not. The rivalry between the BCS and Public Safety and Security in municipal corporations around our sphere of influence is becoming problematic."

"You're the CEO. You can tell them to do whatever you please."

"My power isn't universal, Fiolla. Virtari is a formidable man, and the board listens when he speaks. Corporate politics was born with the advent of the corporation. You learn to navigate those deadly waters, not try to tame them."

Corporations may have replaced governments, but they never abolished the politics found in bureaucracies. Rivalries exist in America Incorporated among employees who share the same goals. Competition may encourage productivity but also spawns distrust.

"How are you planning to handle this?"

"I'm not, Fiolla. You are."

She stops walking, and Valen takes two steps before realizing she's no longer next to him.

"Me?"

"I can't trust the BCS and Public Safety and Security to cooperate. I need you to bridge the gap."

"To what end?"

"Determine if Liberteum was behind the Secaucus attack. If they were, work with Chief Executive Safmor to find a non-violent solution to New York City's urch problem. You can start by bringing his chief guardian here tomorrow morning. Do it quietly."

Fiolla frowns. He might as well be asking her to boil the ocean.

"Sir, with all due respect, I'm not sure I'm the best person for this assignment."

Valen grins. "Eyelash batting aside, you have one of the sharpest minds in this building, Fiolla. I know you can do this. You have a bright future ahead filling critical roles until the board someday realizes that there is one perfect position for you."

"What position is that?"

"Mine," Valen says, turning and heading back into the Oval Office.

Fiolla is left to wonder if his words were genuine or just something he said to get her to take on an impossible task.

CHAPTER
THIRTEEN
LIBERTEUM

Abandoned Subway Station
Somewhere in the Manhattan Underground
New York City Municipal Corporation

Haven returns to a hero's welcome at the old subway station turned makeshift stronghold deep within the bowels of Manhattan. This place is defensible, hardened, and, best of all, entirely forgotten by public safety. It is the perfect place to launch this operation, especially considering its location.

The atmosphere is celebratory among Liberteum's dozen soldiers here. They all take turns slapping Scivix, Nyvar, and Haven on the back for a job well done. Haven doesn't know for sure, but he doubts that many of them thought this would be successful, especially without losing any of his men.

"Welcome back, Haven," Quarren says, hobbling up the stairs from the station's northbound platform to the mezzanine level. "I'm happy to see you and your men back in one piece."

"Thank you. Everything happened according to plan," Haven says as the men around him part to give Quarren room.

"Adiz got what he needed?"

"He seems to think so. He and Jasper took the drives to Valhalla for analyzing."

The old man nods. "No casualties?"

"No casualties," Haven says, thrusting his chin out slightly.

Quarren studies the man. After spending most of his adult life in the underground, he has learned how to measure people. That skill often means the difference between life and death. It has taken a physical toll on Quarren, but his mind is still sharp.

"I need to sit down. Why don't you give me the rest of your update in my quarters?"

"Nyvar, take Scivix and check on the outposts. I'll join you at the north tunnel when I'm done," Haven says before following Quarren down to his temporary room off the platform. He has made it home, or as close as possible.

While the rest of Liberteum was making other preparations, the old man ensured this site was ready. As a result, he knew he would be here for a while and sought to make it as comfortable as possible.

"Why did it take so long to return here?"

"We abandoned the stolen vehicle in Manhattan," Haven explains. "After ensuring Adiz made it to Valhalla with the drives, we stopped at the armory this morning and then headed south. The PSS laid a few video traps in three of the main tunnels, and that forced us to take longer routes."

Quarren nods. The PSS has been hunting urches since the first of them fled to live in the city's tunnels and sewers. One of their tactics is to install motion cameras in tunnels that they know to exist. Most urches take alternate routes, but that is even more exhausting and time-consuming than navigating the labyrinth of underground passages typically is.

"Congratulations on your mission's success. You did well, Haven."

Haven smiles briefly before looking at the ground. "Would your daughter think so? Where is she?"

"Michele and Freya are out at the moment. And yes, she would agree. Except for one thing. You were told zero body count."

"There wasn't one."

Quarren steps in front of Haven and stares into his eyes. He nods, pulls back his right hand, and slaps him.

"Your eyes betray you, Haven. Do not ever lie to me. How many?"

"Besides the guardians who caught us at the junction? The two guards at the tech company."

"I see. Were they resisting or in some way jeopardizing your mission?"

"No."

"So, you killed them out of bloodlust. Were your instructions in any way unclear?"

"They were unreasonable," Haven snaps. "If Michele were willing to place herself in harm's way, she would know that. They needed to die."

"No, they didn't. Murdering biojacked guards with so much PSS presence in the area jeopardized the mission, but you already know that," Quarren says, walking across the small room and staring at the map pinned to the wall. "Who do you think issued the order?"

Haven stares at the ground, realizing his error. While he often openly disregards Michele's instructions, the same doesn't apply to the man he considers a father figure.

"I know you and my daughter have your differences, but she's as invested in this operation as you and I are. Do you understand that?"

"Yes."

"Good. So, when she issues instructions, they might as well be coming from me. Do you understand?"

Haven scowls. He understands but doesn't like that one bit. Michele is not her father. Not by a long shot.

Quarren recognizes his apprehension. "Do you remember when we first met, Haven?"

"Like it was yesterday."

"For me as well," Quarren says with a warm smile. "You were filled with hatred and rage – a man without purpose who only wanted to lash out at the world. With Liberteum, you found that purpose. I was thrilled when you chose to join our ranks. Others were not as enthusiastic."

"You mean Michele wasn't."

"Among others. She recognized your tactical brilliance but thought you were unpredictable and reckless. She thought that you would eventually jeopardize our mission. Is she right?"

"No, she isn't."

Quarren steps back in front of Haven. "Then prove it. This is the last stand of Liberteum. When this is over, we will have either succeeded in bringing change to this miserable world or died in the process. The difference between success and failure may come down to you and you alone."

"I won't let you down. Ever."

"I know, son," the old man says, placing his hand on Haven's shoulder. "You've had a long day. Get some rest. The rave will be the last chance you all have to enjoy yourself before the operation commences."

"Are you going?"

"No, I'm far too old for those things. I will stay here and rest. We have much to do, and the PSS will be searching for us after what happened in Secaucus. Stay alert. No place is safe for us now."

Haven nods and leaves. He admires and respects Quarren, but the man places too much faith in Michele's ability to execute their plan. When the time comes, Haven knows he'll need to step up. Their lives will depend on it.

CHAPTER

FOURTEEN

THE PATRICIANS

ICX Headquarters
Midtown Manhattan Geographic District
New York City Municipal Corporation

Intercorpex was chartered in Zurich and headquartered there for the first years of its existence. Most of the trading was conducted in New York once operations were underway, and there was a push to move exchange leadership closer to Wall Street. The first administrator-general refused, fearing a conflict of interest. The chief executive of America Incorporated offered this location, and the perfect solution presented itself.

This campus housed the former United Nations until the Great Collapse. Extensive renovations were required before the exchange could move in, and it took several years to complete them. Assembly Hall was repurposed to host general meetings with executives from the world's corporations, and the Secretariat Building houses all the back-office staff. It is also home to the office of the administrator-general that Lyris rushes into.

"You're late, Executive Director Lyris," Raimius says, not looking up from his display.

"My apologies, Administrator-General. I wanted to ensure the handoff from Frankfurt went smoothly."

"You have a staff capable of performing their assigned duties, correct?"

"Yes, sir."

"Then, when I summon you, be on time, or you'll find yourself sweeping the NOC floor instead of overseeing it."

"Understood, sir. It won't happen again," Lyris says, knowing the threat isn't an idle one.

Raimius has almost autocratic power and a penchant for exercising it. He is maniacal about preserving total control and has demoted people for lesser infractions than tardiness.

"They're on their way up, Administrator-General," Nevala announces from the door. Unlike almost every global executive, the leader of the world's lone stock exchange refuses to use the computerized assistants found in most corporate offices.

"Let's get this over with," Raimius grumbles.

Lyris and Raimius take the elevator down a floor in silence. Intercorpex has had a tense relationship with the powerful patrician families. The Zurich Canon was enacted to rein in their unruly behavior, and shifted a considerable amount of power away from them in the process. The rift between Intercorpex and the global elite has only widened during Raimius's reign.

The doors open to the room, and Nevala acts as a facilitator by taking a position between the two parties. Most meetings are not this formal, but patricians like to remind everyone how superior they are.

"Administrator-General Raimius, Executive Director Lyris, it's my honor to introduce to you Patricians of the *Gentez-Majorez* Denali Keating and Shalius Covington."

The patricians are impressive men dressed in the finest traditionally cut silk suits and high-collared white dress shirts. Both wear silver replicas of their family crest where the knot of a traditional necktie would be. It's the pretentious and absurd means of announcing to the world that they are members of the *gentez-majorez*.

"Gentlemen, it is an honor to host you here today. Would you like something to eat or drink before we begin?" Raimius says in a tone that isn't as polite as his words.

"The offer is appreciated, Administrator-General," Denali says, "but we're not here for brunch. We prefer to get down to business."

"As you wish. That is all, Nevala."

"Of course, sir," she says, giving Lyris a brief flirtatious glance before returning to her duties.

"What can we do for you, gentlemen?" Raimius asks as their distinguished guests take their seats.

"I believe you already know," Shalius says, the icy edge to his voice further chilling the conversation. "You can start by explaining what happened yesterday."

"Of course. We had an unfortunate technical glitch resulting from some random violence outside our New Jersey data centers."

"Technical glitch?" Denali muses.

"Yes. It's something we're working hard to rectify. Isn't that right, Lyris?"

Lyris knows that Raimius is using him as a human shield. He came into this meeting expecting that.

"We executed a series of recovery protocols to rectify the situation, yes," the director says, keeping his answer vague.

"Gentlemen, you're treating us as fools, and I resent it," Denali scolds, realizing no further explanation was coming. "Unless you're telling me that Intercorpex experiences 'technical glitches' regularly."

Lyris looks to his boss for guidance but gets none. Instead, Raimius glares at the patricians with boiling hatred in his eyes. He doesn't like answering to them any more than he does the Board of Regents.

"No, sir. We rarely have transmission issues between facilities. Our first course of action is to fall over to our secondary links in the event the primary circuits fail."

"Only those were severed as well," Shalius says.

"Which left routing traffic over our tertiary point-to-point microwave system."

"A far less secure mode of communication, and why you balked in ordering an immediate cutover."

Lyris is dumbstruck. There isn't any way he could know that information unless there's a mole in the NOC. Denali flashes a smile as Lyris works it out in his head.

"Yes, sir, that is correct. My intent was not to delay returning to full operational status, but I wanted to ensure our actions were prudent from a security standpoint."

Denali Keating leans forward on the sofa. "There were three explosions triggered outside those data centers within seconds of each other. How did whoever placed them know it would cripple both circuits?"

"We're investigating that," Lyris says.

"We believe it was the work of Liberteum," Raimius quickly adds.

"Administrator-General, I find it hard to believe that thugs could have such intimate knowledge of Intercorpex's network."

"Patrician Keating, are you implying we're somehow involved?" The resentment drips from Raimius's voice.

"You must have a guilty conscience. I stated no such thing," Denali replies with a satisfied smile.

"And to be clear, the explosions weren't directed against the exchange. They were directed against us," Shalius adds.

Lyris can feel the heat of Raimius's anger, but he knows the two men aren't wrong. The attack severed high-frequency trading connections but spared the Intercorpex Trading and Quotation System. Lyris now understands the point of this meeting: Denali and Shalius believe that this was a deliberate attack on them.

"Who would want to do that?" Raimius asks.

"That's the question we expect you to answer before we consider this issue resolved," Denali says, rising from his chair. "And we expect that answer in short order. Good day, gentlemen."

"Administrator-General," Shalius says with a nod. "Executive Director Lyris."

Nevala escorts the two patricians out, and Raimius walks over to the table to pour himself a coffee. He returns to the sitting area and sips it in silence as he stews in his anger.

"Pretentious bastards," he mumbles, breaking the long silence. "How do they expect us to find out who orchestrated the attack? Do they want us to invite Liberteum in and ask them?"

"No, they already know. They want us to take action against them."

"What are you talking about, Lyris? Take action against whom?" Raimius demands.

"The *gentez-minorez*. Denali and Shalius are convinced that lower patricians conspired with terrorists to level the financial playing field."

"And you know this how?"

"It's a feeling."

"Okay. Since you're playing Nostradamus, Lyris, why the hell would patricians sabotage their peers?"

"Because they aren't peers, sir. You've read the security reports coming out of Zurich," the director says, sure his boss hasn't read them. "A patrician war is brewing, and we're now getting caught in the middle of it."

"That's a little overstated, don't you think?" Raimius says with a sneer. "Let the patricians fight among themselves, so long as they leave us out of it."

"We're already involved. If the BCS doesn't find and eliminate Liberteum, we should prepare for additional attacks."

Raimius glares at Lyris before standing, forcing Lyris to do the same. "Global corporations resent the expansion of our power. America Incorporated is the worst offender. They think they hold dominion over us because they helped create the exchange. Nothing could be further from the truth. It's time to show them that."

"I agree, sir."

"We cannot count on Valen to have our best interests in mind. We cannot rely on the security services of our host corporations to protect us."

"ICX Security can employ more robust security at our—"

"That's not good enough," Raimius interrupts, shifting his gaze to the windows and view of the East River behind them. "We need to be proactive. Zurich assigned a security inspector to investigate the attack. Expand his mandate and oversee it personally. Pull in whatever resources you require, but I expect results."

"Yes, sir," Lyris says, nodding before Raimius leaves him alone in the ornate room.

The corner of his mouth curls up. He led the administrator-general right where he wanted him to go. Now it's time to move a couple of pieces on the chessboard.

CHAPTER
FIFTEEN
REGISTRANT RYKOS

Central Park
New York City Municipal Corporation

Like every other, it was a day filled with modules teaching us marketing, accounting, statistics, and history. None of our instructors mentioned what happened in Secaucus. It's like the explosions never happened. Even the news dismissed them as an infrastructure failure and moved on.

Balin and I don't say much until we clear out of Dinsmore and walk through the park. It's nearly impossible to have a private conversation in this city. Even when you think you're alone, someone is either watching or listening. It's the world we live in. At some point, even our thoughts won't be private. Balin is half-convinced that they are somehow monitoring those, too.

"Do you think they'll ever fix that sensor?" Balin asks, pointing at the cast iron black streetlamp with the broken camera dangling from it.

"They fix it every week. The urches break the cameras as soon as they're repaired. Most of them live under this park."

"How do you know?"

"My father has brought his work home with him my entire life. I've listened to the Real-Time Command Center's operations reports. This is a manmade park built on top of the old manmade park. There are a lot of voids to hide in, and urches don't like being monitored, so they break the cameras when they look for food."

"Do you believe the reports?" Balin asks.

"I have no reason not to."

"You have every reason not to. All the corporation does is control the information we see. They don't want us thinking or making decisions. They tell us a version of what's happening and then what to think about it."

"Here we go again," I say, moaning. "Your cynicism is becoming legendary."

"Yeah, but I'm not wrong, either. We learn the history they wrote, watch the news they approve, and read the books they allow to be printed. Everything about this society is meant to control us while they extract every ounce of productivity to do what…enrich patricians?"

"Executives are self-serving. They're not patricians."

"They become them when they retire. That's why they protect the system."

Balin isn't wrong, but he is lucky that there are no microphones or cameras here. If he ever got caught saying that, they would engrave his name on his cell door at one of the reeducation camps. Every word out of his mouth is treasonous.

I had never thought of it that way. Corporations serve themselves, but also the wealthy patricians who created them. The promise of elite status for corporate CEOs ensures that they don't change the system in exchange for the promise of retirement. It's a powerful motivator. The world has always been infatuated with wealth.

"The system isn't perfect, but it's what we have," I say.

"It's the one we live under. It's not ours."

"Is there a difference? What alternative do we have?"

Balin smiles. "The urches found one."

I shake my head. "Yes, leave the comforts of society and become a scavenger. No thanks."

"That's what we're told they are. We don't know if it's true. What I do know is that there are no cameras, Maester systems, or corporate control down there. If their existence is that miserable, how do they throw amazing dance raves?"

So, that's what this is about. I grimace. He isn't going to like this.

"I can't go, Balin."

"You can. You just won't," he argues.

There's nothing he loves more than pushing the distinction between "can't" and "won't." He knows he can't fly. He won't throw himself off the roof of a building to prove it, even though he could. It just wouldn't end well, like me attending a rave.

"We speculate about urches every day on the way home. Wouldn't it be refreshing to find out the truth?"

"Is that why you want to go? To see for yourself?"

"Don't you? Nothing we are told makes sense if you spend thirty seconds thinking about it. It's like those explosions across the river. AME News is reporting that they were gas main breaks. Really? Three of them at the same time? Not likely."

"Balin, if my father—"

"You said he's been summoned to Washington."

"He has, but it's not like he isn't coming back. Even if he goes straight to One Guardian Plaza when he returns, he'll be in the city."

Balin gives me a look. He knows that my father will likely be working all night and not checking up on me. "I won't have this opportunity again, and neither will you. Your mother won't check up on you, and your father is indisposed. It's perfect.

You can either take a walk on the wild side, or you can be the compliant little registrant. It's your choice, but I'm going."

I hate guilt trips, and Balin is a master at them. I'm the son of the chief guardian of New York City– not only will I not get special treatment if we get caught, but the punishment will be worse for me than for him. Balin is correct, however. The stars have aligned, and this is my last chance. It's that thought that occupies my mind even after we part ways and I finish the walk back to my domicile.

CHAPTER SIXTEEN

INTERCORPEX

Keflavik Intercorporational Airport
Independent Territory of Iceland

Zyree clutches at his coat, trying to keep it closed against the gusting wind that's tearing through him. Besides signs filled with letters that have no business being next to each other, barren lava fields are all he sees beyond the airport's parking lot. A man pulls his conveyance up to the curb and hops out of the driver's seat without a coat on.

"Good afternoon, Chief Inspector Zyree. Welcome to Iceland."

The driver doesn't introduce himself. Zyree's contact lenses display the man's personal data, and he blinks to make the dossier disappear. The inspector couldn't care less who the man is so long as the heater is on in his conveyance.

"It's still morning for me."

"What time did your flight leave?"

"Almost midnight, New York time."

"That's rough. Well, there's nothing like fresh Icelandic air to wake you up. You have no luggage?"

"I won't be here long," Zyree informs him. "How far away is the data center?"

"It's in Hafnarfjörður, just outside of Reykjavik. We'll be there in thirty minutes."

Zyree climbs into the passenger seat, and the driver pulls out onto the road between Keflavik and Reykjavik while launching into a monologue on Icelandic history like he's an overcaffeinated tour guide. Zyree doesn't listen, choosing to enjoy being warm.

A half-hour later, the nameless driver pulls up to the front door to the hulking, non-descript facility set far back from the road. Security doesn't seem to be much of a concern here. After what happened outside New York, Zyree expected Commissioner-General Jurghen to order a heightened security presence.

"I hope you change your mind and stay. I'd be happy to drive you into town to sample the local nightlife. We have the most beautiful women in the world."

"Maybe I'll take you up on that," Zyree lies, climbing out of the conveyance.

He walks through the front doors and is greeted by a six-foot-three man wearing a black Intercorpex Security uniform. Zyree rethinks his first impression of this place. The guard is shaped like a refrigerator. If a vehicle did breach the perimeter, this man could stop it himself.

"Chief Inspector Zyree, welcome to Iceland. You're here to see the archive. Follow me."

Zyree follows the guard through the floor-to-ceiling turnstile designed to prevent someone from sneaking in behind an authenticated user by revolving in the reverse direction. On the other side is a mantrap consisting of two separate doors with an airlock in between. Each entry employs double authentication security measures—in this case, retinal and keycard authorization—which his escort dutifully provides.

Rows of cabinets containing hundreds of servers flank the corridor on both sides. It's loud but not deafening in the cavernous room as his escort ushers him to a small office tucked away in the rear corner of the building. He opens the door and gestures him in. Zyree enters, expecting to find a room full of boxes or stacks of hard drives. That's not at all what he sees.

A diminutive man wearing a black metal exoskeleton over his legs is standing alone in the otherwise unfurnished room. Zyree taps him on the shoulder. Startled, the man turns, allowing the facial recognition software to do its work and display his biographical information in Zyree's peripheral vision. An accident cost him the use of his legs. He had good grades in school, with high marks in science and mathematics, and worked most of his adult life for the exchange.

"Are you Zyree?" Ortan shouts, even though they are alone in the soundproofed room.

"I'm right here. You don't need to—"

"What? Oh, wait, sorry. Turn music off," he calls out into the air. "There, that's better."

Zyree looks around in confusion. "I didn't hear any music."

"Cochlear implants," he says, pointing at his ears. "I have music pumped directly to them."

"What were you listening to?"

"Something called death metal. It was popular a hundred years ago. I like it."

"Uh, huh."

"Access to old computer records is one advantage of this job. These songs are in an ancient MP3 format, but I can still play them. And trust me, Chief Inspector, you won't find anything in my biography of any interest to you."

"How did you know I was reading it?" Zyree asks, a little taken aback after scanning the file.

"You guys get a weird look in your eye when you're processing the information that pops up on those things."

There is nothing physically intimidating about Ortan, even with the exoskeleton that provides him with his mobility, but he is sharp. At thirty-seven years old, he's also an unhealthy pasty white with brown hair that hasn't seen a comb in ages. The scruff on his face makes him just as out of compliance with exchange grooming standards as Zyree is.

"I think there's been a mistake. The message from Jurghen was to report to the archive."

Ortan smiles. "You've found it. I'm the archive. I'm also the chief architect of Intercorpex's computer network. That's why the commissioner-general sent you here."

"I see," Zyree says, not understanding at all. "Nice room. Do you stare at blank walls all day?"

The stark white walls are like cotton paint canvasses artists put on an easel before applying paint to them. There are no windows to the outside world. Ortan lives in his own reality back here.

"Blank? Oh, my apologies," he says. "Huldufólk, reset all displays to visible light."

All four walls fill with network schematics, systems monitoring statistics, and data flow charts. It's a mind-boggling amount of information.

"Whoa."

"You aren't the only one with special lenses, Chief Inspector. Yours interface with the exchange security database for relevant information on whom you interact with. Mine process infrared pixels projected on the walls. I don't like people watching me work."

"Impressive," Zyree says, noting that only about five people are working in this building. "What did you call your digital administrator? Huldaflock?"

"Huldufólk," Ortan says with a laugh. "It's not my computer. It's the ancient term for the elves that run this display."

"Elves?"

"Yes. Shall we start?"

Zyree lets it go. Something tells him getting into an argument about the existence of mythical creatures with Ortan would be a waste of time.

"Sure. You can begin by telling me why the commissioner-general sent me to see you in Iceland."

"Because you need to know how the attack in New Jersey managed to do so much damage, and nobody understands Intercorpex's network better than I do. Let's see...."

Ortan stands in the middle of the room and swipes his hand like a conductor at the head of a symphony. Each motion moves the graphical displays around until the space in the center is empty. A single diagram emerges in the center with a snap of his fingers. Zyree moves closer to inspect it. Boxes and lines are everywhere, but he has no frame of reference for what any of it means.

"That looks complicated."

"It's not complicated, just complex."

Zyree shakes his head. "There's a difference?"

"Absolutely. An aircraft is complicated. Safely moving hundreds of airplanes in, out, and around an airport is complex."

"Fine. Complex it is. What am I looking at?"

"This is the circuit diagram for our New York Exchange. Highlight Intercorpex data centers," he commands his elf, causing them to become outlined with a bright red line on the screen. "Reference incident number NCI000413 and highlight."

The four data centers change from gray outlines to solid red boxes, and the lines running from three of them to a single trunk begin pulsing with the same cherry hue. Within a few seconds, the complex diagram becomes simpler to understand.

"What you're looking at are the primary and secondary circuits that run between these data centers. By design, they take different routes to their destinations. They even use different access routes out of the building. To achieve redundancy, they should never intersect. But there's a problem. Huldufólk, show the detailed circuit map."

Zyree moves closer to the wall to get a better look. The problem is obvious. "All three intersect before taking separate routes to their final destination. You said that wasn't supposed to happen."

"Precisely! It isn't. I designed the routes for an upgrade two years ago."

"Then how did it happen?" Zyree asks.

"Here," he says, doing his maestro thing again. Before long, a list of work orders pops up on a different wall.

"Huldufólk, isolate work orders for the identified circuits and display."

Ortan manipulates the list to the center of the screen and enlarges the three work order numbers and corresponding project descriptions. The titles are different, but each contains "circuit" and "routing."

"Display forms."

A "NO DATA AVAILABLE" message in red lettering pops up on the screen. Zyree looks over at Ortan, confused. Intercorpex is the gold standard for data management. Every document drafted gets stored on incorruptible solid-state drives in multiple locations, including this one. They haven't lost so much as an e-note in decades.

"The circuits got rerouted five months ago," Ortan says. "Then, somehow, the work order forms were purged from the file."

"And you didn't catch it?"

"How could I? The work orders don't exist, and operations raised no issues. I changed the Secaucus diagrams to reflect the reality of the network yesterday. Until then, all three circuits ran on separate paths according to my original design. I spent a whole night in this room trying to figure out how both sets of redundant links could go down. It wasn't until I found these that I knew."

"Just so we're clear, you're saying someone within Intercorpex ordered them to converge? Who?"

"I don't know. Our work order numbers are sequential. They can be canceled but never deleted. These were executed, but all supporting documentation was scrubbed, including the requestor's name and the approval chain. Figure out who ordered those cables moved, and you'll know who leaked the information to the saboteurs."

Alarm bells are going off inside Zyree's head. He thought Jurghen sending him to Iceland was a waste of time. Now it makes sense. Ortan's evidence is hard to refute. Someone within the exchange is involved in the attack, and that's why Jurghen wanted this visit conducted in person and kept quiet. Nobody in the NOC can be trusted.

"Thank you, Ortan."

"You're welcome. Just remember one thing: You never saw me here."

"Understood."

"Zyree, there's one more thing," Ortan says, manipulating his mechanical legs to walk over to him. "This was not a random attack executed by a group of disgruntled urches. These explosions were designed to cripple those specific links."

"Yeah, the question is, why?"

"Investigating why is your job, and I suggest you get to it. I have a feeling that whoever did this has something much bigger planned."

CHAPTER SEVENTEEN

AMERICA, INC.

The White House
Corporate Governance District
Washington-Arlington Municipal Corporation

Teman takes a deep breath as he processes the significance of this room. Once coined the "Roosevelt Room," after a former president of the United States, this is the spot where America Incorporated was born. After restoring order following the Great Collapse, the corporations merged into one entity. A year later, the new "Charter Room" bore witness to the dissolution of the United States of America for the newly created America Incorporated.

"Is the White House always this empty?" Teman asks, rising from his seat when Executive Fiolla enters.

"It's six o'clock, and most staff don't report until nine. My apologies for being late. Is this your first visit to the White House?"

"My duties rarely take me out of New York. It's a treat coming to the center of corporate power."

"I'm sure. Please have a seat. Would you like some coffee?"

Teman shakes his head. "No, thank you. I've had too much already. I hate to be blunt, Executive Fiolla, but why was I summoned here?"

"I'm not hung up on my title. Please call me Fiolla. Why do you think you're here?"

"I assume to answer for the explosion across the river in Secaucus."

"Chief Guardian, I think—"

"Teman," he interrupts with a grin. "I'm not hung up on my title, either."

Fiolla smiles. "Teman, if you were called here to answer for that, it wouldn't be with me. Secaucus is outside of your municipal corporate jurisdiction. Nobody is placing the blame for the incident on you or the Secaucus PSS."

"Tell that to corporate security."

"Well, yes, they blame you," Fiolla admits, "but nobody *else* does. BCS agents are mass-produced at West Point to be arrogant divas without souls."

"That's comforting. Then why am I here?"

His host leans forward. "We need your help."

"You could have gotten me on VidLynk to ask for it."

"This request isn't something I would've been comfortable discussing even over a secure communications channel. You cannot repeat anything about the contents of this meeting. Do you understand?"

Teman nods. "Okay."

"This is about Liberteum."

The chief guardian winces at the name. "If you want to know if I think they were behind the explosions," he says, anticipating the direction of the conversation, "the answer is yes, I do."

"Good. Then you understand why you're here. You wrote a series of cautionary memos to New York City Corporate Hall executives warning that Liberteum was still a viable entity. You even requested permission to hunt for them. Those memos were ignored."

"I wasn't persuasive enough."

Fiolla folds her hands on the table. "Maybe. Teman, you're the closest thing I can find to an expert on that terrorist group. Why do you think they did it?"

"They have a long history of being disruptive," he surmises.

"Disruptive to us, yes, but they've never interfered with Intercorpex before. They've also never left Manhattan. Secaucus is new territory for them, both literally and figuratively."

"I wasn't aware they interfered with ICX."

"That's the second reason we're not discussing this over VidLynk. The explosions in Secaucus served a purpose."

"What purpose?"

Fiolla offers a disarming smile. "When was the last known attack by Liberteum?"

"A couple of years ago. They were devastated in an ambush shortly after that. Most executives were content to believe they were eradicated."

"And in the two years since, they've managed to recruit, rearm, train, and then execute an attack outside Manhattan. I can't believe they did that on their own. Is it possible that outside influences are aiding them?"

"You think someone is pulling their strings," Teman concludes, leaning forward.

"We think it's a possibility," Fiolla admits. "This was a sophisticated attack utilizing intelligence that Liberteum couldn't have known. If something more sinister is afoot, we don't want to be caught looking in the wrong direction."

"Or not looking at all," Teman says, leaning back. If only those in power had listened to him years ago, he wouldn't have had to fly down here to have this conversation.

"Chief Guardian, you're charged with ensuring the safety and security of our employees in New York City. Our job is to shield employees from the games world corporations and patricians like to play. It's a global chess match that we can't afford to lose."

"I thought Intercorpex enforces corporate behavior?"

"You enforce employee behavior, but crimes are still committed, correct?"

Teman takes the comment personally. Crime is a tiny fraction of what it was before the collapse, reaching almost zero over the past twenty years. Most criminal activity occurs in what used to be Northern Mexico, where America Incorporated meets Central America's corporate control.

"Fiolla, Liberteum mixes into the urch population. We've never had good intelligence about their membership. They're ghosts, and anyone supporting them will be too."

"You characterized them as a 'cancer silently growing in the city.'"

"Yes, I said that," Teman croaks, less sure about where Fiolla is going with this conversation.

"Cancers must be eradicated. Chief Executive Valen will instruct Chief Executive Safmor to handle the city's urch problem. In a classified directive, you will be tasked to identify, capture, and interrogate the members of the rogue terrorist group Liberteum and determine if they're operating on behalf of any foreign entities."

"An operation of that scale will be highly visible."

"We'll take care of the optics."

"What will happen to the urches who aren't part of Liberteum?"

"You will remand them into BCS custody," Fiolla says, rising from her chair and extending her hand. He takes it and receives a firm shake. "Focus on your assignment. We will handle the rest. Good luck, Teman."

The chief guardian is escorted from the building. It was a long trip down here without knowing what to expect. Now that he does know, it was better when he didn't. The aircraft will be much heavier on the flight back to New York with the weight of the world on his shoulders.

CHAPTER

EIGHTEEN

PATRICIANS

The White House
Corporate Governance District
Washington-Arlington Municipal Corporation

The Oval Office holds symbolic meaning to the employees of America Incorporated. It was the office of the president of the United States before the collapse and the chief executive officer now. For most, it's a privilege to stand in here. To a patrician, it's just another room.

"It is a pleasure to meet with both of you," Valen says after formal introductions are made, and the facilitator steps out of the office.

"Thank you for agreeing to host us on such short notice," Shalius Covington says as the three men take their seats on the sofas.

"We take our relationships with members of the *gentez-majorez* very seriously. However, it's irregular to meet without Prima Bettancourt being present."

"She's indisposed at the moment," Denali assures him. "I've spoken with her, and she's supportive of us having a constructive conversation."

"I see."

While it's true that Denali and Shalius spoke with Talya Bettancourt, they weren't completely honest about wanting to have a constructive conversation. She didn't need to know that ahead of time.

"In truth, Chief Executive Valen, we would rather have this discussion without your largest shareholder present. As I'm certain you've heard, the attack in Secaucus severely damaged our interests."

"Assuming it was an attack," Valen says, smiling to appear non-confrontational.

"Your assumption is different?" Shalius asks.

"I believe it's prudent to let the investigation run its course."

"Fiber optic cables don't explode, Valen," Denali concludes, his voice rising. "Nor is it a coincidence that they wiped out our high-frequency trading abilities."

"The cause of the explosions hasn't been determined, and I won't insult you by pretending to be an expert. I also can't speak to how this unfortunate event interfered with Intercorpex operations. You would have to speak to the exchange about that."

"We have," Denali snaps.

"Excellent. Then what can I do for you two gentlemen?"

Denali and Shalius exchange a brief look. Denali leans forward and rests his elbows on his knees as he meets the CEO's eyes.

"We want to know what you're doing about Liberteum."

"Liberteum was neutralized two years ago," Valen says, unflinching.

"Only a fool would believe that. Are you a fool, Chief Executive Valen?"

Now it's Valen's turn to lean forward to meet the glare of his adversary. "I hope you didn't come down to Washington to insult me in the Oval Office during a *constructive* conversation."

"Of course not, but I also didn't come here to get lied to by the chief executive of the world's most powerful corporation. We can pretend that our reality doesn't exist, but it does. Liberteum is alive and well and attacking our interests outside Manhattan."

"We have no confirmation of who, if anybody, caused the explosions in New Jersey. However, we are directing the NYCMC and their public safety to investigate the matter thoroughly."

"Is that so?" Shalius asks.

Denali leans back into the sofa, breaking eye contact with his host. Valen does the same, employing the old sales technique of matching body language to establish rapport.

"Isn't a terrorist threat an issue for the BCS?" Shalius asks.

"The Bureau of Corporate Security will become involved if something is uncovered. For now, the PSS will take the lead."

"How does Director Virtari feel about that?" Denali sneers.

"The director does what's asked of him, just as all America Incorporated executives do."

"Failing to employ the BCS makes me feel like you aren't taking our concerns seriously," Shalius complains.

"Patricians typically concern themselves with results, not process. I intend to leverage whatever resources are needed to deliver them."

Denali smirks. Valen has never failed to live up to his reputation as a smooth executive. He's right. In general, patricians only care about the bottom line and not how it's reached. Continuing to force the inclusion of the BCS will only cause Valen to question their agenda.

"We eagerly wait to hear what you've learned," Denali says, rising. "One more thing, if I may, Chief Executive."

"Please," Valen answers graciously.

"Has anyone in the *gentez-minorez* reached out to you?"

"It would be unusual for lower patricians to contact my office without first discussing the matter with Prima Bettancourt."

"We live in unusual times. Wouldn't you agree?"

"Yes, I suppose I would. I've not been made aware of any contact. May I inquire as to why you ask?"

"I just have a feeling that they'll be contacting you," Denali admits. It's more than a feeling. He's sure of it.

"Thank you for your time, Chief Executive Valen," Shalius says before the two patricians are escorted from the Oval Office.

Staffers scurry from the corridor, taking great pains to steer clear of the powerful men. Most corporate executives avoid contact with them for a good reason. Patricians have been known to insist that employees be terminated for something as simple as a wrong look.

Shalius and Denali remain quiet until they reach their vehicle. Eavesdropping countermeasures are employed once they take their seats in the back, allowing them to speak without fear that the BCS is listening in.

"He knows more than he's saying."

"Of course he does," Denali concludes. "It doesn't matter. We accomplished our goal. All we need now is patience."

"We need retribution."

"And we'll get it in time, old friend. Intercorpex and America Incorporated will trip over each other investigating what happened. At that point, our path forward will be revealed."

"And if it isn't?" Shalius asks.

"Then we'll forge one of our own."

CHAPTER NINETEEN

LIBERTEUM

"The Foundry"
Midtown Geographic District Underground
New York City Municipal Corporation

There are millions of places to hide under the streets of Manhattan. Some of them, like the area they call Valhalla, would never be found by the PSS. This place is an exception. Haven is surprised that nobody has ever uncovered its location.

Located to the north of the city's largest transit hub, "the foundry" was constructed right under one of the city's most iconic avenues. The ambient noise of the high-speed rail line perfectly masks what they're doing here. In essence, they're hiding in plain sight.

Haven opens the steel door and enters the machine room. The metal storage shelves are lined with parts and raw materials as a half-dozen large 3D printers work on their assigned components. A couple of chemists at the far end of the room are busy mixing raw materials for the gunpowder that will fill the casings. The finished products ready for transport are placed on shelves along the far wall.

One of his men turns off the radio in the corner after they enter. Haven walks over and inspects a lower receiver that was just completed by one of the printers. It amazes him how these old machines can create parts with such precision.

"How long until this run is finished?"

"A day, maybe two," one of the fabricators says.

"Good. Transfer the weapons to Valhalla when they're completed. How are we doing with the explosives?"

"We built the detonators and wired them up. They're all waiting in the staging areas. All you need to do is power on the detonator and emplace them."

"You know that separating the caches makes it more likely that one is discovered," Scivix warns.

"Leaving them consolidated in one spot increases the chance of losing all of them."

"Do you have any idea what I could do with this much explosive? Why are we hitting targets with no tactical value?" Scivix asks, picking up a brick.

"Because Quarren says they have strategic value."

"Are we heading back to the station?" Nyvar asks, walking over to them.

"There's no rush."

"You afraid to face Quarren again?"

Haven eyes his subordinate. "Why would I be?"

"You disobeyed orders and killed the guards in Secaucus. He said zero body count."

"It was Michele's order, not his," Haven argues. "Despite what he says. I know that he's covering for her."

"She's his daughter. It might as well have come from Quarren."

"So I was reminded," Haven grumbles.

"Why did you kill them?"

"Are you going soft on me, Scivix?"

"Hell no. When it's my turn to leave this Earth, it'll be in a blaze of glory, taking as many as I can with me. They can all roast in hell. I'm just wondering."

Haven stretches his neck. There is no good answer. He just felt like killing them. That's not something he'll admit in front of his men and give them any ideas about disobeying his orders.

"I don't like leaving witnesses. Dead men tell no tales."

"You don't believe in Archimedes, do you?" Nyvar asks.

"I believe in Quarren. That's all that matters. I've never met another man like him in my life. I don't know if his scheme will work or not, but I get to participate by doing what I do best."

"And that's good enough?" Scivix asks.

"It is for now. One way or another, the time will come when we can put these weapons to good use."

"You know that we're all with you when that time comes."

Haven smiles. Nyvar and Scivix can always be counted on. He can't do anything to Michele while Quarren is around. He is Liberteum, and Haven won't betray him after everything the man's done for him.

His daughter is another matter. She's weak and will find herself in charge someday unless Haven gets his way. Michele doesn't understand or respect what Haven and his men do. She isn't a leader – she's the leader's daughter and nothing more.

"We should go," Haven says, staring at the door. "We're going to have to avoid the main tunnels. The PSS has been emplacing sensors and cameras again. It's going to take a while to get downtown."

Nyvar and Scivix bid farewell to the foundry workers and leave to scout the tunnel. Haven runs a hand across the weapons rack. It's only a matter of time before he gets to exact his revenge on the world. Nobody will stop that – not Quarren, and definitely not Michele.

CHAPTER TWENTY

INTERCORPEX

Bettancourt Intercorporational Airport
Queens Waterfront Geographic District
New York City Municipal Corporation

Bettancourt Intercorporational Airport, named after one of the founders of America Incorporated, is the primary air travel hub for the New York metropolitan area. Three airports served the city before the collapse. Since the number of approved travelers has dwindled to less than a quarter of turn-of-the-century volumes, only this state-of-the-art facility on the footprint of the former John F. Kennedy International Airport remains in use for passengers.

"Chief Inspector Zyree, I'm—"

"I know who you are, Director Wyeth," Zyree says, greeting the uniformed exchange employee standing in the arrivals hall after passing through the electronic security measures.

"I'm sure you do," Wyeth says, gesturing at his eyes. "I was going to say I'm your ride."

"I don't need a ride. The SpeedRail system is perfectly capable of delivering me to my hotel."

"Of course. The pedestrian transport system in this city is the envy of every corporation. It would get you to your hotel, only you aren't going there. My instructions are to deliver you to the NOC."

"Why am I needed on Wall Street?" Zyree asks with a sigh.

"Executive Director Lyris wasn't obliged to provide me with an explanation."

"I bet he wasn't. All right, let's go."

The driver holds the door for the two men outside the terminal as they climb into the back seat of the conveyance. Wyeth grabs a sealed bottle of water from the console and takes a swig from it. Zyree scans the console for something stronger and frowns when the only offerings are fruit and vegetable juices, colas, and water. There's not even a dram of whiskey to be found.

Zyree settles in for the ride to Manhattan and admires the skyline. New York is a fascinating place. It was once an epicenter of the unrest that brought down the

United States government. Thousands of buildings were looted or destroyed during those turbulent times. America Incorporated spent a significant amount of time and resources rebuilding the city into its crown jewel.

The transportation networks, including roadway and underground rail systems, were completely rebuilt. The dingy streets were replaced with splendid tree-lined boulevards or dedicated pedestrian walkways. It's an astounding transformation from the squalor and misery that defined the city fifty years ago.

The driver pulls up to the rear of the NOC, and the men are waved past a security screening checkpoint. Three minutes and one elevator ride later, they arrive at a conference room manned by a small staff posted at glass terminal displays.

"This is your war room, Chief Inspector," Wyeth says. "It's ground zero for your investigation. The personnel here are operationally tasked to you for the duration of your assignment."

"I prefer to use my Zurich staff," Zyree informs him, blinking away all the biographical information popping up on his contacts.

"These are the only personnel cleared to work on this investigation. I'm afraid that's non-negotiable."

"Where's Lyris?"

"That's not your concern. Focus on your mission," Wyeth says, tapping Zyree on the shoulder before moving into the corridor.

"Director Wyeth, are you involved in this investigation?"

The man stops and turns. "No, why?"

Zyree grins and closes the smoked glass door in his face. It was a childish stunt but satisfying nonetheless.

"All right," the chief inspector announces, "you all have the unfortunate luck of being assigned to me."

"We're happy to—"

"Shut up," Zyree commands, holding up his hand to silence the man. "The next person who tries to stick their nose up my ass is going to be spending the rest of the day at the medical center getting it reattached to their face. Understood?"

"Where do you want us to start, sir?" one guy asks from the back of the room as the rest nod their agreement.

"I want access to New York Public Safety and Security's internal systems."

"Are you serious?" a woman asks.

"Dead serious. One of you needs to hack into their system without getting caught. By tomorrow, I want to know everything they do. Then I want updates in real-time without them knowing it. Can you handle that, or do I need to find another team?"

"I can do it, sir," the guy who spoke up before volunteers.

"Good. I also want the surveillance feeds from every street camera and drone in this city piped into this room."

"Sir, we don't have the bandwidth for that."

"Who are you?"

"Tsinnial. I work for network engineering."

Zyree looks him over. The kid's hair hasn't seen a comb in months. "Tsinnial is a dumb name. You're 'Bird's Nest.' A gazillion people work in this building, Bird's Nest. One of them must know how to run fiber optic cable. I also want the name of whoever's investigating for the PSS."

"Why do you want that?" another guy in the room asks. His voice sounds like a duck quacking and seems mismatched to his beefy stature.

"Because I'm going to go to his house and screw his wife," Zyree offers. "Your new name is Duckballs. Does anyone have any other stupid questions?"

Intercorpex prides itself on being professional and businesslike. They aren't used to being spoken to like this, and their reactions betray that fact. It's just the way Zyree wants it.

"No? Good. Get busy."

CHAPTER TWENTY-ONE

REGISTRANT RYKOS

SpeedRail 3 Line
Chinatown Geographic District
New York City Municipal Corporation

The SpeedRail hurtles toward its next stop before suddenly decelerating and gliding to a halt. Passengers embark and disembark through the sliding glass barrier separating the train and the platform. Ridership is light this time of night, and the train immediately accelerates once the doors close. I'm not sure if my queasiness is from the motion or what I'm risking.

"I'm surprised you agreed to this," Balin says, speaking for the first time since we left Central Park. "I didn't think you would. You know better than anybody how many policies we're breaking."

"Yeah, stop reminding me. My father will cite me for all of them before he kills me."

I lean my head back against the rest. My father despises me. I will never reach the gold standard Varella set no matter what I do. There's no point in explaining to Balin what living in my sister's shadow is like. He's an only child and wouldn't understand.

The SpeedRail pulls into the Canal Street Station, and we exit the train onto the impeccably clean and gleaming platform. We ride the escalator out of the station and begin walking east. I don't venture downtown very often. It has a very different feel than our part of the city.

"Do you know where we're going?" I ask as we enter a quiet park off Essex Street outside a series of skyscrapers.

"More or less."

"Are you sure? Because this is quli housing."

Balin glances over at me. "What did you expect?"

Qulis are the working class—plumbers, electricians, and construction workers. They are corporate citizens but aren't subjected to the same rules as other employees. One of the worst-kept secrets is that they consort with the urches because many of them come from the ranks of the qulis.

A lone figure sits in the bleachers next to the ballcourts minding his business before Balin walks over to him. He looks us up and down before shaking his head.

"Little late for you two princesses to be out without your mommies, ain't it?" the guy asks.

"Not if we're looking to have our tiaras polished," Balin responds with a grin.

"Get outta my face, Ivy," he spits, using the derogatory term for Ivy League undergraduates, and by extension, their prep school brethren like us.

"Business first," Balin says, pulling the two silver coins out of his pocket and holding them up.

"Where did a good corporate citizen like you get a pair of slugs?"

"Why does a quli like you care? Are these the price of admission or not?"

Three more people emerge on the other side of the court. The stranger eyes them closely before turning his attention back to us. I get the impression this guy can spot a BCS agent or a guardian from two blocks away.

"Let me see your right hands." He takes the slugs, and we do as instructed, getting a black scorpion ink stamp in return. "There's a foreign goods wholesaler on Orchard. Walk straight there, but avoid Canal Street."

"Nervous?" Balin asks as we head through the park toward Hester Street.

"You're damn right I am."

We arrive at the wholesaler occupying a five-story brick building and look around. There's nobody to be found. I jump when the basement entrance opens up from the sidewalk. A severe-looking urch wielding a torchlight checks our hands for the stamp and leads us into the dark bowels of the building.

We climb through a hole carved through the foundation wall and into a tunnel. After a couple of turns, a trail of green chemical lights guides us closer to the sound of computer-generated music. At the end of the passage, another urch opens a steel door, and a blast of smoke, strobes, and loud synthesized music smacks me in the face. Balin smirks as he steps forward into the chaos. We're finally here.

The main dance area is larger than I thought it would be. Scantily clad women in short skirts and tops gyrate under the strobes and laser lighting. The men wear modified corporate clothing styled into something much more subterranean cool. No corporation would ever permit this style of dress.

The one advantage of living off the grid is nobody gets to tell you how to live your life. You can eat what you want, dress how you want, and party all you want. It's the compelling upside to this existence. The downside is that you can starve or freeze to death and face summary execution if you're ever caught.

"Let's get a drink," Balin yells over the music.

We make our way through the intertwined bodies toward a makeshift bar along the wall. The pretty-boy look of a few partiers leads me to believe some patricians are enjoying their time here. It must be great to live without fear of corporate rules or the harsh punishment of violating them.

Jugs of clear liquid are stocked on portable shelving units behind a table where a gorgeous woman in a skimpy outfit fills little plastic cups from one of them. We take two and toast each other before tossing them down. That was a mistake. I cough violently as the swill burns my throat. Balin's eyes bulge out of his head.

"Ya boys must be new here. That's how everyone looks the first time they try urch shine," a blonde woman in an impossibly short skirt and tube top says as she sidles up to Balin. "Oh, you're a cute one."

Balin looks like he wants to say something but is still recovering from the effects of the shine. His new urch friend rubs up against him and caresses his chest with her hand before moving it far lower than is customarily acceptable.

"Oh, and so well-equipped, too," she says, grabbing at his crotch. "Come on, baby, show me a good time."

He whispers something in her ear, causing her to frown and saunter away.

"Why didn't you go for it?"

"I don't have the slugs to pay her. Oh my, oh my," Balin breathes as two more hot women walk past us. "C'mon. Let's explore."

There must be a few hundred people jammed in this basement. Hand after hand grabs at me as we push through the crowd. This is almost worth getting caught here.

"Ever wonder where all these urches live?" I ask Balin as we reach another bar and are poured two more cups of shine.

"New York City is huge, Rykos. There are plenty of places underground for them to live."

Some urches are born underground and don't know any other way to live. The rest committed a corporate capital crime by cutting out their biojacks. If these "freejacks" are ever caught, they'll be arrested, prosecuted, and executed at Rikers Island by the time the sun goes down.

"Let's check out the side rooms," Balin says after his second shot of liquid courage.

Before I can protest, he struts down a hall where the crowd thins out. I catch up to him as he pushes a heavy curtain aside and stumbles into a room furnished with battered leather couches and small tables. Candelabras perched on small tables provide the lighting.

"This is a private room, pal," a sinister-looking urch threatens.

"Whoa, relax, man, we're all friends here," Balin says in a smug voice no one in the room seems to appreciate. "From the looks of your women, you're about to get real friendly, too. Maybe we'll join—"

The urch standing closest to Balin moves toward him like lightning and presses a knife against his neck. I am about to protest when I'm grabbed from behind and punched in the gut. The blow pushes the air out of my lungs, and I gasp to refill them.

"Want me to kill them, Haven?"

"You have a big mouth," the guy who hit me says to Balin. "I wonder how well you'll use it after we cut your tongue out."

"I…I didn't mean any offense," Balin stammers, sounding stone-cold sober now.

"You assumed my friends are whores. That *is* offensive."

"We didn't mean—"

Another punch to my abdomen cuts the apology short. My knees buckle, and only the vice grip from the wiry man holding me keeps me upright as I double over in agony.

"I'm not talkin' to you," the man they call Haven says.

"I'm sorry!" Balin wails in panic.

"You're not, but you're about to be. Take a slice out of him, Scivix."

The urch grins devilishly as he brandishes the knife.

"Let him go!" I sputter between gasps, struggling against the man holding me.

"Or what, Ivy? Oh, I get it. You want more attention."

Haven steps in front of me. His short brown hair, unshaven face, and creepy green eyes make him the most intimidating person I've ever seen. He rivals the hardened agents serving in corporate security. He winds up, and I brace myself for another punch when a female's voice rings out from the corner.

"Haven, stop."

"He insulted you, Michele. He thinks you're a whore."

"Don't confuse ignorance with intent," the angelic voice calmly says.

A moment later, she glides into the light of the candelabras. The warm glow illuminates her long dark hair, olive complexion, and almond-shaped eyes. She's the most beautiful woman I've ever seen. My mouth just hangs open as I gaze at her.

"What? You've never seen a woman before?" Haven asks, mocking me to the amusement of his comrades.

"Uh…no…I mean…yes," I stammer unintelligibly.

"Is this guy for real? Let's put them out of their misery."

Two more men emerge from behind an opening in the back corner of the room. Their hair, clothing, and demeanor mean one thing: patricians. I would never have thought they would be so chummy with urches. Unless…

"Are you an urch?" I ask Michele, finally finding my ability to speak.

Laughter breaks out in the room at the dumb question. I force a nervous laugh of my own.

"We really don't like that term," she states coolly. "Sheathe your knife and show them out, Scivix," Michele commands, turning back to the other woman in the room.

"This isn't the kind of situation people usually walk away from," Haven says, grabbing my shirt. "I suggest you be on your way."

I look down at the rippling muscles in his forearm. I also notice something else. Tattoos are forbidden by corporations and are thus popular within the urch community. Haven's is a sleek black torch with a flame from the top, making it look like it's in motion. Underneath is a phrase that looks like Latin. My heart jumps into my throat.

"We're going! We're going," Balin shouts as Scivix pushes him into the hall.

"That woman you called a whore saved your life," Haven says in a chilling tone that matches the terrifying look in his eyes. "The next time I see you, she won't stop me from carvin' you both into little pieces."

Haven disappears behind the curtain. Balin and I waste no time scrambling away from the room toward the dance floor.

"Are you okay?" I ask, trying to settle my heart rate.

"Yeah, you?"

"Scared out of my mind. We should get out of here."

"Are you kidding?" Balin asks, gesturing around the room with his arms. "This place is big enough not to run into them again. Come on. We came here for booze and loose women. Let's find both and try to forget that just happened."

I don't share his enthusiasm. I just met the most beautiful woman I've ever seen and endured a confrontation with her friends. Balin wouldn't believe it if I told him, but we were in the company of the most dangerous terrorists in the world. I know in my heart that we just escaped an encounter with Liberteum.

CHAPTER TWENTY-TWO

AMERICA, INC.

The White House Situation Room
Corporate Governance District
Washington-Arlington Municipal Corporation

Over two centuries' worth of major geopolitical decisions were made in the Situation Room of the White House. The president of the United States met here with top advisors to weigh the consequences of countless military operations. Since then, the room has changed, but its purpose hasn't.

"I guess I'm late to the party," BCS Special Agent Caylem says after entering. Nothing about his tone was apologetic despite being ten minutes late and the last to arrive.

Among the groups represented here by executives are Human Resources, Corporate Information, Public Affairs, Information Technology, and Corporate Development. Valen is sitting in his customary position at the head of the table.

"That's a more appropriate statement than you know. We'll have to bring you up to speed quickly," Valen says. "The New York City PSS has uncovered actionable intelligence and is about to launch an operation to apprehend a large gathering of urches in the underground."

"So, whose authority?" Caylem asks, glancing over at the VidLynk featuring Chief Executive Safmor.

"Mine. Is there a problem, Special Agent?" Valen snaps.

"No, sir. Who's in charge of the raid?"

"I am," Teman replies on the adjacent display. "My name is Chief Guardian Teman, and I'm posted in our mobile command vehicle about ten blocks from the rave."

"Ten blocks?" Valen asks.

"It's not as far as it sounds," Caylem says. "Fine. Walk us through your plan, Chief Guardian."

A twenty-block map section of lower Manhattan pops up on the adjacent display. Two concentric rings encircle a central building that turns red. The map zooms in further, and three dots are illuminated a block away.

"We've identified the main access and two other ingresses to what they call a 'rave.' It's nothing more than an alcohol- and drug-filled dance party. The target is located beneath an old school scheduled for demolition and replacement in the Chinatown geographic district."

"Are you certain there are only three exits?" Caylem asks, shaking his head.

"We have a high degree of certainty based on ground-penetrating radar from our drones," Teman explains as three paths leading from the school to the square are drawn on the map.

"Continue, Chief Guardian," Valen orders.

"A guardian has infiltrated the rave to locate any urches that may be associated with or have information on the group Liberteum. Once we confirm we haven't been detected, we'll secure the tunnels and use a laser charge to punch a hole in the floor above. Two concentric perimeters are set up. Every inch of ground in a quarter-mile radius is covered with video, infrared, and thermal surveillance if anyone slips out."

"What about resistance?" Valen asks as the map zooms back out.

"We're taking full precautions in case any of them are armed, sir. Guardians will be outfitted with energy dispersion plated body armor, night and thermal optics, and assault weaponry with full ammunition load."

"That's a lot of armament to deal with people living under the streets, Chief Guardian. Especially if you don't intend to use it," Special Agent Caylem observes.

Every set of eyes shifts around the room as awkward silence blankets it. The implication of Caylem's comment was clear. Despite the withering stares, he makes no effort to amend or justify it.

"You don't approve?" Valen asks.

The agent leans forward over the table. "I would love to understand how the urches have enough freedom of movement to throw underground parties, but that's a question for another time. We know that they're a growing problem throughout our sphere of influence. Data shows urch black markets lead to corporate losses, sap productivity, and drain our economy. And then there's the crime. The bottom line is that they should all be eliminated."

"We've been down that road once before, haven't we, Special Agent?" Fiolla argues, speaking for the first time. "If memory serves, it caused more problems than it solved."

"I don't think that's an accurate assessment, Executive Fiolla."

"You don't think months of riots and billions of Bytecoin in lost productivity is an accurate assessment? How about the loss of corporate prestige and the devaluation of our stock?"

"The problem was solved. That's what matters."

Fiolla smiles pleasantly. "The BCS has never been about the big picture, has it?"

Caylem glares at her. "I resent the—"

"All right, enough," Valen interjects, shutting down the argument. He's heard enough. "You're approved to commence your operation when ready, Chief Guardian."

"Yes, sir," Teman acknowledges, turning to someone behind him in the command vehicle. "Tell all units to assume final positions and prepare to breach."

CHAPTER
TWENTY-THREE

LIBERTEUM

Urch Rave
Chinatown Geographic District Underground
New York City Municipal Corporation

Nyvar has been to dozens of these raves. He can spot anyone out of place with ease. Right now, he's nursing a drink watching something that isn't quite right.

"Everything good?" Scivix asks after tapping his shoulder. "You look locked onto something. What's wrong?"

"I'm not sure," Nyvar says, scanning the dance floor. "What do you make of him?"

Nyvar points his small finger in the direction of a man standing against the wall.

"An urch who's had one too many?"

"He's not drunk, and I don't think he's an urch. He's acting like he doesn't want to be here."

The two men watch as something catches the man's attention. His demeanor changes, and he pushes away from the wall, moving toward the two boys who stumbled into their room an hour ago.

"Are those our two heroes from earlier?"

"Yeah, they are."

The Ivies spot the man, and concern flashes on their faces. They end their conversation with a couple of women and check over their shoulders as they skirt the edge of the dance floor.

"That's an interesting development."

"Let's follow them," Scivix suggests.

Nyvar and Scivix push through the middle of the dance floor and pick up the pace when they reach the other side. There are only two directions the two kids could have gone. Both are dead ends.

Nothing can be heard over the thumping bass, so they go left around a corner and venture deeper into the corridor. The two men stick close to the walls, making themselves nearly invisible in the low light. Halfway down the hall, they know they guessed correctly.

The bored man from the dance floor has the two punks cornered. He shines a light into their frightened faces. Nyvar glances at his counterpart, making out his silhouette in the darkness. Nobody brings a torchlight to a rave.

"Rykos? What are you doing here?"

"What are *you* doing here?" one of the kids replies.

Scivix was wrong. It wasn't fear on their faces: It was shock.

"Aw, hell. You've got to be kidding me! I need to call this in."

"No, please don't."

"You don't understand, Rykos. I *have* to."

The man pulls up his sleeve and reveals a tablet device. Scivix has seen enough. He draws his knife and crouches low, creeping to within ten feet of his quarry. Moving in from behind, he stands and yanks the man's head back by his forehead. In one easy motion, he draws the knife across the man's throat, causing his open carotid artery to spray blood on the two kids.

"No!" one of the kids screams as he lurches forward.

Scivix drops the body and moves for his gun as the dead man's torchlight hits the ground. The light shines upward, providing enough illumination to see Nyvar standing with his gun pointed at the kid's chest. He stops moving.

"You have some explaining to do, Ivy. Walk," Nyvar commands.

Nobody at the rave gives the quartet a second look as they push through the dance floor back to their makeshift room. Nyvar and Scivix give the scared boys a shove into the middle as Haven fiercely glares at them.

"What's this about?" Michele asks, rising from the couch.

"How do you know that man?" Scivix asks, holding a knife to the smaller kid's throat. "I'm talking to you, Ivy. He called you by your name."

"Nyvar! Scivix! Answer me!" Michele shouts.

"We identified an infiltrator," Nyvar explains, staring at Haven. "He then followed these two to the end of one of the dead-end corridors."

"Guardian?"

"I think so."

Haven nods and pulls his gun, holding it to the larger kid's head before looking at the other.

"You have three seconds to talk. Three. Two. One."

"He was a guardian," the kid says. "I think you're in danger."

"Don't try to concoct some fancy lie to get yourself out of this," Haven cautions. "I'll make your death take four hours."

"In danger? How?" Freya asks, her voice healthy with skepticism as she comes up alongside Michele.

"I think the PSS is about to conduct a raid."

"And how would you know that?" Michele asks.

The kid swallows hard. The larger one closes his eyes as Michele patiently waits. Whatever secret these two kids have, neither wants to reveal it.

"Because my father is the city's chief guardian."

Haven's fist lands on the kid's head with enough force to spin him around. He drops to a knee and stares into the barrel of a gun when he looks up.

"I should have killed you!" Haven barks, moving his finger to the trigger.

"Wait!" Michele orders, gently pushing the gun away. Haven glares at her but doesn't resist. "How do you know the PSS is coming?"

"My father went to Washington and then straight to work. He got special orders down there because of the explosions across the river. That guy you killed was on the PSS tactical team."

"Collecting intelligence?" Freya asks.

Haven nods. "Microdrones can't see through smoke and are obvious down here. The right person can blend in."

"It's a response to Secaucus," Freya concludes.

Michele exchanges a glance with the others. Her father was right, but that's something to worry about later. She nods at Nyvar, who bolts back out through the curtain.

"What's your name?"

"Rykos. My friend is Balin."

"Okay, Rykos. Why would the son of the chief guardian come to an urch rave?"

"It's a long story."

"Well, Rykos, I'm going to want to hear it. For your sake, we'd better not find out you're lying. You have no idea what you're getting mixed up in."

"Michele, he's right!" Nyvar says, throwing the curtain aside. "They must have moved in when they lost contact with their asset. Guardians just seized the main entrance."

"Jesus!" Freya exclaims, pulling out her weapon. The others do the same.

"Stay calm, everyone," Michele says. "Haven? Where's Farron?"

"I haven't seen him. He can fend for himself. We can't. Guardians will seize the exits and secure the building. Then they'll tighten the noose."

"What are we going to—"

Screams echo over the thumping bass in the main room. The techno music cuts out, and urches scramble in a panic. The entire rave descends into pandemonium as urches trample each other to reach the exits.

"They're using lasers to cut through the floor above us," Scivix reports.

"They can drop in surveillance pods," Freya concludes.

"Or use gas to incapacitate us," Haven mumbles. "If we stay here, we're goners. We have to make for an exit and hope for the best."

"I agree," Michele says, clearly not liking the sound of those odds.

"Scivix, kill these two and prepare to move."

"Move where?" Freya asks. "The exits are blocked. It's suicide."

"Upstairs," Rykos offers.

The group looks at him. Haven frowns and gets into his face. "Without rifles, we don't have the firepower to penetrate their armor. I'm not getting into a firefight that I can't win."

Rykos shakes his head. "Their strength will be on the inner and outer perimeters during the breach. Once they feel they have the objective contained, they'll collapse inward."

Michele eyes Haven, who nods. "How do you know that?"

"My father brought me to training exercises when I was little," Rykos admits.

"It's as good an idea as any," Freya says.

"What do we do once we're up there?" Nyvar asks. "Assuming we make it."

"Improvise," Haven says, checking his weapon. "Can I kill them now?"

Michele looks at Balin and Rykos. If they were associated with the raid, they'd be severely punished for divulging that information. Scivix watches as she entertains the idea that they may be who they say they are. There's no time right now to confirm it.

"No. Take them with us. They may still prove useful."

CHAPTER
TWENTY-FOUR
THE PATRICIANS

Keating Family Brownstone
Manhattan Upper West Side Geographic District
New York Municipal Corporation

Denali leans back and admires his New York residence's ornate moldings and trim. He has countless homes scattered worldwide in climates ranging from deserts to tropical islands. Despite its diminutive size, this brownstone is a favorite outside of his estate in Greenwich.

He opted for a night in to resume this game with his old friend. Connected chess is older technology, but the feel of the carved medieval pieces in his hand makes it more rewarding than watching a computer move holographic pieces.

Shalius makes his move, and the computer signals the board. Two lights illuminate, one telling him which piece to move and the other to where. In this case, Shalius's knight jumps to F5.

"You're going to regret that move, old friend," Denali says, using his best foreboding voice.

"You forget yourself, Denali. You may fancy yourself a grandmaster in the political realm, but you are a novice at the actual game."

The patrician laughs. Shalius isn't wrong. Of all the chess games the two men have played, Denali can count on a few fingers the times he's won. It's okay. He might not like losing, but he wins at the things that matter.

Denali is making his move when Abbot enters the room. "Pardon the interruption, sir, but Commander Lacune wishes to have a word. He says it's urgent."

"The commander often has a warped sense of urgency," Denali says, annoyed at the interruption. "What is your opinion of the request? Is it important or nonsense?"

"I am in no position to judge that, sir. However, I believe you should listen to his briefing and make that determination yourself."

Abbot has been at Denali's side for most of his adult life. He's far more than a butler. Part administrative assistant and part confidant, Abbot is the one man on Earth Denali truly trusts to look after his interests. The patrician considers him family, and despite his far lower station, treats him accordingly.

"It's okay, Denali," Shalius says. "I have other things to attend to. You are eleven moves away from being checkmated, and I can finish beating you later."

Denali stares at the board. He doesn't see it. "You will eat those words when we speak again."

Shalius smiles and shakes his head before signing off. Denali stands and moves to the bar to refresh his drink.

"Show him in, Abbot," Denali says, and his trusted butler does as instructed. "What's the problem, Commander?"

"The New York Municipal Corporation's public safety and security organization is conducting a raid on a suspected urch rave in Manhattan."

"Where in Manhattan?"

Commander Lacune calls up a map on his wrist tablet and sends it to the main display. "Chinatown Geographic District."

"We have no business interests in that area of the city. Why are you so flummoxed?"

The commander stares at the ground. "Your son is there."

Denali closes his eyes and curses under his breath. "Are you certain?"

"Yes, sir."

"Has he been apprehended?"

"We haven't received notification through official channels, nor do we know his status. He hasn't responded to any of our VidLynk requests."

Unlike corporate employees, patricians do not have biojacks that report their location. The technology is considered too insecure for them to use. Considering the security forces and medical personnel they travel with, there's no need for those devices. No patrician belongs at the end of an electronic leash.

"That's not out of the ordinary for Farron. He dodges requests from me all the time. If he's at that rave, I want him extracted. Mobilize your men, Commander."

"Sir, that's not possible."

Denali lowers his drink and shoots a nasty stare at the head of his security forces that the man averts his eyes from. "Excuse me?"

"We don't have the manpower in the city to conduct an extraction. Even if we did, it would interfere with America Incorporated's security operation. Intercorpex would consider that a breach of the Zurich Canon."

The Zurich Canon has Denali longing for the old days. The elites should never have agreed to its adoption. No organization should have been permitted to place a yoke on them, least of all the God-complex administrator-generals at the exchange.

"Damn Intercorpex and their ridiculous rules. Why was my son at that rave? Does he not realize that the guardians were bound to strike back at the urches after what happened in Secaucus?"

"I can't speak to his motives, sir."

"It was a rhetorical question, Lacune. Locate my son and inform me the moment you know his location."

"Yes, sir. At once," Commander Lacune says before departing the room.

Denali tunes into AME News to see if there's any coverage. There isn't, and he should have known as much. America Incorporated doesn't share breaking news unless they know how to spin it to their benefit.

He takes a sip of his drink. Farron will ruin this plan if he doesn't get his life in order. Too much is riding on this for him to be this reckless. He may need to be taught a lesson sooner rather than later.

CHAPTER TWENTY-FIVE
REGISTRANT RYKOS

Urch Rave
Chinatown Underground
New York City Municipal Corporation

We charge across the almost vacant dance floor and crash into a wave of fleeing urches pouring out from a tunnel. They're all screaming bloody murder and clawing at their skin like it's on fire. There are no physical indications of trauma, but nobody would know that by listening to them. Their wails of pain are terrifying.

"The PSS is using a thermal deterrent in the tunnel to keep everyone penned in," Haven says. "Come on."

We struggle through the crowd to another door as the twin lasers cutting the hole above us cease. Nyvar dives out of the way as a thirty-six square-foot section of the ceiling drops onto the dance floor. A spinning black drone drops through the hole and spews cylindrical objects that embed into the walls.

"We only have seconds!" Haven screams, pointing at a metal door opposite the corridor that the guardian cornered us in.

"Hurry!" Michele shouts, urging Balin and me along.

When we reach the exit, the most horrible sound I've ever heard nearly splits my head open. I cover my ears and bend over, begging for the sound to stop. I lift my head enough to see an urch fight through the pain to fire a weapon at the guardians above. Bullets rip through his body, and he collapses to the floor.

Scivix grabs my shirt and pulls me through the door before slamming it closed behind me. This area of the basement is coal black. Nyvar powers on a small torchlight to provide some illumination. Huge rusting steel boilers line the far wall as a remnant of the ancient heating system for the building above. In the opposite corner is a small service stairwell.

"Moment of truth," Michele says. "Haven, Scivix, do your thing."

They peek up the stairwell and slowly creep up it until they're out of sight. I jump when gunshots ring out from above. After a couple of tense minutes, Haven returns.

"All clear. Two guardians down. Scivix is securing the stairs and watching for any response. It won't be long before they're missed."

"What do you mean 'down'?" Balin shouts.

"Shut up," Haven orders before turning to Michele. "We can fight our way out, but it's long odds that we'll make it."

"I have a better idea," Freya says. "Strip off the guardian uniforms and armor and put them on. That will buy us some time."

"Then what?" Nyvar asks.

"There's an opening to the Canal Street sewer from a set of buildings two blocks east," Michele says, turning to look me in the eyes. "How far out will your father set up the perimeter?"

"I don't know."

"Nyvar, I need your light."

He complies, and Michele begins drawing a map in the years of dust that has settled on the boiler. I can see her working through whatever comes next in her mind.

"What have you gotten us into?" Balin asks me in a whisper.

"Okay, let's go," Michele orders, wiping the map away.

We move up the stairs and stop at the landing. They continue up into the darkness of the second level. Michele and Freya keep watch as Nyvar helps Haven and Scivix don the tactical gear, already having stripped the uniforms off of the corpses.

"What's the plan?" Haven asks.

"You're going to march everyone out of here like we're prisoners and head east."

"They're going to have hundreds of surveillance feeds, Michele," Haven argues.

"Yeah, but little capacity to process them in real-time, even with computer assistance. It's a short walk to the tunnel, and we can use that to get to Canal Street and escape."

"There's a tunnel under Canal Street?"

"There are tunnels everywhere, Ivy," Scivix informs me.

"I'm not going. I'm done with this!" Balin shouts as he pushes past Nyvar.

"Balin, calm down—"

"I'm not calming anything. You're all crazy!" His voice rises to a screech as he continues to struggle against the urch.

"We don't have time for this," Haven says with a heavy sigh.

He clubs Balin over the head with the butt of his weapon, causing his knees to buckle. He lands on the ground face-first and doesn't move.

"Damn it, Haven!" Michele complains.

"It had to be done."

She closes her eyes and takes a deep breath. "All right. We'll leave him here."

I'm not sure I heard her right. "What? You can't do that! They'll think he was helping you."

"That's true," Haven agrees, aiming his weapon at Balin's head. "I have a better option."

"No!" I lunge for the weapon as the shot rings out. I stare back at Balin in horror. Blood is oozing from a wound in his right arm, but he's still alive.

The gun comes up, and the barrel is pressed against my forehead. I close my eyes, fully expecting this to be the end. I thought providing them a way out could buy me some time to get out of this mess. Now that time has run out.

"You're next, Ivy."

"Hold your fire, Haven."

"He can identify us, Michele. You know that's true. This is the only way."

"Maybe not," she says, getting close to my face. "Rykos, you can come with us, or Haven will shoot you and your friend in the head. It's your choice. Make it."

I glare at her. I never intended for anyone to get hurt. Not Balin, and not the two guardians who won't be going home to their families. I don't want to go with them, but there's no viable alternative. I nod, ashamed for agreeing.

"Stupid," Haven decrees, withdrawing the weapon from my face.

"March us out," Michele commands. "Remember, we're prisoners."

We don't encounter any guardians as we exit the far northeast corner of the building. Sirens pierce the air, and there isn't a single employee on the street. I can hear the high-pitched whine of aerial drones hovering overhead. With my hands clasped behind my neck, I follow Michele and Freya in a single-file line under the watchful eyes of Haven and Scivix. All is quiet for the first block, and then our luck runs out.

"Who are they?" a guardian in tactical gear asks, getting the attention of his partner.

"Urches who tried to escape," Haven says, his voice calm and authoritative.

"Move them to the holding area per the briefing," the guardian relays as we keep walking.

"Roger."

"You're heading in the wrong direction, guardian," the other man shouts at Haven.

"Hey, why aren't those urches in cuffs?" a sergeant says, appearing from around the corner. "Guardian, I'm talking to you! Why aren't those prisoners secured?"

This is not good. I make eye contact with Haven as we stop. One transmission and every guardian in the vicinity will run in our direction. We won't make it ten feet, much less another block. That's when the corner of Haven's mouth curls up.

He nods at Scivix and whirls around, spinning on his heels. The round Haven fires off catches the sergeant in the throat. Before the other two guardians can react, he pumps another round into the face of one while Scivix takes down the other, walking over and finishing him with a headshot.

My legs get weak beneath me. Three men just died right in front of me. Any further thought of helping leaves my mind as I collapse to the ground.

"We need to run for it. Go!" Freya shouts.

Nyvar grabs me and pulls me toward the entrance of a bodega situated on the corner of the block. Haven smashes the bottom pane of the door and unlocks it. We all file inside.

"Find the basement access fast," Michele demands. "The PSS will come looking for their men."

Nyvar finds the stairs, and we head down. The basement has a door that leads to an adjoining building, then another. After a few minutes, we come to a wall with a bookcase. Haven slides it out of the way, uncovering a narrow tunnel leading into desolate blackness.

"We should head west and then south into the park. That gives us the most travel options," Michele explains.

"What about him? We can't bring him where we're going," Freya says.

"And we can't leave him alive, either," Scivix says.

Michele looks apprehensive, but she isn't arguing the point, either.

"He knows who we are. Facial recognition may or may not identify us, but he can with absolute certainty," Haven adds, pulling his gun out again.

"I'm sorry, Rykos. They're right," Michele says, brandishing her weapon.

"Wait, I—"

"I'm sorry, but this is going to hurt a little," she says, an instant before my vision explodes and then, nothing.

CHAPTER TWENTY-SIX

INTERCORPEX

Lyris's Office Suite
ICX New York Exchange
New York City Municipal Corporation

The double office doors swing open, and Lyris checks the time. It's been almost a half-hour since he summoned Zyree. The director doesn't hide his annoyance when the arrogant inspector walks in eating an apple and parks himself in a chair. The disdain only grows when he props his feet up on the desk.

"Make yourself at home, Chief Inspector."

"You wanted to see me?" Zyree asks, taking another chunk out of the fruit.

Lyris stands and moves around the desk. He reaches out with his left hand and sweeps Zyree's feet off the desk. The inspector offers a satisfied smirk.

"I got off a VidLynk with the administrator-general thirty minutes ago."

"Oh, yeah? How is the boss?"

"Impatient. You've made no progress since you've been here. That means you're either the laziest or most incompetent investigator in Intercorpex Exchange Security's ranks. Give me one good reason I should keep you around."

"My winning personality."

"We'll see how far that gets you when I report your failure."

"What makes you think I've failed?" Zyree asks, getting a skeptical look in return. "Have you read the old books?"

"What?"

"You heard me. Have you read the old books? You know, the ones printed before the Great Collapse turned the lights out on the world, and corporate historians rewrote history for the masses."

"I run the global operation of the world's sole stock exchange. That doesn't leave free time for frivolous reading."

Zyree snickers, unimpressed. "You really should make time. In the 1960s, the United States got tangled up in a war in Vietnam. At the height of the conflict, they had over a half-million men combing the jungle for enemies to kill."

"So what?"

"Their enemy was adept at hiding," Zyree continues. "The Vietnamese fought on their terms to negate the advantages of their foe's stronger military. The result was a bunch of rice farmers winning a war against the most powerful country on Earth."

"What's your point, Zyree?"

"America Incorporated is on the verge of repeating history, and so are you. If you want Liberteum eradicated, it takes time to do it right."

"Let me clue you in on the real lesson of that war," Lyris says with a sigh. "The United States lost because politicians didn't listen to the wise advice of their generals and the defense industrial complex. They failed to wage war using tactics that would guarantee victory. Modern books paint a more accurate picture of the truth. What's the point of this history lesson?"

"We identify Liberteum and then beat them at their game instead of doing precisely what they think we will."

"You have no idea how much pressure is being applied, Zyree," Lyris says. "Patricians are livid, Administrator-General Raimius is crankier than usual, and we need this problem solved. You've done nothing to help."

Zyree smirks. "I don't need to. New York Public Safety and Security launched an operation to round up urches in the search for Liberteum."

"What? When?"

"It's happening right now. They throw these big underground raves attended by hundreds of people. The PSS just crashed the party in the hopes that Liberteum is there."

"Why aren't you monitoring their activities?"

"I was until you summoned me here."

Lyris is steaming mad. Had he been aware of any of this, he would have had this conversation in the war room. That's probably why the chief inspector didn't say anything about it.

"That sounds like a Bureau of Corporate Security operation. Why is PSS executing it?"

"Chief Executive Valen issued a corporate directive giving the NYPSS authority. Or so the memo said."

There is a tense moment of silence between the men.

"How would you know that?" Lyris asks, his curiosity getting the better of him. He never learned that you never ask questions that you don't want to hear the answer to.

"We hacked into their systems."

"You what? I explicitly told you…never mind. Where's the raid?"

"Chinatown Geographic District."

"Well, I'm rooting for them."

Zyree shakes his head. "They won't succeed. If everything I've heard about Liberteum is true, they won't get caught in a dragnet. The bigger problem is that they'll go deeper underground, and we won't find them until it's too late to stop the next attack. Now, if you'll excuse me, I have work to do."

"What makes you think they have another one planned?" Lyris asks before the obnoxious chief inspector reaches the door.

Zyree surveys the room and launches his apple core across the office toward the small trashcan positioned next to the coffee service. Against all odds, it goes in.

"Call it an instinct. Until now, Liberteum was running a marathon. Now they're sprinting. You don't do that unless you see the finish line."

CHAPTER TWENTY-SEVEN

AMERICA, INC.

Chinatown Geographic District
New York City Municipal Corporation

Guardians continue to escort apprehended urches bound at the ankles and wrists to the park between Canal and Delancey Streets. The number of those in custody has grown exponentially over the past hour. These urch raves were far more popular than Teman thought. He expected a couple hundred tonight, but the number is closer to three times that.

Most surprising is how many qulis were there, which explains how they powered the sound system and light show down there. There are also nearly a dozen patricians in custody, not that it matters. The privileged sons of the elite will walk away without punishment or recrimination, and they know it.

"Chief Guardian Teman, we have a problem."

The urgent appeal is not what Teman wants to hear. The operation is an unqualified success. The intelligence that can be extracted from these urches is almost limitless. Dead or captured Liberteum terrorists would be the cherry on top of this night.

"What is it?" Teman asks into his microphone as he observes his guardians process another group of urches.

"There's something you need to see in the command truck."

"Okay. I'll be right there."

He hustles back through the field to the command truck parked on Chrystie Street. Despite the difference in technology, the vehicle doesn't look much different from what the NYPD used a century ago. The guardians in the back can monitor video feeds and run facial recognition, behavioral analysis programs, control surveillance, and command tactical assets in real-time.

"What is it?" he asks, climbing inside and closing the rear door. The looks on the faces of the guardians betray them. He knows this is going to be bad.

"Five guardians are down, sir."

"What? Where?"

"Two in the northeast corner stairwell next to an unconscious employee suffering from a gunshot wound. The other three were a block away. All five were shot dead."

Every pair of eyes in the truck is trained on Teman. Losing guardians is just not something that happens anymore. He fights the urge to lash out in anger and focuses on the response.

"How long ago?"

"Their biojacks went offline seven minutes ago, and we sent a squad to investigate."

"Search the video from that street and find the footage of the shootings."

"Yes, sir," a female sergeant responds.

"Sergeant, contact the RTCC. I want every resource dedicated to this. They can run facial recognition on the urches later."

"Roger."

"I want every surveillance feed on the east side of the perimeter monitored. Have all available units shut down a ten-block radius from the school. If a rat crawls out of a sewer, I want to know about it. The moment a target emerges, I want a tactical team on top of them in seconds."

"Yes, sir!" Captain Spirak responds before issuing the new orders.

"I have the video footage, Chief Guardian."

The display comes to life. The green night vision video shows two guardians confronting six figures. The streetlights provide ambient illumination, but not enough for standard video. The details get lost with the night vision. Teman shakes his head. He knows what happened. The urches used the uniforms from the dead guardians in the stairwell to bluff their way out.

The ruse almost worked. Flashes of gunfire erupt, and his men are dead three seconds later. A technician switches camera views. The group moves east and disappears into a small shop.

"Do you have a clearer view?" Teman asks.

"Send me the file," a technician at a different terminal offers. "I can use filters to clean it up."

"Nobody left the building they entered. They may still be in there," another tech suggests.

"I doubt it," Teman says, rubbing his chin. "Send a tactical unit in and search every building on that block. Lift the ROE restrictions. Lethal force is authorized."

The rules of engagement were discussed at great length before this raid. Chief Executive Safmor's directive was to use non-lethal force to the extent possible. Now that they're dealing with armed urches, the game has changed, and so have the rules.

"Sir, the computer has 3-D modeled rough faces from the footage for all targets except the ones with visors. It's as close as we're going to get."

"Run what you have, starting with current HR databases. If they're freejacks, they'll be in there."

"I have a hit on one of them," the technician says, sounding surprised.

"What? So soon? Who is it?" Teman demands from across the command truck.

"Uh...sir, you should see this."

Teman complies, leaning in to see the display. His eyes grow wide in surprise as he studies the image and the biographical data outlined in red next to it. His mouth goes dry as nervous energy pulsates through his body.

"That has to be a mistake."

"It's a ninety-three percent match," the technician reassures quietly, pointing to the confidence index at the bottom of his display. Teman knows from experience that these facial recognition programs are rarely wrong when over ninety percent. Still, it must be.

"There's no way. Confirm Rykos's current location."

After a few keystrokes, an error comes up on his display. "There's no biojack information available, sir."

Teman takes a deep breath. Rykos was outside the rave with the urches who killed his guardians. His biojack would register his location unless it was removed or he's dead. Both options nauseate the chief guardian.

"Where was the last signal location?"

The technician stares up at him. "The bodega."

Teman closes his eyes. "Run the location of Registrant Balin. Cross-check with Rykos's known acquaintances to ensure accuracy."

Teman wrings his hands to control his emotions as he paces back and forth in the cramped truck. The technician types the required commands, and a display with latitude and longitude coordinates comes up. He translates it to a map, but Teman knows the location before it's announced.

"New York City Advanced Medical Center."

"He was in the stairwell with the two murdered guardians," Teman whispers. "Who else knows about this?"

"Just us, sir."

"Let's keep it that way for now."

Teman pats the technician on the shoulder and exits the command truck. He stops a dozen meters away and stares up at the hazy sky. Only a few stars can be seen through the city's light pollution. He needs to wish upon a few of them right now to get out of this nightmare.

Captain Spirak emerges from the command truck and comes alongside him. Teman closes his eyes and inhales deeply. The cleansing breath doesn't help alleviate his angst.

"We can't hide this forever, Chief Guardian."

"I know. I'm not asking you to," Teman says without looking at him. "I don't know why Rykos was here tonight. All I know is that he's in imminent danger."

"Sir," the captain says, leaning in closer to his boss. "This is a serious violation of protocol."

"Yes, it is, and one that I will likely get terminated for. Those are my orders, Captain, and I assume full responsibility for the consequences."

"I understand, sir, but it's not that simple. Your son wasn't resisting. He was helping them escape."

"You're wrong."

"You watched the same video I did, Chief Guardian. Don't let your emotions compromise your judgment. I need to report this."

Teman walks a couple of steps away before stopping. He closes his eyes and hangs his head. He needs to think this through but can't force himself to focus.

"Captain Spirak, you did your duty and reported it up the chain of command. Now, I'm ordering you to find my son. If it turns out that Rykos was helping them, so be it. Until then, treat this as a kidnapping. Understood?"

It's clear from his body language that the captain disagrees. Employees are programmed to follow the rules without exception. How the PSS deals with kidnapping is much different than with a collaborator. Teman knows his order is more than a process deviation – it's sedition.

"Yes, sir."

Teman walks away from the command vehicle and back toward the processing area. His stomach turns at the thought of Ilaria's reaction when she hears about this. Rykos is her favorite, just as Varella is his.

The park is chaotic but under control. Urches in all manner of dress, and some barely dressed at all, have been separated into small groups around the park. The thought of his son being around these dregs is sickening. The possibility of his helping the worst of them is terrifying.

Teman stares again at the sky. "Rykos, what have you done?"

CHAPTER TWENTY-EIGHT

LIBERTEUM

Lower Manhattan Underground
New York City Municipal Corporation

Michele and Freya are the first to climb through the tunnel's wall access into the station. Haven follows Scivix and Nyvar, who are dragging the unconscious Rykos. The men heft him up to the platform and carry him to the mezzanine level where the ticketing area was.

"What happened?" Quarren asks, noticing the ragged and exhausted group and rushing over to them.

"The PSS raided the rave," Michele explains. "We were lucky to escape."

"Who's this?"

"Our good luck charm."

Haven scoffs as his men lay Rykos on the ground. "We should have dumped him on the way here."

Quarren looks at Michele for an explanation. "He's the son of the chief guardian. He warned us about the rave moments before it happened."

"There's a lot more to the story," Haven says.

"I bet."

"Do you want me to get rid of him?"

Michele shoots Haven a glare before sharing a pleading look with her father. He recognizes its intended message.

"No. Put a cot in one of the utility rooms off the platform. He'll be our guest for the time being."

Haven throws his hands up as Scivix and Nyvar scowl. "You can't be serious! He's a threat to the operation."

"So was going to that rave, Haven," Quarren says evenly. "That didn't stop you."

"You agreed to let us go...your daughter even went."

Quarren grins. "Part of being free means you have to live with the opinions and decisions of others, even if you disagree with them. We all knew there would be repercussions for Secaucus. I warned you of the dangers. You evaluated the risks and assumed them to cut loose one last time before enacting our plan. Who am I to tell you no?"

"And now you're willing to assume one yourself?"

"Yes. I don't know what the young man's motivations were, but if your lives were spared because he helped you escape capture, then we will spare his."

"That's not what happened!" an exasperated Haven shouts. "He gave us a couple of seconds' warning. That's all. We didn't need him."

Quarren nods slowly. "A couple of seconds is often the difference between life and death, Haven. You know that better than most men."

"If he's the son of the chief guardian, they'll come looking for him," Scivix interjects.

"And I know you and Nyvar and Haven and the others will be ready to defend us if they do. I assume you already removed his biojacks."

"The ones we know about," Haven mumbles. "Who knows if that kid has one we missed?"

"If he does, then it's already too late," Nyvar admits. "They'll know that we're here and will be coming."

Quarren nods at Haven.

"I'm going to check the tunnel. Scivix, Nyvar, check the other accesses and our street-level outposts," Haven commands.

The three men head in different directions. Michele helps her father pull Rykos off the ground and bring him to a utility room. She retrieves one of the cots from the bunkroom and lays him on it.

"You warned us not to go to the rave. Why weren't you more insistent about it? It's almost like you knew this would happen."

"I don't have a crystal ball, Michele. I cannot see the future any better than you or Haven. Even if I could, it was your decision. You're no longer my little girl. The hardest thing for a father is watching a child grow up to make their own decisions. It's also the most important thing."

Michele takes a deep breath and looks up and down the dimly lit tunnel that runs through the station. Her father has a knack for making her feel guilty, even if it's unintentional. The decision to go to the rave was hers to make and ultimately come to regret.

"Was that the real reason you brought this boy here? It wasn't because he warned you about the raid."

"You know me too well. He could be the one, Father."

"The son of the chief guardian?"

Michele nods. "Nobody is more surprised about that than me. Could you think of a better candidate?"

Quarren rubs his chin and joins her in staring down at their unconscious guest. The Archimedes plan has always had an Achilles' heel. It's a variable that can't be solved for, so they need an outsider who can do the math for them. Michele thinks he's the one, and she may be right. Unfortunately, they gave up on that piece of the puzzle long ago.

"Then we'll have to find out quickly. Time is running short."

CHAPTER
TWENTY-NINE

INTERCORPEX

The "War Room"
ICX New York Exchange
New York City Municipal Corporation

Zyree stands and stretches. There has been an insane amount of information for the team to process since the raid ended. His team could use a break, but they need to find something useful first. Nothing in the interviews they've downloaded from the PSS servers points to Liberteum.

"Have all the captured urches been identified by the PSS?"

"Negative," Bird's Nest says, staring at his display. "The processing is complete, but the RTCC shifted resources to another tasking."

"Another tasking? Does that have something to do with the guardians who were killed?"

"Unknown, Chief Inspector. There's little information on it," Duckballs says.

"The information is being suppressed, even within the PSS itself," Zyree says, taking a seat and rubbing his chin as he stares at the main display. "Odd. It should be all hands on deck to find their killers."

They can sift through the video and read the PSS interrogations, but he already knows that the urches who murdered those guardians were Liberteum. The PSS must know that as well, so why be so secretive? There's something more to it, and that has Zyree intrigued.

"Duckballs, where would the guardians' bodies be taken?"

"An NYCMC mortuary facility, probably."

"Where?"

"Uh, there's one in the Bronx, one in Queens, and one on Houston Street."

"Bingo. Bird's Nest, get into their systems and see if you can find anything. Start with the Manhattan mortuary, but check them all. What about the street footage of the killings?"

"I still can't find it, Chief Inspector," a woman announces, "but I will."

"No, you're wasting your time," he says with a sigh. "It's gone."

Between street cameras, body cameras, and drones, there were more than three hundred video feeds of the raid. Any corporation's most sensitive work environments employ strict controls to safeguard information. This is achieved by "air-gapping" computers in many instances, meaning the terminals are not networked. Zyree nods as he concludes that the NYPSS has those videos secured on one of these air-gapped systems somewhere in their headquarters.

"What do you want me to do?"

"Comb through other video feeds in the area. It's a long shot, but maybe we can catch them emerging from a manhole or something."

"Yes, sir."

"What about you?" Zyree asks her partner.

"I've been searching for suitable footage from inside the rave to run through a facial recognition algorithm. Most of it is either infrared or night vision. There's not enough data for the computers to create a profile without compositing images manually, and that takes time."

"Chief Inspector, this feed has promise," a third technician says. "The farther you get from the strobes and dust kicked up when they drilled through the floor, the better the quality. This angle covers a hallway off the main room."

She points at the display as the video rolls. Figures are visible, but bad angles obscure faces. Zyree watches as a small group stops at the open dance floor.

"That's interesting," he mumbles, leaning in. "They're using security tactics."

A face on the display causes his contact lenses to go nuts. A biography pops us, and he can't believe what he's reading.

"Stop the video. Back it up five seconds and advance frame by frame. Freeze it!"

She complies and watches Zyree stare intently at the display. He shakes his head. It wasn't a misidentification. He's watching a ghost.

"Creating a 3-D facsimile now," the tech says, as a series of green lines on the screen takes facial measurements.

"Don't bother," Zyree says, crossing his arms. "Just process the raw image through the ICX database."

The technician does as instructed, and the results pop up a few seconds later.

"Senior Inspector Haven. This urch is one of ours?"

"Was one, as in past tense. Haven's been dead for almost three years."

"You knew him, Chief Inspector?" Bird's Nest asks.

Zyree nods. "I gave his eulogy."

Everyone in the war room stares as the chief inspector moves to the front of the room and stands in front of the main display. The video at the raid plays up next to Haven's bio. They just found a key piece to the puzzle, and the revelation is terrifying. With Haven involved, this investigation just catapulted into a whole different reality. This assignment just became personal.

"This group with Haven is our top priority. I want every shred of information about them we can find. Someone call Director Lyris and tell him to meet me in his office."

"Sir, it's two in the morning," one of the technicians informs him.

"Yeah, that's why I'm not calling him myself. Tell him we found the break we were looking for."

Zyree finds a chair in the corner and closes his eyes. This can't be happening. Haven was more than just an inspector – he was a friend that he'll now have to bury a second time.

CHAPTER THIRTY

AMERICA, INC.

The White House
Corporate Governance District
Washington-Arlington Municipal Corporation

Fiolla fidgets in her chair as she waits in the Oval Office. She has been summoned here many times and always finds Chief Executive Valen waiting for her behind his desk. This morning was different. She was told to take a seat and get comfortable.

The door swings open, and Valen storms in, fresh from his Situation Room conference. He slams his tablet computer on the large wood desk before looking out at the Rose Garden.

"I was called into that briefing at six this morning. It's a good thing because every news outlet in the world except ours is reporting what happened in New York. On the other hand, our executives are keeping employees in the dark. Do you see the error in that logic?"

"Patricians get global news feeds."

Valen turns and points at her. "Bingo."

"I don't know who ordered the lid or why," Fiolla offers.

"Me neither. It was the first question I asked public affairs, considering this was a propaganda opportunity. They said that they didn't have enough information to craft a narrative. What do you think of that?"

Fiolla lowers her eyes and exhales. Valen is a master at asking questions that have no correct answers.

"AME News presents what they're told to. Either Public Safety didn't release the information or the BCS suppressed it."

"Astute analysis, Fiolla," Valen says, flashing a smile as he sits in his high-backed leather chair. "It was both. Per my directive, the PSS released an informational notice addressing the growing urch problem. Details of the raid were sparse, so the New York desk editor contacted Corporate Hall and One Guardian Plaza who never responded. Then they tried the BCS's New York office and were told to kill the story completely."

"The BCS never should have ordered that."

"I agree. These organizations often forget they play for the same team."

Intercorporational rivalries are not unheard of. They're commonplace in many Asian companies, especially Japan, where subsidiaries are organized into keiretsu that compete against each other as much as foreign corporations.

"Would you like me to coordinate with public affairs and corporate communications to air a package about the successful operation last night?"

"No, because the raid wasn't successful," Valen says. "It was a complete failure."

"With all due respect, sir, why am I here?"

The CEO looks up at Fiolla from his desk. "I want to find out why."

"Sir?"

"Five heavily armed guardians in full tactical gear were killed. The informant inside the rave was also found murdered. The perpetrators escaped through an airtight perimeter. I want to know how that's possible. Most of all, I want to know if they were Liberteum. Have you heard anything from Teman?"

Fiolla shifts her weight as she wrings her hands. "He sent me a data file with detainee information, but nothing tying them to Liberteum or the guardian killings."

"What useful information does he have on the urches he apprehended?"

Valen's strategic mind craves information. Fiolla knows she needs to give him something worthwhile before he targets her with his frustration.

"None, except not all of them are urches. There were countless qulis and almost a dozen sons of prominent patricians."

"Interesting," Valen says, rubbing his chin. "Get me their names. Is Teman hiding something?"

"Hiding something?"

Valen leans back in his chair. "There's always a reason for withholding information. We do it to control the narrative. I want to know what narrative Chief Guardian Teman is controlling."

"I'll find out, sir," Fiolla says, rising and straightening her tunic.

"No, I won't ask you to do that. I will. It's time to pay the chief guardian a visit in person," Valen decrees, picking up the tablet he slammed down on his desk when he walked in. "We're going to New York tomorrow. Set it up."

CHAPTER THIRTY-ONE

REGISTRANT RYKOS

Lower Manhattan Underground
New York City Municipal Corporation

My eyes struggle to open. Once they do, I wait for them to adjust to the darkness. The dank smell of mildew and stale air fills my nostrils. I lift my head off the cot and immediately regret it. The dull throbbing in my temples seizes my whole head.

It's only now that the memory of how I landed here rushes back. I sit up and notice the crimson dots at the center of white gauze taped to the top of my right hand and around my left wrist. What did these savages do to me? A second later, it hits me: They removed my biojacks.

"You never should have brought him here," I hear the muffled voice say outside the door as it echoes off the dingy white tile walls.

"We didn't have a choice," Michele retorts.

Shadowy figures become silhouetted from makeshift construction lighting haphazardly strung up behind them.

"Are you serious? We could have left him with his friend. We could have killed both of them. There were plenty of other choices."

"Haven's right, Michele," a third voice that sounds like Nyvar adds.

"We only got out because he warned us," she argues. "Don't forget that."

"We got out because we were lucky," Haven argues. "If he's the son of the chief guardian, the PSS will turn the entire city upside down looking for him. If he's still transmitting, we're in grave danger just staying here. Both those outcomes jeopardize our plans."

"You guys cut out his biojacks."

"His father is the *chief guardian*. He might have an extra one that we missed."

I glance at my bandages. Biojack locations are kept secret for reasons like this. They found both of mine, even if they don't know it. Nobody will find me here.

"Archimedes is in motion. There's too much at stake. We need to get rid of him."

"What do you want to do? Put a bullet in his head and dump him on the street?" Michele asks with an exasperated tone in her voice.

"I was thinking in the river, actually," Haven deadpans. I hate this guy.

This conversation isn't encouraging. The second worst mistake I've ever made was going to that rave. The worst was giving them information that helped them escape. One act of disobedience and an error in judgment will cost me my life.

"I'm sorry to disappoint you, Haven, but Rykos stays here and is not to be harmed. That's the end of this discussion."

"You need to take this to Quarren," Haven demands. I watch him grab Michele's arm as she starts to walk away.

"I already have. He left the decision to me, and I just made it."

"Are you planning on reforming him or using him as a plaything?" Haven asks, getting a chuckle from Nyvar.

In the time it takes me to blink, Michele has a knife to Haven's throat.

"Touchy, touchy," Haven mocks with amusement.

"My father believes that you're a valuable tactical expert, Haven. I wonder how good you'll be with your throat cut."

"You and your threats," he says, slowly easing her knife away. "Daddy won't be around to protect you forever. When that day comes, maybe we'll see who gets the best of whom."

"Fortunately for you, that day is not today."

Haven disappears from my sight, and Michele heads in the opposite direction. Nyvar stands outside the small room and turns to catch me staring at him. Crap. I should have pretended to be unconscious.

"Aw, hell," he exclaims before stomping toward me.

My mouth is as dry as a desert. I want to say something, but the words don't come.

"What are you doing awake?" he asks, checking behind him.

Before I can respond, he brings the butt of his weapon up and slams it down on my head. My vision explodes into stars….

CHAPTER
THIRTY-TWO
THE PATRICIANS

One Guardian Plaza
Municipal Governance District
New York City Municipal Corporation

Farron Keating stares at the chief guardian and knows what he's thinking: The only thing worse than a teenage patrician is an entitled twenty-something patrician. The superiority complex comes when sons and daughters play more significant roles in their parents' empires. Farron is no exception and knows that he's untouchable.

"Do you think this is funny?" Teman asks after his last question results in a derisive chuckle.

"There's nothing funny about this, Chief Guardian. My father won't think it is, either."

The chief guardian leans back in his chair. Farron checks the clock on the wall. It's getting close to ten o'clock, and his father still isn't here. He must be letting him sweat this interrogation out as a penance for getting caught in the raid.

Farron looks around. The interrogation room is not much different from what would have been seen a hundred years ago. It measures ten-by-ten and features a single aluminum table and two chairs in the middle. A two-way mirror adorns the far wall, and an ultra-bright LED light in the center of the room makes it brighter than is comfortable. Like everything in this corporation, everything is monitored by video and audio.

"I'm asking simple questions. Your father would expect you to give me straight answers."

Farron shakes his head slowly. "I doubt that. You have no jurisdiction over me."

"That's true. I don't."

"Then let me go."

"Not until you answer my questions," the chief guardian says, leaning forward and clasping his hands in front of him.

"That's not going to happen. You don't even have the right to question me."

"Come on, Farron. Are you telling me that your fancy tutors never forced you to read the Zurich Canon? Article two, section seven specifically relates to patricians' responsibilities when detained or questioned by corporate security personnel following the commission of a crime."

"Does it?" Farron asks with a smirk.

The Zurich Canon is Intercorpex's governing document that defines the protections and entitlements of all patricians. The second article specifies that no patrician can be prosecuted or detained by any established corporate security organization unless it is determined that an act that violates the canon has been committed.

"I can't arrest you but can ask questions if I believe you were involved in an illicit activity."

"Consorting with urches is not a crime under the canon, Chief Guardian."

"Murder is. I lost six men last night. If you know who committed that capital crime, it's abetting. So, you can cooperate, or I will refer your family to Intercorpex. It's your choice."

"I'm sorry for your men, Chief Guardian. I am. But I can't help you."

Farron stares at his interrogator impassively. Chief Guardian Teman uses the remote in his pocket to activate a display on the wall showing the picture of a teenage kid.

"Have you ever seen this person?"

"No."

"Okay, what about these people?"

He calls up a second picture, this one of a group outside the Chinatown rave. It's not the best quality, but it is clear enough for someone to identify the woman if they know her.

"Nope. They don't look familiar."

"Are you sure? Not even the woman? I mean, she's beautiful. How hasn't a wealthy, strapping young man like yourself not crossed paths with her at one of these raves? She'd be tough to miss."

"I've never seen her," Farron maintains, leaning back in his chair and folding his arms.

A rap on the door interrupts Teman before he can press him further. He looks over when it opens.

"Sir, Patrician Keating is here to see you," a guardian announces from the threshold.

"Time's up," Farron says, smiling.

The chief guardian rises from his chair and heads out of the interrogation room before turning and striding down the hallway. No patrician likes to be kept waiting. Denali Keating is among the worst of them.

* * *

"Good morning, sir. I'm Teman, Chief Guardian of New York Public Safety and Security."

"I know who you are, and you know who I am. What's unclear is why you think you have the right to question my son."

"We should talk in private," Teman says, leading the patrician to a small sitting area.

The two men sit on a pair of sterile office couches before Teman launches into explaining the raid and how it was executed. He concludes with actions taken once his son was identified as a patrician, including removing restraints, providing breakfast, and notifying him about what had transpired.

"The questioning is intended to determine if Farron can provide information that would lead to the apprehension of known terrorists who may be connected to the murder of six guardians. That is permitted under the canon."

"You were looking for Liberteum?" Denali inquires with a raised eyebrow.

"It's possible they're responsible."

"So, you must think that my son, a patrician of the *gentez-majorez* and heir to the Keating empire, is involved with terrorists?"

"No, sir, but I believe he knows who they are."

Denali's demeanor changes. He was patient through Teman's explanation and more cordial than usual. He has more of an edge now.

"He said this?"

"No, but—"

"Then he denied it, and you think he knows their identities anyway? So, now my son is a liar?"

"No, sir. I never meant to imply that. I apologize."

Denali is amused but doesn't show it. The chief guardian was wise to stop justifying his questioning. There's little doubt that his mentioning Liberteum had the opposite effect than intended.

"Release my son, Chief Guardian Teman," Denali says, standing. "I don't believe he's of any further use to you or your investigation."

"Right away, sir."

The chief guardian walks back to the interrogation room. Farron is standing and checking his hair in the two-way mirror when he enters.

"You're free to go."

"Well, it was wonderful to meet you, Chief Guardian. I hope you find the people you're looking for," Farron says before stopping and leaning in to his ear. "But you never will."

Teman turns his head and locks eyes with the arrogant young patrician. He knew it. Unfortunately, there's nothing more that he can do about it.

"I'll see you again soon, Farron."

CHAPTER
THIRTY-THREE
AMERICA, INC.

The America Tower
Manhattan Financial Geographic District
New York City Municipal Corporation

The America Tower is the tallest skyscraper in the Western Hemisphere following the destruction of Chicago during the collapse. Situated at the northwest corner of the old World Trade Center site, the "Freedom Tower" was renamed in 2042 after the corporate charter was adopted and the ten-year infrastructure plan was announced. Restored to its previous glory, it now stands proud as the crown jewel in America Incorporated's most important city.

"I didn't know you were going to be in New York today," Teman says, looking resplendent in his uniform.

Public safety and security in every municipal corporation adopted distinct uniforms to set them apart. The guardians in New York City sport a design that is a throwback to the dress uniforms of the old United States Marine Corps.

"Neither did I," Fiolla says. "It was a last-minute decision."

"I figured. I assume you want a debrief of—"

"Not here."

She motions him to the elevator bank. The pair are joined by a man in a ceremonial BCS uniform who swipes his hand across the reader and presses the button for the building's top floor.

"Are we going to your office?" the chief guardian asks as they rocket to the top of the skyscraper.

"I don't have an office in this building."

"Okay, so where are we going to meet?"

"We're not meeting, Teman," Fiolla explains as the elevator doors open. "You're here to see Chief Executive Valen."

A shiver runs down Teman's spine. The CEO doesn't meet with lowly public safety officials. It's almost unprecedented, and that's what scares him.

"Fiolla, what's this about? What aren't you telling me?"

"No, Teman, it's more like what aren't you telling us? The PSS has been less than forthcoming with the details about the raid. Senior executives are now wondering why."

"I never meant to—"

Fiolla holds up her hand. "Let me give you some advice. Valen plays the political game at a level you couldn't reach in three lifetimes. Don't lie to him. If he thinks you are, your next stop when you leave here will be Rikers Island. Follow me."

There's no need to wait for an acknowledgment. Chief Guardian Teman dug this hole and will either heed her advice or he won't. That's his problem as she leads him past the reception area and into an ornate outer office.

"He's waiting for you, Executive Fiolla," the executive secretary informs her.

A pair of large wooden doors automatically swing open. Valen stands at the floor-to-ceiling windows and admires the view of Manhattan that stretches past Central Park. Introductions are made, and the two men shake hands.

"Why don't we all sit?"

The group moves to the seating area. Teman selects a sofa, and Fiolla sits opposite him. Valen eases into one of the upholstered chairs and studies him intently.

"Chief Guardian, I've been briefed on the Chinatown operation. I'm sorry to hear about the guardians who were killed. Please extend my condolences to their families."

"Thank you, sir. I will," Teman responds, his voice jittery.

"Is there any new information on who killed them?"

"We're working to identify the shooters. We've identified one person seen with the escaping party."

"You're talking about your son, Rykos," Valen says. The blood drains out of Teman's face. Fiolla is equally surprised.

"How did you know that?" he finally stammers.

"You don't become CEO of the world's most powerful corporation without knowing how to get information. Tell me about your son."

Teman starts from the beginning and explains every detail leading up to when he realized his son was trying to escape the raid with the urches. He concludes with his reason for not divulging that information. Fiolla listens intently. The chief guardian made some bad decisions but is man enough to own up to them. That's increasingly rare in the modern business age.

"Do you think he was kidnapped or working with them?" Valen presses.

"I...I honestly don't know."

"You didn't rise to the rank of chief guardian because you have bad instincts," Valen presses. "What do you think?"

"I think whatever happened that night was not what he expected. I believe he's in danger, and I have to find him."

"That's why you've been so secretive?" Fiolla asks.

"I didn't mean to deceive you. I needed time to figure out what happened."

"Were the suspects that killed your guardians and kidnapped your son members of Liberteum?" Valen asks.

"There's a high degree of probability. They used illegal weapons to kill the first two guardians. Most urches aren't armed with sophisticated weapons, nor do they know how to use them."

Valen gets up and moves to a credenza where the coffee service sits. He pours himself a cup and adds some milk and a sugar cube. He stirs the brew, appearing lost in thought.

"You detained the sons of some patricians," the CEO says, still stirring.

"Yes, sir. They were released."

"I heard one of them was Farron Keating. How much do you know about his father?"

Teman shifts in his seat. "I know that he has a residence in the city but spends most of his time at his Greenwich estate. Rumor has it that he's trying to steer Intercorpex policy."

"He's the most influential patrician of the *gentez-majorez*. You took a considerable risk holding his son once you learned who he was."

"Farron Keating was at an illegal gathering of urches and might be abetting a dangerous terrorist group. I treated him as prescribed by the Zurich Canon."

"You played fast and loose with the spirit of the canon, and you know it," Valen says. "That's why the first VidLynk Denali Keating made when he left your building was to the Oval Office."

"Sir, I—"

"You didn't lie to me earlier, Chief Guardian, and that's the only reason we're still having this conversation," Valen says, his hand raised with two fingers extended, indicating that he's not finished speaking. "But your initial deception concerns me. You may have felt it justified, given the circumstances surrounding your son. I assure you that it wasn't. I have little patience for people I cannot trust."

* * *

Valen lets his statement hang in the air for Teman to sweat over. The pause has the desired effect.

"Executive Fiolla convinced me that your familiarity with the city would overcome your tactical and technical inexperience in sensitive operations. I'm not sure that was a wise move in hindsight. Tell me, Fiolla, do you still have confidence in the chief guardian?"

"I don't like being kept in the dark," she confesses, staring directly at her boss. "Ordinarily, I would question whether he's up to the task. However, his son's involvement makes this a special situation. The chief guardian is personally invested, and I think we should let him proceed in tracking down Liberteum."

Valen regards his junior executive for a moment before taking a sip of his coffee. Fiolla can't read what he's thinking. It's either what he expected her to say or the opposite.

"Interesting. Well, it looks like you are getting a stay of execution, Chief Guardian. Fair warning, if you repeat past mistakes, you'll receive less mercy from me than Executive Fiolla is showing you. Are we clear?"

"Yes, sir," Teman croaks.

"Good. You're dismissed. Executive Fiolla will be out in a moment to escort you to the lobby."

The chief guardian wastes no time fleeing the office. The doors slowly close behind him. Fiolla turns her attention back to Valen once they're shut.

"That was a gutsy decision, Fiolla. I expected you to advise me to get rid of him."

"I think this is the best course of action, even if it's one that you didn't expect or want."

"That's why I like you, Fiolla," Valen says with a laugh. "You don't suck up. Most executives would have stumbled over themselves backtracking. Do you think his son is involved with them?"

"I don't know, but Teman will be more motivated to find and destroy Liberteum than anyone. He'll search every corner of this city himself if that's what it takes."

Valen takes another sip and nods. He returns to his desk and sets the cup and saucer on it. He looks up after a long moment.

"Okay. Escort him out. Understand that you're married to this now. If Chief Guardian Teman fails, you fail. Ensure you're putting your trust in the right place."

Fiolla's heart seizes for a second, and she nods. She understands what that means. She's now in charge of the eradication of Liberteum. It was her choice to spare Teman, and she must live with the consequences. Teman had better love his son enough to risk everything to get him back.

CHAPTER THIRTY-FOUR

LIBERTEUM

Abandoned Subway Station
Somewhere in the Manhattan Underground
New York City Municipal Corporation

Of all the advantages of this abandoned station, the one disadvantage is the lack of privacy. There are rooms that people can retreat to and quiet spaces on the opposite side of the tracks, but very few of those areas are illuminated. Michele assumes that's why Haven has some of his men gathered on the mezzanine.

"What's going on?" Michele asks, climbing the stairs from the platform.

The men look at each other and then at Haven, who glances up briefly before returning to a map spread out on a folding table. "We're planning something."

"Planning what?"

"The assassination of Chief Executive Valen. We found a way to take him out."

"Out of the question," Michele says, shaking her head.

"What? Are you going to dismiss it that quickly? Hear me out at least."

Michele crosses her arms and nods at Haven.

"Valen will convoy from America Tower to the airport. He can take only a few routes over the East River, but I'm betting on the most direct one. We will place spotters here, here, and here," Haven says, pointing at the map of Manhattan. "That will confirm the route and number of vehicles. If he crosses at Midtown like I think he will, we can ambush him here. He'll never know what hit him."

"You want to set up a surface ambush in broad daylight while the entire PSS is hunting us? You don't have the manpower for that," Michele says, poking the first of many holes in the plan.

"We don't need much. We'll use one of the trucks equipped with a transponder in the motor pool. We can load it up with explosives and drive right up alongside him."

Michele shakes her head. Now it's Haven's turn to cross his arms. He waits for the balking and inevitable useless questions he knows are coming. He's thought this through. Some details need to be ironed out, but this isn't his first operation. He knows they can pull it off.

"What do you think that will accomplish?"

The question throws him. "We'll chop off the head of the snake."

"And then what? We run for our lives while another grows in its place? The chief executive officer is more than one man – it's an institution. The board of directors will replace Valen within hours and galvanize people against us and all urches. Assassinating Valen doesn't solve anything."

"And your plan does?" Haven seethes, his jaw tightening.

"There needs to be a fundamental change in this world. That change must include the people, not just taking down the system."

"The people?" Haven asks, nodding and looking around the station. "Are you serious? We're surrounded by enemies who hate us. You can daydream all you want, but that will never change. I see an opportunity to kill their leader, and I'm going to seize it."

"The hell you will," Michele says, taking a step toward him.

"Stop me."

Haven's men stand by his side and glower at Michele. This wouldn't be a fight she could win, even if she wanted to try. Haven would be a challenge one on one.

"We have a plan, Haven. You agreed to help execute that plan. If you go back on your word, you aren't the man of honor you think you are."

His face turns red as he gnashes his teeth. "You think you have the right to judge me?"

"My daughter is right, Haven," Quarren booms as he labors up the opposite side of the stairs to the mezzanine level. "You looked me in the eye and said that you would support Liberteum until the day you died. Do you remember that conversation?"

Haven lowers his eyes. "I remember."

The men step aside as Quarren reaches them and places his hand on Haven's shoulder. It's a fatherly gesture and one that Michele has seen him use to defuse tempers before.

"Then what's the problem, son?"

"Quarren, I respect you, but all this...this plan...it's not going to have the effect you think it will."

Michele feels her anger energize her spine. "How do you—?"

Her father holds up a hand, and she instantly falls silent.

"Why not, Haven?"

"Because these people can't be saved. I've watched and interacted with corporate employees for years. This system is all they know. They rely on it to take care of them because they can't care for themselves. The world died in 2038, and its soul perished with it. All that's left is a corpse being kept on life support."

Quarren nods. "I understand why you feel that way."

"Do you?" Haven challenges.

"Yes, but I think you're wrong. You're here. Freya, Adiz, Jasper, Koltayne, Scivix, Nyvar…even the son of the chief guardian is here. He warned you when he was programmed to hate you."

Haven shakes his head. "That's a handful of people. How many call this planet home?"

"Some of the greatest revolutions in world history started with a handful of people. The Renaissance, the Enlightenment, the American Revolution… all began with ideas that took root and changed the world. Work with us to do the same, Haven. Let us try. If we fail, you'll be free to exact whatever revenge you deem necessary."

"And if I refuse?"

Quarren frowns. "So long as you stay here, you will follow our path. But you're a free man. You can make your own choices. If you feel that your plan is what you must do, then pursue it without our help or resources."

Haven lowers his head. The freedom of choice is powerful. A part of Michele hopes that he'll leave, but it doesn't look like that's the decision he's arrived at. He signals his men to follow and stops as he reaches Michele.

"You had better hope this works."

CHAPTER THIRTY-FIVE

INTERCORPEX

The "War Room"
ICX New York Exchange
New York City Municipal Corporation

Zyree sits in the back of the converted conference room and watches his team. Lyris chooses his people well. They're task-oriented, mission-focused, and have an impeccable work ethic. The men and women here are earning his respect, and that's not easy to do.

It's been forty hours since the raid, and not a single member of this task force has left the building. They ordered in when they were hungry and took turns crashing out somewhere in the building to catch a little sleep. They're sifting through the mountain of digital material for this briefing. As good as they are, Zyree is happy some reinforcements of his own have arrived.

"How big a wanker is this senior director?" one of his men asks moments before Lyris swings open the door and stomps in.

"You're about to find out," Zyree says, walking to the front of the room.

"Who are these guys?" Lyris demands, pointing to the two junior ICX Security inspectors.

"The big one is Malkor, and the little one is Parold."

The sarcastic comment was meant as a joke since they're both beefy guys with no necks. Lyris either didn't get it or didn't find it funny.

"I asked who they were," Lyris reiterates with a stern look that Zyree doesn't find remotely intimidating.

"They're with me."

"I brought you in because you work alone," Lyris whispers, turning his back to the others in the room. "I didn't authorize additional people."

"No, you didn't. While I appreciate the job your staff has done, when it's time to do fieldwork, they won't be much use to me. Malkor and Parold are operators that Commissioner-General Jurghen specifically assigned. I'm going to need them before this is over. Now, do you want to continue this debate, or shall we begin?"

Lyris shakes his head, sits in a chair at the front of the room, and waits for Zyree to get on with it. Zyree nods at Bird's Nest, who dims the lights and brings the large display to life.

"Public Safety and Security's raid on the urch party in Chinatown was not the bust we originally thought it was," Zyree begins. "We've sifted through countless hours of footage and have identified some presumed members of Liberteum.

"The first I briefed you on yesterday," Zyree continues, pointing to a screen capture from inside the rave. "Inspector Haven was a seven-year veteran of Intercorpex Security. Four years ago, he was presumed killed in an explosion while on an assignment."

"It looks like he was well-trained," Lyris says after the tech posts Haven's bio to the main display.

"Haven was at or near the top of every training class he ever attended. He's an expert marksman, skilled in hand-to-hand combat, surveillance techniques, and espionage. His fitness reports were stellar. He was a loyal inspector with a promising career in front of him, or so we thought."

"Is he running Liberteum?"

Zyree glances back at his two men staring at the display with fire in their eyes. Neither man knew Lyris, but Intercorpex Security is more of a brotherhood than a security department. They don't take betrayal lightly.

"No, he's probably the tactician—and a dangerous one. Then there's this man. He goes by Scivix and is a former member of the New York PSS. Scivix is Haven's opposite. He's a violent man who was reprimanded on countless occasions for reckless behavior, abuse of employees, and suspicion of corruption. He was on the verge of termination when he disappeared."

"Until now. Do the PSS have any idea he's involved?" Lyris asks.

"No, we don't believe so. As bad as Scivix and Haven are, this woman may be the scariest."

A new image comes on the screen, grainy and dark like the others. Zyree watches the blood drain out of Lyris's face when her comprehensive and complete biographical information shows up. He might not recognize the woman, but he knows the uniform better than anyone.

"This is Freya. She was a member of Intercorpex operations right here in New York until eighteen months ago."

"Oh my God," Lyris breathes, still shaken by the revelation. "Doing what?"

"Intrusion detection and systems penetration defense."

The fact that a member of the exchange operations staff disappeared and turned traitor on Lyris's watch is not lost on him. Zyree watches him mentally put the pieces together. These are not members of a street gang looking to create havoc. They have professional resumes that could make a terrorist organization capable of unspeakable damage.

"That leaves this woman. We haven't been able to uncover any record of her."

The grainy picture of an attractive brunette pops up on the main display. After watching the video dozens of times, it appears that Haven is almost deferential to her. That makes her a leader or an essential member of the group.

"Is the information classified?"

"Given her age, it's more likely that she was born an urch," Zyree concludes.

"Are these the only five members of Liberteum?" Lyris asks, wagging a finger at the display.

"These are five of the six that killed the guardians and escaped into the underground. We don't know if more were present."

"The PSS doesn't have any of this?"

"Not yet."

"Good. Keep it that way," Lyris says, rising from his chair.

"That's not the best approach," Zyree says, folding his arms as a stare-down erupts between the two men. "Manhattan is just over twenty-two square miles. The underground is an unmapped labyrinth. If you want Liberteum found, we'll need the manpower the PSS can bring to the search."

"What makes you think they would help?" Lyris asks in a condescending voice, getting a knowing smile in return.

"Put up the kid's official file," Zyree orders the technician. A moment later, the official corporate biographical record fills the main display. "This is Registrant Rykos, the second child and only son of the New York Public Safety and Security Chief Guardian."

"So what?" Lyris asks, exasperated.

"Pull up the video and freeze it. This is Registrant Rykos with Haven and Scivix at the rave. The footage of the murders has been removed from their servers, but I'm willing to bet he was the sixth person that fled with them."

"He's a member of Liberteum?"

"He was with them. I'm guessing Chief Guardian Teman knows that, which is why there's no information about the killings. He wants to keep his son's involvement a secret and has all the incentive in the world to help us."

Lyris thinks about the implicit request for a moment. He understands leverage. It's a prudent course of action to meet the exchange's objectives. Zyree is hopeful that even an egomaniac like Lyris will recognize that.

"No."

"What do you mean, no?"

"Are you deaf? The PSS cannot know that Intercorpex hacked into their systems. You're going to have to do this without their assistance," Lyris concludes, a sinister grin crossing his lips.

"I don't have the resources."

"You're a resourceful man, Zyree. I trust you'll find a way."

That was executive-speak for "it's your problem, not mine." Executive Director Lyris may be competent, but he's nothing more than a functionary in the world's most backward bureaucracy. Zyree knows if he succeeds, Lyris will take the credit. If he fails, he escapes blame.

"My mission is to identify the members of Liberteum and eliminate them. I used your people to accomplish the first half of that goal, and now I will use whoever I see fit to accomplish the second."

"Don't deceive yourself into thinking that you give orders around here," Lyris barks. "You work for me, and nothing is stopping me from informing Raimius about your insubordination. You know how much he loves that."

Zyree shuts up. There's nothing to be gained by arguing with the senior director in front of his staff. Lyris threatened to rat him out to the schoolmaster like the fink he is. Not that it matters. Zyree has never been good at following directions.

"Very well. Have it your way."

Lyris makes his way out of the makeshift war room. The majority of the staff here averts their eyes, pretending to find something interesting on their displays. Zyree understands their reactions. Lyris is their boss and has their loyalty out of necessity.

"What's the move, chief?" Malkor asks as he and Parold join Zyree in the front of the room.

"Cherry pick the best people in this room and dig through the PSS archives for everything they have on Liberteum. I'm betting that woman is the daughter of a former terrorist. I want to know which one."

"Roger that. Search for a needle in a needle factory. Anything else?"

Zyree scans the faces of the staff engrossed with whatever they are using as an excuse to look busy. Some of them can be trusted, and others are undoubtedly reporting to Lyris. Their conversations need to stay vague.

"No. We stick to the plan."

CHAPTER THIRTY-SIX

AMERICA, INC

Chief Guardian Teman's Domicile
Manhattan Upper West Side Geographic District
New York City Municipal Corporation

When Teman steps out of the elevator into his apartment, there is no greeting. For years now, his daily routine has included cursing the metallic, British-accented voice of his Maestro system when it greets him. The silence is deafening on a day when he could use any semblance of normalcy.

"Hello?" Teman calls out into the dark emptiness.

"In here," Ilaria whispers from the living room.

Every light in the apartment is out. The city's ambient light coming through the large windows facing downtown provides the only illumination. It still does little to provide anything more than a vague outline of their furniture.

"What happened to the Maestro system?" Teman asks, easing his way over to the living room couch and sitting next to his wife.

"I muted it," Ilaria says without looking at him.

"Why are you sitting in the dark?"

"I didn't want the lights on."

"Maestro, lights," he commands, getting an immediate response.

Ilaria looks terrible. Even without her usual application of fashionable makeup, she's a lovely woman. Not right now. Her eyes are red and puffy from crying, and a rash has formed under her nose. The stylish hairstyle she pays a fortune for is nothing more than a stringy mess atop her head.

"Are you okay?"

His wife looks at him in horror. "Am I okay? They have my son, Teman! They have my son! And you couldn't be bothered to tell me yourself!" she screams, hysterically beating him against his chest.

"I need you to settle down, Ilaria. It's—"

Ilaria slaps him across the face. She stands and paces around the living area. His guardians told Teman that she handled the news about Rykos well when they informed her. Maybe she was in shock, and reality has now set in.

Teman stands and turns in time to see Ilaria pick up a decorative vase from the end table and hurl it at his head. He ducks as it sails past him and shatters against the wall.

"Don't you dare tell me to settle down! He's my *son*."

"He's *my* son, too!"

"Then act like you give a damn about him! For once in your life!"

The main display flickers to life, and the image of a guardian seated at a desk appears. Thanks to the Maester, the PSS can peek into anyone's life at any time. This is one of those moments.

"This is Guardian Trulog of the Department of Domestic Intervention and Arbitration. We have been alerted by your Maestro to a violent dispute. Can I be of service?"

"No, everything is fine," Teman says, staring at his wife.

"That's great to hear. Still, I believe it would be prudent to dispatch a unit as a precaution," he says in the pleasant-yet-firm voice he was trained to use.

"That's not necessary."

"I'm afraid it is," Trulog advises.

"Guardian Trulog, I'm the chief guardian of New York. I said it isn't necessary."

"Yes, sir, I'm aware of that, and I'm very sorry, but protocol dictates—"

"I wrote the recent revision to the protocol and was present at Corporate Hall when Chief Executive Safmor approved it. Intervention isn't necessary. Do you understand, or do I need to discuss this with your supervisor?"

Trulog shifts in his seat. Teman put him in a bad situation but doesn't care at the moment. His missing son and hysterical wife are more immediate priorities.

"I'm sorry for the interruption, sir. Have a good evening."

Ilaria shakes her head and takes a seat on the couch. She reaches for a glass and takes a swig of something that's not water. Alcohol may be forbidden, but the well-connected can still acquire it in import shops or through urches. Teman has no idea how or where his wife got hers.

"Ilaria, I care just as much as you do about getting Rykos back. I've spent every moment since they took him searching for leads. I've met with Safmor…hell, I discussed it with Chief Executive Valen. It's our…my…highest priority."

"Have you heard anything?"

The name drops had the desired effect of calming Ilaria down. "We're still searching. Look, I know what you're going through. I feel it, too."

"You have no idea what I'm going through. You didn't give up a promising career because you committed the sin of getting pregnant. Come to think of it," she says, swirling her glass, "have you ever wondered why it's always the wife who raises the children, even if she's on the better career track?"

"I don't set corporate policy," Teman says, thinking she sounds more and more like Rykos. "Is that what this is about? You're angry with me because you got pregnant with Varella?"

"Giving birth to my children were among the greatest moments of my life, but I would have been happy to stop with Varella. You wanted a son, so my career plans were put on hold that much longer."

"Yes, I wanted a son, and—"

"You got Rykos," she finishes. "The boy who could never live up to your lofty expectations."

Teman runs his hand through his hair. Ilaria needs to know that their son may be involved with a terror group and not the victim of one. That uncomfortable truth might shatter her belief that Rykos is some angel being held down by his oppressive father.

Unfortunately, she's not cleared to hear that information. Maestro would report the transgression immediately, and Teman would be relieved of his command. She likely wouldn't believe him anyway.

"I'm tired of you believing that I play favorites with my children."

"And I'm sick of you pretending that you don't."

Teman folds his arms. He's not in the mood to travel down that path again.

"Rykos put himself in this position."

"You wouldn't be so quick to judge if it was Varella," Ilaria says with a scoff.

"Varella would never have gone to an urch rave," he argues. "Listen, I'm going to do everything in my power to get him back. I promise you that."

"Then don't waste time talking to me," Ilaria says, turning away from him. "The next time I see you, it will be with our son. If he's not with you, don't bother coming home."

Teman nods slowly. With the weight of the world already on his shoulders, not dealing with Ilaria may be a blessing. He crosses the living room and heads for the elevator.

"Maester, de-luminate."

The lights go down, leaving Ilaria in the darkness once again.

CHAPTER THIRTY-SEVEN

REGISTRANT RYKOS

Lower Manhattan Underground
New York City Municipal Corporation

The sudden blast of cold on my face jars me awake. I jerk upright, and cold water drips off my nose and chin. I look up to see Scivix standing over me with a bucket.

"Wakey, wakey," Haven taunts from behind him.

Scivix hefts me off the cot. My head starts pounding again when I stand. The pain commands more of my attention than the fear over what's happening.

"Don't even think about runnin'," Scivix warns. "There's no place to go, and Michele is the only thing standin' in the way of us slittin' your throat."

We walk out of the dank room along a narrow strip of elevated concrete running parallel to rusting iron rails. The men support me from each side as I will my knees to work. I know where we are now. This is part of the old underground train system before the SpeedRail was built.

I'm shoved toward a small staircase leading up to a mezzanine that looks to be the ticketing area. Haven and Scivix are dismissed, and I look around. My captors have makeshift tables along a wall with banks of old computers and even older displays. The man at the terminals glares at me before turning to Michele.

"You're sure you want him seeing this?"

"I'm sure he's seen computers before, Jasper," Michele says, studying my face.

She pulls a bottle of water from the case on the floor, uncaps it, and hands it to me. I chug it so fast that a small stream pours down my chin. It's warm but the best I've ever tasted. When I finish, she retrieves the empty bottle and hands me another.

"Sip this one," she commands. "You're dehydrated. The water needs to get absorbed, or it'll just get pissed out."

"Okay," I croak between sips.

"I apologize for your treatment. Haven wanted to be sure you weren't transmitting."

"I never should have warned you," I say in a raspy voice as I inspect the bandages on my hand and wrist. "I wish my father had caught all of you."

"Your situation would be different, but perhaps not better," an old man says from a chair in the corner. "You know this. It's why you warned Michele and the others in the first place. It was your best chance to get out of there undetected. Let's sit. I'm afraid I don't have the stamina I used to."

The man at the terminal jumps into action and pulls over a beat-up office chair for me. "Who are you?"

"My name is Quarren."

"Where are we?"

"An old subway station. It served as part of New York's MTA system until the economic collapse. It was sealed and long forgotten after the SpeedRail was built."

"Are you Liberteum?" I ask, trying to confirm who's holding me captive. Quarren and Michele look at each other. The old man finally smiles and shows me the black torch tattoo on his forearm.

"Liberteum is loosely derived from the Latin word '*Libertas*' meaning freedom and independence. It's not a group, Rykos. It's an idea."

"I don't understand."

"I don't expect you to. At least not yet."

"What do you want with me? You say freedom is an idea, but you're holding me hostage. That makes you a hypocrite," I say with a sneer.

"You were brought here for your safety."

"My safety? I was knocked unconscious. My friend was shot and left behind. Haven wants to kill me. You call this safe?"

"Rykos, there is little doubt public safety has you on video escaping the rave," Michele says. "Your father can't protect you from the repercussions."

"What do you think will happen if we release you and you suddenly appear outside One Guardian Plaza? Do you think you will run into your father's open arms, and all will be forgiven? Trust me, son, the world doesn't work that way. I think you know that."

He's right. My father would be the first to report me to human resources or send me to reeducation. He would consider it a lesson I should learn for my insolence.

"I did nothing wrong."

"I doubt the corporation will agree."

"How would you know? You're an urch."

"Because, Rykos, that's why I became one," Quarren says. "I once had bandages when my biojacks were removed. America Incorporated convinced everyone that those microchips are implanted for their benefit. That's not true. They're instruments of control used to keep you enslaved."

"Or they're safeguards to keep law-abiding employees from disappearing at the hands of terrorists," I practically spit.

I'm trying to rattle this old man, but he's unflappable. This is a game to them. He's only being nice so I will confide in him. My father taught me the tricks, and I'm not going to fall for them.

"'Terrorist' is an old term and one that I wouldn't expect you to know the true definition of," Quarren says.

"And you're going to educate me?"

"We're going to show you a truth different from the one you know," Michele answers.

"You've been told that Liberteum is a dangerous threat to the corporation," Quarren adds. "That we want to destroy the society employees have worked so hard to build. I also know that you don't believe everything you hear."

"You went to an urch rave, Rykos," Michele says. "Good corporate employees don't do that."

I can't argue with that. They're right about me, and the thought makes the fear well up again. I need to get out of here before it's too late.

"Let me go."

"We will when the time is right."

I'm about to protest when someone climbs the stairs behind me. I think Haven and Scivix are returning and ignore the pain as I strain my neck to see. It's neither. This man has a slight build, softer face, and with a bit of luck, a sunnier disposition.

"Rykos, I don't believe you've met Adiz. He's one of our computer experts."

He nods before bending to whisper into Michele's ear. "Go rest, father. I'll escort Rykos to his room and get Adiz's full update."

"Son, I know you have no reason to trust us," the old man says, struggling to his feet. "All I ask is that you keep an open mind. You may find answers to many of the things you question."

"It's hard to keep an open mind while being held captive," I say, trying to get them to understand that I'm a prisoner.

"I understand why you feel that way. You have yet to realize the truth."

"What truth?"

"That you're freer locked down here with us than you ever were up there."

CHAPTER THIRTY-EIGHT

THE PATRICIANS

Keating Family of the Gentez-Majorez Estate
Greenwich Geographic District
Southern Connecticut Municipal Corporation

Greenwich is a stone's throw from New York City and was the ideal location for wealthy patricians to establish their estates following the collapse. Existing mansions were expanded, and large swaths of middle-class dwellings were bulldozed to accommodate the new elite. Today, Greenwich is almost exclusively populated by patricians.

Denali watches the helicopter circle the estate from the second-floor balcony of his mansion. Exterior illumination highlights the size of the imposing structure that resembles a massive stone fortress. The lights on the helipad flicker to life, and the helicopter swoops in and gently touches down. The blades of the chopper slow their spin before the door opens.

"Show our guest to the study, Abbot," Denali commands.

"At once, sir."

Denali retreats inside the mansion and passes through the foyer with its grand staircase, antique light fixtures, and priceless art hanging on every wall. The entire house is old world-beautiful, like something out of the nineteenth century. The patrician is not in his study for more than a couple of minutes before the oak doors swing open.

"Senior Director of Intercorpex Global Operations Lyris," Abbot announces formally.

"I apologize for the brusque nature of the invitation, Senior Director," Denali says from the far side of the room.

"With all due respect, sir, I was taken from the NOC at gunpoint, stuffed into a car, and brought here by helicopter. That's an abduction, not an invitation."

"Yes, you're probably right. Leave us," Denali orders the pair of gorillas who picked Lyris up outside the NOC. Abbot joins them in exiting the room.

"What do you feed those guys?"

Denali chuckles. "In return for their support, I don't ask about their food bill."

"How many men like them do you employ?"

"Thousands. My global interests require protection. It's an unfortunate reality of these times."

"You have an army?" Lyris asks, astounded.

"That is such an antiquated term. I think of them more as an insurance policy against loss. Please, have a seat, Senior Director. Would you like a drink? I have a brilliant thirty-year-old single malt scotch from our family distillery in the Highlands."

"Uh…I'd like that, sir, thank you."

Many corporations have banned alcohol. While employees of the exchange are not required to follow corporate directives, the prohibition makes acquiring such beverages complicated. They seize the opportunity when it presents itself, which is why patricians always offer high-end stuff.

"You're undoubtedly wondering why you're here," Denali says, pouring the scotch into a crystal tumbler and handing it to his guest before sitting in the red leather chair across from him.

"It crossed my mind. I assume that you're wondering what progress we've made in the week since the Secaucus attack."

"I already know that you've made none. This is about our meeting with Raimius. You walked into a difficult situation and acted with professionalism."

"Thank you, sir, but you didn't fly me to Greenwich to tell me that."

"No, of course not. What do you think of the administrator-general's performance during that meeting?"

Lyris shifts in his seat. The cardinal rule for employees of Intercorpex is never to disparage the man running it. Raimius wields unspeakable power and has no compunction about exercising it against anyone daring enough to slander him.

"I think he responded…."

Denali smiles after Lyris's voice trails off. "You think he was lacking."

"I didn't say that."

"It's what you want to say but won't. Loyalty is a precious commodity. Most employees are coerced into investing it in the undeserving. Those who are faithful due to their own volition are worthy of admiration. Which category do you fall into?"

"Are you questioning my loyalty?"

Denali leans forward with the drink in his hand. "I would never be so imprudent. I *am* questioning whether it's misplaced."

"Sir, I—"

"Please, call me Denali."

Lyris lurches backward. Deference to patricians is expected of anyone outside the ranks of the global elite, even in casual settings. A patrician offering someone to use their first name is an unheard-of break in established protocol.

"Okay, Denali. I've heard rumors that some patricians are quietly working to remove Raimius. If I may be candid, is that what this meeting is about?"

"You have excellent sources. Yes, several of my peers are attempting to convince the Board of Regents that Raimius isn't suited to run Intercorpex. No, that's not what this is about, per se."

"Per se?"

"I'm not involved in my peers' efforts, although we share the same reservations about Raimius. He's a power-addicted micro-manager with a pathological need to control everything. Worst of all, he's unstable. That's dangerous in the times I fear are ahead."

"You're referring to Liberteum?" Lyris asks cautiously, eliciting a devilish smile from his host.

"His response to their most recent attack was inadequate."

"Sir, I'm not on the Board of Regents. I have no say in whether he stays or goes."

"The Board of Regents," Denali says with a sigh, rising and moving to the bar for a refill. "A dysfunctional conglomeration of morons if there ever was one. They aren't fit to mop the exchange floor, let alone set its policy. They can't be trusted to do the right thing."

Denali catches a glimpse of Lyris as he shifts his weight and sips his scotch. The conversation is making him uncomfortable, which of course, is the point. The patrician wants it that way.

"What is the right thing?" Lyris finally asks.

"Choosing a leader instead of a politician. The regents take care of themselves. They elevate someone from their ranks to administrator-general instead of finding the best person for the job. Someone with a unique understanding of how Intercorpex works and already has the necessary respect. Someone like you."

Lyris nearly chokes on his scotch. "Denali, I'm never going to be considered for AG."

"You've never thought of it?"

"Every director at Intercorpex wonders what it would be like to run the exchange," Lyris confesses. "But it will never happen."

"I shouldn't need to explain to you that stock exchanges were originally conceived to benefit the public interest. They allowed companies to raise equity from investors by providing them a marketplace. Intercorpex operates under the same principle, only to benefit patricians, who saved humanity."

"Yes, sir, I understand all that."

"My family fortune relies on Intercorpex, as do those of my peers. We are forced to trust an oligarchy that has forgotten its purpose. We need to remind the regents of whom they were created to serve."

Denali is practicing a little revisionist history. The Board of Regents ensures patricians cannot exert undue influence on exchange leadership. They are insulated from political maneuvering and choose the administrator-general from their ranks for that reason.

"Lyris, I did not fly you up here tonight to get dirt on your boss. I can find that on my own. I'm looking for someone to bring Intercorpex into the next century. I think that someone is you."

"When do you see this happening?" Lyris croaks, still unable to process what the powerful patrician is saying.

"There is no timetable. It could happen next week or next year. How events unfold will dictate that. What's important now is whether you would accept the role."

Lyris sets his drink down and stares at his hands. Denali is offering an opportunity that no director could ignore. If he does, others can be approached. He hopes it doesn't come to that.

"You're asking a lot of me."

"I'll be asking a lot more of you should you decide to take the reins of Intercorpex. Take some time and think about it. I don't need an immediate answer. However, when I do ask for one, you must be prepared to give it to me."

"Yes, sir."

The study's large oak doors swing open. Abbot appears and nods.

"The helicopter will take you back to Manhattan. It should go without saying that the subject of this meeting is to be kept between us. Any disclosure will bring serious consequences."

"I understand."

"Excellent. I sincerely hope you accept the offer," Denali concludes, extending his hand, which Lyris accepts. "I believe you are the right man to safeguard the future of the exchange. I think you know you are, too."

CHAPTER THIRTY-NINE

INTERCORPEX

Outside One Guardian Plaza
Municipal Governance District
New York City Municipal Corporation

It's hard to loiter outside any building in New York City without attracting attention. It's one of the most monitored metropolises in the world, and a mountain of computers run programs designed to track every soul living and working here. The area around One Guardian Plaza is crawling with uniformed members of the PSS at the seven o'clock shift change. It's not the smartest place to try to look inconspicuous.

Zyree expected to see his target coming into work and instead watches him leaving the building. He follows him down the street and around a corner, watching from fifty feet away as he enters a small deli. There were at least a half dozen places closer to headquarters, so either he likes the coffee here or has another reason for the long walk.

Minutes later, he exits the shop with a coffee and makes another left, continuing away from One Guardian Plaza. Zyree trails him down the block and loses him on a side street for a moment. Not wanting him to be out of sight for too long, he speeds up and peers around the corner. The road is empty.

Zyree scans the sidewalk and curses to himself as he picks up the pace. Two hands grab his shoulders from behind and shove him inside a bakery. The female clerk behind the counter shrieks as the man pins him against the front wall. Zyree crashes his fists down on his arms to break the grip.

The move is immediately met by a series of quick strikes that Zyree deftly deflects. His assailant changes tactics and rushes a jab that Zyree blocks to catch him off guard. He simultaneously grabs the man's wrist and straightens his arm. Before completing the move, the man shifts his weight and elbows Zyree in the abdomen, causing him to release the hold.

Zyree has had enough of the fun and games. This fight is a draw but will go on for another twenty minutes unless it ends now. Before the man can come at him again, Zyree pulls out his holographic identification.

"Chief Inspector Zyree?" the chief guardian asks, dropping his guard after studying the credentials. It's only then that he notices the uniform.

"That's right," Zyree says with a smirk.

Teman types the name into his wrist tablet. The biographical data it returns is probably similar to what Zyree's biocomp relays onto his contact lenses. Tablets were cutting-edge technology for Intercorpex two decades ago. Of course, they are far better funded.

"Why are you following me, Chief Inspector?" Teman demands.

"We need to talk."

"Make an appointment."

Zyree shakes his head. "What we need to discuss can't be done in your office. It's in both our interests that there's no record of it."

"What could you possibly have that I would be interested in?"

The chief inspector leans in close to him. "The identities of the people holding your son."

* * *

"This place doesn't have video surveillance," Teman assures as the men slide into a booth at the run-down eatery.

"Good. Trust me, Chief Guardian, I have more to lose than you do. My superiors have expressly forbidden me to speak to you."

"How did you know about my son?"

Zyree stares at him. This meeting is a risk, but if he's going to earn Teman's trust, he needs to be honest with him.

"We have access to the intelligence from the Chinatown raid."

"How did you get that?"

"It's not important."

"You hacked our systems, didn't you?" Teman demands after some thought.

"How and why we obtained that information is one reason I'm forbidden to talk to you. Now, we can waste time discussing that, or you can come to understand that I'm here to help you."

"I didn't become the chief guardian by trusting anybody who claimed they wanted to 'help' me. If you have the same information we do, what makes you think you know more than us?"

"Because if you had identified the members of Liberteum who killed your guardians and are holding your son, you'd be acting on it."

"And because you have our intel, you would know if we were," Teman says under his breath.

Zyree suppresses a smile. "Something like that."

"Why help us? What do you want in return?"

"I've been charged with finding out who was behind the attack on our data center circuits in Secaucus and neutralizing them. Since we are after the same people, our goals are mutually inclusive."

Teman's eyes narrow. There is a healthy distrust between security services, and Intercorpex is no exception. While Teman and his guardians may despise the BCS, they have no affection for ICX Security either.

"Why don't you eliminate them yourself? Exchange security has a top-notch special tactics team that—"

"Has no remit to operate with impunity in America's sphere of influence," Zyree finishes.

"Request it through proper channels."

"My superiors aren't convinced it would be approved, and your BCS would demand to know our intelligence sources before granting it. For obvious reasons, we can't share that. I'm willing to provide you with the intel because you command the resources required to take down Liberteum."

Teman leans back and shakes his head. He has a right to be suspicious. Security aside, the political relationship between Intercorpex and the corporations is frosty. With America Incorporated, it's closer to an ice age.

"Okay. What do you know about my son?"

"You want to know whether I think he's working with them. The answer is, I don't know. I will help you find him. What happens after that is up to you."

Zyree's answer seems to satisfy the chief guardian. "If I agree to this, how do we proceed? Create a link between our two teams?"

"My team can't know that I'm working with you. Their loyalties lie elsewhere."

"Then how do you plan on sharing intel?"

"You need to bring me to One Guardian Plaza."

Teman's reaction speaks volumes. Zyree knew he wouldn't like this idea.

"You can't be serious."

"It's the only way."

Teman mulls the idea over for a moment. He wants to agree but is weighing the risks.

"If I find you are usurping my authority even once, our cooperation ends, and I'll report all of this. Are we clear?"

Zyree watches the voice stress analysis displayed in his periphery. The returns confirm what he already determined: Teman is a straightforward guy and isn't deceiving him. The threat is valid.

"Yes, we're clear."

"Good. I can't walk you through the door. It will raise too many eyebrows."

"Are you going to sneak me in as a maintenance worker or something?"

"Not exactly," he explains, giving Zyree a onceover. "What are your sizes?"

CHAPTER FORTY

LIBERTEUM

Abandoned Subway Station
Somewhere in the Manhattan Underground
New York City Municipal Corporation

The one nice thing about living in the underground is that there are millions of nooks that someone can hide in when they want to be alone. Liberteum has several strongholds that serve this purpose. This isn't one of them.

Michele stepped over the rusting tracks and climbed up to the platform on the northbound side of the station to get away for a bit. This is the only place in this old station where she can be alone with her thoughts. Or so she thought.

"What are you doing here, Chele?" Freya asks, pulling herself up from the railbed and sitting next to her on the platform's edge.

"I need some alone time."

"Well, I'm ruining that," Freya says with a smile.

"Yeah, you really are," Michele says with a laugh. "Adiz and Jasper keep prattling about computer stuff. It's hard to concentrate."

"They are annoying, aren't they? What's on your mind?"

"What isn't? This plan...it's a long shot if everything goes right. I'm worried about all the things I haven't thought of that will make it go wrong."

"Archimedes is complex, Michele. It's also brilliant and well thought out. You can't expect yourself to account for every contingency. You have good people you need to trust to adapt to the unexpected."

Michele folds her hands in her lap and stares at one of the construction lights they wired to the electrical conduit snaking through the old station.

"The success of this operation rests on every detail."

Freya scoffs. "You're too hard on yourself, as usual. That's why everyone thinks you're an obsessive pain in the ass."

Michele jerks her head around. "That's blunt."

"Because I'm your friend, I can be. These people are risking their lives. They need a leader, not a perfectionist."

Michele nods but doesn't think there's a distinction. In her mind, planning is leadership. She needs to be prepared, and so do they. That means mitigating as many risks as possible. Freya is right – they're risking their lives, but she refuses to roll the dice with them.

"Why did you come to the underground? You never told me."

"You never asked," Freya says, leaning back and supporting herself on her arms behind her. "I was raised on a small Bavarian farm. My mother taught me how to bake and cook when I was a child. I thought that's what I would spend my life doing. I was wrong. I tested exceptionally well in mathematics and logic. Obviously, that meant more to the German corporation than a baker did."

"They forced you to leave your home?"

"That's how it works. I was sent to Munich for primary school and Berlin for university. They spent years training me on everything there was to know about computer networks. I rarely saw my family."

"I can't imagine what that's like."

"How could you, Chele? You were born an urch who could make her own choices in life. Others chose mine."

She's right. Everything Michele knows about corporations was explained to her by her father and friends. She was born free, or as free as a person can be while spending a lifetime fleeing the authorities and wondering where and when their next meal is coming from.

"How did you end up in the city, Frey?"

"Intercorpex acquired my services from the German Corporation, and I was shipped to New York. I hated the network operations center. The men and women who work there are robots – they do a task, go home, and return the next day. There's no joy or happiness. It's an existence, nothing more. I wanted more."

"You wanted freedom."

Freya nods. "People have forgotten what that feels like. They're comfortable with someone watching everything they do and making decisions for them. Humanity has lost the will to live…to truly live. When I heard about Liberteum, I had to find out if it was real. So, one day, I left the NOC and never returned. After a week in the underground, I found you."

Michele remembers that moment well. There was this beautiful girl who had no idea what she was doing. Freya was lost and ripe for exploitation down here. Michele wasn't about to let that happen and took her under her wing. That was long before she learned what the scared young woman could do with a computer.

"Everyone thought you were a spy," Michele says with a laugh. It wasn't funny at the time.

"Trust needs to be earned. It's one of the few similarities urches and employees still have."

"Is that why you volunteered for the most dangerous part of our plan? You think you need to prove yourself? Because you don't."

"Would you trust Adiz or Jasper to do it? They'd wet themselves before they even get to the server room."

"That's true, but you didn't answer my question."

"I knew long ago that I would never again knead dough or smell fresh bread straight out of the oven. I will never again romp among the Bavarian Alps, inhale fresh alpine air, or gaze upon the edelweiss. I will never live the life I wanted. If I have to make a sacrifice so that some young girl never faces that lack of choices, then it's a price I willingly pay."

Michele averts her eyes. She has never thought about the world outside Manhattan. All she's ever seen of it comes from old books. If this plan works and she survives, maybe seeing the world she's trying to save isn't a bad idea.

"I don't want you to have to make that sacrifice, Frey."

Freya pats Michele on the knee and jumps down to the railbed before looking up at her. "Then get back to work obsessing over every detail."

CHAPTER FORTY-ONE

AMERICA, INC.

Battery Park
Battery Geographic District
New York City Municipal Corporation

Fiolla loves mornings. There's no part of the day more peaceful or serene for her. The air is fresh and crisp, and the world is still quiet before the chaos of the commute begins. It's the perfect time for her to be alone with her thoughts.

Battery Park is almost devoid of people at this hour. A few joggers are finishing their workout, but most have already cleared out to start their day. Commuters will begin their daily sojourn soon, and this waterfront will be packed during the lunch hour. Fiolla will be back in Washington by then.

A strong hand covers her mouth as she's grabbed from behind. Fiolla immediately panics, trying to scream without success. She desperately tries to wriggle free from the grip, but it's too strong.

"Give me your money, lady," a raspy voice whispers into her ear from behind.

Fiolla stops struggling briefly as she processes his order. Money doesn't exist anymore, at least in physical form. The conclusion that he's deranged drives her urgency to break free.

Almost as if he read her mind, the man releases his hold. Fiolla is about to start running when she hears the man laughing. Against her better judgment, she turns to face her attacker. When she recognizes his face, she punches him hard in the arm.

"Ow!" he exclaims between laughs.

"That wasn't funny, Farron! You scared me half to death!" she shouts.

"Fiolla, you're in one of the safest cities in the world. Cameras cover every inch of this park from five different angles. Did you really think you were getting mugged?"

"Six guardians were killed this week. It's not as safe as you think."

"Then you had better kiss me now before we both die."

She doesn't need a second invitation. Fiolla grabs Farron and kisses him hard, enjoying every second of it. Corporate society would disapprove of their relationship, but Fiolla doesn't care about the age discrepancy or that he's a patrician. He may be eleven years younger and a member of the elite. To her, he's perfect.

"I missed you," she says when their lips finally part.

"I missed you, too," he says, taking her hand as they start walking along the edge of the water. "I didn't think you were staying in the city overnight."

"Valen had meetings that ran late and then agreed to dine with some subsidiary CEOs. We'll head back to Washington today. You should have stayed in the city last night."

"I wish I could have. My father wanted me in Greenwich after my run-in with the PSS."

"What the hell were you thinking going to that rave? I warned you that those are dangerous."

"I had business there."

Fiolla shakes her head. Farron is cryptic about Keating family dealings. She learned a long time ago not to press him on it. Patricians live in their own little world, but she wishes he would let her in a little.

"You're Denali Keating's son. What business could you possibly have at an urch rave?"

"Just because America Incorporated cast the urches out of society doesn't mean they're useless to my family's endeavors. I was careful."

"Not that careful. You got caught," Fiolla says.

Farron waves her comment away. "All they could do was detain me and clean out their underwear when my father showed up."

"Was he angry?" Fiolla asks. She knows her father would have been livid, and she wasn't born a patrician.

"I got the typical lecture. It wasn't my first. Has there been any fallout in Washington? I know the story is circulating on the GlobalNet."

"China and Russia are pouncing on the news. The CEOs of a few other corporations are trying to take advantage of our perceived weakness. And, of course, there's the internal bickering. Corporate Security is kicking public safety in the teeth. I'm helping with damage control while Valen navigates the waters."

"Sounds like you're busy. Are you getting any vacation time soon?"

"I don't know," she says, feeling herself blush. "I mean, I'm due for one, but I don't know where yet."

Farron stops and turns to face her, taking her hands in his. "It doesn't matter. I'll meet you wherever they send you."

After another long kiss, the couple turns and continues their stroll along the water, hand in hand.

"It must be nice to be a patrician with unlimited resources," Fiolla muses.

"It has its advantages and disadvantages."

"More advantages, I think. Regardless, I won't be going anywhere until this thing with Liberteum is over."

"How long is that going to take?"

Fiolla shrugs. "I have no idea. Even if I did, you know I can't talk about it," she says, fully aware of the corporate protocols about divulging sensitive information.

"Telling each other about our days is what couples do. Besides, I couldn't care less about the internal workings of America Incorporated."

"Your father might."

Farron lets out a little laugh. "My father's interests are far grander in scope. Our concerns are more global. We're from different worlds, honey."

"You don't need to tell me that," Fiolla says, uniquely aware and fearful of their differences.

"Then I guess we should be happy that love exists in both of them."

They kiss again, sending Fiolla to paradise for another blissful moment. When they finally part, it's too soon. It's always too soon for her.

She checks the time on her tablet. "I need to get back before I'm missed."

"Keep in touch, and please, let me know if you need anything," Farron says. "I'm here to help you through this. All you need to do is ask."

After their goodbyes, Fiolla walks away with pep to her step. A rendezvous with Farron always makes her giddy. The sooner this current crisis subsides, the sooner she gets to see him again. If a speedier resolution means taking him up on his offer to help, it's something she's willing to consider. It's one of the advantages of dating a patrician, so she may as well leverage it.

CHAPTER FORTY-TWO

AMERICA, INC.

One Guardian Plaza
Municipal Governance District
New York City Municipal Corporation

New York City is safer now than at any point in its history. Anyone entering the fortress that is One Guardian Plaza wouldn't know it. All visitors are scanned, identified, and checked for weapons by an array of hidden sensors. Teman knows the system flagged the chief inspector as an "unknown." The spare guardian uniform Zyree is wearing will fool a casual observer, but the computers cannot be spoofed. Fortunately, the analysts tasked with checking building access won't question the chief guardian.

"This is an impressive building," Zyree says as they pass through the foyer's invisible security area.

"We try. The architects designed this place to promote feelings of security among the employees who live in the city."

"Yeah, well, it worked."

The headquarters of New York's Public Safety and Security is located on the former site of the NYPD's One Police Plaza. Like most government buildings, rioters destroyed it during the Great Collapse. Instead of rebuilding the brutalist-style building, it was razed, and this magnificent structure was erected.

The new building is part Mayan temple, part medieval castle. It features a tapered, pyramid-like effect that extends five floors. From there, the main building extends straight up another ten stories. Each corner of the building juts out, creating an effect of square castle turrets stretching up to the tenth floor. The structure looks solid, right down to the two-inch-thick gray windows blended seamlessly into the façade.

"Where's your office?" Zyree asks.

"On the top floor, but that's not where we're going."

The two men climb into the elevator and step into a small, eighth-floor reception area with a sign that reads, "Real-Time Crime Center."

"Welcome to the RTCC."

"This is your emergency operations center?"

"No. We maintain an EOC at another secure location. This is one of two places that analyze every video feed and Maestro report in the city. Computers flag problems for our analysts to check, and investigators are dispatched to address issues."

"Preemptively?"

"Sometimes. Mostly we gather evidence, make arrests, and package cases for tribunal hearings. I've ordered a dedicated team to assemble in the crisis room to chase down leads on Liberteum."

The main crisis room is used when transferring operations to the emergency operations center isn't warranted. The circular room is about fifty feet in diameter, with two exits in the back and one at the front. Large curved displays affixed to the back wall show AME News and relevant crime data. Three concentric rings of workstations encircle a workstation for the crisis captain. A round fixture over the middle ring and accent lights on the walls illuminate the entire room.

Each workstation is complete with a virtual keyboard, dual glass displays, and a wireless communications unit. The state-of-the-art room is superior to what any other PSS has and is equal to what the Bureau of Corporate Security uses to conduct their operations.

"Guardians, can I have your attention?" Teman announces as he steps to the crisis captain's dais. "What I'm about to tell you is not to leave this room. Despite the uniform he's wearing, the man I'm with is not one of us. He's Chief Inspector Zyree of Intercorpex Security, and his presence here is unsanctioned by the exchange. Despite that, he has approached us with unique perspectives on the targets we're looking for. Give him your undivided attention. Chief Inspector?"

"Thank you, Chief Guardian. You have an impressive operation set up here, but computers and video feeds will not help you find Liberteum."

"Why do you say that?" a sergeant asks from the front row.

"Because they detonated an explosive device outside our data center across the river and managed to slip back into the city undetected. Then they escaped an airtight cordon during a raid."

"They made it to an underground passage. It's how urches live. Sooner or later, they'll make a mistake," a woman in the back row concludes.

"We're not talking about typical urches here. They have tactical training and advanced computer skills. They understand logistical support and how to employ security. Most importantly, they know how to be ghosts in the most monitored city in the world."

"How do you know that?"

"Because I know who they are."

There's an audible gasp in the room. Zyree delivered that news with the subtlety of a sledgehammer. Guardians look over at Teman to gauge his reaction. They don't get one.

"Can someone load this on the main display?" Zyree asks.

He hands a chip to a technician, and his presentation loads. A moment later, the chief inspector takes the room through the information on his old counterpart Haven and the two computer geeks, Jasper and Freya. The mood of the room changes when he gets to Scivix, a man who once wore a guardian uniform. By the time he finishes, the room is dead silent.

"How do you know all this information?" someone whispers.

"Intercorpex caters to the world's elite. Developing a robust intelligence operation was a necessity and a trade secret."

Teman gives Zyree an appreciative look for not divulging the actual source of the intelligence. His guardians would not respond well to knowing his team tapped into their systems, regardless of whether the intrusion was well-intentioned.

"Assuming what all you just told us is true, how do you suggest we proceed?" a guardian in the middle ring asks.

"Stop thinking of Liberteum as common urches and start thinking of them as a group that shares the same capabilities you do. They're organized, trained, and careful. To catch them, you need to think outside the box."

"We're expanding monitoring to the underground areas we know urches transit to get around the city."

"You're assuming they're mobile."

"They have to be," another guardian offers. "That's how they acquire resources."

"That's an assumption. What if they're getting outside support?"

"Who?"

Zyree shrugs. "I don't know. That's where we can use your expertise."

Teman watches the interaction with interest. Zyree didn't come here with the swagger of the arrogant bastards over at the BCS. He's treating the guardians as equals to the powerful Intercorpex Security. The apprehension in the room is fading away as a result. He won them over in a short period.

"We can access biojack data and have the algorithms search for any anomalies in people's routines," the sergeant offers.

"That's not going to be easy," one of his technicians argues.

Zyree smiles. "Anything you can do will be helpful. There's one more thing. With the chief guardian's permission, someone here needs to liaise with the BCS."

Teman is caught off guard by the request as an audible moan resonates around the room.

"They aren't our biggest fans right now, Chief Inspector," Teman says. "Why do we need their help?"

"Corporate Security is responsible for America Incorporated's computer networks. Considering Liberteum's skillsets, there may be an attempt to hack your corporate networks. The BCS needs to be prepared for that. I'm doing the same thing on my end."

Every set of eyes turns to Teman. They're out of questions and are waiting for guidance. He slowly returns to the center of the room and stands next to Zyree.

"Guardians, the employees of this city and the corporation we work for are looking to us to bring these miscreants to justice. Let's make this happen. Team leaders, get us set up."

Every guardian in the room springs into action. Zyree and Teman watch as they break into teams to hunt down and destroy Liberteum once and for all. The first step is figuring out how to find them.

"I have to head back to Wall Street," Zyree says as Teman walks him to the elevator bank.

"Don't forget to change uniforms," the chief guardian warns with a smile. "How do I reach you if we find anything?"

"Have someone in the RTCC send you an e-note. We'll see it," Zyree says, grinning as he steps into the elevator.

"You're reading my e-notes, too?" Teman asks, his voice a little distressed.

Zyree winks as the doors close.

CHAPTER
FORTY-THREE
REGISTRANT RYKOS

Abandoned Subway Station
Somewhere in the Manhattan Underground
New York City Municipal Corporation

I climb down the standpipe and brush off my hands. The brackets securing it to the wall make convenient footholds to reach a brick near the top of the wall that I thought might be loose. It wasn't, and with that went my last hope to find an escape. I've searched every square inch of this dimly lit room for a way out that isn't through the door. There isn't one.

The steel door swings open with a loud creak, and Quarren enters. He studies me for a long moment without saying a word. A smile eventually creeps across his lips.

"There's no way out of this room, Rykos, or this station for that matter. Please, have a seat."

I sit on the cot that I have spent countless hours in as he sets up the folding chair leaning against the wall.

"Where's Michele?" I ask, trying to fill the uneasy silence.

"She's attending to some business."

"Haven and Scivix must be busy, too. They haven't hit me in the head for a while."

"I apologize for your treatment," Quarren says with a sigh. "Haven does a difficult job for us. He often releases that stress in the wrong way."

"A job doing what?"

"Keeping us safe, for starters, but enough about all that. I brought you something."

Quarren hands me a hefty tome that was tucked under his arm. I glance down and read the title: *Discovering America*. I look at him in surprise after realizing what he just handed to me.

"This is one of the old books. I thought these were all destroyed or locked up."

"Most of them were. You'd be amazed what you can find down here if you know where to look."

"It's forbidden to read this, let alone possess it."

"We don't concern ourselves with such things. Besides, it's only forbidden for employees; it's required reading for many high-level executives."

"How do you know that?"

"Because I was one. I was a senior program manager."

His answer floors me. He must be lying. Executives don't end up living beneath the streets of Manhattan as urches. It just doesn't happen.

"Program managers aren't executives," I argue.

"They were during the early days of the rebuilding. Much has changed since then. It was a long time ago."

"Then how did you end up down here?"

"That's a story for another time," he deflects, leaning back in his folding chair.

"Yeah, right. Why would I believe anything you say?"

"You wouldn't. There is no reason to trust me, Rykos, but that's not the problem. You don't trust or believe what anyone says."

I fidget as a tingling sensation rolls up and down my spine. He thinks he knows me just because I went to a rave. He doesn't.

"I don't want to talk to you, and I don't want to read this book," I say, tossing it on the floor at my feet. "It's probably fake."

"That's your choice, Rykos. However, you will never know unless you open it and make that determination for yourself."

"I learn history in school," I argue, as Quarren struggles to bend over and retrieve the textbook from the dingy floor. I almost can't believe those words came out of my mouth.

"My grandfather was a soldier in the United States Army before the collapse. He told me when I was a boy that history is written by the winner. The history you know was manipulated by corporate interests to control people. You learned what they *wanted* you to learn. I think you know that."

Take away the tragic circumstances, and this conversation sounds like my talks in Central Park with Balin. Our venting was a way to cope with a hypercompetitive race for an Ivy League education and the executive status that follows it. Maybe it was always more than that. I lean over and pick the book up off the ground when Quarren gives up.

"And this is going to, what? Enlighten me?"

"It will explain things from a different perspective. That's all. Rykos, if you truly want answers about the world you live in, this will help you figure out what questions to ask."

"What I want is to be released."

"And you will be. You have my word. In the meantime, you can continue your futile search for a way out of this room, or you can read something you may never again have a chance to. The choice is yours."

Quarren struggles out of his chair. He stares at me for a long moment and offers a weak smile. I realize that I'm clutching the book with both hands.

"Breakfast will be served in another hour. We will talk again at dinner tonight," he says before leaving the room and closing the door behind him.

I stroke the book's faded cover. Balin and I always dreamed about reading one of these. I wish he were here now. It's the unsanitized history of the world before the crash. The pages of mildewed paper in my hands were written before the modules that focus on the benevolence of corporations. Quarren is right: I will never have another chance.

I open the cover and flip past the title page. On the backside, printed along with a bunch of nonsense, is the date I was looking for: Copyright 2025. I leaf through the text, recognizing familiar events along with images and headings that I've never seen before. With a deep breath, I flip back to the first chapter and begin reading.

CHAPTER FORTY-FOUR

INTERCORPEX

ICX Headquarters
Midtown Manhattan Geographic District
New York City Municipal Corporation

A summons to report to headquarters while in the middle of the Beijing hand-off was the last thing Lyris expected. He had to squelch his nervousness during the car ride up here and had nearly beaten it into submission until he saw the concern on Nevala's face. She never wears emotion on her sleeve.

"Did you take a car here, Senior Director Lyris?" Nevala asks from behind the desk outside Raimius's office.

"Yes, I did."

"Did your driver know about the new vehicle security policy?"

Lyris squints. He has no idea, but Nevala flares her eyes to warn him not to say that.

"Uh, I don't believe so, no."

"I thought so," she says with a sigh. "We're trying to get the word out. If you don't mind, please give him this IntraLynk address. The page explains the new procedure."

Nevala scratches a note on a piece of paper. It's an analog solution in a digital world, but an effective one. She hands it to Lyris, rolling her eyes around the ceiling as a reminder that a dozen cameras are watching them.

"I'll be sure to give it to him."

"Thank you, Executive Director Lyris. Please make yourself comfortable. The administrator-general will be right with you."

Lyris walks over to the upholstered chairs in the waiting area and takes a seat before unfolding and reading the note: *He knows about Denali.*

Raimius was eventually going to find out about his trip to Greenwich. People in power know everything, and Raimius fancies himself at the top of that pyramid.

"You may go in now, Senior Director," Nevala says with a slight nod.

"How was the trading day?" Raimius asks, staring out the window at the East River when Lyris enters.

"Average."

"No after-effects from the Secaucus attack?"

"All trading and reporting systems are working within normal parameters, Administrator-General."

Raimius couldn't care less about the trading day and knows that Intercorpex's systems are operating as they should. This is just the appetizer. Lyris wants him to get to the main course now that he knows what's being served.

"And the investigation? Any progress?"

"The team hasn't made significant progress yet. I will get an update when I return to Wall Street."

"I see. Maybe you're too busy consorting with Denali Keating to make it a priority," Raimius says, firing the opening salvo.

"With all due respect, sir, 'consorting' is not an accurate description. Denali Keating insisted on speaking directly to me. Given our last meeting, I didn't think it was in our interests to offend him by declining."

"I'm sure it wouldn't have been," he agrees, his tone conveying a different message. "And I'm sure there were countless reasons you did not inform me immediately afterward."

"There was nothing to report, sir. Patrician Keating wanted an update on our investigation. Their concerns haven't gone away."

Lyris waits patiently for a response. Nothing he says here will make a difference. The administrator-general imagined the worst possible reason for the visit and concluded that Lyris conspired against him.

"He could have reached you on VidLynk for an update."

"He thought dragging me to Greenwich would be more intimidating."

"That's all he wanted?"

"He wants more progress, and ultimately someone's head."

Raimius turns to look back out the window, and Lyris relaxes a little. "Yeah. He wants mine."

"Sir?"

"I have a long history with the Keating family. Along with the Covingtons, they fancy themselves the primas of the exchange if there were such a thing. He's using the Secaucus attack as leverage to force me out. Apparently, he wants your help."

Lyris's mouth goes dry. He put that together fast.

"I don't see how, sir."

"Lyris, do you think you're the first person in Intercorpex to be wined and dined by a patrician looking to exert influence on our operations? I'm surprised he hasn't reached out to you earlier."

"Sir, I don't believe—"

"I've facilitated the buying and selling of trillions of Bytecoin over my career. It taught me a valuable lesson: Money doesn't make the world go round – relationships do. The most valuable commodity isn't currency or stock, or even information. It's loyalty."

"Are you questioning mine, sir?" Lyris asks, trying to sound offended.

"Check that indignant tone before I demote you so low that you'll covet the job of the man who shines my shoes. This is now a one-way conversation. I don't know what Denali Keating promised you, and I don't care. He won't win, and I will crush anyone who takes his side. Understood?"

"I understand completely."

"Good. If I so much as hear a rumor that you're conspiring against me, it won't take any imagination to figure out what'll happen."

Threats are desperate acts to maintain control. Unfortunately, Lyris knows that the administrator-general will follow through on them. He knows where this road ends if Raimius uses his imagination to fill in the blanks about what transpired.

"You won't, sir."

"Good. I'll be watching you, Lyris. You're dismissed."

Lyris spins on his heels and strides through the door. He gives Nevala a quick wink as he passes by her. He will bide his time until Denali calls upon him to help destroy that son of a bitch. When he does, Lyris knows he'll be ready.

CHAPTER
FORTY-FIVE
AMERICA, INC.

The White House
Corporate Governance District
Washington-Arlington Municipal Corporation

The trip back to Washington with Valen was a short one. He didn't say much on the flight, leaving Fiolla to review the plethora of issues awaiting her return. Now back in the office, she starts plowing through the work piling up.

"Executive Fiolla, you have an incoming secure VidLynk from Patrician of the *Gentez-Majorez* Denali Keating. Do you wish to accept?" Rosie's metallic voice asks.

Fiolla sighs. She doesn't have time to go twelve rounds with Farron's father. The request was made over a secure channel, so it must be important. At a minimum, Denali Keating thinks so. Those are often two distinctly separate things.

"Accept. View on my workstation display only."

The magnetized locks on her office doors energize with a click. A red hue emanates from the crown molding as a visual cue that a secure call is in progress. Every office in the White House employs these measures, including the Oval Office, which takes it countless steps further.

Her display flickers to life. She expects to see Denali Keating staring at her. When the image appears, her mouth hangs open.

"Farron? Are you crazy? You can't contact me here!" she scolds, using a hushed tone that's unnecessary in the soundproof office.

"I just did. Valen is about to call you into the Oval Office."

"Why? And how could you know *that*?"

"Because he's been summoned to Corporate Hill this evening and needs you to accompany him."

Corporate Hill was once called "Capitol Hill." The Capitol Building was rebuilt, renamed, and repurposed for board meetings and stockholder office space. The prominent suite below the foyer belongs to the *prima*, a title bestowed upon the largest shareholder of a parent company. The same family has owned a majority of America Incorporated's shares for decades. Fiolla is surprised it hasn't been renamed Bettancourt Hill.

"But how could you—"

"My father has a seat in the chamber, and he gets privileged information. Talya Bettancourt is rallying shareholders to apply pressure on Valen."

"Is this about Liberteum?"

"She's embarrassed about the Secaucus attack and the bungling of the Chinatown urch raid."

"It wasn't bungled. Liberteum fought their way out, and guardians died in the process. That wasn't foreseeable!" Fiolla almost shouts, losing control of her temper.

"I know that, and you know that, but patricians have their version of reality. They'll twist the facts to suit their narrative. It's nothing new."

Fiolla rubs her temples. The high and mighty confer judgment from comfortable chairs in the halls of power without any fundamental understanding of what happens on the ground. The elites are far removed from how the world works.

"It's just politics, Fiolla," Farron says, consoling her.

"What should I do?"

"Warn Valen. He doesn't know what this is about. If you prepare him, he's adept enough to avoid Bettancourt's talons when she swoops in for the kill."

"How can I warn him about something I shouldn't know about?"

"Fiolla, you're as smart as you are beautiful. You'll think of something."

She closes her eyes and exhales. "Thanks. I owe you."

"I'm going to hold you to that. Good luck," he says with a wink before ending the VidLynk.

Fiolla leans back in her chair and stares at the ceiling. She does owe him. He's provided her information before and never asked anything in return. She would hate to think there could ever be a quid pro quo in this relationship. Patricians rarely date outside of their ranks. The fear of being used has always kept her from opening up to Farron, despite him never being anything but helpful.

She makes her way down the corridor to the Oval Office, forcing thoughts about their relationship from her mind. She has work to do, which involves helping Valen navigate his impending confrontation with a powerful patrician.

* * *

Corporate Hill is magnificent. The original Capitol Building, Supreme Court, Library of Congress, and legislative office buildings were gutted by fire during the Great Collapse. Engineers and architects preserved the original buildings as much as possible during the rebuild. The idea was to foster a sense of continuity for those who remembered the old government.

Shareholder Hall, built on the Capitol footprint, consists of two large meeting areas separated by a grand foyer featuring a modern dome that replaced the original. The board of directors meets on one side of the building. The other side is reserved for patricians of the *gentez-majorez* who acquire seats by maintaining a large percentage of shares. They meet infrequently, but their interests are represented by the *prima*.

Petite and in her fifties, Talya Bettancourt is the elegant, sophisticated, and professional head of her family. She's also as cutthroat and political as patricians come.

"Executive Fiolla, could you please give *Prima* Bettancourt an update on the status of our operations?" Valen asks after formal introductions are made.

For the next couple of minutes, Fiolla walks her through the events beginning with the attack on Intercorpex and ending with the urch raid in Chinatown. She manages not to stumble through it, despite the awkward feeling of being caught in the political machinations of two giants.

"You authorized New York's PSS to conduct the raid?" she asks Valen.

"Yes, I did."

"That was an error in judgment."

"That's an interesting conclusion," Valen says, signaling the start of their battle.

"An accurate one. Corporate security conducts operations of that nature."

"The BCS doesn't have the experience in dealing with the urches that public security does," Valen argues.

"That's irrelevant."

"I disagree."

"The BCS would not have allowed Liberteum to escape," Talya argues, no longer masking the contempt in her voice.

"The facts don't support that assumption."

Fiolla watches the patrician intently. She intended to ambush Valen and catch him off guard. Instead, he's parrying her accusations with ease. The verbal combat is wearing on their host's patience.

"You will transfer operational control in the hunt for Liberteum to the Bureau of Corporate Security immediately," Talya decrees.

"I will do no such thing."

"You mistake an order for a suggestion."

"And you mistake me for someone you are in a position to order," Valen counters with a knowing grin.

"You will do as I say, or I will have you replaced."

Valen leans back into his chair, almost looking relaxed. The break in protocol infuriates Talya that much more.

"Hollow threats are beneath you, *Prima* Bettancourt."

"Threats are beneath me. Promises are not."

"The result is the same, Talya."

Fiolla watches her struggle to avoid going ballistic. "Do you think not referring to me by my proper title is a wise course of action right now, *Valen*?"

"No less wise than you summoning the chief executive officer here to intimidate and threaten. I have allies on the board of directors as well. You can't replace me, and you know it. Now, we can have a long, drawn-out battle for the reins of this corporation, or you can agree that we share the same goal."

"That's not always the case."

"We both want America Incorporated to be the most valuable and productive corporation in the world, correct?"

This is a heavyweight boxing match. They're dancing around each other, each throwing the occasional jab without landing it. Valen and Talya are experts at this game, but one of them will get hit eventually. The question is who.

"And you think recent incidents promote that?" Talya says with a hint of disbelief in her voice.

"You need to look at the bigger picture," Valen says, leaning forward. "Every corporation in the world deals with terrorist groups advocating anarchy and chaos. Some are more organized and militant than others. I believe the short-term volatility of our stock is worth being the first corporation to solve that problem."

"Assuming you can find and eliminate them," she responds, leaning back deeper into her chair.

"I was not elevated to the chief executive position because I didn't deliver," Valen says with a confident grin.

"Fair enough," Talya says after a long moment. "I said what I needed to, and you made some bold promises in return. I'll be expecting results. Good evening, Chief Executive Valen."

"Thank you, ma'am," Valen says, bowing slightly along with Fiolla after they rise from their seats.

The pair leave the *prima's* spacious office and return to the foyer. The sun is almost down, and the streetlights struggle for dominance against the encroaching dusk. The CEO takes a moment to enjoy the view before climbing into the limousine.

"Thank you for warning me about that conversation," Valen says as they get underway. "How did you know?"

"I heard a rumor and then saw the meeting on your schedule. I put two and two together," Fiolla says, hoping he doesn't sniff out the lie.

"I pride myself on avoiding ambushes. Without you, I would've walked in there unprepared," Valen confesses.

"If I may ask, sir, what just happened? She dismissed us rather abruptly."

"Talya got what she wanted. One thing you learn about corporate politics at this level is when you get the answer you want, end the meeting."

"So, she supports what you're doing?"

"No, Talya enticed me to make a promise she can use against me if I fail. She's planning on convincing the board to replace me regardless," Valen says with a wry smile. "Making the promise buys me time to make plans of my own."

Fiolla doesn't understand politics at this level. The prima and the chief executive officer of the company should be able to work out their differences for the good of the company. That's never the case. To them, it's about power and control, and they always covet more.

"What are you going to do?" Fiolla asks.

"Talya Bettancourt wants a pawn beholden to her sitting in the Oval Office. This issue with Liberteum is a chance for her to chase that dream. I need to move my pieces around the chessboard. Contact Chief Guardian Teman as soon as we get back to the White House and impress upon him that we expect results. If he can't deliver them, I'll get the BCS involved."

"Certainly, sir."

"One more thing. We need to squelch the rumors out there. I'm ordering corporate communications to put you on AME News during the seven o'clock hour to state our position on the raid."

Fiolla's mouth hangs open. "Sir, that's outside my area of expertise. Shouldn't it come from our public affairs executives?"

"It will carry more weight coming from you. The interview questions will be drafted and cleared ahead of time."

"Of course, sir. I'll handle it," she says, her voice wavering as the limousine pulls into the drive leading to the West Wing.

"I know you will. You're one of the few people I can trust right now, Fiolla. Welcome to the inner circle."

CHAPTER FORTY-SIX

LIBERTEUM

Abandoned Subway Station
Somewhere in the Manhattan Underground
New York City Municipal Corporation

Quarren stares at the old map on the wall as light from the flickering candles dances around the room. He prefers the soft-orange warmth to the construction lighting illuminating most of the old station. This is not home for him, despite his daughter bringing some of his belongings down from Valhalla.

A knock at the door precedes Rykos's arrival. He offers the young man a seat at the table with two cooked dinners. He accepts, suspicious at the show of kindness as he sets the old textbook down on its edge.

"You eat well for an urch," Rykos says, picking up a fork.

"Not always, I'm afraid. I'm glad to see you're making the most of your time with us," Quarren says, nodding at the book.

"I'm a hostage. There isn't much else to do to pass the time."

"You aren't a hostage, son. You're a guest with limited freedom of movement."

Rykos frowns and looks around the room as he takes a bite of his chicken. It's his first decent meal since before the rave.

"Where did you get all this stuff?"

"I told you. You can get almost anything down here. Cellars were widely used for storage before the collapse. The new city was built atop the old, so much of it was entombed. We opened them."

"I don't recognize most of this stuff."

Quarren joins him in surveying the room. There are posters of historical figures, events, and slogans. There is even a replica of the "Betsy Ross Flag" from the American Revolution on the far wall.

"How far into that book are you?" Quarren asks.

"Not far enough, I guess. I've skipped around. I know about most of the events I'm reading about, but the context is different."

"Give me an example."

"The American Revolution. We were taught that the war was fought by business owners who were mistreated by Britain's abusive government. They financed an army to drive them off the continent. Was that a lie?"

"I'm afraid it's not that black and white, Rykos. Many of the United States' founding fathers were merchants and plantation owners, and yes, laws passed by the British government did hurt colonists financially. However, the struggle was more about the people having a say in their governing. Do you remember reading the line, 'no taxation without representation?'"

"Yes."

"Most colonists didn't want to separate from the crown; they wanted a voice in parliament. When that was denied, they began to believe they would be better off governing themselves. The fight for independence was made up of people from all walks of life and social standings."

"And World War II was the same thing?" Rykos asks, paying rapt attention between bites.

"That was a battle for liberty against fascism and tyrannical rule. For obvious reasons, history was rewritten into something entirely different. Modern corporations don't want their employees being reminded of one of life's fundamental truths."

"What's that?"

"That the struggle for freedom never ends. It must be fought for and won by every generation."

Rykos sets his fork down and clasps his hands. "Corporations gave us freedom from war and conflict, racism and sexism, and the perils of economic uncertainty. They have achieved what thousands of years of human endeavors failed to."

"You were taught that, but do you believe it in your heart?"

"It's hard to believe what's written in here," Rykos says, tapping the book on the table.

"It's not easy for anyone to accept. Ask anyone down here. Historical truth conflicts with corporate programming. Everything you've been taught is a carefully concocted lie meant to bring about a specific end."

"What end?"

"Your unwavering loyalty to the system."

Quarren watches the young man. He can see the conflict in his eyes. It's the same one he faced decades ago and has coached countless other people through since. Sparing his daughter from that struggle was the best decision he ever made.

"Why rewrite history at all?"

"Because the past is the key to the future. The world was once filled with different political ideologies. Most governments exercised their power only through the consent of the people. It required compromise. That's unheard of today. Corporate executives don't permit different perspectives or ideas. They can't have people questioning their authority, and the study of history encourages critical thinking. The only opinions allowed now are the ones they provide you."

"I have my own," Rykos snaps.

Quarren can't hide his amusement. "You have the one they gave you. It's the reason you're so conflicted right now. I know because I saw it in myself once upon a time."

"Before you became an urch?"

"Before my eyes were opened to the truth."

"You said you would tell me why you came down here," Rykos says before the door opens and a trio of figures enters.

Scivix and Haven flank Michele. All three are covered in dirt and mud. Haven eyes Rykos hard before turning his attention to the leader of Liberteum.

"I did, but sadly, there isn't time for it right now," Quarren says before turning his attention to his daughter. "Is everything set?"

"We're as ready as we're going to be."

Quarren nods. Michele helps him out of his chair, and he kisses her on the forehead. Rykos stands and picks the textbook up, cradling it in his arms.

"I'm afraid I need to cut our dinner short, Rykos. Michele will take you back to your room. I'm going to rest now."

"Can I ask you one question, Quarren? How many times have you read this book?"

"More than you can count."

"So, if this is the only source of your information, isn't it true that maybe you've been brainwashed, too?"

"You're finally starting to understand," Quarren says with a smile before moving to the bed in the corner and lying down.

Rykos follows Michele out of the small room with Haven and Scivix pulling up the rear. For once, they aren't pushing him along.

"Does your father always speak in code?" Rykos asks Michele as she escorts him down the platform.

"I hope he isn't tormenting you too much," she says with a warm smile.

"It's an improvement over being hit in the head."

"That can be arranged again, Ivy," Haven barks from behind. "Keep flapping your—"

"Return to the tunnel, Haven," Michele commands over her shoulder as they walk.

"Your time is coming," he warns before moving off with Scivix up the platform in the opposite direction.

"It would be easier if you didn't antagonize him," Michele says, stopping.

"It would be easier if you just let me go," Rykos counters. "You could have killed me or left me with Balin. Why bring me down here?"

Michele starts walking again, and they pass the raised ticketing area, where the hackers are hard at work. She can't tell him. Not yet.

"I thought you might want to see what's going to happen."

"What do you mean?" he asks. "What's going to happen?"

"The beginning of the struggle for the soul of humanity."

Rykos shivers at the statement. "I don't understand."

"You will soon," Michele says as they reach his room. "Get some rest. Tomorrow is going to be a long day."

CHAPTER FORTY-SEVEN

AMERICA, INC.

"The Cellar"
SoHo Geographic District
New York City Municipal Corporation

In modern times, what passes for a bar is a throwback to an old 1920s speakeasy. America Incorporated's ban on alcohol forced drinking underground just as the Prohibition Era did. Most employees would not risk their positions to frequent these establishments, but the qulis have much less to lose.

"Chief Guardian...dis is a surprise. I ain't expectin' to see you down here so soon," the barman says as Teman and Zyree emerge down the dimly lit stairway.

The few customers here make for exits to the underground. Teman smiles. Places like this exist throughout the city. He occasionally orders a raid to send a message about discretion. Overall, they cause few problems and can prove useful in other ways.

"I'm full of surprises, Gyell. How's business?"

"Slow since ya rounded up a chunk of my clientele in dat raid of yours. Now ya here scarin' my usuals away. What da ya want? Ya lookin' for info?"

"Do you have any?"

"Nah, all I's got now is an empty bar," Gyell says, gesturing around the decrepit room with his arms to prove his point.

Most purveyors of illicit spirits would panic if the chief guardian of New York City walked in. Not this one. Gyell and Teman have an understanding.

"Would you tell me if you did have information?" Teman asks, leaning on the rickety bar.

"Ya know I would. I ain't wantin' trouble. Who's ya friend? Bodyguard? Boyfriend?"

"Psssh," Zyree scoffs while Teman doesn't bother masking his amusement.

"We just need a quiet place to talk."

"Da place is empty now, so sit where ya like. Want ya usual?"

"Yeah. Bring two." Teman slaps a pair of slugs on the makeshift counter. "This should cover the drinks and make up for your inconvenience."

Gyell snaps the slugs up from the bar and nods. The two men head over to a dilapidated booth in the corner and slide into the bench seats. Zyree looks like he's making a mental note to ensure his hepatitis vaccinations are up to date.

"I thought slugs were illegal."

"They are," Teman says with a grin.

"Here ya go," the bartender mutters as he sets two small glasses of clear liquid on the table and goes back to the bar.

"Not a bright one, is he?" Zyree asks after he's out of earshot.

"I don't think he did well in his modules before going off the grid, but education doesn't matter here. Street smarts keep you alive in the underground, and he has those."

"I have to be honest, Teman. I never would've expected you to frequent a place like this. You seem so…."

"By the book? Illegal speakeasies like this are the best places to find out what's going on under the streets of the city."

"Does this one have a name?"

"The Cellar."

Zyree looks around. Teman always found the name appropriate. Hidden in the basement of an ages-old building in SoHo, The Cellar's modest illumination is choked by dark brick walls. The place has a medieval feel, and the vibe would be cool if it were on purpose.

"I'm surprised the urches and qulis come here if they know Gyell is selling them out."

"Nothing he tells me can get traced back to him. I rarely act on any of it," Teman explains. "It's not worth burning him as a source."

"So, he's an informant?"

"And a purveyor of the finest urch shine in the city," he says, taking a sip of the clear liquid and feeling it burn down his throat. "It's how I found out where the rave was."

"What is this stuff?" Zyree gasps after taking his own sip.

"Vodka. Single filtered."

"Like hell it is. I've had vodka in Europe and it didn't taste like this," he complains before looking back at the bartender. "I didn't think urches or qulis would turn on each other by sharing information with you."

"The underground shares a lot of similarities with society aboveground. They have a class system, can be cutthroat, and do what they must to survive. The only real difference is that they don't have the comforts we do."

"Or the controls."

"Yeah, or the controls. Controls are necessary in an orderly society."

"Is that why you hate them?" Zyree asks. "Because they chose to come down here and live outside the system?"

Teman presses his lips together. He's never been asked that question and doesn't know how to articulate an answer.

"I hate them because they have no reason to live outside the system. Most of human history was marked by misery. Corporations solved society's problems and provided everything a person needs: a steady income, a comfortable place to live, safe streets, a good education, and even entertainment when performance merits the reward."

"What about freedom?"

"Freedom was a myth propagated by governments. There was never any such thing."

"Something tells me that the urches would disagree," Zyree says.

Teman shakes his head and nods over at the bar. "Like Gyell over there, they aren't very bright."

"Touché. How have so many avoided capture? I mean, New York is a big city, but you have the technology to hunt them down."

"The city's underground is a labyrinth that they've learned to navigate. Subfloors of skyscrapers go down to the bedrock and every apartment building has a basement. Then there are old train lines, sewers, and maintenance tunnels that connect them all. Avoiding us, even with our technology, isn't much of a feat once you know the lay of the land."

"I would have thought you'd order every guardian in this city to grab a torchlight and search every inch of it," Zyree says, earning a glare from the chief guardian.

"I want to find my son, but I won't sacrifice countless guardians to do it without actionable intelligence. I can't fight a subterranean guerilla war just because I'm personally invested. You didn't ask to meet for a philosophical conversation about urches, Zyree. What do you want?"

"To give you this."

Zyree unbuttons one of the fasteners on his tunic and pulls out several sheets of paper folded in half. He slides them across the table to Teman.

"Hard copy? I'm not sure we even own a printer anymore. What am I looking at?"

"The head of the snake," Zyree says, causing Teman to raise his eyebrows before he nods. "His name is Quarren. He was an executive-level senior program manager in New York."

"Yeah, I can read. So what?"

"He messed up. The details are vague, but the projects he was managing during the rebuild of the city failed. As a result, he was targeted for termination on the grounds of gross incompetence. Before the PSS could execute the order, Quarren and his wife went off the grid."

"I'm still not following you."

"I ordered my team to research the origins of our target. I thought it would take a while to find anything, but once the pieces started falling into place, it moved fast."

"Are you telling me…?"

"Quarren is Liberteum's leader."

Teman's mouth hangs open. Neither the PSS nor BCS made any progress in identifying members of Liberteum, much less its leader. This can't be right.

"We've been trying to identify this guy for years. Do you really want me to believe that you managed to do it in less than a day?"

"Don't be offended, Teman. We had fresh eyes and tackled it from a different perspective," Zyree says.

Teman scans the pages. It all looks circumstantial to him.

"Walk me through it."

"For starters, Liberteum's first attack was on an office building in the city housing the construction firm Quarren was working for."

"That could be a coincidence."

"You know better than that, but let's assume you're correct. Let's skip ahead to the good part. When Liberteum was thought to have been annihilated in that raid a couple of years ago, all their gear was processed for trace evidence. Most of the DNA matched the dead terrorists. One sample didn't."

"I know all this. The DNA wasn't in our database."

"Because Quarren's wife went underground with him *before* she gave birth. The DNA you found belongs to their child. We compared the sample you took with Quarren's DNA profile. It was a paternal match."

"Okay, so he has a kid that belongs to Liberteum, but it's still a reach to claim he's leading them."

Zyree smirks before finding the paper with the picture of a man in a camouflage uniform with a patch on his shoulder. "We found that after a search through your databases for his family background."

"It's an old picture. So what?"

"Look at the writing on the patch."

"*Ex gladio libertas*," he mutters, not getting it at all.

"It means 'the sword of freedom' in Latin. It's where he derived the name. Liberteum is a misspelling of libertatem, meaning—"

"Freedom?" Teman asks, perplexed.

"The -eum means 'them' in Latin, as in 'free them.' Free the world. Teman, I don't think this group is engaging in random violence. Quarren assembled a group with a singular goal: to take down the whole system."

Teman sits back in his rickety chair. Liberteum has always been considered a nuisance, and nothing more. It's a considerable shock to the conventional wisdom to regard them as something far more dangerous. It wouldn't be the first time in history that's happened.

"It's compelling, but still speculation, Zyree. I can't do anything with this. Even if you're right, my superiors will laugh me out of the room."

Teman slides the papers back across the table. He stares at them for a long time. It may be speculation, but his gut tells him that Zyree is spot on.

"Then don't brief them, Chief Guardian. This is our guy."

"All right. What do you suggest we do?"

"Wait until their next move and be ready to react at a moment's notice."

Teman throws his head back in disgust. "That's a lousy plan. The CEO will never settle for me being less than proactive in the search. He's demanding results, and their next attack could be years from now."

"That's where I think you're wrong. Quarren is an old man. If we're right about them planning to take down the system, then the Secaucus attack was the first step and your raid may have accelerated it. Trust me, they're going to make a move soon. We need to be ready."

CHAPTER
FORTY-EIGHT
AMERICA, INC.

AME News Studio
Midtown Geographic District
New York City Municipal Corporation

Broadcasting from New York, *American Morning* is the most-watched news show in the corporation. Whereas the evening news was once the primary program people relied on for information, the dawn of the Corporate Age created a new paradigm where employees tune into the news before their commute. While not everyone works standard business hours, plenty of them do.

"Do you have the questions we provided?" Fiolla asks the anchor as she reviews notes on a tablet under the anchor desk.

"This isn't my first interview," Kassaya says without looking up. "Although public affairs executives don't dictate the questions like this. I guess the White House is more insecure."

Fiolla winces at the slight. "Maybe we're more concerned about getting the truth to our employees without the typical useless AME News commentary."

Journalist Kassaya has one of the most recognizable faces in the corporation. She's viewed by employees as a trusted source of information around the sphere of influence. To Fiolla, she's just arrogant and condescending.

Kassaya is about to respond when a producer begins the countdown. She scowls at the lost opportunity seconds before a beaming smile lights up her face when the cameras roll. Fiolla shakes her head at the immediate transformation.

"Welcome to *American Morning*. Today is Tuesday, March sixteenth, and it is now the seven o'clock hour. With us to lead off this morning's update is Executive Fiolla, the staff vice-president of Corporate Affairs for the White House. Thank you for joining us today."

"Thank you for having me."

"Analysts in corporate accounting are expecting a strong third quarter from the parent company based on key subsidiary growth in the raw resources and transportation sectors. Is America still on track to deliver?"

"Yes, I'm pleased to say we are. Recent productivity mandates resulted in increases that offset downturns in other sectors. We also benefit from increased exports to the Central and South American Corporations as part of a trade deal negotiated last year. We will meet or exceed this quarter's projections."

"There's been a lot of volatility in AME over the past week, which is rare for the parent company. Is there a weakness that has caused these wild fluctuations?"

Fiolla fights the urge to wring her hands. There's a reason Public Relations handles this sort of thing. She knows what she's talking about, but being on camera and heard by hundreds of millions of people is unnerving.

"America Incorporated has historically been one of the IGI's most stable and reliable stocks. Unfortunately, every stock is prone to periods of volatility. We're confident that we'll settle into a growth trend moving forward."

"So, there are no concerns?" Kassaya asks.

Fiolla stares at the journalist. The question bothers her. It's not what she asked, but how she asked it. The tone of her voice was almost…hostile.

"None at all. Looking at our technical analysis, the simple and exponential moving averages are still trending upward. There is no indication that a downturn is coming."

Kassaya looks unimpressed. Fiolla knows her biography well. She's an admirer of old-school journalists and longs for a return to how the media reported stories before the turn of the century. They would press to drag the truth out in an interview. Unfortunately for her, that model died at the turn of the century and is incompatible with the corporate need for a perfectly crafted message.

"There has been a lot of speculation about the action by New York's Public Safety and Security against a gathering of the city's urch population. Much of that speculation has come because of a lack of information. Can you comment on that?"

"Of course," Fiolla says, appreciating her perfect recital of the question she was instructed to ask. "The White House authorized Chief Executive Safmor to direct the PSS to take action against the urch population. I think we should make it clear to all employees tuning in that urches are illegal in our sphere of influence. They commit criminal acts, and their existence has been tolerated for far too long."

Kassaya stares at Fiolla for a long moment. Dead air on television is awkward and difficult for viewers to watch. An evil smile crosses her lips, causing Fiolla to shift slightly in her seat.

"Executive Fiolla, intercorporational media outlets reported that the terrorist group Liberteum was the target in the raid. Is that true?"

Fiolla clenches her fists. She now knows why she hesitated: Kassaya brazenly strayed from the approved script.

"Our competitors in the global marketplace like making false accusations to bolster their positions within the corporate community."

"Then you deny that Liberteum was behind the explosions outside Intercorpex data centers in Secaucus?"

"I cannot speak to what those explosions were. The investigation seems to point to catastrophic equipment failure. Despite attempts to portray it otherwise, nothing indicates an attack of any sort."

"You still haven't answered the question. Was this Liberteum?"

Fiolla forces a smile. Kassaya is playing a dangerous game. Valen won't be happy with this interview and will take it out on AME News. Liberteum was not to be mentioned, but now that it has, Fiolla improvises an answer.

"Liberteum was decimated two years ago," she says before looking at the camera. "There cannot be a threat from them because they no longer exist."

CHAPTER FORTY-NINE

REGISTRANT RYKOS

Abandoned Subway Station
Somewhere in the Manhattan Underground
New York City Municipal Corporation

A cheer erupts when my captors hear the executive's proclamation. I was escorted to the mezzanine level to watch the seven o'clock news hour. In addition to Michele, her father, Haven, and Scivix, hackers Jasper and Adiz are gathered in this subterranean stronghold with about two dozen others that I don't recognize. Liberteum is a bigger group than I thought.

"Did you hear that? We don't exist," Haven says, pointing at the ancient display on the makeshift table.

"They're about to find out the hard way that we do," Jasper says with a guttural laugh. Something about his reaction sends a shiver down my spine.

I look toward the platform behind me. Escape is unlikely, and fighting them is out of the question. Part of me wants to make a run for it, but another wants to know what this is all about. My curiosity is winning.

"Can I have your attention, please," Quarren announces over the din as he rises from his folding chair.

The subway station quiets to absolute silence. It's the measure of the respect the group has for this man. When he speaks, nobody else dares to.

"Over two decades ago, I fled certain death at the hands of the corporation. It was the right decision, but it had consequences. It cost the life of my wife, whom I loved with all my heart. The day she died, I made a vow: to form a group that could shine a light in the darkness corporatism ushered in. That group is Liberteum, and that day has arrived."

Everyone offers up wild cheers, many of them holding weapons over their heads. The men and women in the room are dressed in clothes I have never seen on urches before. Some are clad in black vests, cargo pants, boots, and tactical gear my father's guardians would wear.

"Michele?" Quarren steps aside and allows his daughter to take center stage.

She's also dressed for war. Her long black hair is tied into a single braid that falls halfway down a paramilitary-style jacket. Olive drab pants with two large pockets on either thigh hug her at the hips, completing the intimidating look.

"We've been planning for this day since I was a child. We've had to work together, bleed together, survive together, and dream together. Today, we make that struggle worthwhile," Michele decrees, eliciting another enthusiastic cheer.

"My friends, we all share a love of freedom, a need for independence, and a desire to show the world that the light of liberty still burns. Today marks the first step of that journey. Our small flame will grow into a raging inferno, consuming our enemies and freeing the world from its perpetual bondage.

"We all know our missions and what must be done," she continues. "There are also risks. Some of us may not survive to celebrate our victory. Believe me when I say that your sacrifices will not be in vain."

"Hear! Hear!" the crowd cries.

"Archimedes once said, 'Give me a lever long enough and a fulcrum on which to place it, and I shall move the world.' We have the lever. We have the fulcrum. Now, we move the world. Friends…patriots…ready yourselves. Phase two of Project Archimedes is about to begin."

Everyone moves with a purpose except me. Jasper and Adiz sit down at the makeshift table and begin tapping away at their keyboards. Haven and Scivix conduct a weapons check with about a dozen other men and women. One group sets off down the stairs toward the train platform while the rest take the dark passage off this level.

Quarren leans against the far wall and watches his small army. Michele issues some last-minute instructions, and I realize that her father is passing her the mantle of leadership.

"What's Archimedes?" I ask when she makes her way over to me.

"You're about to find out. Freya? Are you all set?"

"I've been waiting for this for a long time. I'll never be more ready."

Freya is almost as beautiful as Michele. Her blonde hair is woven into a similar braid, and she's dressed similarly. A smile lights up her face as her bright blue eyes twinkle.

"You have the most dangerous part of this operation," Michele warns. "Please be careful. I want to see you in Valhalla when this is over."

"You know I will. I need to get in position. It will take a while to get there," she warns, receiving a warm embrace from Michele. "I'll see you soon."

"Are you okay?" I ask, noticing the anguish on her face.

"Freya is one of my closest friends. It scares me to think that I might not see her again."

"Why? What is she going to do?"

"Here you go, Michele," Scivix says, handing her the meanest-looking weapon I've ever seen. It doesn't appear that I'm going to get an answer to my question.

The dark gray long gun is like nothing I've ever seen. It has a sturdy shoulder stock, trigger guard, and a high-capacity magazine. Its simple design has no apparent integration with its bearer like modern weapons do. There's no doubt that it's equally effective, though.

"Where did you get all these weapons?" I ask, hoping that I'm overreacting.

"We acquired a fifty-year-old 3D printer that can fabricate metal components. This rifle is based on a 2025 military design. Once we acquired the plans, we could produce all the arms and ammunition we need."

"Where did you get the gunpowder?"

"We made it," she says, eliciting a surprised reaction that amuses her. "You don't have any practical skills up there, do you, Rykos? All you need is potassium nitrate, charcoal powder, sulfur powder, and some basic chemistry skills to get the formula right. Haven't you noticed that we can adapt to anything?"

"I'm starting to."

"Good, because you're about to learn another lesson."

I meet Michele's eyes. They're beautiful but have a hardness to them that comes with determination and deadly intentions. I'm almost afraid to ask.

"What lesson?"

"That a small group of determined people can change the world."

CHAPTER
FIFTY

INTERCORPEX

Global Network Operations Center
Manhattan Financial District
ICX New York Exchange

Zyree is shown into the spacious office and is greeted with a scowl. Lyris doesn't have a sunny disposition on a good day and isn't in the mood for another round of sarcastic banter this morning. That's too bad. He'll get it anyway.

"You summoned?"

"I did. Don't sit."

Zyree grudgingly complies, straightening himself and placing his hands behind his back. The director of operations continues scanning the display on his desk to make him wait a few moments.

"It's just before eight in the morning. I should be with Wyeth on the NOC floor. Instead, blowing a two-bit security guard back into his place is a higher priority right now."

"Anyone I know?" Zyree quips.

"Don't get cute with me."

"I'm not. You're wasting time with a useless preamble. What do you want, Lyris?"

"To chop your balls off and stuff them down your throat."

"I guess I should be grateful that you don't always get what you want," Zyree counters.

"You were explicitly told *not* to work with public safety. I know this because I gave the order. Instead, you saw fit to share proprietary exchange information...not with a low-level functionary, but the chief guardian of New York himself. What do you have to say about that?"

"They have sharp uniforms."

Lyris looks like he's about to explode.

"Listen, smart ass," Lyris says, pointing a finger at Zyree. "I'm only dealing with you because of your reputation for getting results."

"I get results because I'm willing to do what it takes to get them."

"Only you haven't gotten them! All you've managed to do here is defy my orders."

Zyree shrugs. "Your orders were idiotic."

"My orders are to be unquestioned," Lyris responds sternly, "and followed to the letter."

"Yeah, that's not going to happen. This may come as a surprise, but I don't work for you."

"You wouldn't last five minutes here if you did."

Zyree holds his hands out and stares at the ceiling. "We finally agree on something."

The director takes a deep breath. He's on the cusp of completely losing his temper. Zyree wonders how much further he needs to go to push him over the edge.

"How do you think Raimius will react when I inform him of your insolence?"

"Probably the same as when I report your incompetence."

"I'm the senior director of global operations!" Lyris shouts. "You're a nobody pretending to be a big shot. Who do you think the AG will side with?"

"Bureaucrats think that their titles and relationships matter more than delivering outcomes. Sentimentality is dead. It's all about business in this world, and business runs on productivity and results. That's what Raimius understands."

Lyris shakes his head and crosses the room, stepping directly in front of Zyree and closing to within an inch of his face. The chief inspector doesn't flinch.

"You know, Zyree, I'm getting tired of your attitude."

"You'd better take a step back before something bad happens to you that the best doctors in the city can't reverse."

Lyris is about to challenge him on the threat when the double doors to his office swing open. Malkor charges through as the administrative aide does everything he can to stop him. It was a losing battle from the start.

"This looks cozy," Malkor says, grinning.

"What the hell do you want?" Lyris snaps.

"I have some urgent business to discuss with the chief inspector."

"What business?"

"I'm sure you'll find out when you get down to the NOC floor," Malkor says, shaking his head. "They'll be calling for you at any moment."

"Executive Director Lyris," the system announces, "you're needed in the network operations center immediately."

"Acknowledged."

"What's going on, Malkor?" Zyree asks.

"A series of explosions just rocked Manhattan."

CHAPTER
FIFTY-ONE
AMERICA, INC.

The White House
Corporate Governance District
Washington-Arlington Municipal Corporation

It's already been a long day with lots of dashed dreams. She couldn't arrange a lunch date with Farron or go to her domicile for a hot bath to reduce the stress. The message recalling her to Washington came immediately following her tussle with Journalist Kassaya, and a car ferried her straight to the White House after she landed. Such is the life of a corporate executive.

"Executive Fiolla," an aide greets her in the foyer of the West Wing. "Your presence is requested in the Oval Office. I'm to show you there immediately."

"Lead the way. Is this about the interview?"

"I was just directed to bring you right in, ma'am."

Fiolla knows this can only be about one thing: Valen saw the interview. He's about to take his frustration out on someone, and she hopes it's Kassaya and not her. Chief Executive Valen doesn't look up as she crosses the carpet and adjusts her clothing while he pecks away on his virtual keyboard.

"You've had a long morning," he says, still typing away. "I know Journalist Kassaya went off-script. I'll deal with her and her producers, but they aren't my concern. I want to know if someone put her up to it."

"I can't imagine why someone would."

Valen peers up at her. "I can."

"Sir, I think—"

The doors to the Oval Office burst open and Special Agent Caylem storms in with four armed men wearing the protective uniforms of the BCS. They take up positions on either side of the desk and at the doors leading out of the room. Caylem stands in front of the CEO.

"Sir, there were three explosions in New York City with unconfirmed reports of a fourth. We've upgraded the defensive posture of all corporate buildings in the sphere of influence."

"Explosions?" Fiolla asks, feeling a shock to her nerves. "Where?"

Caylem stares at his tablet. "A retail store, two apartment buildings, and a SpeedRail platform that caused a train to derail."

"Casualties?"

"Undetermined at this time, sir," Caylem says, checking his wrist tablet. "The PSS issued a precautionary mass casualty expectation order to area medical centers."

"Chief Executive Valen, you have a VidLynk request from Director Virtari of the BCS," his digital assistant informs him.

"Connect on the main display, Hallie," Valen orders before the image of the director comes to life on the far wall. "Tell me you have news, Virtari. Have the causes of the explosions been identified?"

"Not yet, Chief Executive. The PSS informed us that Maestro systems reported gas leaks at the two apartment buildings. We won't know if that was the cause until the fires are out and a forensic investigation is conducted. However, there were no gas mains near the SpeedRail station or the retail shop."

"Director, are you saying that this is another attack?" Valen asks.

"Given what happened in Secaucus, it fits Liberteum's M.O."

"I don't want speculation or best guesses, Director. I need facts. Get me some. I'm going to monitor this from the Situation Room. Get over here as soon as you can."

"Yes, sir."

"Hallie, have all key executives assemble in the Situation Room immediately."

"Of course, Chief Executive."

"You're dismissed, Agent Caylem. Fiolla, please follow me."

Valen walks across the room and opens the door to the adjacent private study. The BCS agents don't move from their posts, and those assigned to guard Valen stand outside the door. This is the most privacy he'll have until the protection order is lifted.

"Fiolla, I need you to open a backchannel with Chief Guardian Teman. Find out directly from him what's going on up there."

"I will do so immediately."

Fiolla tightens her jaw. She doesn't like the request. Valen distrusts Virtari, and the head of the BCS despises Valen. She would rather stay out of the crossfire. If this is what the CEO's inner circle is like, she'd rather stand outside it for the rest of her career. That's not the only thing that's bothering her.

"Sir, I just went on television and told the world that Liberteum doesn't exist. If this is an attack, it could mean—"

"I'm aware of what that could mean. We'll deal with all that later. The BCS will want to seize control from the PSS, who will fight them. I need you to referee that. I'll worry about what AME News and our subsidiaries disseminate over the InterLynk."

"Of course, sir."

"Fiolla, I'm counting on you. This is going to get worse before it gets better," he says, adding even more weight on her shoulders.

* * *

The RTCC is staffed by professionals who identify and respond to criminal incidents around the city. They aren't trained to deal with catastrophic events. While the scene behind Teman isn't utter chaos, it's desperately urgent. The man himself looks frazzled.

"This isn't a good time, Fiolla," he says, clearly distracted.

"No kidding. The BCS is about to start hounding you, and you're going to want to talk to me first. What do you know? How bad is it?"

Teman tightens his jaw. "See for yourself."

Videos of four plumes of smoke are fed onto her display. Emergency vehicles and PSS personnel have already responded to each. The most chaotic scene is at the SpeedRail station. It was rush hour and choked with commuters.

"The BCS has provided Valen with their analysis. What's yours, Chief Guardian?"

"One explosion is an incident. Two is a suspicious coincidence. Three is a tragedy. Four is an attack."

"Do you think it's Liberteum?"

Teman looks away from the camera. There is conflict in his eyes. Fiolla understands his predicament. An admission could mean termination.

"Yes," he states, finally looking back at her.

"Okay. What are you planning to do about it?"

"I have ordered the EOC to be brought online to run tactical operations. The RTCC will handle the emergency response to the explosions and general city security. I'm about to head over there now."

Fiolla nods, pleased to hear that he isn't sitting on his hands, mired in indecisiveness.

"You know the city. Why those locations? Any ideas?

Teman calls up a map and sends it to Fiolla's display. The grid of buildings and streets is overlaid with the crisis data. Fiolla stares at the data. The locations look desperately random.

"Other than the SpeedRail station, there was no impact to critical infrastructure or explosions in locations likely to produce mass casualties. If they have a purpose, I don't see it."

"Could this be a prelude to something else?" Fiolla asks.

"It's possible, but it will require more investigation. I have some people that can look into that."

"Then don't let me get in your way. Good luck, Teman."

Fiolla signs off, and her standard office lighting is restored. She leans back in her chair. Farron likely wasn't at any of those locations. At least she can be thankful for that. It's one of the only things about today that's gone right. She hopes that Valen's suspicion is wrong. She can't imagine things getting any worse.

CHAPTER FIFTY-TWO

LIBERTEUM

Non-descript Office Building
Tribeca Geographic District
New York City Municipal Corporation

It took Haven three months to find a way into this building. It was remodeled twenty-five years ago, and like most structures, an entirely new physical plant was installed. Instead of removing the old infrastructure, the new systems were installed on a higher sub-level.

Employees and executives call them "urches," but they should be called "moles" since they are experts at tunneling. This one was built off an old sewer and only took a couple of weeks to complete. They broke through the foundation wall and then reconstructed it to erase any trace of their intrusion.

Not that anyone comes down here. There are no cameras or sensors on this sub-level. Like in much of the city, old infrastructure was abandoned, hidden, and forgotten. Freya pushes through the access into the old boiler room and shines her torchlight from the mouth of the tunnel.

"So far, so good," she mumbles.

That was the easy part. She lugs the canvas bag through the opening, pulls out some fresh clothing, and changes quickly. Only one stairway leads out of this room, and there is likely a camera at the top of it. The stolen uniform will look convincing on a camera feed. If anyone stops her and looks closely, it's game over.

Freya climbs the stairs and enters the utility sub-level like she owns the building. She makes her way to one of the three utility rooms housing the HVAC plant and lets herself in. Sensitive areas of this building are heavily monitored and have unbeatable intrusion detection measures. Nobody knows what she'll find once she's inside; if she manages to get inside.

There are several two-by-two foot air conditioning returns in the ceiling. On this level, all the returns branch off a master trunk that leads to the evaporator and air handling units. She can go anywhere on this floor from here, or so Jasper thinks.

Freya drags over a work table and stands on it to unscrew the vent cover. She grasps the edge and manages to pull herself into the duct in one fluid motion. It was something she's practiced for months. She makes a mental note of where she has to go and starts sliding forward on her stomach.

After fifteen minutes, she realizes that this is taking too long. She picks up the pace and makes the hard left down a feeder duct blasting air into her face. This has to be it. She'll lose a lot of time if she's wrong.

Server rooms require a lot of power and cooling. Adiz determined from the plans they acquired that this room uses three air conditioning systems for redundancy. She peers through the thin slats but can't see much. This has to be the right place.

There's no way to know if there are cameras in here. If there are, Freya's break-in will rank among the shortest in history. She withdraws the hammer from her bag, struggling to move her arms in the tight space. She slams it against the vent a dozen times before a corner gives out. A half dozen hits later, the second screw pops. She bends the vent down and peeks her head into the room.

There are no signs of cameras. That's good. In another well-practiced move, she grasps the edge of the vent, pushes her body forward, and does a flip to the ground, landing on her feet.

Freya couches and scans the aisle between two long rows of server cabinets. She glides over to the edge of the aisle and scans the wall. Again, no cameras. Freya changes direction and does the same at the other end. Nothing. This room is unmonitored from the inside. Perfect.

She makes her way over to a work area and rips free the small laptop taped to her back. Adiz and Jasper built this for her from spare parts, and she'll be surprised if it even powers on. The device took a beating on the way here and wasn't in good shape when it was handed to her back at the station—fortunately, the clunky machine boots.

"Okay, here goes nothing," she whispers to herself, jacking a cable into a switch.

Freya types a few commands, and the machine runs a script. After a few moments, she has an admin account. She rolls her chair over to one of the crash cart computers used to recover systems and inputs her new credentials. The interactive menu pops up, and she's amazed at what she has access to.

"Now we're talking," she whispers.

The first order of business is to update her status before getting to work. Freya sends a command from the laptop that she knows the hackers will pick up. There are several vital tasks to complete, and time is short. How quickly she finishes them will determine whether she gets out of this building alive.

CHAPTER
FIFTY-THREE

INTERCORPEX

PSS Emergency Operations Center
Lower West-Side Office Building
New York City Municipal Corporation

In comparison to their headquarters, the facade of the PSS's emergency operations center is unimpressive. Located in a nondescript office building on the lower west side of Manhattan, it has no distinguishing features from street level. Of course, that's why the site was chosen – it's meant to be inconspicuous.

Zyree quickly learns what it lacks in grandeur it makes up in functionality. Opposite the modern reception area is a man trap designed to deter intruders and hardened doors that lead to the main floor. The setup isn't dramatically different from the Real-Time Crime Center.

The room has workstations arranged in rows facing the front instead of the concentric rings to promote collaboration. The entire EOC is cast in an eerie blue glow from the high ceilings above, and accent lighting underneath each workstation adds to the mystique of the room.

"Glad you could make it, Chief Inspector," Teman says as Zyree is escorted in.

"I wish it could be under better circumstances. Where do we stand?"

"You mean besides fighting the BCS for jurisdiction?" Teman asks, frustrated. "The explosion in the retail shop is a mystery, and the SpeedRail station is still a rescue mission. We confirmed that ruptured gas lines caused the apartment building explosions."

"Gas lines?"

"Much of the city's infrastructure has been replaced, but there are some old pipes out there that could have ruptured."

"You don't *really* believe that, do you?"

Zyree studies the chief guardian. One of the critical lessons he's learned during his countless investigations is the power of denial. Many executives and employees refuse to believe the irrefutable facts staring them in the face. In almost every instance, that denial has led to bad decisions.

"Only a fool would believe it's a coincidence."

"Chief Guardian," the incident commander interrupts, "we have reports of small detonations in Times Square and outside Grand Central Terminus."

"Fatalities?" Teman asks, massaging his temples.

"Injuries are reported. Guardians assigned to Times Square claim explosive devices were placed in trash receptacles."

"Pull the video footage of that area from the past twenty-four hours. I want to know the name and title of every employee who walked within ten feet of them."

"Camera feeds are offline in those areas, and the video isn't accessible."

Teman turns and stares at Zyree, who nods. The camera systems employed throughout America Incorporated cannot be easily disabled. It takes someone with remarkable hacking skills to accomplish that. Unfortunately, Liberteum has a couple of those.

"Get tech on it and deploy drones," Teman barks. "I want every inch of this island covered. Double our presence at all critical transportation centers and river crossings. Recall every guardian assigned to this city and put them to work."

Teman joins Zyree in staring at the map overlay on one of the large displays. His guardians are capable of moving assets around the city. It's up to him to figure out where they should be going next.

"They're targeting every part of Manhattan," Zyree mutters.

"Yeah, but why? We're scrambling but are on high alert now. What's their end game?"

"I have no idea, but we need to figure it out."

"Our analysts haven't found any link between the sites. Times Square and Grand Central make sense but didn't cause many casualties. Other than spreading our emergency response thin, there's no logic to this."

"And you're wondering if somehow Intercorpex is involved?" Zyree asks, getting a nod in return. "Let me contact the NOC."

Zyree studies the map again. No alerts pop up on his contacts that indicate any impact on critical exchange systems. That isn't always the whole story. He knows someone who might provide some insights and has a guardian place the VidLynk.

"What do you want, Zyree?" Lyris barks.

"Your help."

"Yeah, right," the director moans. "That'll be the…. Where are you?"

"Public safety and security's emergency operations center."

Lyris sighs and shakes his head. "When you disobey a directive, you don't go halfway with it, do you?"

"Do you want to waste time lecturing me about policy, or do you want to get to the bottom of this attack?" Zyree asks, getting a knowing smirk from one of Teman's guardians seated at the workstation.

"Why do I care? It's an America Incorporated problem. Exchange operations aren't affected."

"Are you sure?"

Zyree's question has the desired effect. Lyris turns his head to check the status of exchange systems and networks on the NOC display. There are no alarms, and nothing seems out of the ordinary.

"There is no impact to our primary systems and networks."

"That's not what I asked, Lyris. Have the explosions caused *any* disruptions?"

Lyris checks the event log. There is only one informational entry. "Network engineering reported the secondary and tertiary order input circuits are down. They're not critical infrastructure; primary routes are unaffected."

"What do you mean by 'order input'? The matching engines are across the river in Secaucus."

"Yes, but the *gentez-minorez* use the Intercorpex Trade and Quotation System hosted here. The orders are then sent across the river for matching and execution."

"So, you're telling me that all ITQS orders get routed through Wall Street?"

Lyris rolls his eyes. "Isn't that what I just said? What's going on? Is there a threat to exchange operations I need to know about?"

"I don't know yet," Zyree says, rubbing his stubble. "What would happen if you lost the primary circuit right now?"

"We would be forced to fail our operations over to London."

"Okay. You need to aggressively monitor all network traffic for anomalies. I'll contact you when I know more."

"Zyree, you don't give me orders—"

The chief inspector makes a slashing motion across his neck, and the guardian smiles as he cuts Lyris off mid-sentence. That should have been satisfying but wasn't. Zyree turns back to the live feed of smoke billowing from what is left of a building and steeples his hands in front of his mouth. This feels bigger than random mayhem. If these explosions are connected to those circuit outages, he hopes Lyris figures out how and why before there's any unrecoverable impact.

CHAPTER
FIFTY-FOUR

THE PATRICIANS

Keating Family of the Gentez-Majorez Estate
Greenwich Geographic District
Southern Connecticut Municipal Corporation

This day has been a long time coming. Denali wasn't as nervous during the attack in Secaucus as he is now. Years of planning have gone into this endeavor. All of it rests on what happens in the next couple of hours. It's terrifying. And exhilarating.

Denali Keating is not a man who stands on the sidelines as most elites do. He likes to be in the action and yearns to be the one calling the shots. He has to put both of those inclinations aside. He not only isn't on the front line in this battle, but isn't in control of anything that happens. Placing faith in others to do what needs to be done has never been one of his strong suits. That even applies to Farron. Unfortunately, for this to work, he must do precisely that.

Abbot opens the door to the study as he stares at the market data on his display. He has a financial team that can mind his extensive portfolio. He has other concerns, and he's sure that Commander Lacune will address some of them.

"Public Safety and Security activated their Emergency Operations Center. The RTCC is handling incident response and the EOC is coordinating the search for the perpetrators."

Denali exhales and smiles. That's one variable solved for. He was assured during the planning that they would take that measure, but when it comes to a crisis, corporations and their security forces are nothing if not unpredictable.

"Good. What else?"

"Farron says that the resource is in position."

The corner of Denali's mouth curls up. He didn't think that the terrorists were capable of that, so several contingencies were constructed. He doesn't mind being pleasantly surprised about them not being needed.

"That will make for an interesting day in the city. What about the explosions?"

"An investigation is underway, but it doesn't appear that either the PSS or BCS has connected any of the dots. AME News is continuing to report them as accidents."

"I would be surprised if they said anything to the contrary. At least until they have to. Has my son given you any insights?"

"He is actively working with his source in the White House. He says everything is going according to plan."

Denali checks the time on his grandfather clock. Not everything.

"Thank you, Commander. Keep me informed."

Lacune bows slightly and marches out of the study. He's made a lot of visits up here. Denali is going to have to venture down to the operations center for the next one.

"Abbot, have we received any contact from Talya Bettancourt?"

"No, sir."

"What the hell is she waiting for?" Denali mumbles. He expected her to act by now.

"Would you like me to request a VidLynk with her?"

It's tempting, but the conversation would likely not end well. Talya Bettancourt isn't someone who takes orders or likes reminders. She knows what her responsibilities as Prima are. Denali knows that she will act, even if she's taking her sweet time about it.

"No."

"Very well, sir."

"Where is my son?"

Abbot places his hands behind his back. "Still in Manhattan, although he isn't at the brownstone or his domicile."

"I'm sure he isn't. Tell me, Abbot, have you noticed a change in him over the past six months?"

Abbot rolls his shoulders back slightly. Denali doesn't like making him uncomfortable by putting him on the spot like this, but he wants to know the truth. Abbot, despite is his unwavering loyalty, can always be relied upon to give it when solicited.

"Farron is a young man learning to find his way in the world. His changing should not be unanticipated."

"Do you think his relationship with the White House executive and interaction with the urches is affecting him?"

"I'm afraid I don't know much about Fiolla, sir, other than she's beautiful and intelligent. It would not surprise me if his relationship with her is becoming deeper than what was originally planned." Denali grunts but doesn't say anything. "As for the urches, they have a unique way of planting ideas in people's heads. Their way of life is deplorable and alluring at the same time. Farron is strong-willed but still young. I would not discount any influence they may have on him."

Denali nods slowly. That's what he fears. "Thank you, Abbot. That is all."

Abbot bows and leaves the study, pulling the door closed behind him. Control. Denali feels like he has none, including over his own son. Fortunately, something can be done about that. It may be the only action he can take by the time this day is over.

CHAPTER
FIFTY-FIVE
REGISTRANT RYKOS

Abandoned Subway Station
Somewhere in the Manhattan Underground
New York City Municipal Corporation

The mood here has changed from enthusiasm to trepidation. I have no idea what they are doing or what "Project Archimedes" is, but everyone is on edge. Michele is pacing around the mezzanine as the two hackers peck away at their ancient keyboards. Even the usually stoic Quarren wrings his hands as he watches from his chair.

"Talk to me, Adiz," Michele says as she stops and looks over his shoulder.

"They haven't detected our intrusion, but if they investigate the drop in power, they're going to know someone tapped in."

"The attenuation is only a few tenths of a dB," Jasper explains, "but it's detectable if they know their baseline."

"They will be monitoring their network closely with the secondary circuits down," Adiz says, pushing his glasses up his nose, "but they'll never suspect a tap until it's too late."

"Let's hope you're both right," Michele says, exhaling sharply.

I have no idea how they managed to tap into the fiber optic lines leading to the exchange. I've always thought that Intercorpex's network was impenetrable. Even if it isn't, there are other safeguards to protect their information.

"The data's encrypted," I say from my chair.

The two hackers exchange a knowing grin. "For now."

I shake my head. These hackers know that the more sensitive the information, the higher the level of encryption. Intercepting and decoding a simple e-note would take years. Penetrating the exchange's order system like they're planning is impossible.

"How do you know they're going to use the cable you tapped?" I ask, desperate to get answers to the questions raging in my head.

"You ask a lot of questions," Jasper mutters as he works.

"We took measures to ensure it," Michele says, pointing at the display tuned into AME News. Images of smoke billowing into the sky and emergency vehicles from the various attacks seem to be playing on a continuous loop.

"You killed people just to do this?"

"We weren't trying to kill anybody."

"But people died."

"Don't be naïve, Rykos. People always die. Corporations kill thousands of people a day, and it's business as usual."

"You really believe that, don't you?" The reality that this woman is delusional starts to set in. I inhale and puff my chest out. "You'll never get past their encryption."

Michele grins. "We already have."

My mouth hangs open. These are only urches. "What?"

"Intercorpex is pioneering quantum encryption, but it's not ready for production use," Jasper says after Michele nods at him. "Instead, they use a 4096-bit RSA to secure their data. We cracked it by employing acoustic cryptanalysis."

"It's a side-channel attack," Adiz continues for his partner. "It's like cracking the passcode on a door lock by looking at the greasy fingerprints on the keypad. The CPU's voltage regulator generates an acoustic signal as it fights to maintain a constant flow during varied loads. We listened to those high-pitched sounds as it decrypted the data.

The explanation is way over my head, but I can't help being amazed at their technical ability. My father would never have expected this. The corporate narrative is that urches are stupid. How wrong they are.

"Wouldn't you have to be at the exchange to do that?"

"Let's just say that we had some special help," Quarren says.

A breaking story from Times Square pops up on AME News. Another explosion happened. I'm about to press for more information when Haven comes bounding up the stairs.

"Mission accomplished. The remaining team returned from its target. No casualties or apprehensions."

"You put a bomb in Times Square?" I ask, standing. "Was killing people on the SpeedRail not enough for you?"

All the anger of being kidnapped and buying into their propaganda feeds a surge of rage. No longer able to keep my emotions in check, I lunge for him.

He's ready for it, artfully deflecting my rush and dropping an elbow on the back of my neck. I crumple to the ground in a heap. I roll onto my back and am kicked hard in the ribs.

I cough hard, roll back over, and almost manage to climb to my feet when I'm kicked in the face. I drop to all fours and struggle for oxygen, swallowing the blood streaming from my nose. When my vision focuses, Haven stands over me with a weapon inches from my face.

"Make your peace with God, Ivy."

"Haven, don't!" Michele orders.

"I'm done listening to you, Michele. He's not one of us. You made a mistake bringing him here, and I'm going to rectify it right now."

"If you pull that trigger, it will be the last act you have on this Earth," Quarren decrees in a calm, smooth voice.

I watch Haven pull his eyes off me and turn his head to find himself staring down the barrel of Quarren's handgun.

CHAPTER
FIFTY-SIX

AMERICA, INC.

PSS Emergency Operations Center
Lower West-Side Office Building
New York City Municipal Corporation

Modern corporations don't expect results; they demand them. America is no different. They provide housing, guaranteed employment and an income. However, the stress of meeting the obligations they ask for in return can be overwhelming. This is one of those moments.

The chief guardian takes a deep breath and gets Fiolla up to speed on the four main attacks and two secondary incidents at Times Square and Grand Central Terminus before launching into the PSS response. She doesn't look impressed when he finishes.

"Chief Guardian, I warned you to get ahead of these attacks."

"We're not sure they're directed at us," Teman states flatly. "Let me introduce you to Chief Inspector Zyree of Intercorpex Security. We've been working together trying to find Liberteum."

"I've been in contact with Executive Director Lyris," Zyree says. "These explosions disrupted two fiber circuits that feed orders to the exchange."

Fiolla gives him a puzzled look. "We haven't heard that."

"It's not something Intercorpex would communicate. They're only secondary and tertiary feeds."

"Then why is that important?"

"Those four explosions severed each circuit in two places," Zyree calmly explains. "Liberteum wanted those two fiber cables destroyed. We're still trying to figure out why."

"Attention in the EOC!" a guardian bellows, his words amplified by the speakers in the room. "Chief Guardian Teman to the aerial ops desk, urgent!"

"What's going on, Teman?"

The concern in Fiolla's voice mirrors his feelings. This can't be good. Assuaging the fears of the bureaucracy will have to wait.

"I'll get back to you, Fiolla."

"No, wait—"

"That won't make her happy," Zyree deadpans after Teman disconnects the VidLynk.

"Fiolla told everyone watching the seven o'clock news this morning that Liberteum was destroyed. My hanging up on her is the least of her problems. What's going on?" Teman asks once they reach aerial operations.

"I...I can't...I can't explain it."

"Explain what, Lieutenant?"

"I'm losing control of our drones, sir. Eleven and counting."

"What?" the two men say in unison.

"We're systematically losing positive control of deployed drones over the city," Lieutenant Ashalai explains.

Teman watches the boxes that identify drones switching from green to yellow to red. He can't believe his eyes.

"Five are offline, three have crashed into buildings, and three made ground or river impacts."

"What about the rest of the drones?"

The lieutenant stares at him with dread in his eyes. "They're being rerouted to the Midtown Geographic District... Forty-Second Street, along the East River."

"Intercorpex Headquarters," Zyree mumbles.

Teman runs his hand through his scalp and to the back of his neck. He gives it a couple of squeezes in a futile attempt to alleviate tension.

"Two more have gone unresponsive," the frantic voice of another guardian calls out.

"Someone talk to me! How is this possible?"

"It's not, sir. The signals can't be intercepted. They're designed with a fail-safe to return to base if we lose control," the lieutenant explains.

"Where's the control point?" Zyree asks.

"One Guardian Plaza, but tactical control was transferred here when we stood up the EOC."

"Someone hacked into your network," Zyree warns.

"The drones are controlled over a closed network. It can't be hacked from the outside," the lieutenant says.

Zyree stares at Teman. "This building isn't as secure as One Guardian Plaza. What about hacking it from the inside?"

Teman's eyes grow as wide as saucers. Artists have epiphanies. Guitarists find the perfect riff, and lyricists pen the perfect coda. It happens for men in the security field when they learn the enemy is right under their nose.

"Ground all the drones now! The entire fleet! Land them in the streets if you have to."

"But sir—"

"It's not a suggestion. Do it!"

"Three more down," the guardian narrates as he watches his display. "One of them just crashed into an office building."

"Attention in the EOC!" Teman bellows at the top of his lungs, causing heads to turn in his direction. "Lock this building down and organize a floor-by-floor sweep. Search every office, bathroom, and utility closet in this building and detain anyone suspicious."

"We don't have enough personnel to conduct that kind of sweep," the EOC commander warns.

"Maybe we don't have to," Zyree says. "Call up a blueprint of this facility on the holo."

Teman follows the chief inspector over to the circular holographic generator near the commander's workstation. About the size of an old oil barrel, it's cutting-edge technology that renders a complete, three-dimensional skeletal diagram of the Emergency Operations Center.

"All right, show me the utility layer view, removing plumbing and HVAC. Focus on electrical and data trunks."

Yellow and green lines spider their way throughout the hologram. Zyree walks around the diagram studying the routes, trying to make sense of them. Teman's impatience grows as the aerial surveillance desk announces that drones not already hijacked have been secured.

"Where's the transmitter?" Zyree asks the lieutenant.

"On the roof."

"We're wasting time, Zyree," Teman complains.

"No, we're not. The fiber optic cable to the antenna doesn't go straight to the roof. It follows this path down to Sub-basement Level Three," he explains, tracing the route with his finger.

"It's where the networking gear is kept," the EOC commander interjects.

Teman shares a knowing look. "There's no way that area is secure. I want a security team in full tactical gear assembled in the lobby by the time I get down there. What do you say, Zyree? Want to go hunting?"

"Absolutely."

"Attention in the EOC!"

The two men stop in their tracks. They turn back to see the battle captain, who is stark white.

"We have just initiated the emergency alert system! Building alarms have been activated across the entire New York City Municipal Corporation."

They check the main display to see the emergency message scrolling along the bottom of the AME News broadcast. The text is a simple order to evacuate every building in the city due to an imminent threat of a bombing. There's no way the employees would ever think it's not the PSS ordering it.

"That's being sent to every display and device in the city," Teman mumbles.

Zyree slaps Teman on the chest. "Come on. We need to find this hacker before millions of people clog the streets."

CHAPTER
FIFTY-SEVEN
INTERCORPEX

PSS Emergency Operations Center
Lower West-Side Office Building
New York City Municipal Corporation

A team of five guardians in tactical gear arrives at the lobby when Zyree and Teman
do. Zyree is impressed at the public safety and security's foresight of having one on
standby when the EOC was stood up. Bringing in an external team would take time
that they don't have.

"Make sure I get this back," Teman says before passing Zyree a handgun as they
load into the elevator.

"There's no security down there?"

"Only the standard intrusion detection measures. One reason the EOC was
located here is there are no corporations in this building worthy of attention."

The elevator slows, and chimes as 'SB3' glows on the display panel. Zyree checks
to ensure his weapon is ready and takes a cleansing breath. The doors open, and the
team pours out, taking positions in the small lobby.

"Where's the equipment room?" Teman asks the detail commander.

"Left out of this foyer, down the corridor, make another left, and it's the second
door on the right."

They fluidly move around the corner and down the hall in a rolling "T" tactical
formation modified for seven members instead of five. Zyree clenches his teeth.
There is no cover in this whitewashed corridor, and they are sitting ducks if
ambushed.

When they reach the second left, the point man uses his seventy-degree tactical
sight to peer around the corner and gives the all-clear. It's improvisation. Tactical
teams have tiny drones that could scout ahead, but Teman ordered those to remain
unused just in case.

"Stop!" Zyree whispers with urgency only ten seconds after rounding the corner. The team freezes in place, and the men in front look back in confusion about the order.

"What's wrong?" Teman asks.

"There's a tripwire strung across the corridor from that trash can."

"How can you possibly see that?"

"I was expecting it. That garbage pail doesn't belong here. It was moved from the far corner."

Teman presses his lips together and orders the team down the hall. They move with great care and step over the hair-thin wire. If a proximity fuse had been attached to whatever explosive is set in the small silver and black container, the whole team would have been wiped out.

"We need him alive," Teman reiterates when they reach the utility room.

The point man pushes against the door handle. It's secure, and Teman moves forward.

"Watch for more booby traps and be ready for anything. On three. One, two...." Teman waves his biojack in front of the reader, and the lock clicks. A second later, they burst through the door.

Zyree swings his head left and right, his weapon moving with it. He expected to be met with a hail of gunfire. Instead, all he hears is the whir of hundreds of cooling fans and the overhead clanging of the air conditioning.

The team splits in two and travels to opposite ends of the row of data equipment that runs parallel to the front wall. The ambient noise masks their movements as they round the corner and check the aisles between rows. At the end of the fifth thirty-foot length of cabinets, Teman spots the intruder.

"Don't move!" he commands as the guardians fan out and train their rifles on his head. "Make one more keystroke, and you die. Raise your hands above your head."

The hacker complies without turning. "Stand and turn slowly to face us."

Again, he does as requested and faces them. Zyree's mouth hangs open as the beautiful woman stares back at him. He hazards a glance at Teman, who's equally stunned.

"Search her," the detail commander orders.

Teman taps his earpiece and opens a channel to the EOC. "The hacker is in custody; network room is secure. I need EOD down here to defuse an explosive device and some computer experts to see if they can use her equipment to regain control of our drones."

"She's clean," a guardian confirms after searching her. He slaps a set of electromagcuffs on her wrists.

Similar to the handcuffs used for centuries, these restraints use electromagnets instead of mechanical locks. As a result, they can't be picked.

"Return control of our systems," Teman says, putting the barrel of his handgun against her forehead.

Zyree studies her face. She's expressionless and has no hint of fear as her information displays on his contact lenses. Freya, the intrusion specialist, left Intercorpex for the underground. She may crack if the right kind of pressure is applied.

The chief guardian withdraws his weapon and slaps her across the face. The blow splits her cheek open, but the woman remains silent.

"Do it, or I will make the rest of your pathetic urch life a living hell."

She doesn't even twitch. No fear. No defiance. No emotion at all. Nothing but an impassive thousand-yard stare.

"She's not going to talk without persuasion," Zyree says.

"Yeah, I'll persuade her," he says, turning to the detail commander. "Is there a custodial room down here?"

"Three doors down on the right."

"Bring her there and secure her to a table."

The guardians do as instructed. Zyree follows Teman to the small room lined with industrial shelving storing cleaning supplies. Teman grabs a mop bucket and fills it from the dump sink. The chief inspector places a hand on his shoulder.

"What are you doing?"

"There are ways to make people talk."

"Teman, you know as well as I do that torture—"

"Liberteum is tearing my city apart! If that isn't enough reason to do this, don't forget that they also have my son. She's the one chance I have to solve both of those problems. She's going to talk whether she wants to or not."

"You're losing your perspective," he admonishes.

"Last chance," Teman says to Freya as he sets the bucket on the ground before pulling a cleaning rag off the adjacent shelf. "Let's start simple. What's your name?"

"Go to hell."

"Well, at least she's talking now," Teman says.

"Chief Guardian, don't do this. It's not going to—"

"You're wearing out your welcome, Zyree. If you don't want to be here, then leave. I can handle this myself."

Teman puts the rag over her face, picks up the bucket, and starts pouring water over it. The woman screams and gets a mouthful of water. He stops when her gagging becomes uncontrollable.

"Hurts, doesn't it? Do you feel the burn from that water when it hits your lungs? There is nothing I won't do to safeguard the employees in this city. Now, let's try this again. What's your name?"

"I said go to hell."

"This is going to be a long day for you," the chief guardian says with a mock sigh and begins pouring the water again.

Zyree has seen enough. He leaves the room, not wanting to be a party to this. The instinct to resort to these measures is understandable when the circumstances are dire. He has used questionable tactics during past investigations. The one thing he learned was the information you get is unreliable. He hopes Teman figures that out before this goes too far.

CHAPTER
FIFTY-EIGHT
LIBERTEUM

Abandoned Subway Station
Somewhere in the Manhattan Underground
New York City Municipal Corporation

Adiz sighs and rubs the bridge of his nose before replacing his glasses. He spins his chair around, hanging his head for a moment. Jasper watches him with the same sullen look on his face. Nobody wants to deliver this news.

"Michele? Freya missed her check-in. She was likely captured."

Michele closes her eyes, purses her lips, and nods. "Okay."

When she turns, Rykos is staring at her. Quarren stopped Haven from shooting him in the head, but the outburst landed him chained to a support column. There is more anger in his eyes now than when he was first brought down here. Michele needed more time, but there just wasn't enough. She shudders at the thought that Haven was right – they should have left him.

"You knew she would be captured, didn't you?" Rykos asks.

"It was a dangerous assignment. It was a likely outcome."

"Did she know that? You said you would see her when this was over. You knew that was a lie. You sent her to her death, didn't you?"

"She knew the risks," Michele almost whispers.

"She was your friend!"

"Yes, she was. She chose to make the sacrifice because what we're doing here is bigger than her. It's bigger than all of us. Liberty is an ideal worth fighting for; worth dying for. I don't expect you to understand that."

"Michele, this location could be compromised. We have to accelerate the timeline," Adiz says.

"She would never talk."

"You can't be sure," the hacker argues. "We need to assume the worst."

"Intercorpex will detect the intrusion sooner or later. We might as well go now," Quarren says, speaking for the first time in a long time.

"Are you going to try to kill more innocent people?" Rykos asks, an edge to his voice.

"Our intent wasn't to kill anybody," Quarren assures Rykos. "The SpeedRail casualties were unfortunate, and the Times Square and Grand Central bombs were only meant to be distractions. This isn't about harming people."

"I don't believe you. You didn't have to bomb an underground near rush hour. If you didn't want to kill people, you wouldn't have."

Quarren shakes his head slowly. "Unfortunately, it was necessary for Archimedes to be successful. This isn't about destroying the world, Rykos. It's about saving it. I would have hoped you'd understand that by now, but perhaps you needed more time."

"Understand what? Replacing corporations with the old governments? I read your book, Quarren. They were just as bad, if not worse."

Everyone in the room just stares at Rykos. It's not anger. They almost look like they feel sorry for him.

"Democracy failed," Rykos continues, undeterred. "People traded away their freedoms willingly. It wasn't forced on them. Corporations may have rewritten history, but that part is accurate."

"We don't have time for a civics lesson right now," Adiz interjects.

"Nyvar, send word to Haven and Scivix to prepare for any guests that crash the party," Michele commands. "It's go time, Jasper."

Rykos stares at the hacker but holds his tongue. His eyes trace the route of the bundle of cables from the workstations to where they disappear into the tunnel.

"You're right," Quarren says, standing in front of Rykos. "People did trade away their freedom. They had it for so long that it eventually lost its value. That doesn't mean that the flame of liberty has been vanquished. It still burns inside them. It burns inside you."

"You're wrong."

"Maybe. This is the first step in finding out."

Quarren puts a hand on Rykos's shoulder before returning to his chair.

"Here goes nothing," Jasper murmurs.

He types a command on his keyboard and hits Enter.

CHAPTER
FIFTY-NINE

AMERICA, INC.

The White House Situation Room
Corporate Governance District
Washington-Arlington Municipal Corporation

At this level, everything is a political battle. Executives who climb the corporate ladder to the highest leadership rungs will do anything to keep their positions. Fiolla glances over at the display on the wall as the VidLynk to the EOC connects, and she watches a news anchor try to explain what's going on. Events like this end executive careers.

"You disconnected me, Teman," she says, once the link establishes.

"Apologies, Fiolla. I was busy managing this crisis," he says, sounding annoyed.

"Part of managing this crisis includes reporting back to me. The Situation Room is full of executives clamoring for someone to blame. You're making yourself the easy target."

"Fine."

Teman launches into a rapid-fire account of the events that transpired over the last forty-five minutes, and how they determined there was a hacker in the EOC. He describes how she was apprehended and explains that he's in the middle of her interrogation.

"That's a serious security breach. What about the evacuation alert?"

"She locked us out of the system. Once we get back in, the current message will be replaced with one instructing employees to return to work."

Fiolla frowns. Teman isn't giving her anything useful. She needs solid results that the chief executive can use as leverage.

"What have you learned from this hacker?"

"Her name is Freya, and she is a member of Liberteum. She says Liberteum is planning to detonate a large truck bomb at Intercorpex Headquarters. I've notified the BCS and doubled security at major transportation hubs and landmarks in case she's lying and targeting us."

"Teman, the BCS won't stay out of this. They're going to press for operational control. Valen will agree to it."

"We'll lose valuable time if the BCS assumes command. My guardians are already in place, but we're spread thin. If the BCS wants to help, they can secure Intercorpex."

Fiolla types an encrypted note to Valen and sends it before leaning back in her chair. An incoming VidLynk pops up. She rubs her temples, trying to push the stress headache aside.

"We cannot allow an attack on Intercorpex to happen. I will ensure the BCS helps ICX Security lock down their campus. Be ready to hand over command to them and offer your full cooperation if it's ordered."

"Fine."

The VidLynk disconnects and Fiolla accepts the waiting request. She recognizes the identification.

"Farron, I'm sorry, but this isn't a good time.... Where are you?"

"Standing in the middle of the street with about ten thousand other people!" he shouts over the din.

"You're in Manhattan?"

"Yes, and wishing I was almost anywhere else right now."

Fiolla has bigger concerns than a patrician being inconvenienced, even if it is Farron. He has more than enough resources to take care of himself. She turns her attention back to another e-note she's crafting.

"Farron, listen, I really can't talk right now."

"You need to hear this. Talya Bettancourt has enough support on your board of directors to remove Valen for gross incompetence. She's looking to get a quorum to hold a vote today."

"What? We're in the middle of a crisis!" Fiolla shouts.

"That's modern politics. The best time to stab an enemy is when they aren't facing you. Talya never wastes an opportunity to get what she wants, and that's Valen gone. This crisis is giving her the excuse she needs."

"I have to let Valen know."

"Yes, you do. Go."

"Thank you, Farron. I owe you another one."

Fiolla terminates the VidLynk. She says that a lot – probably too much. That's a concern for another time. She locks her workstation and charges down the corridor for the stairs that lead to the Situation Room.

She's not accustomed to this level of security. While a small number of agents is required to deter disgruntled employees or corporate espionage attempts, it isn't anything like what the old president of the United States needed. The ordinarily empty desk outside the Situation Room is manned by a uniformed member of corporate security who watches her swipe the back of her hand in front of the sensor to gain access.

Many of the highest executives in the parent company are in the throes of a full-throated argument. She slides between a pair of shell-shocked aides near the door, doing their best to be invisible. Valen sits at the end of the long table, rubbing his chin as he absorbs the arguments.

"Where is the chief guardian? Why isn't he answering these questions?" Virtari asks.

"He's conducting an interrogation," Chief Executive Safmor responds from the main screen on the wall. On the screen beside him is a PSS captain who bristles at the BCS director's question.

"That's not his job! He has people who can do that."

"He felt the critical nature of this threat demanded his involvement," the guardian says, defending his boss.

"He's incompetent and needs to be removed from his position."

"That's enough," Valen interrupts, noticing Fiolla inching toward him. "Let's not lose focus on the problem. This threat needs a swift and coherent response. I'm stepping away for five minutes. When I return, I want an update on preparations for the defense of Intercorpex and what's being done to neutralize Liberteum."

Valen rises from his chair and nods for Fiolla to follow him into the corridor as the bickering around the table restarts.

"Tough crowd," she observes.

"Never let a crisis get in the way of politics," he laments, shaking his head before looking at her. "They're more interested in advancing themselves than solving problems. Thanks for the heads up on the possible truck bomb. Do you have anything more on that?"

"No, sir, not yet. There's something else you need to know. A source informed me that Talya Bettancourt is pressing members of the board to remove you as we speak."

Valen grimaces. "I'm not surprised."

"I'm not either, sir, but the timing…."

"As I said, never let a crisis get in the way of politics. There's blood in the water, and Talya Bettancourt is a Great White. It doesn't matter that people are in danger in New York. For her, this is an opportunity. I need some time to think. Thank you for the information. We'll talk later."

Fiolla deals with politics at the executive level, but nothing like this. She's at a loss for what to do, and the hopelessness is overwhelming. Only one person is able to help her, but that would require going back and asking for his assistance…again.

CHAPTER
SIXTY

THE PATRICIANS

Keating Family of the Gentez-Majorez Estate
Greenwich Geographic District
Southern Connecticut Municipal Corporation

This is ridiculous. Denali has been watching AME News coverage of the explosions in New York. If it can be called that. Outside of their admission that something happened, there are almost no details. His own people are providing better information about what's happening.

One of the feeds Commander Lacune sent to him is from a building on Wall Street. It clearly shows a sizable crater in one of the nearby streets. America Incorporated can call for all the information blackouts they want. They won't be able to escape the noise that Liberteum is making in Manhattan.

Abbot steps into the room and stands off to the side of Denali's chair.

"What is it, Abbot?"

"You have received a VidLynk request from the administrator-general of Intercorpex."

Denali smirks and checks the time on the antique grandfather clock situated in the corner of his study. He's wondering what took Raimius so long.

"Shall I decline the request, sir?"

"No, Abbot, please transfer it here. Thank you."

The butler complies immediately and exits the study as a harried and disheveled man fills the display. Stress is unhealthy, and the man is under a lot of it. Denali plans to add some more.

"Administrator-General Raimius. I wouldn't have thought you had the time to reach out to me, considering your difficulties."

"We have everything under control," Raimius says in a response that sounds automatic from overuse.

"The ticker says otherwise."

"Patrician Keating, market fluctuations should be expected considering the happenings in New York. Unless you know something that I don't."

The metaphorical bell sounds following the comment. Raimius may fancy himself an excellent administrator, but he's a novice when it comes to diplomatic strategy. It only took him a few sentences to betray the nature of this VidLynk. Still, Denali knows that he needs to be careful. Raimius may be petulant and unstable, but he isn't stupid.

"I know a great many things that you don't, but nothing about what's happening on your exchange. I do find it hard to believe that the unfortunate incidents with terrorists could cause this level of market volatility. It appears to be collapsing."

"The market isn't collapsing."

Again, another automatic answer. "That's good to hear. What can I do for you, Raimius?"

"The Secaucus attack hit your interests hard."

"You're wasting time reciting what I've already told you. Unless you're contacting me with the satisfaction I requested against the perpetrators."

"No, I'm not."

Denali frowns. "That's unfortunate. Then we have nothing to discuss."

"The word among the patricians is that you hold the *gentez-minorez* responsible," Raimius says, rushing the sentence before Denali could disconnect. "Is that true?"

Denali leans back and inhales. He could deny it, but why should he?

"It's a working theory."

"One that you're acting on?"

"How would I be acting on it, Raimius?"

He offers a weak smile. Probably his first today. "It's no secret that you have a sizable security force to protect your interests. Some would call it an army."

"Are you looking to borrow them?"

"We don't need them."

"Again, all evidence to the contrary," Denali says, causing Raimius's stupid smile to disappear.

He leans in to the camera. "I want to know if you are exacting your revenge against them."

"Administrator-General, you are beginning to try my patience. My army, as you put it, defends *my* interests. It does not attack others. That's not really what you wanted to discuss, is it? You want to know if I'm somehow responsible for the trading difficulties you claim you aren't having."

Raimius chews on his lower lip and looks away briefly. "The timing is suspicious."

"What timing? Are you saying there is a problem?"

"As I said, it's under control."

"That's good to hear. I will ask you again…what can I do for you, Raimius?"

Denali is amused and isn't sure that he's hiding it well. The administrator-general is making this too easy. The more frustrated he gets, the more he contradicts himself. That makes it easier to make him even more frustrated. It's the perfect circle.

"Liberteum is behind the attacks in New York City. Even brainwashed employees can figure that out."

"I figured. I assume that means you are close to eliminating them."

"The PSS—"

"Doesn't run Intercorpex. You do. I would have thought you and Valen could have agreed on some manner of action against terrorists that threaten both of your interests."

"We spoke," Raimius snaps.

"And?"

The question is met with a prolonged silence. They didn't agree with anything because, why would they? Those two egomaniacs have no desire to work together, even for the common good.

"I'm a busy man, Administrator-General. Since you have nothing to offer, you're wasting my time with baseless accusations and futile questions. The next time you contact me, it will be with news that Liberteum has been eradicated and whoever they are working with disciplined. Until then, we have nothing more to say to each other."

Raimius doesn't have the time to protest. Denali ends the VidLynk and leans back in his red leather chair. He smiles. This is working even better than he planned.

CHAPTER
SIXTY-ONE
INTERCORPEX

*PSS Emergency Operations Center
Lower West-Side Office Building
New York City Municipal Corporation*

Zyree leans against the wall as he watches EOD disarm the explosive device in the trash can. It was crude but would have channeled its energy down the corridor and killed all of them. His contact lenses alert him to an incoming call from the NOC. He sighs and connects it.

"What the hell are you doing, Zyree?" Lyris shouts.

"There isn't much going on, so I dropped by a spa for a pedicure."

"I'm not in the mood for your antics. We just received a VidLynk from the BCS. They say—"

"That there may be a truck bomb on the way to headquarters. I know. The chief guardian informed me when he extracted the information during interrogation."

"Whose inter—? You know what? Never mind. You didn't think that it was important to report the threat to me?"

"The PSS had already informed the White House and BCS before telling me. Also, there is no truck bomb."

"How do you know?" Lyris ask, using his best condescending tone.

"First, look at your external security feeds. See all those people? The entire city looks like that right now. If your goal is to drive a truck bomb up to a building, would you put that many obstacles in your path?"

"The PSS issued that alert."

"The PSS was hacked. Liberteum issued the phony evacuation order. The woman the PSS captured hacking their systems is lying. Something else is going on."

"What?"

"I don't know yet."

Zyree closes his eyes. That's the problem. He knows in his heart that the truck bomb is a ruse, but he needs to be able to prove it. Lyris has no appreciation for gut instinct, especially his.

"What the hell is wrong with you, Zyree? The BCS is surrounding headquarters like it's under siege. You're the only one who isn't taking this seriously!"

"I'm well aware," Zyree moans. "What's the market doing?"

"The market's fine. Why do you keep asking?"

Zyree sees the ticker scroll in his peripheral vision. AME's stock price is bouncing around due to the explosions, but otherwise, it looks like a typical trading day.

"Two circuits were taken out, and I'm still not convinced that was accidental. You're telling me there hasn't been any other alerting?"

"There were alarms earlier for light trading volume," Wyeth says, coming up behind Lyris.

"Light trading volume on a day like today?" Something in that statement piqued his interest.

"It correlated with the evacuation order," Wyeth continues, earning a furious look from Lyris. "Trading has returned to normal levels, if not higher. It's expected behavior."

"You're desperate, Zyree. Stop chasing phantom conspiracy theories and help stop this bombing. If you fail—"

"Keep me advised if anything changes," Zyree says, ending the conversation when Teman emerges from the custodial room. "Did you get tired or something?"

"The White House interrupted me. We got what we needed."

"Did we? It's my experience that torture leads to dubious results," Zyree says, pushing himself off the wall. "You'll get the information you want. It won't be the information you need."

Torture techniques in the corporate era are less violent than in the Middle Ages, but the results are equally questionable. Some corporations swear by its effectiveness, but Zyree's own experiences taught him that what you learn is often a bunch of lies.

"Well, her name's Freya, which we knew, and she admitted that Liberteum is planning to detonate a truck bomb against Intercorpex. That's actionable intelligence."

"I think you need to consider that she's telling you what you want to hear," Zyree says in a tone laden with disbelief.

Teman shakes his head. "I know when people are lying."

"So do I," Zyree says, pointing at his eye. "I also know that people will say anything to make the pain stop. The pieces don't fit. It's too small."

"Trying to blow up a building is small?" Teman asks.

"I think Liberteum is more nuanced than you think. The attack in Secaucus was specific in its effects. The Manhattan explosions severed circuits in two different places. None of that makes sense if launching a car bomb is their goal."

Teman scowls. "They were a distraction for the main attack. A hit on Intercorpex would be symbolic."

The chief guardian takes the evidence in front of him and formulates a theory without questioning why he has the evidence in the first place. He's looking at this as a criminal act, not an organized effort by a group with a tremendous ability to execute tactical operations. Zyree needs to convince him of that, and fast. He takes two steps toward the custodial room before Teman blocks him.

"What are you doing?"

"I'm going to find the truth. I'm also going to find out where your son is. You can let me find out if I'm right or live with the regret if you're wrong."

"All right," Teman says, stepping to the side. "You're the cyborg with the built-in lie detector. Don't let me stop you."

Zyree brushes past Teman and enters the custodial room to find Freya shivering on a folding table with two of its legs propped up to give it a slight incline. She is bound with nylon straps to immobilize her. One of Teman's guardians holds a white rag that they've been using to cover her face.

"Round two," Teman says, entering behind the chief inspector and moving to the sink to fill the bucket. "Unless you want to start talking now. What's your name?"

"I told you my name," she says, wearing her rage like a mask. "It's Freya."

The voice stress analysis in Zyree's vision indicates no stress in her voice to indicate deception. Now he has a baseline.

"Very good. Keep this up, and maybe we won't have to strip you naked and use the picana on you. What size vehicle is this bomb in?"

"A standard truck."

"A truck? Like a box truck?"

She nods. Even the most hardened people trained in counter interrogation techniques crack under the stress of waterboarding. The only real question is how long it will take and how accurate the extracted information will be.

"And the target is Intercorpex?"

"Yes."

"Where is it launching from?"

Freya doesn't answer. Teman places the rag over her face and pours the water. Although the method isn't designed to drown a subject, too much water can get into the lungs. He's pushing that envelope.

"Where is the attack launching from? When is it going to hit? Is my son there?"

"Your son?" she asks, coughing.

"His name is Rykos. Your group kidnapped him after the Chinatown rave. Is he there?"

"He's with the truck," Freya says.

Teman puts the bucket down. "Satisfied?"

"No. Is Quarren the leader of Liberteum?" Is Haven a member? Do they have Rykos with them?"

Freya's eyes grow wide in surprise. Even Teman picks up on that signal. Zyree's contact lenses display the rest of the story. It can recognize deception now.

"Were the bombs in Manhattan meant to sever Intercorpex circuits?" Zyree asks.

Freya doesn't speak. She doesn't have to. His biocomp sensors immediately pick up the increased heart rate and faster breathing.

"Is your plan to disrupt the exchange? That's what I thought."

"Zyree! What did you learn?" Teman asks as Zyree opens the door to leave.

"You need to find a new method, Teman. The only thing she didn't lie to you about is her name."

CHAPTER SIXTY-TWO

REGISTRANT RYKOS

Abandoned Subway Station
Somewhere in the Manhattan Underground
New York City Municipal Corporation

The two hackers stare intently at their displays. Now and again, one of them makes a few keystrokes, but otherwise, they're just watching. Adiz finally turns his chair and looks at Michele, who waits patiently for an update.

"We've captured about twenty percent."

"That's it?" Michele's reaction to Adiz demonstrates more than surprise. It's distress.

"So far. The high-frequency traders are the only ones active right now. Volatility is great for them, but most patricians aren't risking trades until they know which way the winds are blowing."

I don't know much about Adiz, but he understands how the market works. There are modules taught at Dinsmore to recognize trading patterns. Whatever Liberteum is up to, the patricians are the key. They aren't grasping why the elites aren't trading right now.

"If you're destabilizing the market, you'll see less volume, not more," I say from my position at the column. The chains holding me here are starting to chafe.

"We need to give the *gentez-minorez* a reason to log on. Throttle it up, Jasper," Michele directs.

"That will only make it worse," I call out.

"Don't be so sure about that," Michele fires back.

"It will increase the chances that the exchange recognizes a problem," Jasper warns.

"It's only a matter of time before they do, anyway," Adiz argues. "Their switchboard must be lighting up by now. If they shut us down before we hit the goal, this was all for nothing."

"He's right. We've come too far for half measures. Do it."

I shake my head in disgust. The only thing more frustrating than being chained to a support column is having no idea what they're doing. I could be watching the end of the world from ten feet away, and I'm powerless to stop it. Quarren must sense my frustration and leaves his seat to join me.

"How are you, Rykos?"

"I'm fine. Can't you tell?" I ask, jingling the chain against the column. "What are they doing?"

"Changing the world," he responds with a look of fatherly pride.

"Why is it important to have patricians log in to the exchange?"

"It's just a piece of the puzzle we need to accomplish our goal."

"You mean Archimedes? What is that?" I ask, giving in to my curiosity.

"It's not a what; it's a who. Archimedes of Syracuse was considered the greatest scientist of the classical age. He was a Greek mathematician, physicist, astronomer, engineer, inventor, and weapons-designer killed by a Roman soldier when the outer city fell following a prolonged siege."

"Why does whatever you're doing have that name?" His rambling explanation makes no sense.

"My daughter picked it. She has affection for historical events."

I still don't understand the reference, so I join Quarren watching the crew assembled at the workstations. There is more to Michele than just her beauty. She has both strength and vulnerability. She's decisive yet still uncertain. It's alluring.

"Quarren, I still don't understand why you're showing me this. I'm not one of you. I don't share your beliefs or agree with your agenda."

"I thought I already explained that."

"I don't believe you."

"Ten percent over the threshold," Jasper announces from his seat at the table along the wall.

"That's the problem, isn't it? You don't know who or what to believe. You never have. Rykos, when this is over, your father will put you in a room and debrief you. He'll want to know everything you saw and heard down here."

"And I'll tell him," I say, lifting my chin defiantly.

"Good. Tell him everything. I want him to report everything he learns to his superiors."

Quarren's answer catches me by surprise. "Why? You're responsible for killing people and hacking Intercorpex. You'll be the most wanted man in New York."

"I already am."

"Twenty percent over the threshold," Jasper announces.

"Why do all this? You at least owe me an answer to that."

"If I tell you the answer, it's propaganda," Quarren says, offering a smile. "If you figure it out for yourself, it's understanding."

"Thirty percent. We have their undivided attention now," Adiz says, getting a nod in return from Michele, who is watching my conversation with her father.

"Hang in there, Rykos. You'll be back with your father in a matter of hours," Quarren advises me, returning to his seat.

I don't doubt him. I know my father will come for me, but what if that's part of their plan? And what if they succeed? What scares me most is the world I'm going back to.

CHAPTER
SIXTY-THREE

AMERICA, INC.

PSS Emergency Operations Center
Lower West-Side Office Building
New York City Municipal Corporation

The chief inspector looks a little surprised anyone in the EOC is willing to cooperate with him. The PSS and the BCS despise each other, and neither is inclined to work with Intercorpex Security. To them, they're unwelcome outsiders.

"Can I help you with something, Chief Inspector?" the EOC commander asks, noticing him standing at the holo generator.

"Yeah, how do you use this thing?" Zyree asks as he taps the controls.

"I'll help," a technician offers. "What do you want to see?"

"Let's start with a map of Manhattan."

"Coming right up."

Using a small wrist device, Zyree places a VidLynk to Malkor. The implant cancels the background noise in his ear as the line connects.

"What's up, boss?"

"Where are you?"

"I'm in the war room with Parold watching the insanity going on in this city."

"Is anyone there with you?" Zyree asks.

"No. Lyris reassigned the entire staff to monitoring assignments on the NOC floor."

"Yeah, okay. Do you guys have your tactical gear with you?"

"Chief Inspector, we're door kickers. We brought three Alpha kits with us."

Zyree smiles at their foresight. Intercorpex Security is not allowed to pre-position equipment in most corporations. As a result, they travel with their equipment. This was an excellent time to bring the heavy package with the latest toys.

"Good. Get suited up, full tactical load. And prep the third kit for me."

"Are you expecting trouble?" Parold asks.

"Chance favors the prepared mind. I'll be in touch."

Zyree disconnects and dials up the address that Ortan gave him before he left Iceland. When the secure audio-only VidLynk connects, the blaring sound of classical music fills the chief inspector's ears.

"Ortan, turn that off! I can barely hear you."

"I'm sorry, Chief Inspector. I don't usually get VidLynks. You should be happy that I moved on from death metal." Ortan squints at the display. "You're on audio-only. Where are you?"

"New York's Public Safety and Security's Emergency Operations Center."

"Oh, fancy. I want to see it."

"There's no time," Zyree argues, wanting to get to the point of the call. "I need something from you."

"Hold on."

Zyree loses his patience after thirty seconds elapse. "Ortan!"

"What?" a voice booms over the room's speakers.

Every guardian in the EOC stops what they're doing and looks up. To Zyree's horror, Ortan stares down at them from the EOC's main display.

"What the...? How did he do that?" the commander demands.

"I'm a man of many talents."

"Ortan, say hello to everyone so we can get on with this," Zyree says, waving a dismissive hand in the air.

"Hello, everyone," he sings out with a goofy wave of his own.

"This is unauthorized access to our facility!"

"But not your first today, it appears," Ortan says, causing the commander to no doubt wonder how an Intercorpex employee could know that.

"Ortan, I need to know the routes of the three fiber circuits in Manhattan used by the ITQS."

"Aw, I thought this was going to be hard. That should take two seconds."

"They need to be displayed on this holograph generator," he says, pointing to the device with the rotating three-dimensional image of Manhattan.

"Okay, well, that might take a moment longer," he says, leaning forward.

"Do you need the IP address?" the technician graciously asks.

"No, I have it." The nonchalant comment earns Zyree a few nasty looks that he tries to ignore.

A tense minute later, one green and two red lines appear on the map. Each snakes through different routes beneath the city. The two red ones move north, one passing over the Hudson River around Midtown. The other continues up into the Bronx across the Harlem River. The third circuit, the green one still active, comes out of the exchange and heads directly over the East River into Brooklyn.

"Can you highlight the buildings and the SpeedRail station that were destroyed by the explosions?" Zyree asks the technician. A moment later, those locations turn orange.

"Ortan, is there anything special about these circuits?"

"Not really. They carry trade data for the ITQS."

"Is there anything about this that would prevent a failover to London if the third circuit went down?"

The network engineer shakes his head emphatically. "No, nothing. Switches would automatically reroute ITQS requests across the Atlantic."

"Thank you for not being too condescending with that explanation," Zyree says, glancing up at the main display.

"No problem. I understand you're an idiot."

The guardians all smirk. Zyree ignores the playful retort, resolving to get even with the cybernetic freak show later.

"Have there been any incidents reported downtown?" he asks the guardians in the room.

"Everything happening today has been in midtown or uptown," the EOC commander confirms.

"We're looking at this all wrong," Zyree says, resting his hands on the holographic generator and leaning forward. "Ortan, has any work been done on these circuits in the past six months?"

"Let's see...oh boy. You're creepy. There's a work order for network engineering to do a turndown and turn up, only there's no hardware maintenance associated with it."

"Who authorized the work orders?"

Zyree already knows the answer to the question. He glances up to see Ortan's eyes peering back at him. His look says it all, and they can't mention it in the present company.

"The data has been erased."

Everything since Secaucus is related, and they just found the common thread. Someone in Intercorpex is helping a terrorist group, but addressing that comes later. Right now, they need to find Liberteum.

"Do you guys have a map of the lower Manhattan underground?"

"It's nowhere near complete. There have been a lot of—"

"Just show me what you have," Zyree says.

It comes up a moment later on the holographic renderer, and Ortan takes it upon himself to show the route of the live fiber cable. It doesn't take long to find what they're looking for. The irony won't be lost on anyone that it's right next to the Wall Street NOC.

"What is this?"

"The old Broad Street subway station. It was decommissioned after mass transit was rebuilt. Now it's a utility junction."

"That's right on Intercorpex's doorstep. Can it be accessed?"

"Both ends of the tunnel and the station's pedestrian accesses were sealed, but there should be a maintenance access," a guardian says.

"Bingo. Thanks for your help, Ortan. I'll take it from here."

Zyree makes a slashing movement across his throat, prompting the guardian in charge of communications to cut the feed to the main display. The move is short-lived. A few seconds later, Ortan reappears.

"Are you sure you don't need me to—"

"You have your *own* work to do," Zyree says, shooting him a look of warning. "Goodbye, Ortan."

"He's a strange bird," the EOC commander says after the link is severed a second time.

"You don't know the half of it." Zyree smirks. "Patch me through to Teman."

"He won't answer."

"Fine, I'll find him the old-fashioned way."

Teman sprints off the EOC floor to the elevator bank and takes it down to Sublevel Three. He passes the remnants of the explosive ordnance disposal team and makes his way to the custodial room. He enters to find the chief guardian holding his pail with his face inches from Freya's.

"Where is the truck bomb launching from?" Teman screams at her.

"Up-uptown," she stutters.

"Where uptown? Where is my son?"

"He's at the old Broad Street subway station," Zyree says, leaning against the door. "There is no truck bomb. They're launching a cyberattack on Intercorpex."

"What? That's not what Freya says."

"And I warned you that she's lying."

Teman turns his head and stares at the ground. Zyree remains silent, giving him time to work through his thoughts. Corporations put a lot of pressure on their employees, and mistakes aren't easily forgiven. This is a decision that Teman can't rush even if time were on their side.

"How sure are you about this?" Teman asks.

"As sure as I can be without going there and seeing for ourselves," Zyree concludes without missing a beat. "Everything she has told you is a red herring to buy time so that Liberteum can finish what they started. Or am I wrong, Freya?"

Her reaction is telling. The sensors in his biocomputer relay the information to his contact lenses. He's spot-on and nods at the chief guardian.

"Remove her restraints and sit her up," Teman orders. The guardians comply before taking a couple of steps back. "I'm going to ask you one more question. Do you believe in God?"

Freya stares at him. Zyree watches her pretty blue eyes squint as she formulates an answer to the question. At last, she thrusts her chin out.

"No."

Teman draws his weapon. Freya's mouth only has time to open in surprise as he squeezes the trigger and puts a bullet into her forehead. The sound echoes off the walls as the round goes through her skull and punctures a bottle of drain cleaner on the shelving behind her.

Her body crashes onto the table, and the blood from the exit wound begins streaming onto the floor. The acrid smell of gunpowder wafts through the cramped space.

"Too bad," Teman says, turning to his guardians. "Dispose of the body and clean this up."

"Was that necessary?" Zyree asks. He's seen death before, but that was more akin to murder.

"It was more humane than what the BCS would do once we turned her over. Trust me, that was merciful. How do you know Liberteum is at Broad Street Station?"

"It's the best place to disrupt the exchange without anyone knowing while maintaining the ability to conduct a defense. Haven would have insisted on that. Everything that's happened is designed to get us looking for the wrong attack in the wrong part of the city. And it's working."

Teman taps on his wrist tablet and opens a channel to the EOC upstairs. "Commander, how many tactical teams do we have in lower Manhattan?"

"Fifteen five-man teams are posted at SpeedRail stations below Canal Street. Everyone else is staged around midtown. We have additional personnel available, but they aren't equipped to—"

"Roll available tactical teams into a perimeter around Broad Street and Wall and instruct them to hold positions. Have all other available guardians create a supporting perimeter. Get the RTCC to analyze all camera surveillance in that area. Can we get a command vehicle down there?"

"The streets are jammed with people from the evacuation alert. It will take forever just to move personnel on foot down there, much less a truck."

"Do what you can and stage it outside Trinity Church."

"Yes, sir!"

Teman turns to Zyree. "We're betting everything on this. God help you if you're wrong."

CHAPTER
SIXTY-FOUR

INTERCORPEX

Global Network Operations Center
Manhattan Financial District
ICX New York Exchange

Lyris is getting bombarded. He had no idea why patricians are whining, but there are other pressing problems to deal with. Zyree got into his head, and he's barely taken his eyes off the displays since speaking to him. If the chief inspector is right about Liberteum attacking the exchange, he's not about to let a warning sign go unnoticed.

"Director Lyris? This is the Service Desk. The call volume from angry patricians is growing exponentially."

"Do they not see what's going on? Volatility is to be expected."

"They aren't calling about volatility, sir. They claim something is wrong with the ITQS."

Lyris's heart skips a beat before jumping into his throat. The sinking feeling in his stomach accompanies the realization that the complaints he's been ignoring are the warnings he was looking for.

"I'm conferencing in Director Wyeth." Lyris stands and signals the director, who connects to the channel. "What are they seeing?"

"Sir, they claim orders aren't being fulfilled. Several of them describe resubmitting trades with similar results. We searched for their confirmations, but what we found wasn't what they submitted. It's strange."

Lyris is about to ask if they received a processing confirmation when alarms sound on the NOC floor and red strobes erupt around them. "Director, we have a volume alert. There is a twenty percent spike in trading over average. Make that twenty-five percent," the voice goes on to correct.

"Director, this is operations," another voice chimes in as a second alarm sounds in the NOC. "We are receiving volatility alerts. Above-average price swings on IGI securities."

"Service Desk, let me get back to you. Operations, what kind of price swings?"

"Sir, matching engines are processing massive buy and sell orders for vastly different prices. It's causing huge price swings on the ticker."

"That's not typical behavior, even in a crisis," Wyeth says as they both watch the candle graph on the secondary display.

"No kidding," Lyris mumbles.

Volatility on the corporate subsidiaries exchange is typical, but the Intercorpex Global Index never behaves this way. In this case, it's reversed. The secondary market is trading normally, making this that much more disturbing.

"Director, this is the Trading Desk. We have a problem."

"You're not the only one," Wyeth says. "What is it?"

"Computer processing queues are alerting 'over-threshold.' Logs indicate that they're having problems matching trades to account numbers."

"What?" Lyris shares a confused look with Wyeth.

"It's as if the trades were made from ghost accounts. They're valid, but when we go to reconcile them against the account number, the computers determine that it doesn't exist."

"That's not possible."

"I know it isn't, sir, but it's happening," the panicked woman states.

Lyris exhales, taking stock of the situation and wondering how this could be happening. The quiet professionalism and efficiency that are the hallmarks of this operation have evaporated in the NOC. The room has descended into absolute chaos as the number of issues mounts.

"Director, this is the Service Desk. Call volume just tripled."

"Acknowledged. Trading Desk, is it possible that a virus somehow faked these unreconciled trades?"

"I don't know how, sir. Archangyl would have eradicated it."

A near artificial intelligence protects Intercorpex's systems and trading platforms. It's not an exaggeration to say that Archangyl is the perfect defense system. It learns, adapts, and changes itself to combat threats without human input or intervention. If malicious code were introduced to their systems, the software would immediately delete it and trigger an alarm.

Lyris stares at his workstation. Intercorporational news has picked up on the market volatility. There are still no VidLynk requests from Raimius. If the situation isn't bad enough, his silence makes it more unnerving. He should have reached out by now.

"What are your instructions?" Wyeth prompts from next to him.

"Director, the queue is growing," the Service Desk says.

"Director Lyris, we're approaching forty percent increase over average volume and climbing rapidly," Exchange Operations advises him.

Lyris stands as everyone looks to him for guidance. He has none. There are no apparent actions to take, and Lyris doesn't know what to tell the analysts to look for. In fact, for the first time in his professional life, he's at a complete loss for what to do.

CHAPTER
SIXTY-FIVE
LIBERTEUM

Old Broad Street Station
Lower Manhattan Underground
New York City Municipal Corporation

Two myths are being shattered before Michele's eyes. The first is the invincibility of Intercorpex. Her father used to say that if corporations were a car the world was riding in, then the exchange was the engine that propelled it. Humanity serves corporate masters, who then use Intercorpex to benefit the global elite. They are as fallible as Quarren said they were.

The second is what Liberteum has managed to accomplish. Employees regard urches as dirty, uneducated, underground gypsies with no practical skills other than scavenging and terrorizing civilized society. She wishes whoever subscribes to that characterization could see them in action now.

"This is crazy," Michele says, looking over Adiz's shoulder. "I never would have expected this!"

"I've created tickets that yield the widest spread," Jasper says. "Sell orders for ten thousand shares of China at a hundred Bytecoin. Buy orders for five thousand shares of Russia for ten thousand Bytecoin. I'm doing the same thing with every stock in the IGI."

"And they aren't filtering them?"

"They don't know how to. Our fake trades are indistinguishable from real ones that the patricians are sending in," Adiz explains. "We're at fifty-nine percent and rising. Patricians must be getting concerned about their positions."

"That will encourage the *gentez-majorez* to play the high-frequency game, adding to the chaos," Michele concludes. "Perfect."

"This was never about destroying America Incorporated, was it?" Rykos says from his spot on the floor next to the column.

"Corporations are only part of the problem, Rykos," Michele explains. "Since its creation, Intercorpex has increased its influence over everyone. Their charter gave them power, the Zurich Canon gave them dominance, and a single currency gave them complete control."

"They don't control the currency," he argues.

"You know better than that, Rykos," Quarren interjects, interlacing his fingers. "Everything is intertwined. When corporations assumed the mantle of governance, they required a single, stable currency to facilitate trade and a financial market to enrich the elites. Bytecoin may appear to be decentralized, but Intercorpex controls it."

"You make it sound like they control everything."

Quarren twists his mouth in a knowing smile. "Before the collapse, people feared something called the 'New World Order.' It was believed that powerful elites were conspiring to replace nation-states with a global totalitarian regime. That's what happened with Intercorpex."

"If what you're saying is true, then why don't the patricians and corporations ally to fight back against the exchange?"

"Because they both benefit from the system. So long as Intercorpex doesn't expand its power too quickly, there isn't enough political will for corporations and patricians to fight them."

"So, what are you doing?" Rykos asks.

"Giving them a reason to fight," Michele says from her spot behind Adiz.

Haven charges up the stairs from the tunnel and frantically rushes over to Quarren. Whatever the reason for his hasty return from his post, it's important.

"Our position is compromised. Spotters report teams of guardians moving in this direction. A command truck was seen pushing down Broadway through the crowd."

"How long do we have before they try to breach?" Quarren asks.

"It depends on how good their intelligence is. They'll establish a perimeter first, just like at the rave. Once resources are in place, they'll find an access route."

"The PSS canceled the evacuation alert, so people will start moving back inside," Jasper adds, pointing to the display showing AME News.

"We won't have much time once those streets clear," Haven finishes.

"Clock's ticking, guys. Make the seconds count," Michele advises her two hackers.

"Haven, make sure our escape route is secure. We don't want to run into them when it's time to clear out of here."

"You got it," he says, nodding at Quarren before rushing back toward the platform.

Michele stares at her father. There's nothing that needs to be said. They have a good plan, but a thousand things could go wrong with it. Fate will decide whether they succeed or fail, and the world will get that answer in the next couple of hours.

CHAPTER
SIXTY-SIX

AMERICA, INC.

Church Street South of Vesey
Lower Manhattan
New York City Municipal Corporation

From the EOC's location on Chambers Street to the corner of Trinity Place and Broadway is a leisurely fifteen-minute walk on most days. Despite pushing and shoving people out of their way, it has taken Teman and Zyree that amount of time to cover half the distance. Liberteum deserves some credit for initiating a fake evacuation order to flood the streets with people. It was a masterstroke.

The chief guardian considers himself in good shape and figures that Zyree doesn't cheat himself in his workouts, either. Both are winded from fighting their way through the crowd. Needing a break, they pull up at the back of Saint Paul's churchyard. Teman seizes the opportunity to stand on a short, two-foot wall and cling to the black wrought iron gate as he surveys the mass of humanity ahead of them.

"Why are we stopping? You tired, princess?" Zyree jokes, resting with his hands on his knees as he sucks oxygen in.

"This is taking too long. I need to send the tactical team in now."

"Is the command truck in place?"

Teman consults his tablet. "No, it's stuck on Broadway, but it's closer than we are. There are enough tactical personnel on-site to conduct a raid now."

"You don't have eyes or ears on that station," Zyree says, clearly not liking that idea one bit. "You'll be sending your guys in blind."

"Yes, and I'm willing to take that risk. We don't even know if Liberteum is there. The sooner we know for sure, the better. Having a command truck in place doesn't change that."

"You know better. The command vehicle can analyze the feeds from the drones you send in to sweep the tunnels."

"We're not using drones. If they're spotted, Liberteum will have more time to prepare a defense."

"You don't think they've done that already?" Zyree argues, dumbfounded.

Teman is in no mood to argue the point. This is his operation and his men. It's his son down there. If Liberteum is holed up in that station, they can finish them once and for all.

"The longer we wait, the more likely we lose the element of surprise. My guardians can handle themselves."

Zyree shakes his head and hops on the wall to look at the clogged street.

"Captain, this is the chief guardian," Teman says, opening a channel on his tablet. "Are you in position yet?"

"We're at the Fulton Street SpeedRail station. From what the EOC has briefed, we'll enter the old subway tunnel and proceed south to where it's sealed. Engineers have assured us that there's an old maintenance access hatch in the wall fifty meters north of the abandoned station. That will put us right on top of them."

"All right. Move with haste. You're cleared weapons-free once you're en route to the objective. Shoot on sight. Do you understand?"

"Yes, sir. Any other special instructions?"

"Yeah. Don't take chances with your lives. Good hunting."

Zyree joins the chief guardian as he ends the conversation. "What about the south?"

"There's no access that way," he says with a shake of the head.

"Liberteum is going to have multiple escape routes. I'm telling you, you should wait to send your team in until—"

"I'm not waiting! This is my operation and the order has been given. Are you going to complain about it or are you coming?"

Teman starts making his way south when Zyree gets a call. The chief guardian appreciates everything Zyree has done, but he's out of his depth. He doesn't know the city or their enemy. Not like Teman does. He is going to lose men, but he will lose even more by waiting. That's what Liberteum will expect him to do.

"Malkor! Where are you? Good. We're trying to get down there now. Hell no. Meet me at the rally point," Zyree says, ending his VidLynk.

Teman picks up speed. They travel another few blocks before noticing that there are fewer people to move out of the way.

"Is the crowd thinning, or is it my imagination?" Zyree asks.

"The EOC rescinded the evacuation order. Employees are returning to work," Teman shouts between pants.

The command vehicle is parked in the middle of the avenue with a dozen guardians around it. Captain Spirak appears in the entrance at the back of the truck.

"Chief Guardian, we're glad you're here. We're just coming online now. Two ten-man teams are moving down through the tunnel toward the objective. There's nothing on night vision or thermal. The tunnel is clear."

Zyree looks for his men, and not seeing them, follows Teman up the metal stairs leading into the truck. Feeds from helmet-mounted cameras are shown in a grid on the large display. They've halted at a concrete wall. One of the men moves to inspect a three-foot by three-foot access hatch through the barrier. It's been recently used.

The tunnel is littered with debris and rusting junk. Infrared beams attached to the team's weapons illuminate the area with the help of their night vision. It's still tough for the guardians in the command truck to make out what they're seeing.

"I thought this tunnel was used for utilities," Zyree says, checking the displays. "Why aren't there any pipes or conduit?"

"It's all on the other side of the barrier. The station is used as a junction for electrical power, water and natural gas mains, and data lines. This old section of tunnel serves no purpose anymore," the lieutenant explains.

"No wonder this city has an urch problem," Zyree mutters.

"You're preaching to the clergy," Teman agrees. "If the corporation spent a fraction as much time focusing on security as they do turning a profit, we wouldn't be in this situation."

The captain gets on comms with the team leader and discusses the possibility of the access hatch being rigged with a booby trap. The commander of the second team about fifty feet behind the first moves his head to look at some cylinders tucked against the tunnel wall.

"Wait! What is that?" Zyree asks, pointing. "Have that team leader turn his head back to the right."

"Lieutenant, pan right," Spirak says into the microphone after punching a button to open a channel. He does, and everyone fixates on five metal drums perched next to a concrete support column.

"They're old oil barrels, I think," the team leader says. "They look new. I'm going to investigate."

"Get them out of there!" Zyree shouts.

Teman recoils at the urgency. "It's just debris from the—"

"Move them back now!"

An arm reaches out to touch one of them when a bright light flashes over the displays. A split second later, the ghostly green images turn into static. A deafening roar echoes off the buildings on Wall Street, and Teman looks at Zyree in horror.

The two men shoot out of the back of the truck just in time to witness panicked people fleeing a cloud of dirt and smoke billowing down Broad Street and spilling into the intersection with Wall Street. Teman places his hands on his head and looks down the street in utter disbelief.

"What the hell was that?" one of Zyree's men asks when the pair toting a large equipment box arrives.

Zyree rubs his forehead. "The price of stupidity."

CHAPTER
SIXTY-SEVEN
INTERCORPEX

Global Network Operations Center
Manhattan Financial District
ICX New York Exchange

The building shakes, and the lighting in the NOC flickers. Technicians scamper under their desks while others grab their desks and look apprehensively up at the ceiling. Lyris shifts his gaze between the main displays and the ones perched on his workstation, wondering if they'll stay online. They do. Everyone in the room is thinking the same thing.

"What the hell was that?"

Wyeth looks at the director and shrugs.

"Director, ICX Security. There was an explosion on Nassau Street, just to the north of the intersection with Wall."

Lyris's worst fear has been realized. Zyree's assurances that the NOC wasn't a target were flat wrong. It must have been a truck bomb that the BCS intercepted.

"Systems check! Was the primary circuit for the ITQS severed?"

"Sir, this is NetEng. The circuit momentarily flapped but is stable. We lost some packets but still have connectivity."

"Director, Ops. All servers are operational. Everything is stable."

"Our systems are about the only thing that *is* stable right now," Wyeth quips, staring at the main display showing the current stock prices.

"Director Lyris, this is ICX Security. I patched you into the video feed from our Broad Street cameras. Whatever just happened there ripped a massive hole in Nassau Street."

"What?" Lyris leans in for a better look.

It's a block away, and the director almost didn't recognize it. Wyeth moves around the divider that separates their work areas and joins him. The video is obscured with a layer of smoke and dust, but amidst the scene's chaos, they can see a forty-foot hole where the street once was.

"Was it a truck bomb?"

"Undetermined, sir. It could have been, but I would have expected more street-level casualties and damage. It was more likely a subterranean detonation."

ICX Security personnel are trained in explosion effects, but they aren't experts. Lyris is convinced it's a truck bomb, but the buildings lining the street only have shattered windows. If it were one, there would be far more damage.

"Get in touch with PSS and find out what the hell is going on!" Lyris barks.

"We need to transfer operations to London," Wyeth says.

Lyris dismisses his suggestion with a wave. "I would have done that twenty minutes ago if it was that simple. London isn't equipped to deal with this trading problem."

"If it's a virus—"

"We can't make that decision based on a hypothetical. Let's assume it is a virus that Archangyl didn't eradicate. All we'll accomplish is sending hyper-trading patricians into a fit of rage and double the number of elites screaming at us."

The telltale chirp in Lyris's earpiece announces an incoming VidLynk. He glances down at his display and sees that it's from the office of the administrator-general. It's about time Raimius reached out.

"Sir, I was wondering when—"

"You've made a mess of things, Lyris," Raimius says without a trace of the usual panic that an incident a tenth this size would incite.

"I'm sorry, sir?"

"There are threats to Intercorpex property, the market is a mess, and I have every patrician in the world contacting my office. I entrust you to handle these problems. Instead, you've managed to turn this into a complete disaster."

"Sir, I—"

"I don't need excuses, Lyris. You wanted to be the global director of exchange operations, and you've failed miserably. Fix this, or I will relieve you of your duties and do it for you."

That explains Raimius's radio silence. This has everything to do with the Denali Keating meeting. Lyris understands the game now. Raimius will let him fail if it offers a reason to ask for his resignation when the dust settles. He needs a way out of this.

"Sir, we may need to transfer operations to London. There was an explosion outside the building."

"Did the explosion affect trading?" Raimius asks.

"No, but—"

"Then what good will transferring operations do? Lyris, don't make me question your decision-making abilities more than I already am."

"We have a problem with trading right now."

"You don't think I know that? Fix it, or your next job will be mopping the Iceland data center's floors."

The VidLynk disconnects. Lyris knows that the AG is counting on him to either succeed or fail. If it's the former, Raimius will take all the credit. If it's the latter, he removes a threat. It's a win-win. All Lyris needs to do is find a way to disappoint him.

"Trading Desk, any luck reconciling those trades?"

"Negative. We were going to contact you before the building shook. The server isn't artificially manufacturing these trades. They're coming over the wire, correctly formatted with proper ITQS transaction numbers."

"So, transferring to London won't solve the problem?"

"Not until we find a way to filter them."

Lyris curses under his breath. So much for that. Until they find the source of the trades, the NOC is helpless to combat them. By then, the whole market might collapse. The volatility is off the charts.

"I'm out of ideas," Wyeth says. As the head of New York Operations, his job is also on the line. He'll likely be taking Lyris's if they don't find a solution – and fast.

Lyris closes his eyes and shuts out the world around him. A worst-case scenario deserves a last resort. Only one person has been ahead of this from the beginning. He opens his eyes and tugs on the bottom of his tunic.

"Get me Zyree on a VidLynk."

CHAPTER
SIXTY-EIGHT
THE PATRICIANS

The White House
Corporate Governance District
Washington-Arlington Municipal Corporation

For obvious reasons, the Broad Street explosion isn't being reported over AME News or the InterLynk. Public Affairs is toiling to craft a message that paints the situation positively. The reality is that the corporation is getting bested by basement dwellers. At least, that's what competing corporations are reporting to their employees.

Fiolla needs answers. She also needs advice. She places a VidLynk to get one, if not the other.

"I'm surprised to hear from you," Farron says after they connect. "Are you okay?"

"I'm fine. It's quieter now. Are you back inside?"

"Yes. The evacuation order was lifted. Is this about the explosion downtown?"

"How do you know about that already? I just got word of it myself."

"We have contacts in that area. Word travels fast when the street outside your building is a crater."

"I'm sure. No, it isn't about that, but I do need your help with something else."

"This sounds serious," Farron says, the grave tone in his voice lowered to match hers.

"It is. I hate to ask, but do you know of any way to get Talya Bettancourt to stop calling the board of directors?"

"With all that's going on, I didn't think Valen would be worrying about that," Farron says after a long pause.

Fiolla nods. "He is, thanks to your information. I'm sorry. I know that I'm putting you in a terrible position, but Valen can't manage this crisis in New York and fight a political battle on Corporate Hill at the same time."

"I understand, but this…I don't know if I can help, Fiolla. Talya Bettancourt is the *prima,* and we can't risk ending up as a target for a family that powerful."

"I understand. I'm desperate, Farron."

"Is this a professional conversation or a personal one?"

The question catches Fiolla off guard. She rubs her hands together and lowers her eyes. "I don't know what you mean."

"Are you asking me as Fiolla, the woman I love, or as an executive with an office in the West Wing of the White House?"

"Why would you ask that?"

"You are an ambitious woman. It's one of the things I love about you. But now I'm beginning to wonder if I'm nothing more than the boost you need to earn your next promotion."

Fiolla closes her eyes. His words cut deeply. She has never considered herself like the other executives who have risen through the ranks of America Incorporated. She works hard and would never sink to such underhanded tactics. The man she loves doesn't understand that, and the thought is forcing her to fight back the tears.

"That has never been the case. You have to believe me," Fiolla pleads.

"I want to, but this needs to be a relationship built on trust. We need to start acting like partners. You have to let me into your life all the way. No more secrets."

Fiolla lifts her eyes and stares at the man in her display. She fully understands what he's asking. "I can't share corporate secrets with a patrician."

"Then I can't share information about patricians with a corporate executive. Goodbye, Fiolla."

"Wait! Okay, you win. I'll do whatever you need me to. I don't want to lose you."

"I don't want to lose you, either," he says in a soothing and sincere voice that washes Fiolla with a sense of relief. "Intercorpex."

"What?"

"The answer to your problem is Intercorpex. They're having issues with their trading system, and that's what's causing all this market volatility. I'm guessing they haven't informed you of that."

"No, not a word," she says, tapping on her virtual keyboard to bring up recent exchange communications. There aren't any.

"Rumors are swirling among the patricians that Liberteum is behind it."

"How do you know that? Wait, your business with the urches…. You aren't involved with Liberteum, are you?"

"Of course not. I have contacts in the underground that provide information crucial to our business. Urches know more about what happens in this city than the CEO of New York does."

"What do I do with that information?" Fiolla asks.

"Leak it. If that news breaks, patricians will feel threatened that their positions in AME are being diluted and scream at Talya to pressure Raimius for a solution. She'll have to shift focus away from her efforts on Corporate Hill."

Fiolla's mind is racing. That could work long enough to allow Valen to talk to the board. The only problem is that she can't leak it directly to AME News. It would be too obvious. It has to be another news agency that AME is willing to source for the story. Fortunately, she knows someone that can quietly set that up.

"Thank you, Farron."

"You're welcome, my love. Go handle business. We'll talk again when this is all over."

Farron disconnects and Fiolla leans back in her seat and stares at the ceiling. She may have saved her relationship with him, but she could be selling America Incorporated out in the process. He's afraid that she's using him, but that street runs in both directions. Fiolla forces the thought from her mind. She has work to do.

"Hello? Executive Fiolla? To what do I owe the pleasure?" a saccharine voice says after the VidLynk request is accepted.

"Journalist Kassaya, we need to talk."

CHAPTER SIXTY-NINE

REGISTRANT RYKOS

Old Broad Street Station
Lower Manhattan Underground
New York City Municipal Corporation

It's taken a full ten minutes for my ears to stop ringing. The dust and smoke that enveloped the station have finally dissipated. I can actually see what's around me. I thought I was going to choke to death.

I thought this decrepit piece of aging infrastructure was going to collapse on itself. Large chunks of concrete fell all around us and it's a small miracle I wasn't killed. Michele and her entourage were more concerned about the hack still being in progress than checking on my safety. Even Quarren ignored my desperate pleas about what happened.

"The tunnel is sealed," Nyvar proclaims after feeling his way back up the small stairway leading to the mezzanine level. "They won't be coming from that direction without using heavy machinery."

"We should hear that no problem if they do."

"What was that?" I ask, trying once again to get their attention.

"It was an explosion. Are you a moron, Ivy?"

"What triggered it?" I press. I don't understand why they would set one off so close to us.

"More like *who* triggered it. The PSS, probably. Well, what's left of them," Nyvar says with a laugh.

My heart sinks into my gut. I know many of my father's men and have attended countless ceremonies and dinners with them over my life. It's what is expected when you grow up as the son of a distinguished guardian. What are the odds that I knew the men who just perished?

"What? Why?"

"We can't let them breach this location. At least, not yet," Michele says.

"So, you blew them up? You bastards! My father could have been with them!"

"So what?" Nyvar grins.

I jerk against my chains. I want to rip his tongue out. I hate him. I hate all of them.

"Nyvar, go find Haven and help him back here," Quarren orders. The terrorist complies without another word. "Rykos, I doubt your father was with them."

"How could you know that?" I scream, losing the battle to control my emotions.

"Because the chief guardian won't join a tactical assault team. It's against protocol."

"Even when he knows his son is being held hostage?"

"Especially under those circumstances. His decisions would appear compromised," Quarren says.

I don't know if he's right. I don't know enough about what my father does to argue with him.

"So, you kill all his men instead? How do you justify that?"

"Their deaths were unfortunate, but guardians are trained to protect the system at all costs, even if they didn't realize that's what they were doing. Everything down here…all this…is aimed to unshackle humanity from the chains of that system. Those men won't be the only casualties in that battle."

"You say that like it's okay."

"It's not okay, but it is reality. You read about past wars in that textbook. Some were about power and riches while others were about liberty and freedom. They all had one thing in common: People died."

"You think anyone wants to return to a time of war and chaos?" I ask, falling back on what I learned in my modules. "We've evolved as a global society and created a better way to live. The system may not be perfect, but it's a whole lot better than what came before it."

"Do you really mean that, Rykos? I mean *really* mean it? Or is that what you were programmed to think?"

I stop arguing and think about what he asked. How many conversations have I had in Central Park with Balin decrying the very system I'm defending now? Is Quarren right? Are my words a conditioned response?

"Father, we need to think about leaving here," Michele interjects. "The explosion only slowed them down. It won't stop them. They'll be coming again."

"We're not leaving yet. It will take them time to regroup and find another way down here. We'll be ready."

I'm sick to my stomach. They are so nonchalant about murdering people. How could I ever have gotten involved with them? I collapse to the floor and hang my head, knowing that this will get worse before it gets better.

CHAPTER
SEVENTY

AMERICA, INC.

Trinity Church
Lower Manhattan
New York City Municipal Corporation

Trinity Church has become a symbol of spiritual values in Manhattan's long-thriving financial district. A place of worship has occupied this site since 1697, although this building is only around two hundred forty years old. It survived the most calamitous events in the city's history, including the plane attacks in 2001, several major floods, and the Great Collapse. Now it stands vigil over today's events.

"This is a beautiful building, isn't it?" Teman says, staring at the exquisite altar when he hears Zyree come up alongside him. "Using stone as a building material may be a thing of the past, but it possesses a natural beauty symbolic of a different time."

"It's breathtaking, but you aren't in here to admire the architecture. You need to set aside what happened to your men, Chief Guardian. There will be plenty of time to mourn later."

"That's easy for you to say. Twenty men, gone," Teman says. "You warned me and I didn't listen. Now they're dead, and I'm responsible."

"Liberteum killed them, not you. They died doing their duty."

Duty. Teman shakes his head. How many of them would have chosen to be guardians if some primary school aptitude test hadn't put them on that career track? How many would have chosen this career, no matter how honorable it is to protect their fellow employees? Law enforcement used to be a calling. Public safety is just another job.

"Have you ever lost men before?" Teman asks, still staring straight ahead at the altar.

"You don't do what we do and not lose men. We need to honor their sacrifice by finishing what they started."

"Chief Guardian?" a voice from behind calls out. "I'm sorry to interrupt, sir, but you're requested back in the command truck. They have something for you."

"We'll be right there."

Teman takes one last long look at the altar before heading back down the aisle with Zyree following. He knows the chief inspector is right – he has a job to do, and they still have his son. He resolves to avenge his fallen brothers and save Rykos. Or he will die trying.

"What is it?" Teman asks after climbing the stairs into the back of the command vehicle.

"The EOC may have found another way into the station," Captain Spirak informs them. "There is a series of underground pedestrian passageways that linked the old Wall and Broad Street Stations. This corridor moves north up to the Equitable Building here," he explains, tracing the route with his finger. "Then it cuts across the Manhattan Bank building to the east and dives southwest until it reaches the station where the N and Z lines terminated. It will bring us straight to the mezzanine level of the downtown platform."

"You're sure these passages still exist?" Zyree asks, leaning in for a closer look.

"The Wall Street passage was likely walled off when the SpeedRail station was constructed. I'm sure the accesses from the two office buildings are likewise sealed."

"The subbasement of the Equitable Building," Teman says, tapping his finger on the map. "I'm betting that's Liberteum's way out. If we can block their escape route, we'll have them trapped inside the perimeter."

"Yeah, but they know that, too," Zyree argues. "These aren't dumb people. They'll be waiting for us."

Teman rubs his chin. It makes sense. They would hear any breaching through the Equitable, but might not be wise to them coming from the SpeedRail Station.

"Find that Wall Street access. We'll have Liberteum outmanned and outgunned. Their weapons can't penetrate our body armor. If we come at them fast and silent from the south, we might catch anyone waiting for us at the Equitable Building off guard."

The chief guardian looks at Zyree. "It's risky, but I don't have a better plan. Did you reconnoiter the southern part of the tunnel?"

"It's sealed tight, Chief Inspector. We'd have to blast our way in."

Zyree nods, but Teman's mind is already made up. "Have two tactical teams meet me over at Wall Street Station. Send the details of that tunnel to my tablet."

Teman exits the truck and pulls the lid off a crate positioned at its side. He dons body armor with energy dispersion plating and mounts night vision and thermal optics to a ballistic helmet. Finally, he jerks a rifle out of the rack, slaps in a magazine, and chambers a round.

"Where the hell do you think you're going?" Teman asks Zyree, who has donned even more impressive-looking equipment and is standing beside the truck with his two men.

"With you."

"No way. PSS protocol prohibits you from coming along."

"What does it say about hunting for a hacker in the EOC or about the chief guardian charging into a hostile zone?"

It's a good point, not that Teman is willing to concede it. "Don't argue with me on this, Zyree. I can't bring you along."

"Chief Guardian, listen to me. I know you feel responsible for your men and want your son back, but this is about more than an attack on your city. This is an attack on Intercorpex. You know we're valuable assets, and you need all the help you can get. Don't make the mistake of not utilizing us."

Teman sighs and checks out the armored and heavily armed men. The two ICX Inspectors almost dwarf Zyree. Their stature is almost as imposing as their firepower.

"You're under my tactical command, no questions asked. Follow my directions or I swear to God…."

"I can live with that," Zyree says. His two men also nod.

"All right. Let's go."

They fall in behind the chief guardian as they head to the Wall Street SpeedRail station.

CHAPTER

SEVENTY-ONE

LIBERTEUM

Old Broad Street Station
Lower Manhattan Underground
New York City Municipal Corporation

Everyone is feeling the effects of the explosion. It doesn't matter that they were on the other side of a thick reinforced concrete wall. It was the worst for Haven and his two men. They stumble up to the mezzanine looking like they went through hell.

"Are you okay, son?" Quarren asks, rushing over to help Nyvar pull Haven back to his feet.

"I'll live. I got my bell rung pretty good."

Jasper hands the three men bottles of water that they suck down. Haven uses some of his to rinse off his face. None of them look injured, but the hacker gives them a onceover to be certain before nodding at Michele.

"The tunnel collapsed?" she asks.

Haven looks back at the tracks. The air is still choked with dust, obscuring the lights strung up in the station.

"Completely sealed."

"That'll teach 'em," Adiz says, grinning.

Haven shoots him a nasty look. "They'll try again. Do you want to be on the front lines when they do? If not, shut your damn mouth before I break your teeth."

Michele steps in to deescalate the situation before Haven rips Adiz's tongue out. The hacker is out of harm's way in front of a computer, at least for the time being. Michele is sure the view is different on the perimeter.

"If they try again, we need to be ready. What do you need, Haven?"

He looks at her and crinkles his brow. "I need to double the guard on the southern access. It's not defensible, but they also don't know about it. Should they discover it, we'll need to execute a fighting retreat."

"That's our primary escape route, Haven."

"We have others," he snaps.

"Unless they find those. The pedestrian passageway shouldn't be hard for them to discover."

"We'll be ready for them. There are only two possible infiltration points and we have ambushes at both. An attempt to push through either will land them in a vicious crossfire."

"And if they get past you?"

Haven nods at the entrance off the mezzanine. "Then we'll blow the section of passageway off the station and turn it into a tomb."

Michele glances over at Rykos and sees the look of shock on his face. This isn't what she wanted for him. Letting him watch what is happening is turning into a mistake. No matter how much mistrust he has in corporatism, he's still not ready for the sacrifices that liberty requires.

"That leaves us with only the southern access and the emergency route, which isn't a good option. Do you have enough men to hold the passageway?"

"It depends on what size force they attack with. I could always use more men."

Quarren moves over to the table where the hackers are seated and picks up a rifle. He checks to ensure it's loaded and dons a modified vest with pockets for extra magazines.

"I'll go."

"Father...."

"I'm a spectator here, Michele. You, Jasper, and Adiz have work to do. If Haven needs more men, I'm the best available option. Let's just hope I don't have to run. If something happens, remember our conversation," Quarren says, shifting his gaze between Michele and Haven. "Make sure Rykos is taken care of."

There's no point in arguing. The man is unmovable once he makes up his mind – Michele and Haven can only nod.

"Rykos, this may be the last time we see each other. I sincerely hope you learned something from me in your time down here. Best of luck to you, son."

Quarren grasps his shoulder in an almost fatherly gesture before turning and disappearing into the dark passageway.

Michele grabs Haven's arm, "Take care of him."

"I will."

"Be safe, father," Michele calls out as Haven joins Quarren in the passageway.

"Taken care of?" Rykos asks as Michele turns her attention to Adiz and Jasper.

"Don't worry. It's not what you think."

CHAPTER
SEVENTY-TWO
INTERCORPEX

Global Network Operations Center
Manhattan Financial District
ICX New York Exchange

The call fails to connect for the second time, causing Lyris to curse. Zyree has always been hard to reach, and he's wanted to knock his teeth out because of it. This is not the time for the chief inspector to ignore him. Lyris waits as the system tries a third time to connect.

"This is not a good time, Lyris. What do you want?" Zyree says after the VidLynk connects.

"Your head on a pike. What the hell is all that noise?"

"We're smashing through a cement block wall. I don't have an update for you right now."

"You were right, Zyree."

Lyris pinches the bridge of his nose with his fingers. He hated the sound of that coming out of his mouth.

"It's loud in here. Did I just hear you right?"

"Yeah, you did. The primary circuit was Liberteum's target," Lyris admits. "They've managed to tap into it somehow and are planting false trades on the wire. It's creating havoc in the markets. Aren't you paying attention?"

"Uh, yeah, I'm glued to the ticker because I have an extensive portfolio to manage. Can't you filter the fake trades?"

"No, they're formatted perfectly. The computers can't tell the difference. We only know because the trades can't be matched to account numbers. Look, Zyree, whatever you're doing, you need to make ending this intrusion a priority."

"We're working on it. Wait, how is creating false trades possible?" Zyree asks.

"We don't know."

"How much time do I have?"

Lyris checks the super high-definition LED board for the market's trade volume and current value. The price swings are massive. How much of it is due to legitimate trading and how many are generated by the false requests is anybody's guess.

"It's hard to say. Best guess, if things don't stabilize, we're looking at a complete market collapse within the hour."

"Okay. We have a fix on their location. They're barricaded in an old subway station under Broad Street."

Lyris pulls up a map of the area on his display. "That's right next to the NOC. The primary ITQS circuit comes from that direction."

"How do you think I found them?" Zyree says.

"Can you reach them?"

"Liberteum isn't making it easy. Our last attempt resulted in an explosion that left a crater and a lot of dead guardians. We think we have another route in, but who knows what we'll find."

Lyris hangs his head and runs his fingers through his hair, pressing hard on his scalp as he does. There's nothing he can do from here. As much as it pains him to admit it, Zyree is the last chance to stop this.

"Zyree, listen to me. You have to end this incursion into our network. Everything else is a secondary priority. The very existence of Intercorpex may depend on it. Do you understand?"

"Yeah. You should know, the chief guardian's son is down there."

"Everything else is a secondary priority," Lyris repeats, expecting an argument. He can't understand how or why that happened, but there's no time to get those details now.

"Acknowledged. I'll update you when I can," he says before disconnecting the call.

"What did he say?" Wyeth asks.

"Director Lyris? This is Public Affairs."

Lyris shakes his head at Wyeth. This is about the only group he hasn't heard from today. This can't be good.

"What is it?"

"Tune into UKBC. They're reporting something you need to see."

Lyris changes the feed on a display as Wyeth moves around the divider. Most people residing on this continent aren't credentialed to get intercorporational broadcasts. Being the lone global exchange, the satellite dish on the roof ensures they have access to every news outlet on the planet.

"Unnamed sources inside Intercorpex have confirmed they are experiencing an issue with their trading system that's creating enormous market volatility," the financial correspondent for the United Kingdom Broadcast Corporation reports from her anchor desk. "Right now, it appears the problems are limited to the Intercorpex Trading and Quotation System, or ITQS, the system where market and limit orders are forwarded to the exchange for execution."

"Oh my God," Wyeth mumbles.

"There has been no confirmation whether the explosions seen around New York today are responsible for the problems, and Intercorpex has not released any official statements to patricians or the global corporate community. At this point, we believe the two are not linked."

"Public Affairs, this is Wyeth. Who else has this coverage?"

"China, Brazil, and Eastern Europe just picked it up and are reporting the story live. Requests for comment are coming from countless others. It went up on the GlobalNet as well."

Every corporation has its version of an intranet. In America, it is called the IntraLynk and serves as a way for employees to share information while conducting business. When discussions between corporations are necessary, it is done via the GlobalNet, a network that most closely resembles its predecessor, the World Wide Web. Once a news story is posted there, it travels around the world in a matter of minutes.

"Keep me informed," Lyris says.

"Did someone leak it from here?" Wyeth asks from over Lyris's shoulder.

"I don't know, but I will personally kill whoever is responsible."

"Even if that someone is Raimius?"

Wyeth read his mind. It would be a huge risk going public about this incident to remove him. It will cause too much reputational damage, considering the administrator-general never needs to justify making personnel changes, including firing his global director of exchange operations.

Another alert goes off in the NOC.

"Aw, now what?" Lyris grumbles, rolling his head to the side.

"Director, this is the Trading Desk. Sell orders now exceed buys by a two-to-one margin and climbing."

"Acknowledged, Trading Desk."

"The patricians are pulling their money out," Wyeth says, staring at the intraday market analysis. "If the ratio of sellers to buyers gets too high—"

"I know, I know. We won't have an exchange left. It'll be the death of Intercorpex."

CHAPTER

SEVENTY-THREE

AMERICA, INC.

Old Subway Pedestrian Tunnel
Wall Street, Lower Manhattan
New York City Municipal Corporation

The lighting in this passage was disconnected long ago. Even advanced night vision optics and infrared torchlights struggle to cut through the almost impenetrable darkness. Punching through the wall to access this tunnel was the easy part. The men pause fifty feet from the opening to ensure the team is assembled and ready. Now comes the hard part.

Clothes, cartons, and bedding from urches who once called this miserable place home litter the floor of the narrow hallway. The lack of maintenance has taken its toll on the walls. Peeling paint has exposed the steel support beams and subjected them to rust and corrosion.

"Multiple team formation, heavies in front," Teman whispers into his throat mic.

Two lines of four men form along the walls, with the second man in each staggered toward the inside. The standard protocol is for the fourth man on each side to face rearward, but it's unnecessary with a second team behind them. They keep their weapons at the low ready.

Teman orders the assault force forward up the tight passageway that twists through the subbasements of several buildings. Each jog to the left or right creates a blind spot that could present danger, and Liberteum could already know they're coming.

Broken wall tiles crunch under their feet with every step. The noise has nowhere to dissipate, and creates an echo chamber of reverberating sound. Instead of a stealthy tactical security unit, the assault sounds like a marching band in a Corporate Day parade.

After five minutes, the point man gives the halt signal, and everyone takes a knee. Teman peers down the passage thirty meters ahead; a set of turnstiles that marks the end of the old fare control area blocks their path. He didn't anticipate that. The revolving aluminum doors will not only be tough to squeeze through with all this gear on but will make a lot of noise.

"Now what?" Zyree asks Teman.

"Number four man on each team forward to investigate," he whispers into his throat mic.

The two men set off, taking slow, deliberate steps to minimize noise. They don't get far.

A hail of gunfire erupts from behind the turnstiles, and the two men crash to the ground. The assault squad drops to the concrete floor as the remainder of the heavy team returns fire with their automatic weapons. The gunfire is loud, even with ear defenders in.

"We're pinned down!" Teman screams over the sound of weapons blasting, watching two more men get hit. "We've got to pull back!"

Their fire isn't indiscriminate; it's aimed and accurate. Ricochets bouncing off the walls and roof of this corridor are equally deadly. They won't last a minute under the withering fire pinned down like this.

"How many do you see?" Malkor shouts.

Zyree lifts his head off the ground and sticks it up over the bodies of the men in front of him. It almost gets shot off. Teman hopes his fancy contact lenses got him the information they need.

"Five, although reinforcements could be farther up the hallway."

"I got this," Malkor says.

He activates the nonlethal countermeasures in his armor. A small launcher pops out of his wrist guard, and three projectiles launch in the direction of the turnstiles. At first, nothing happens. Then, all hell breaks loose.

Two of the projectiles are intense strobes that disorient anyone in the vicinity. Teman squints, his night vision optics now useless. The final projectile emits an excruciatingly painful audio tone debilitating to anyone not wearing ear defenders. The devices have the desired effect. The withering gunfire coming from the barricade ceases.

"Forward, now!" Teman orders the remainder of the team.

"No!" Zyree shouts.

His warning goes unheeded. They rush forward with rifles blazing, stepping over their fallen brothers. They make it halfway to the turnstiles when a salvo of gunfire rips through the corridor, dropping three men and sending the rest careening to the ground. Teman and one of the survivors scurry for cover behind discarded furniture that lines the side of the passage.

Teman pulls a smoke canister from his vest and launches it down the hallway. He exposes too much of his front and is knocked backward by the force of rounds striking his armor. The canister erupts, spewing a thick white smoke that obscures everything in the hallway ahead of them.

"Pull…pull back," he gasps into his comms unit as he lies sprawled out on the ground.

The men pinned down in front of them take immediate advantage of the smokescreen. They grab their wounded comrades by their armor and begin dragging them back down the passageway. An explosion detonates with enough force from the overpressure to push the oxygen out of Teman's lungs. He covers his head as debris rains down on him.

Zyree peeks up to see the countermeasures cease and terrorists return to their firing positions. The antipersonnel bomb was effective in stopping any advance cold. Liberteum is prepared. He ducks as bullets whiz over his head with a popping sound. That was too close.

"This is hopeless, Zyree!" Malkor yells. "If we stay here, we'll be torn to pieces!"

"We won't get three meters before getting cut down," he shouts in reply.

Parold gives the chief inspector a nod. He rises from the ground and breaks into a full sprint, his rifle expending ammunition at its cyclic rate of fire. Bullets strike his body armor as he hurtles toward the turnstiles. When he takes a hit to his leg, he staggers down to his knees.

The men behind the turnstiles start to fall back in disarray, but one stays behind and stubbornly unloads on the hulking figure. Parold fires off rounds until his rifle runs dry. He manipulates the timer on a grenade and tosses it in front of him. He turns to Teman and gives a thumbs-up as three more terrorists begin firing at him.

"Cover!" Teman yells, clenching his eyes tightly and covering his head as the device detonates. The tunnel shakes as support beams give way, and the passage begins to collapse. It's not a complete blockage but will make it impossible to fire through, allowing for a retreat.

"Teman, are you okay?" Zyree asks between coughs after managing to push forward up the passageway.

"I'll live," he says, gripping his side and grimacing as he's helped up. "We need to find another route."

Zyree and Teman pick up the wounded guardians and stagger back to the Wall Street SpeedRail station. There is no need for stealth anymore, making the return trip quicker. A couple of minutes later, they exit the passage with the help of an army of uniformed guardians waiting for them.

CHAPTER SEVENTY-FOUR

REGISTRANT RYKOS

Old Broad Street Station
Lower Manhattan Underground
New York City Municipal Corporation

Michele and the hackers are rattled by the explosions and staccato of gunfire from the passageway. They have their weapons drawn and are ready to shoot anything that emerges. Muzzle flashes provide brief illumination. Then another massive explosion shakes the whole station, almost knocking me off my feet.

The world seems to stop after that. There is no more gunfire. The silence is eerie as the trio waits for something to happen. A minute ticks by. Then another. Is this my rescue party?

"Coming in!" a voice shouts. Michele and the hackers lower their weapons.

Haven and another guy I don't recognize carry Quarren, who has an arm draped over each of their shoulders. He's grimacing from the pain, and I notice the large red splotch over his midsection. All of them look like they've been through hell.

"Oh my God! What happened?" Michele screeches in horror as the battle-worn men stumble into the room and lay Quarren on the floor.

"The PSS found the passage," Haven says, his hands on his knees as he pants to catch his breath. "They came up the old Wall Street tunnel, and we ambushed them using the turnstiles for cover. They used some new countermeasure devices on us. We were lucky to escape."

Quarren's face is ashen, and he's losing a lot of blood. Nyvar retrieves a bag and pulls out some old bandages, not the cutting-edge treatments modern medical centers use. I watch as he applies pressure to one to stop the bleeding.

"What about Scivix?" Michele asks, kneeling and taking her father's hand.

"A man in ICX Security armor charged at us. Scivix covered our retreat. A grenade collapsed the tunnel and would have wiped us all out. Scivix paid for our escape with his life."

Michele gives Haven a couple of nods before turning her attention to the men attending to Quarren. "How is he?"

"He's been shot twice in the abdomen," Nyvar says, a foreboding look on his face.

I'm helplessly chained here to the wall. They killed even more guardians, but I can't help but stare at Quarren. It doesn't look good.

"Michele…"

"Don't talk, father," she says, stifling her tears as Quarren tries to lift his head off the ground.

He shakes his head. "Get out of here. They…they'll be coming again," he sputters.

"We can't move you without—"

"I'm finished," he says, looking down at his blood-soaked shirt. "My work is done. You…you need to go. You need to finish…what we started."

Quarren seems to be a decent man, and he treated me well down here. I can feel Michele's anguish at the thought of losing him. Tears are pouring down her cheeks. Even the psychopath Haven has a grim look on his face. If there was one man he respected down here, it was their leader.

"Haven, what options are left for getting out of here?" Nyvar asks, keeping a wary eye on the passageway.

"We could still exit through the Equitable Building, but we have to assume those passages are compromised. That leaves the south platform or our emergency exit."

"Any news from our guys to the south?"

"No. It's quiet over there as of the last check-in," Jasper relays.

"If they found the transfer passages, how long before they realize there are other ways in here?" Nyvar asks.

"Make the call, Haven," Michele says, stroking her father's forehead. He's looking worse by the second.

"Nyvar, link up with our team over at the south platform. There are more options to get out of the area from that route." Michele looks back at him. "The emergency exit is the last resort. There's only one way out of there," Haven explains.

"Okay," she says, turning her attention back to her father as Nyvar bolts down the stairs.

CHAPTER
SEVENTY-FIVE
AMERICA, INC.

The White House
Corporate Governance District
Washington-Arlington Municipal Corporation

The news about Intercorpex spreads like wildfire once it hits the GlobalNet. The result was well worth the time Fiolla spent convincing Journalist Kassaya to play along. Despite serving the same parent company, greasing palms is still a valued way of conducting business. Threats work as well.

The display on the wall is divided into quadrants, each filled with a competing corporation's news broadcast. The UKBC will get credit for breaking the story, but now the race is on to provide the best in-depth coverage. Even though employees of most corporations are restricted to watching their native news programs, it doesn't mean there isn't a global rivalry among news organizations.

Fiolla's brow crinkles when she sees the VidLynk request pop up. She instructs Rosie to accept it on the main display. Raimius is clearly not happy.

"Are you responsible for this?" the administrator-general asks without a greeting.

"Excuse me?"

"You heard me, Executive Fiolla."

"Responsible for *what*? Administrator-General, I'm not sure why you contacted me or what you're implying."

"You've heard the reports coming out of Europe. I want to know where they got that information."

"You should ask the UKBC. My first guess is that someone within Intercorpex leaked it to them," Fiolla says.

"I can assure you that's not the case," he argues as if having a source from the exchange leak information to the media is a rare occurrence when the opposite is true. "I intend to ask them, but for now, I'm asking you."

"Asking me what? I work for Corporate Affairs, not Public Affairs. If you'd like, I can transfer you over to them."

"Young lady, don't you dare pass me off like I'm calling customer service."

"My name is *Executive* Fiolla. Do not scold me like I'm an elementary school registrant who got caught eating glue, Administrator-General."

Raimius's face turns bright red, and Fiolla thinks he may be on the verge of bursting a blood vessel. The AG has a reputation for being petulant, demanding, and condescending. She now understands how he earned it.

"I demand to talk with Chief Executive Valen."

"I am not his switchboard operator. You can contact his office directly to see if they will patch you to the Situation Room. Now, is there something I can do for you, Administrator-General?"

"I want to know if America Incorporated leaked the information being reported."

Raimius suspects that the White House had a hand in this. That much is obvious. Whether he's making an educated guess or has actual information that Fiolla helped orchestrate it is the question.

"So you said. I imagine if we had leaked anything, it would have been to AME News. They would never pass on a scoop."

"Let me be very frank with you, Executive Fiolla. I believe someone from America Incorporated released damaging information about Intercorpex to the global media. You have the most to gain by it, considering the inability to safeguard your city from a bunch of urches. Rest assured, I will find out the truth. When I do, I wouldn't want to be your CEO if the trail leads back to the White House."

"I will be sure to relay your threat to him," Fiolla says, desperate not to react to the taunt.

"See that you do. Good day, Executive Fiolla, and good luck cleaning up New York."

"Good luck getting the patricians to ever trust you with their money again, you arrogant autocrat," she mumbles after the VidLynk disconnects.

Fiolla returns to her desk and collapses in her chair. Farron's tactic is working. The news reports will force Talya Bettancourt to refocus her energies just as he advised. The question is, at what cost? All that may have been accomplished is solving today's problem now by creating a larger one for tomorrow.

CHAPTER SEVENTY-SIX

INTERCORPEX

Wall Street SpeedRail Station
Lower Manhattan
New York City Municipal Corporation

Zyree sips water and sucks down some oxygen from the mask a medic offers him. He is lucky – smoke inhalation is a small price to pay for being alive. Energy-dispersing plating is less effective against the higher velocity projectiles Liberteum fired from their rifles. The PSS isn't as well-equipped, and Teman's guardians paid with their lives.

"These guys are starting to piss me off," Zyree says, coming up alongside Teman as he watches the medics check out his surviving men. "I thought you said they had no heavy weapons."

"Yeah, well, they found some."

Zyree watches as another team files into the tunnel as a blocking force in case the terrorists are bold enough to attack. He doesn't think they'd be so brazen, but it's a sensible precaution considering how this day is going.

"Command, this is the chief guardian," Teman says, opening a channel on his tablet. "What is the status of the men still in the tunnel?"

"Biojacks are all flat-lined, sir," Spirak reports in a mournful tone.

Teman slams his hand against the wall. He hangs his head and takes a deep breath.

"We need to find another way into that station."

"You're going to run into more ambushes and IEDs whichever route you take," Zyree says.

"What would you suggest, then? Collapse the station with explosives and kill them all, including Rykos? That's what the BCS would be doing right now. Or maybe you want to stand here and accept defeat. I'm going to tell you, neither of those two options works for me."

"Teman—"

"If there's another way in, we'll never find it. This is our best chance. We're going to fight our way through them if we have to."

Zyree grabs him by the shoulder and spins him around. Teman swipes his arm away violently. His nostrils are flaring, and there's rage in his eyes.

"I just lost a man down there, too. We're going to get these bastards, but we have to be smart about it. I promise you that there's another way to get onto that station without running the gantlet."

"Then you go find it! You don't work for me, and I can't stop you. I'm not about to waste time or lives searching for another access that everyone has told me doesn't exist."

Teman turns to see the guardians on the platform looking at him. Zyree notices it, too. They need leadership, and arguing with the chief guardian isn't inspiring confidence in the ranks. Zyree holds his hands up in surrender.

"Command, tell me you've found a way around the blockage in that passage."

"Yes, sir, we think we have," the captain says. "The tunnel runs past a Manhattan Bank storage area in the basement. We can blast through the wall."

"Okay, that will put us on the other side of the cave-in," Teman says, drawing a picture in his mind.

"Yes, sir, but it's also a straight shot to the station without any angles or cover. They'll see us the moment we breach. We don't have the personnel to conduct a head-on assault."

Teman nods. Captain Spirak is right. Liberteum will see them coming long before they reach the station. He can guess what nasty surprises they rigged in that stretch of hallway.

"Command, get guardians in tactical kit over to the Manhattan Building with ballistic shields and the crowd mover."

"Roger!"

"I'm done sneaking around. The shields will provide us cover, and they won't know how many men we have behind that crowd mover."

"You need drones to scout ahead," Zyree says.

"The drones are grounded, including the tactical ones. It stays that way until we're certain our systems are secure. We'll have to make do. We're out of choices."

"Good luck to you, Chief Guardian," Zyree says, placing his fist over his heart in the ICX Security salute. "*Veritatem et honorem.*"

The men shake hands and make their way out of the SpeedRail station. Zyree heads east with Malkor in tow as Teman and his guardians rush northeast toward the Manhattan Bank building. Time is of the essence, and they are running out of it.

CHAPTER
SEVENTY-SEVEN
LIBERTEUM

Old Broad Street Station
Lower Manhattan Underground
New York City Municipal Corporation

Quarren's breathing gets shallower. Nyvar opens another bandage and covers his abdomen. He applies pressure with his hands, causing Michele's father to wince in pain.

"I can't stop the bleeding," Nyvar complains.

"We can cauterize it," Haven suggests.

Nyvar shakes his head. "Even if we had the time, he's bleeding internally. There's no telling how much damage those bullets did."

"Michele?" Quarren whispers.

"I'm here, father."

He waves his left hand before letting it collapse back to the ground. "Tell them to stop."

The two men look at each other as tears begin pouring down Michele's face. They reduce the pressure, allowing Quarren to breathe easier. He lets out a sigh of relief.

"I'm not going to do that. We're going to fight for you. You can survive this."

She looks at Haven, who frowns and shakes his head. The man is as tough as nails and almost completely unfeeling of any emotions outside of hatred and rage. He has a soft spot for her father and respects him more than anyone. If Haven thinks it's a lost cause, then it is. She closes her eyes as waves of sorrow wash over her.

Quarren forces a smile. "We both know that I won't."

"No! You're going to be fine. I'm not going to lose you." Tears stream in thick tracks down her face.

"I'm so very…proud of you. You are my daughter, and you're just like your mother. I'm…going to see her again."

Michele tries to speak but no words come out. She plants her face on his chest and he reaches up and strokes her head.

"It's okay. My time…has run out. Yours is just beginning."

"I can't do this without you. I can't do it alone."

Quarren coughs violently. "Archimedes…was always your plan. You…can see it through. Do it for me…for all of us. Haven?"

"I'm right here, sir."

Haven moves around to the other side of him so that he doesn't need to lift his head.

"You're like a son to me. Promise me something."

"Anything."

"Rykos… You know…what to do."

Haven looks back at the registrant still chained to the support column. He expected to see a smug look on the kid's face. There isn't one. There's sadness in his eyes.

"Promise me…Haven."

"You have my word."

Quarren nods. His breaths grow labored as his lungs begin to fill. Frothy blood oozes from his mouth as he takes his last breath. Michele begins sobbing uncontrollably when his hand goes limp in hers. Haven reaches down and closes his eyelids. He places his fist over his heart. It's a gesture he hasn't used in a long time.

"*Veritatem et honorem.*"

"Goodbye, father," Michele says, kissing him on the cheek.

Jasper places his hand on her shoulder as Adiz looks on. "We have what we need, Michele. We should go."

She wipes the tears with her sleeves and stands. She walks over to Rykos, who hangs his head when she steps in front of him.

"I'm very sorry, Michele."

She nods. "It's what he wanted. Go ahead, Haven."

Rykos's eyes narrow and then grow wide when Haven pulls out his handgun. He points it straight at the kid before lowering it at Quarren and firing three rounds into his chest.

The sound makes Michele jump, and she struggles to hold back her emotions.

"What are you doing?" Rykos screams, wide-eyed in disbelief at the brazen disrespect.

"Protecting you," Michele informs him through her watery eyes.

CHAPTER
SEVENTY-EIGHT

PATRICIANS

Keating Family of the Gentez-Majorez Estate
Greenwich Geographic District
Southern Connecticut Municipal Corporation

Money is the root of all evil. That's what people who don't have it say. Denali has heard that axiom for decades from employees who wish they had a fraction of his wealth and are jealous that they don't. That's the way of the world and always has been.

The argument that money doesn't buy happiness has an element of truth to it. It doesn't unless what you are buying with yours makes you happy. Patricians waste their Bytecoin on all manner of useless things. Denali bought an army. He also built a room to command it from. Both of those things make him immensely happy.

The operations center beneath the mansion was built to withstand a nuclear blast, not that such a happening is a concern in this era. Unlike the fine antiques and ornate décor that adorn his residence above, this space is absent any ornamentation. There are no frivolities here. Everything in this room has a purpose.

Large displays line the walls and workstations are set up in clusters around the two-thousand-foot-space. In some respects, it is set up much like Intercorpex's Wall Street Network Operations Center. The big difference is the eerie red light that envelops the space.

"Commander Lacune, what's happening?" Denali asks as he enters and the men and women rise from their workstations. He gestures to them to sit.

"It appears that the second attempt to breach the Broad Street Station was also repelled. From the looks of the PSS medical response, there were significant casualties."

Lacune selects a video feed outside the Wall Street SpeedRail station. Emergency vehicles are arriving to join the ones already lined up outside one of the accesses. Denali doesn't know why they are there, other than there must be a way into the terrorist stronghold from that location.

"Liberteum is more determined than they thought. Will public safety try again?"

"I don't know, sir. I doubt they'll give up that easily, but they may wait for BCS support considering what they're up against."

Denali looks at the ticker and rubs his chin. His fortune has taken a hit, but he has massive reserves that he can use to regain the losses. He plans on putting the old adage "buy low, sell high" to good use. That's if the market recovers at all. It's in a freefall toward zero.

"Intercorpex must be getting desperate. I don't think the PSS has the time to wait for help."

"We will inform you once we learn more," Commander Lacune says, eliciting a nod from Denali.

"What about our forces?"

The commander brings up an electronic ledger showing the status of their units. Denali stares at the display, noting the disposition and location of each across the globe.

"The ones not in training are on alert. So far, there have been no threats or actions against any Keating interest."

The patrician isn't worried about protecting his assets. That's a short-term concern. It's the long game that he needs to focus on. Denali shakes his head.

"It's not enough."

"Sir?"

"We need more forces, Commander. We should have twenty percent more than this."

Lacune wears a look of concern. "Sir, recruitment has slowed significantly. I don't know—"

"What about other patricians? Have you tried poaching from them?"

Everyone in the room stares at their commander. The Zurich Canon establishes a set of rules that patricians must abide by. Aside from that, there are unwritten rules among the elites. The request Denali made violates both.

"We didn't think that would…be received well."

"That's my concern, not yours. Start making overtures. Target the lower patricians first. With their limited resources, they can't match what we can offer."

"How many more men do you need?"

Denali smiles. "I'll let you know when to stop."

"Very well, sir. There's one more thing that you should see. We completed the transfer of these to our fabrication facility."

Another video is sent to the display and the smile on Denali's face widens. The two huge aircraft would bring joy to any patrician.

"Will they fly?"

"Our engineers think so. Both aircraft are structurally sound. The metal fatigue is far less than the last three. The electrical and hydraulic systems need to be overhauled and the wings rebuilt, but they are airworthy. It will just take time."

"How much time?" Denali asks.

"They stopped making parts for these after the collapse. Everything we need will have to be machined. Even then, neither has flown in a half-century."

"I want progress, not excuses, Commander. Tell the engineers and machinists to get to work. That's what I pay them for."

"Yes, sir. If I may ask…who do you intend on getting to fly them?"

"I'm working on that. Understand, Lacune, that the existence of those two aircraft must remain a secret. If anyone at that facility utters a word to anyone about the existence of these planes, have them shot in the head. Understood?"

"Yes, sir."

Denali stares again at the video of aircraft on the display. They have seen better days, but they are still magnificent machines. They are his pet iron eagles.

"Oh, and when we get them working, I want them painted flat black," Denali says, cocking his head to the side.

Lacune grins. "I'll order the paint myself."

Denali nods and turns to leave the operations center. Men and women can be trained to be soldiers. Military hardware from the world's violent past is tougher to obtain. Tough doesn't mean impossible, though, and this expense is worth every Bytecoin. After all, every army needs an air force.

CHAPTER
SEVENTY-NINE
AMERICA, INC.

The White House
Corporate Governance District
Washington-Arlington Municipal Corporation

Valen excused himself from the Situation Room to get Fiolla's latest update in person. With the BCS still standing watch in the Oval Office, they head into his private study again and close the door. He didn't find anything she said surprising, including the call from Administrator-General Raimius.

"You've done great work, but now it's my turn. You should stick around for this."

Valen sits at his desk, calls up a menu, and sends a VidLynk request to one of his staunchest political allies. At least, he has been one. Who knows what Talya Bettancourt is promising board members to bring them over into her camp.

"Chairman Hammond," the CEO says when the VidLynk establishes, and the aging yet still handsome chairman of the America Incorporated board of directors appears on his display.

"I was wondering when you would finally contact me. You're late to the party."

Every corporation in the world is accountable to a board responsible for making important decisions and representing the interests of patrician stockholders. The composition and number of seats in these bodies vary by company. Small corporations have as few as five members, while Japan has the most with thirty-one.

"Talya Bettancourt reached out to you, I assume?"

"Along with the rest of the board. She's made some *interesting* overtures," Chairman Hammond says.

"I bet she did. What did you tell her?"

"Something along the lines of, 'I'm the chairman of the board for the most powerful corporation in world history and don't take marching orders from a patrician.'"

While most board members have business experience, some corporations rely on nepotism or a political favor system. All fifteen members of the Board of Directors for America Incorporated were former chief executive officers of major subsidiaries who distinguished themselves during their tenure. They make up one of the more active boards in the world, having been made so by a string of chairmen who sought continuous expansion of their influence. As a result, they are also one of the most political boards.

"Not all of the board members share the chairman's unwavering dedication," Zeykala says, stepping into view on the display.

Valen grins. Her hatred for him is legendary among executive circles. On the original shortlist to assume control of the parent company, he beat Zeykala out for the job, and she's been bitter about it ever since. Following her retirement from a prominent technology subsidiary, she was appointed to the board and has become Valen's most outspoken critic.

"Good to see you again, Boardmember Zeykala."

"I sincerely doubt that," she drawls.

She may be north of sixty-five years old, but she still has the fire and drive of a young executive fresh out of the Ivy League. Zeykala is slim and aging gracefully, with tinges of gray accenting short blonde hair. She would be an attractive woman if her acerbic tone and caustic personality didn't send even the most stoic men running for their lives.

"I thought the board might show some loyalty in a time of crisis."

"My loyalty is to the company, not to the individual *temporarily* charged with running it. Imagine a CEO who made a career of being one step ahead of everyone failing to handle the one problem that's been under his nose since before he took over."

"Liberteum was eradicated," Valen says.

"All evidence to the contrary."

"Valen, the board is taking *Prima* Bettancourt's concerns very seriously," the chairman interjects before things can turn nasty. "I know she has a vendetta against you. But her arguments are valid, and she has enough influence to sway board members to see things her way."

"Chairman Hammond, I've presided over an era of unprecedented growth and prosperity. America Incorporated is positioned as a world leader for the next decade. Are you all willing to sacrifice all that?"

Zeykala claps sarcastically. "Bravo, Valen, bravo. You've managed to squander all of that brilliant management by mismanaging the growing threat in New York. After the first attack, I believe you made certain promises that we would not see a repeat. Now, we're watching a second, more devastating strike less than two weeks later."

Valen narrows his eyes. There's no doubt that she's been talking to Talya Bettancourt. It's the only way she could know about the subject of that conversation.

They were probably planning Valen's demise over tea five minutes after he left her Corporate Hill office.

"Whether that is his fault remains to be seen, Zeykala," Hammond cautions.

"And I believe it is and that it's in the company's best interests to seek new leadership."

Zeykala has always coveted the CEO position despite the articles of incorporation forbidding any board member from assuming the role. It's a rule that she has pushed to rewrite since being appointed, arguing that America Incorporated should never be deprived of superb leadership by limiting the pool of qualified candidates. Much to Valen's chagrin, her proposal has been gaining traction.

"We're all rooting for a quick resolution to this incident," Chairman Hammond says, trying to ratchet down the tension. "This exchange volatility and negative publicity of terrorist attacks aren't good for the corporation. *Prima* Bettancourt has insisted on an investigation. We won't be taking any action until that's complete."

Zeykala's face says it all. She wanted a special session to remove Valen tonight. The chairman is taking a risk by holding off, but it's a defensible decision. Unfortunately, if Valen is proved negligent, even Hammond won't protect him.

"Thank you, Chairman Hammond. I look forward to cooperating in any way I can. Now, if you'll excuse me, we're still in the midst of a crisis."

"Of course. Good luck," the chairman says, signing off. Zeykala just scowls in the background.

"That didn't go so well," Fiolla says, frowning.

Valen spins around in his chair. "Sure it did. I got the time I needed to wrap up this crisis before moving to the next. Sometimes, this job is about living to fight another day."

Fiolla shakes her head and exhales. There's no way she can understand. The only people who know how it feels to be the CEO are those who served before him. Everyone else can only guess, assuming they bother trying to understand at all.

"Get another update from the PSS," Valen orders. "With Virtari and the BCS involved, I need to know what's happening in New York directly from them. We need to get this over with and fast."

CHAPTER EIGHTY

INTERCORPEX

Global Network Operations Center
Manhattan Financial District
ICX New York Exchange

Net cash outflow from any stock market usually is less than the reduction in the valuation of that market. Intercorpex is nothing more than an auction house where bids are matched to offers. When patricians dump shares quickly, they only find buyers at lower price points. When there are no buyers, the market crashes. Lyris is staring into that abyss.

"Director," Wyeth says, peering over the divider, "the rate that patricians are pulling money out of the markets is accelerating."

Lyris rubs his chin. "Trading Desk, any luck with a filter yet?"

"None, sir. The legitimate sell orders coming in are so large that we can't distinguish what's real and what isn't."

Lyris checks the board and grimaces. The market is dropping like a rock. If this continues, the life expectancy of Intercorpex can be measured in minutes, not hours.

"Keep working on it. The IGI is plummeting."

"What are we going to do?" Wyeth asks.

"Hope for a miracle."

Lyris signals the communications system to reach Zyree. It takes a few moments to connect, but the director breathes a sigh of relief when it does, even if it's audio-only.

"Zyree, tell me you have news."

"The second raid was a failure. We were ambushed in the passage leading to the station. I lost a man. The PSS lost a lot more."

"We're running out of time. At this rate, the market will collapse in the next half-hour. We can fail over to London, but not until whatever is causing these false trades stops. Do you understand?"

There's a long pause and a sigh. "Yeah, I get it."

"Are you still with the PSS?"

"No, we parted ways. They're attempting another breach down the passageway. I'm with Malkor searching for an alternate route south of the station they claim doesn't exist. We think we may have found a possible way in."

Lyris winces. This isn't a good time for the chief inspector to be the maverick, but he keeps his mouth shut. Like it or not, Zyree is the last hope to stave off disaster.

"What are the odds you can get there in the next thirty minutes?"

"I'll do what I can, but they're entrenched down there. You're going to have to be prepared to do what you have to on your end."

"I can't, Zyree! I'm powerless to stop this attack. The future of the exchange is up to you."

The sound of the silence on the line is deafening. It's also unnerving. Lyris has never felt so exposed or out of control. He prides himself on being ready for any contingency. He could never have predicted this.

"Then you'd best let me get back to work," Zyree says, disconnecting.

"What did he say?" Wyeth asks.

"That he'll do his best."

Wyeth throws up his hands. "His best? Does he not realize what we're up against?"

"He knows. There's one other option we haven't considered. We shut it all down."

"Shut down the exchange?" Wyeth asks after his jaw drops. "The exchange hasn't been closed for even a single day since it opened."

"And we've never faced a crisis like this before."

"Lyris, Intercorpex survived the First and Second Pirate Wars, the Easter Holocaust, patrician espionage that led to the Zurich Canon…. It was our stability that led to Pax Corporaticum. If we go offline, all that unravels."

Pax Corporaticum is a term stolen from Roman antiquity. Executives and patricians use it to describe an era of unprecedented global peace and prosperity under corporate rule. Despite ongoing violence in the Middle East, the rise of Intercorpex is credited for bringing lasting peace to the globe for the first time in over two millennia.

"An offline exchange is a wounded but viable entity," Lyris says, his voice low and gloomy. "A total collapse will kill it for good. It's the last resort if Zyree fails. Brief the department heads. Make sure that the shutdown checklists are handy. I'll give the order when it's necessary."

Wyeth closes his eyes and nods. He just watched the global director of exchange operations put himself on the path to career suicide.

CHAPTER EIGHTY-ONE

REGISTRANT RYKOS

Old Broad Street Station
Lower Manhattan Underground
New York City Municipal Corporation

Haven unlocks my chains, freeing me from the column. He opens Quarren's hand, places the key in it, and closes his fingers around it. I stare at him, not sure what the hell is going on.

"Quarren was releasing you when the rest of us started evacuating. As soon as you were free, you wrested the gun away from him and shot him three times. Understand?"

"What?"

"You are going to be interrogated when you leave here. They will want every detail, including how you escaped," Michele says. "That's your story."

"As if it's believable," Haven mutters.

"It will be if he convinces them. Practice the story in your head. The best lies are the ones the liar believes are true. If you screw it up even a little, they will kill you. It won't matter what your father says."

Nyvar comes rushing back over the tracks to the closest platform and then up the stairs with two other men right behind him. He's worried, and that can't be good. He gulps a deep breath before speaking.

"They're coming. The south maintenance access has been compromised."

"Damn it!" Haven exclaims. "How long until they get here?"

"A couple of minutes, unless they make a wrong turn."

"We have to go now," Michele says. "We'll use the emergency exit and hope for the best."

The hackers don't waste any time descending the stairs to the platform and disappearing around the corner. Nyvar and a few others are right behind them.

Haven removes the magazine from his weapon and strips the remaining bullets out. He then works the slide, sending the remaining bullet popping into the air. He catches and pockets it. Satisfied it's unloaded, he hands me the gun.

"Why are you doing this?"

Haven squints. "Not because I want to. I'd rather put one of those bullets between your eyes. This was Quarren's last request and your 'get out of jail free' card. He liked you."

Michele nods at Haven, and the man makes his way to the platform, leaving me alone with her. She walks over and types a code into a keypad. A series of short beeps follows several long ones.

"You're getting your wish – you're about to be rescued. Tell the men who come that the computers are booby-trapped. You have five minutes to get out of here before the subway station is destroyed."

"Michele, I—"

"Shut up."

She grabs me and kisses me. It's soft and sensual. For a moment, I forget where I am and who she is. Our lips part, and she strokes my face. I can feel the electricity from her fingertips as she caresses my cheek. She steps back and cocks her right arm.

"Take care of yourself up there."

She thrusts her fist forward and lands it hard on my cheek. My vision explodes into a kaleidoscope of bursting colors. I catch the support column in time to stop myself from crashing to the ground. Squinting to restore my vision, I gingerly touch the gash opened below my eye and feel the blood streaming down my cheek. By the time I look back for her, she's already gone.

I stare down at the gun. My father has never let me hold one before. It's heavier than I thought, but the cool steel feels good in my hand. It's an instrument of death, and I'm beginning to understand why people who carry them feel so powerful. It explains a lot about my father.

I walk over to Quarren's body and stand over it. A pang of regret punches at my chest. How much I could have learned from him if I had—

"Drop the weapon!" a man shouts from the platform. I immediately comply.

The man outfitted in thick black body armor doesn't take his rifle off me as he climbs the stairs. A second man approaches from the opposite side of the mezzanine. I don't recognize either of them. Neither is wearing a PSS uniform.

CHAPTER EIGHTY-TWO

INTERCORPEX

Old Broad Street Station
Lower Manhattan Underground
New York City Municipal Corporation

The last thing Zyree expected to see was the son of the chief guardian holding a gun over the body of the presumed leader of Liberteum. He looks shaken. Blood streaming from the fresh wound on his cheek is only now starting to clot. Whatever transpired happened only a few minutes ago.

"Are you okay, Rykos?" Zyree asks.

"I'm okay. Who are you?"

"We're friends of your father."

"Where's Liberteum?" Malkor asks, still sweeping the station for possible threats as Zyree picks up the gun Rykos dropped.

"They went down that way," Teman's son says, nodding toward the platform the opposite way they came from. "They saw you coming and fled. We need to get out of here."

Malkor hurries down the stairs and begins a search of the platform.

"They let you live?" Zyree asks, ignoring Rykos's warning as he tries to figure out how the kid is still breathing.

"They were going to take me with them. Quarren unchained me, and I fought back. I managed to get his gun away from him. Then I…." Rykos hangs his head and stares back at the body.

Zyree's voice stress indicator registers as inconclusive. No matter how far technology progresses, it will never replace human intuition. Rykos may be in shock, but he's also lying. The chief inspector wants to press him for the truth, but there's no time.

He walks over to the table and inspects the old computers and hundred-year-old CRT displays. Even the newer one tuned into AME News predates the collapse. The computers they're using were built by someone using nothing but spare parts.

Somehow, the terrorists have cobbled together a rudimentary system that's threatening the most advanced electronic marketplace ever built.

"Don't," Rykos warns as Zyree reaches for a keyboard. "They rigged it with explosives. That's why I said we need to leave. They're on a timer, but if you tamper with the equipment, it'll trigger the detonation early."

Zyree peeks under the table. An old digital timer is inserted into a homemade plastic explosive. A helpful countdown starts in his peripheral vision, indicating that they have less than four minutes to get out of there. He looks back at the gas mains running through the station. This place will be nothing more than a crater when it blows.

"They didn't leave much time."

"They set it when they saw you coming."

"Of course they did. I hope you can run, Rykos," Zyree says, pointing up the passageway leading off the mezzanine. "Your father is up that way somewhere. Find him and warn him about the explosives. Get him and his men out of there. Go!"

Rykos takes off across the mezzanine and disappears into the blackness of the passageway. Zyree establishes a connection to Lyris while hunting for something to put this setup out of commission. The search ends when he spots the fire ax resting in the corner.

"Zyree! Where the hell have you been?" Lyris barks in his ear.

"Ending the hack. Stand by...."

Zyree aims at the bundle of cables leading down from the ceiling to the equipment at the table. He shears them in half with a hearty swing of the ax. It crashes into the wall and breaks the glass tiles. There's nothing left to do but hold his breath and hope that the station doesn't explode around him. When he opens his eyes, the chief inspector is thrilled that it didn't.

"Zyree! We're at—"

"Fail over to London now!"

"Why? You said the threat is over."

"I don't have time to argue with you, Lyris. Just do it!"

Zyree bolts down the stairs. He sprints over to Malkor, who is checking the frame of a steel door.

"Are you sure they went this way?"

"Not really," Malkor says, "but it's the only one I haven't checked. On three?"

Malkor gives the count. The men burst into the room. LED torchlights embedded on the shoulders of their body armor struggle to illuminate the dingy space. A three-by-three-foot hole is cut into the back wall. Zyree checks his compass: due west.

Malkor shines his light down the access. "Aw, man, tell me this doesn't lead into the basement of—"

"It sure does." Zyree connects a VidLynk as his fellow inspector waits impatiently.

"Time is short, boss. This place is about to blow. Who are you calling?"

"Teman. I need to let him know where we're heading. Worst-case scenario, he'll know where to find our bodies."

"That's reassuring," Malkor moans.

"Zyree, where are you?" Teman almost whispers.

"We're in the station. Liberteum fled, and we found their escape route. Your son is in the passageway leading north out of the station," he explains as fast as possible.

"We're in that passage now!" The sound of relief in his voice is palpable.

"Good. Don't shoot him. Clear everyone out. The station is rigged to explode. It will rupture the gas mains and blow this whole place to hell."

"We turned the utilities off," he argues.

"There's still gas in those pipes. You have about two minutes." Zyree's countdown reads two and a half, but close enough. "I'm going after them. They tunneled out of here to the west. Come find me when this is over."

Zyree disconnects the call and plunges forward to an uncertain fate. Malkor follows him through the access. Neither man has any idea what awaits them in the darkness. They only know what will happen if they stay.

CHAPTER
EIGHTY-THREE

THE PATRICIANS

Keating Family of the Gentez-Majorez Estate
Greenwich Geographic District
Southern Connecticut Municipal Corporation

The helicopter makes a graceful arc to the estate's east before following the shoreline back toward the pad. The boom spins a hundred and eighty degrees as the pilot flares the nose up. Farron likes wild rides. Just watching the machine move like that is making Denali's stomach turn.

They land, and the turbine engine winds down. The elder patrician watches from the back terrace as the rotors slowly stop turning and Farron exits. He smiles as he shakes the pilot's hand.

"Abbot, give me a moment alone with my son, will you?"

"Of course, sir."

The butler departs and returns to the mansion as Farron strides briskly up the walkway from the helipad. He has a bounce in his step, and with good reason.

"Good afternoon, Father."

"It is, isn't it?" Denali asks with a smile. "Intercorpex still hasn't figured out how to fail over to London. The market is crashing."

"I know. The plan worked just as Liberteum expected. They're bringing the entire exchange to its knees with phase two. We couldn't have asked for better results."

"It's an encouraging start, for sure."

Farron studies his father's face. "I thought you'd be happier."

"I'm very pleased."

"Then why aren't you doing cartwheels right now?"

Denali smirks. "Men my age forgo gymnastic pursuits. Take a walk with me, son."

Farron gives him a suspicious glance as they take the east stairs and walk the cobblestone path to the garden. Nothing is blooming in this magnificent space yet. Spring is coming, though, and with it, flowers of every imaginable variety and color.

It's one of the places on this estate that bring Denali peace and serenity during the warmer months.

"Do you know what the Keating name means?"

"I know that it's the Gaelic form of the surname Céitinn."

"That's not what I meant," Denali says with a chuckle. "One of the first things that corporations did when they came to power was eliminate the use of family names. I remember my father talking about how traumatic that was for most people."

"People don't like change," Farron offers, not having the slightest idea why his father is telling him this.

"It was more than just a 'change.' The family unit was the bedrock of humanity for millennia. Up until the end of the last century, the family was the foundation upon which all relationships were built."

Farron shakes his head. "Yes, but it became far less important."

"That's true, but it was still always present. The new society changed the paradigm so that an employee's first obligation had to be to the corporation they served. That didn't sit well with your grandfather and great-grandfather. Our family name had meaning, and they weren't about to give it up."

"I don't understand. Patricians aren't employees; we're owners. The policy wouldn't have applied to us."

The corner of Denali's mouth curls. "That's not the way things started. There was no such thing as patricians in the early days. We may have been among the founders, but we were as much a part of the corporation as the people who worked for it."

Farron nods. "So, what happened?"

"Your great-grandfather insisted on an exemption for our family. At first, he was sneered at and ignored. Then other families like the Bettancourts, Covingtons, and Fontanbleus joined him. Before long, enough powerful families had joined the movement that it couldn't be ignored."

"I appreciate the history lesson, Father," Farron says, stopping. "But is there a point to this story?"

Denali places a hand on his shoulder. "Our family name is everything. It's not a relic of the past but the last vestige of an honored tradition that must always mean something to us. It's where both our hearts and loyalties must always lie."

"I understand."

"Do you?" Denali asks, the smile disappearing from his face. "You've spent a lot of time with that woman from the White House."

"It's what my duty requires."

"Is that all? I've noticed an unsettling change in you, Farron. Are you falling in love with her?"

"No," he says defensively. "I'm playing the part that you asked me to."

"And I must ensure it remains that way. Fiolla is an employee. She works for our staunchest enemy. There's no place for her in our world because she could never understand what it means to be dedicated to a family. Corporate life is all she knows."

Farron feels the knife's edge of those words slice through his soul. There's no point in arguing with his father. Denali Keating is set in his ways, and any objection to his line of thinking is considered rebellious.

"Of course, Father."

"You know, I didn't want to expose you to her brainwashing or the antiquated ideas of Liberteum. I couldn't be certain that they wouldn't corrupt your impressionable mind."

"I assure you, they haven't," Farron says, thrusting his chin out.

"I think they have, at least in part. Their grandiose notions of liberty and freedom are compelling but have no place in our world order. Those days are long past. The people who once clung to those ideas gladly gave up both for the safety and security our world now provides."

"Father, I don't know why you believe I would fall for their propaganda. I tell Liberteum what they need to hear to secure their help. The same with Fiolla. We can't do this without them."

Denali laughs. "We could. It's just better for our cause if they continue being useful idiots."

"Why? If we don't need them, why not keep this in-house?"

"You still have much to learn, Farron. I'm an old man. It will fall to you to shape the future I'm securing. Son, you are going to be the leader of all patricians. Corporations will defer to you. Intercorpex will have no more power than the local supermarket does. I need you to diligently prepare for those responsibilities."

This conversation started weird and has only gotten stranger the deeper they walk into the garden. Farron has never known his father to be open with his feelings.

"I'm not sure what that means," Farron confesses.

"When the time comes, you will end your relationship with Fiolla without question. We will then terminate the Liberteum terrorists together. You cannot let your feelings get in the way of what must be done. Do you understand?"

Farron swallows hard. So, that's what this is about. "Yes, sir."

"Good. Then let us speak no more of this today. A celebration is in order. We have much to be thankful for. Let's head to the study and watch what happens."

Farron follows his father back to the mansion with an uneasy feeling about the future churning his stomach.

CHAPTER EIGHTY-FOUR

INTERCORPEX

Global Network Operations Center
Manhattan Financial District
ICX New York Exchange

The market drops with every one of Lyris's pounding heartbeats. The first corporation will hit zero in a matter of minutes, and the rest will follow. The transfer to London only would have slowed the bleeding but not stopped it. He can only hope that the chief inspector was right about ending the hack.

"Zyree? Zyree?" Lyris shouts before noticing that the link disconnected.

"Director, we're ready to suspend trading operations on your command," the Ops team reports in his earpiece.

"Stand by, Ops. Trading Desk, check incoming on the ITQS for anomalies."

"Roger, Director. Checking...."

Wyeth stares at his boss and outstretches his arms, prompting him to explain. "Zyree told me to fail over to London. He claims he ended the hack."

"Do you trust him?"

Lyris presses his lips together and cocks his head slightly. "Does a snake charmer *really* trust his king cobra? Trading Desk, talk to me."

"Block sizes and bids and asks fit the profile of known good trades, but it's tough to know for sure," the man says, hedging. He doesn't want to be held accountable for giving out bad information.

"Sir, this is Operations. We're still awaiting your shutdown order."

Time is up. Lyris can either go left or go right, but he needs to decide. There's no time for further deliberation or validations. He makes the call.

"Cancel shutdown and stand by for instructions. Wyeth, what was the last status report from London?"

"I checked with them five minutes ago. They're ready for us. Director, if you do this and you're wrong...."

Lyris holds his hand out for him to stop. "All personnel in the NOC, let me have your attention." The communication goes out on the all-hands channel, and the room instantly quiets. "Execute immediate failover to London. Do it now!"

The process to manually transfer exchange operations to the disaster recovery site requires nothing more than typing a series of commands. The devil is in the details. Validating that everything is handed off and communicating correctly is their most important activity.

"Sound off with the status report," Wyeth orders.

"ITQS forwarded."

"London matching engines up and operational."

"Snap quote requests processing."

"Director, the London NOC reports they are assuming control of all market operations," Wyeth reports.

"Keep an open channel with your counterpart over there. I want all eyes glued to the market. If the network so much as drops a packet, I want to know about it."

"You got it. Raimius is trying to reach you via VidLynk," he says, pointing at Lyris's display.

The executive director looks down. That was fast. He was so caught up in the moment that he didn't hear the request chirp in his ear. He closes his eyes and connects the VidLynk. Zyree had better be right.

CHAPTER EIGHTY-FIVE

REGISTRANT RYKOS

Broad Street Station Passageway
Lower Manhattan Underground
New York City Municipal Corporation

I grope along the wall and move as fast as I can. I can't see a damned thing in here. The walls are coated with black grime I can feel rubbing onto my hands. The guy could have given me a torchlight or something. This would go a lot faster, and I need to do just that.

It can't have been more than a minute or two since I left, and I have no idea how far I've gone. It could be a hundred meters or a dozen. Either way, I'm sure it isn't nearly far enough.

My foot catches something, and I tumble forward before losing my balance and faceplanting on the concrete floor. I stumble back to my feet, broken tiles from the walls sliding as I try to regain my footing.

I hear clanging and rattling in the darkness in front of me. The sound carries through the pitch-black veil that surrounds me. That has to be my father and his guardians.

"Father!" I scream at the top of my lungs. "Father!"

I get no response. The noise stops, and all I hear are my footsteps and the crunching beneath me. My heart thunders in my chest, not at the darkness or silence, but the unknown. I have no idea how much farther it is. I don't know how long I have until the timer reaches zero.

My breathing becomes shallow and labored. I try to push forward, but it's harder to keep moving. I...I can't. The panic seizes me and I collapse into a ball on the ground. Maybe it's better for everyone if I don't make it out. I won't have to lie about what happened down here. I won't have to face my father and his questions.

"Rykos? Rykos?" a distant voice cries out.

"I'm here! I'm here."

A light washes across my face. Beams from high-powered torchlights slice through the darkness. They grow closer...closer. The lights are almost upon me until one settles on my face. I shield my eyes, trying to determine who's wielding it.

"Rykos, it's me."

"Father?"

I struggle to my knees as he reaches down to hug me. I've never felt so happy to see him. For the first time in my life, I feel close to him. The sensation doesn't last long as he breaks out of the embrace.

"We have to go. We don't have much time. Can you walk?"

"You…know…about the explosives?" I stammer as he and another man pull me to my feet.

"We have him. Less than thirty seconds," he says, pointing to his ear. "Drop the shields and the people mover and haul ass!"

We start running as well as we can away from the station. Two of his men lead the way, and the torchlights help us avoid the bigger obstacles. We're able to cover more ground in a fraction of the time than I did doing it blindly. Then night turns into day.

I feel the passage shake. A sharp sound precedes a force that almost knocks me over. The passageway quiets before I hear a rumble. It's low at first, then grows increasingly louder and more violent. My father and his men pick up the pace, and I struggle to match them. Guardians in the distance are frantically waving and screaming at us to hurry.

"Faster!" my father screams.

We're not fast enough. The rumble turns into a roar, and a blast of superheated air knocks me to the ground. I cover my head as the force of the explosion rushes past us. A thick cloud of dust envelops us from behind, blotting out the torchlight beams. The air is thick. I gasp for oxygen. I feel the dust and smoke enter my lungs, choking me. I curl into a ball and cough violently. I try to take another breath, searching for breathable air that isn't there. The sound dissipates…the darkness closes in….

CHAPTER
EIGHTY-SIX

INTERCORPEX

Global Network Operations Center
Manhattan Financial District
ICX New York Exchange

This is the angriest Lyris has ever seen the administrator-general. He looks like he's about to explode. It may not matter that Zyree provided him with the perfect cover. At the end of today, Raimius will laud him as a genius or turn him into a scapegoat. A betting man would notice the odds favoring the latter.

"Lyris! You'd better have a damned good explanation for transferring operations to London."

"I do, sir. We received a threat to the build—"

Lyris doesn't get the words out before a massive pressure wave rocks the building. It's the loudest sound anyone here has ever heard. The building shakes violently, knocking everyone standing to the floor. Lyris and Wyeth grab onto the railing surrounding the back of their raised platform and hang on.

The west side windows shatter and fly into the room as the overhead lighting units flicker and switch off. Workstations and displays die when the power cuts out. The room is plunged into darkness. Lyris scrambles under his desk and tucks himself into a ball, covering his ears in a futile attempt to cancel the deafening roar reverberating through the room.

It only muffles the screams…gritty dust permeates the air. He expects the ornate roof of the once-proud trading floor to start collapsing around him. Instead, the noise and shaking finally subside, along with the shrill sounds of genuine terror.

Emergency generators kick in, powering the overhead lighting that wasn't damaged or destroyed. Lyris climbs out from under his desk and joins Wyeth in looking around. It's an eerie sight. He's never seen the displays powered off and the room dark like this. The only sounds are section chiefs checking on their shocked staff members.

"Are you okay, Director?" Wyeth asks, brushing himself off and searching for any signs of apparent injury.

"Yeah, I think so. You?"

"I'm okay, just shaken up."

"Attention in the…." Lyris stops when he realizes that the communications system is offline. "Wyeth, check on the staff."

"I'm on it."

Building security rushes onto the NOC floor and is greeted by Wyeth as he climbs down the stairs. After a brief discussion, they walk through the room, calming everyone and offering medical assistance. It doesn't appear anyone is seriously hurt.

"How did you know?" one of the technicians shouts in Lyris's direction. "How did you know to transfer operations to London right before the blast?"

All conversation in the cavernous room ceases. Many staff begin moving toward his elevated workstation. He doesn't know what to say. What defense would he have for not telling them of the threat that could have cost them their lives? He's about to make up some sort of answer when Wyeth steps forward.

"Because he processed what he knew faster than any computer can. He recognized the imminent threat and made a tough decision that this group executed. It's why Intercorpex isn't facing an outage right now. It's why he's the greatest global director this exchange has ever seen!"

Shouts, whistles, and applause erupt. Lyris waves to his staff before giving Wyeth an appreciative nod. In four eloquent sentences, he gave Lyris everything he needed to protect himself from Raimius's wrath. When the dust settles and subsequent investigations conclude, every report will conclude that Lyris saved the day by ordering the failover. Raimius still has the prerogative to remove him, but the firing would raise eyebrows.

Lyris doesn't know why Wyeth did it. Should the administrator-general pull that trigger, he's in line for a big promotion. That's loyalty that Lyris will have to reward someday.

That will have to wait, though. It will be a long process to put this place back together, and it needs to start immediately. Raimius won't stand for a transfer to London lasting more than a day or two. At some point, he's looking forward to being briefed on what just happened.

CHAPTER EIGHTY-SEVEN

AMERICA, INC.

The White House Situation Room
Corporate Governance District
Washington-Arlington Municipal Corporation

Fiolla is admitted past the BCS agent posted outside and slips into the crowded Situation Room. She assumes a spot along the wall, thrilled that she hasn't had to spend much time here. The room reeks of body odor from flop sweat. That's the pressure of being a corporate executive in a time of crisis.

America Incorporated's exchange proconsul is taking his turn in the spotlight. His anguished face fills the main display as he struggles to find words to answer the latest question. Each exchange-listed company is obligated to appoint a proconsul as a liaison to Intercorpex. Their duties include ensuring a corporation understands and follows exchange rules and acts as an official communication conduit.

"Volatility has dropped significantly over the past few minutes," he informs the executives in the room. His eyes flit to something off-camera for a moment. "Sir, I'm getting word that Intercorpex is transferring trading operations to London."

"Why are they doing that?" Virtari asks.

"I'm not sure, Director. Let me see what I can find out."

The proconsul mutes his mic, and everyone in the Situation Room leans back in their chairs. They've been sitting here for hours. As comfortable as the seats are, backs are getting stiff, and legs are beginning to ache from inactivity.

"Chief Executive Valen, our stock price is still in a freefall," one of Fiolla's colleagues from Corporate Affairs observes.

"Patricians are spooked about the explosions and the unconfirmed reports of issues at Intercorpex," an economic advisor concludes. "Everyone's stock price is taking a beating."

"What are they saying about it?" Director Virtari asks, out of his depth on economic and exchange matters.

"Nothing, either publicly or privately."

"The patricians can arrest the fall," Valen interjects. "Contact Prima Bettancourt and have her convince our largest shareholders to buy chunks of stock. They'll welcome the chance to increase their positions at a steep discount."

"We'll reach out to her, sir."

"Chief Executive Valen," the director of Public Affairs says, "AME News is reporting on Intercorpex's trading problems from outside the exchange on Wall Street."

"Better late than never. Put it on a secondary display."

The reporter stands in front of the main entrance of their Wall Street facility. The streets are emptier than an hour ago. One of Valen's aides turns the volume up.

"There is still no word from Intercorpex as to the extent or cause of the trading problems responsible for today's record volatility. The Intercorporational Index is plummeting, down over twenty-eight hundred points and continuing to fall. Corporations across the globe are—"

A bright flash erupts behind the reporter, who starts to turn before the picture goes black. A couple of seconds later, the broadcast cuts back to the anchor desk.

"We seem to have lost our feed from Wall Street," the AME News anchor stammers, adlibbing instead of reading off the prompter. "We will bring you the rest of the report as soon as we get it back."

"Chief Executive Valen, there has been a massive explosion on Wall Street, just outside Intercorpex," Director Virtari says.

"Was it a truck bomb?"

"Unknown at this time."

"Then find out! Immediately!"

Valen gives Fiolla an apprehensive look that mirrors hers. Many things can be hidden from the eyes of the employees. Explosions aren't one of them. All the work to pivot the narrative back to Intercorpex is for nothing if New York City keeps blowing up.

CHAPTER EIGHTY-EIGHT

INTERCORPEX

Emergency Field Trauma Center
North of Wall Street
New York City Municipal Corporation

Teman lies on one of the hundred triage cots lined up on an office building patio just north of Pine Street. It's nothing more than a thin, plastic-lined mattress on a collapsible aluminum frame, but it beats the hell out of lying on cold concrete. Most of the employees being treated suffer cuts from flying glass or broken bones from the blast.

"You look like hell," Zyree says as he walks over to Teman.

"I'm no worse for wear. Just some bumps and bruises and a little smoke inhalation. How are you?" Teman asks, noticing his bandaged hand.

"The usual symptoms from barely surviving a massive explosion. And junior over there?" Zyree asks, nodding over at Rykos. He's still wearing his oxygen mask.

"The same. We'll get transported to the medical center once they finish moving the urgent cases."

Rykos won't complain about the triage cot. It must feel great compared to what he's been subjected to over the past couple of days. His wrists are raw from his chains, and he looks hypothermic. Comfort is not a priority for Liberteum.

"At least it's going to be a nice night," Zyree observes, breathing in the cool air and looking at the darkening sky as the last hints of sun glint off the skyscrapers. "What happened in the passage?"

Teman explains how he met up with Rykos and how the blast caught them before exiting the passageway. Fortunately, fire safety and rescue reached them before they succumbed to the smoke.

"You were lucky."

"Yeah, lucky. The BCS has temporarily assumed city-wide control. From what I've heard, there isn't much left of the station to investigate."

"Nothing but a smoldering crater."

"One fewer place for urches to hide, I guess," Teman says, searching for a silver lining. "You know for sure that Liberteum escaped?"

"Most of them," he says, looking over at Rykos. "They left right before I got there. I uploaded the body armor video to the RTCC. They'll be able to confirm it, but the dead man was Quarren. Your son killed the leader of Liberteum."

"That will make for an interesting discussion with my wife."

"I'm surprised she isn't here," Zyree observes, looking around the sea of humanity on stretchers and cots.

"The BCS cordoned off the area. I can't get her in. She'll meet us at the medical center. I have a question for you. How did you get into the station?"

Zyree explains that they found a maintenance access that led to a train tunnel that once served a now-defunct line across the East River. That led to the station.

"How many times were you told there was no access from that direction?" Teman says with a slight chuckle. "I'm glad you never accept information at face value. Thank you for saving my son's life."

"Are you guys talking about me?" he asks, removing his oxygen mask.

"We are. Rykos, this is Chief Inspector Zyree of Intercorpex Security."

"We've met, although I barely recognize you without your costume on."

Zyree walks over and shakes his hand with his bandaged one. "It's a brave thing you did down there, Rykos. You must get that from your father."

"Thanks," he says meekly.

"What's next for you?" Zyree asks the chief guardian.

"I don't know. Liberteum is still somewhere in this city, and I plan on tracking them down. They need to answer for what they did today."

"You may have the easy task, Teman. I have to explain to my superiors that the instigators of the largest terrorist attack the exchange has ever witnessed escaped through the subbasement of our own building."

After sending Rykos out through the passageway, Zyree and Malkor pursued the terrorists through a series of voids. They were expecting an ambush that never materialized. They made it into the subbasement of the Wall Street NOC when the explosion ended the pursuit.

"Ouch."

"Yeah, ouch. My orders were to help track down Liberteum. You may be seeing more of me."

"Well, Zyree, I hope we finish that job before you get the chance."

"I'll second that, Chief Guardian."

"Chief Inspector?"

"Yes, Rykos?"

"Thank you. And you too, father. I'm sorry that I... For everything."

Teman nods at his son. "We have a lot to talk about, Rykos."

"I know."

"You're going to be interviewed by my guardians and BCS agents again and again. They're going to want to know everything that happened while you were down there."

"I understand."

"Intercorpex Security will likely want to talk to you as well. Rykos, is there anything you need to tell us before that happens?" Zyree asks.

Teman stares at Zyree and looks like he wants to protest. Instead, he shifts his gaze to his son. The chief guardian wants to believe his son didn't help them escape the Chinatown raid. He wants to think that he wasn't involved in anything that happened. Zyree does, too, but the footage spins a different story.

"Like what? They took me as a hostage when the raid started. They threatened to kill me if I didn't play along. Somehow, they learned who I was and planned on ransoming me later. When I saw an opportunity to escape, I took it."

The chief guardian looks at Zyree, who nods at him. He has seen how effectively Zyree's biocomputer identifies deceit, and the confirmation seems to have put him at ease.

The chief inspector is grateful that Teman doesn't have this capability. Almost nothing Rykos said was truthful.

"*Veritatem et honorem,*" Zyree says, placing his fist over his heart.

"*Fratres in armis,*" Teman replies with a solemn nod, using the appropriate ICX security response. "I'll see you around."

CHAPTER

EIGHTY-NINE

AMERICA, INC.

The White House
Corporate Governance District
Washington-Arlington Municipal Corporation

The walls of the Oval Office are lined with executives standing out of view of the lone camera trained on Chief Executive Valen. He sits behind his desk, exuding the confidence employees expect from their corporate leader. It's the reassurance that every employee and patrician needs to see right now.

"Good evening, my fellow employees. As many of you have undoubtedly heard, a heinous terrorist group detonated a series of explosions in New York earlier today that caused considerable damage and loss of life," Valen reads from the teleprompter.

"These attacks disrupted one of our proudest cities and murdered your fellow employees in the name of advancing a bankrupt cause and seeking the return of a failed political ideology. The terrorists go by the name 'Liberteum,' but liberty for all is not their goal. Their real objective is to satiate their hatred for our ideals and beliefs. They are nothing more than harbingers of death using brutal tactics from long-past and happily forgotten times.

"This attack was not just on the employees of New York or our benevolent corporation. It was an attempt to destroy our way of life because of their inability to conform to it."

There's disgust in Valen's voice, but that's not what makes the line effective. It was the slight lean forward and the squint of his eyes...all nonverbal language that punctuated his words. He is not putting on an act for the camera – he believes every word he's saying.

"These men resent what you have. Liberteum would instead return to a time when people struggled to make ends meet and often failed. They resent where you live, preferring to see the homeless choke our streets in wasted lives spent in squalor and despair. The terrorists resent your success and long for an age of rampant unemployment, unequal wages, and financial struggle.

"Liberteum justifies these beliefs by following the corrupt example of political leaders who marched us into a global economic calamity. They would bring further violence and misery to the world while trampling the livelihood of the masses. They resent the corporatist society that arose from the ashes left by fires their heroes ignited. They believe the system is flawed and must be destroyed, only they have nothing to replace it with. They really preach anarchy, and anyone who does not subscribe to their twisted ideology must be eradicated.

"They showed us the violent face of their bloody quest today. The men and women of New York's Public Safety and Security rose to the occasion in confronting them. Many guardians paid with their lives. As a result of their bravery and courage, the terrorist attack did not cause panic or cripple the corporation. It did not, and will not, alter our way of life.

"Through all the death and destruction, there will be a brighter tomorrow. I am pleased to report that the man who led these monstrous attacks perished at the hands of a young registrant. Rykos, the son of New York City's chief guardian, was kidnapped before the attacks occurred as leverage to stop the guardians from responding with force.

"It didn't work. The guardians did their duty, and Rykos displayed incredible bravery by single-handedly killing the leader of Liberteum. The mastermind of these attacks is dead, and now we will destroy the few leaderless terrorists who remain.

"I have directed Public Safety and Security in New York to work alongside the Bureau of Corporate Security to eliminate any remaining terrorists and urches from whom they draw their support. It is my pledge as your CEO that these attacks will not continue. We will never cower in the face of violence nor bow to their perverse philosophy.

"When the sun rises tomorrow, I expect every employee to attend work as normal. Through the various divisions of this company, I will report back to you on our progress. Until then, good night, America Incorporated, and may all your days be productive."

"And we're out," the producer says from next to the camera. "Thank you, sir."

Valen rises from his desk in the Oval Office and removes the microphone pinned to his tunic. He's joined by employee affairs executives. "Make sure that gets replayed on AME News and during the seven o'clock hour tomorrow."

"Of course, sir. We'll see to it."

"Nice speech, sir," Fiolla says, walking up to him as a hair and makeup technician wipes his face. "It was an inspiring message."

"They're only words, Fiolla. They'll placate our employees, but the patricians will demand action and board members already want my head on a pike."

"Words have power, sir. Look at the market. You finished the broadcast three minutes ago, and our stock is already climbing in Frankfurt. We'll continue that trend when New York trading reopens."

"Assuming it opens," he laments, leading Fiolla by the arm away from the prying ears of executives and staffers still in the Oval Office. "Has Intercorpex made any statements about their operations being disrupted?"

"Only the one released a couple of hours ago. I don't expect them to say much more. They don't gain anything by announcing the actual impact."

Intercorpex released a statement on the GlobalNet admitting the explosions disrupted some non-critical circuits and that the destruction of the old subway station was meant to cripple the exchange. They applauded the efforts of their internal security and the PSS for thwarting the attack long enough to fail over to their disaster recovery site. While they admitted it was a rough market day in New York, they blamed the high volume and volatility on the day's events and not a problem with their trading system.

"No, you're right, they won't. The battle will be fought in the shadows."

"I'm not sure I know what you mean," Fiolla says, too new to the game to understand. She may know the players, but no one has taught her the rules yet.

"It's the way the world works. China, Russia, and other major corporations will use propaganda to reduce our market share in key industries. They'll send sales diplomats into the field to persuade corporations to nullify or curtail trade agreements. Intercorpex will use what happened to enhance its power over the corporations and the patricians. Worst of all, Talya Bettancourt will use every ounce of influence she has to swing the necessary votes to oust me. She thinks I failed to deliver on my promise."

"The leader of Liberteum was killed. That's something," Fiolla offers.

"Yes, but it's not enough. Eliminating Liberteum must be our top priority."

"I understand, sir. Is this something the BCS will run with?"

"No," Valen says after reflecting for a moment. "They believe a change in leadership is prudent. Virtari wants a CEO he can control. They'll drag their feet, hoping the board makes a move. I want the PSS spearheading the effort to find Liberteum in New York."

"I understand, sir. I will do whatever I can to assist."

"I appreciate that, Fiolla. Start by propping up Registrant Rykos. I want him recognized with a corporate award for his bravery."

Fiolla fidgets. "Sir, just so you are aware, there are unanswered questions surrounding his kidnapping."

"Not anymore. He's a hero now – a young registrant who stood up to evil and helped us win a battle. That's the message I want our subsidiaries and AME News pushing."

"Consider it done," Fiolla says with a nod. "Anything else?"

"I'm going to need your help now more than ever," Valen says. "I only wish I had more time to prepare you for what we're going to face next. Liberteum's attacks may be over, but the real battle is just beginning."

CHAPTER NINETY

THE PATRICIANS

Keating Family of the Gentez-Majorez Estate
Greenwich Geographic District
Southern Connecticut Municipal Corporation

Denali grins and moves his bishop forward. Checkmate in eleven moves, his ass. Chess is the ultimate strategy game. It requires vision, understanding your opponent's playstyle, and how to best position your pieces to control the board. It also requires a degree of unpredictability because your opponent also knows what winning requires.

Shalius moves the lit piece to the lit square and stares at the camera. "You're risking everything."

"Are we still talking about chess?" Denali asks, expecting this conversation.

"You are the head of one of the wealthiest families on the planet. You have the best of everything and want for nothing. Why do this?"

Denali leans back. It's not like he hasn't had this conversation before. "Why did you agree to help? Or the others, for that matter? It's because you know what's coming, same as I do."

"You are an undeniable visionary, Denali. That doesn't mean you can see the future."

"No, but I can see the past – the real past, not what the corporations cooked up in the history books to absolve them of any blame for the collapse of society. Governments may have driven the world off a cliff, but the politicians who led them were bought and paid for with corporate dollars."

Shalius steeples his hands in front of his lips. "Only a handful of people on Earth still believe that."

"It doesn't make it less true."

It's one of the slickest examples of mass brainwashing in human history. A scared global population worshipped corporations for leading them out of the darkness. Two generations later, none of them realize that those same corporations led them into it to begin with.

"And I agree with you, but you didn't answer my question," Shalius observes, making a move. "Why do this now? Why not twenty years ago when we were both younger?"

"Maybe I was still optimistic that it wouldn't come to this," Denali says, countering the move and staring at the board. "Look at our sons. Do you believe Narik and Farron have what it takes to maintain our empires?"

"No previous generation thinks the next is worthy."

"Exactly. My legacy must be more than expanding my family empire. It must be safeguarding it."

The two patricians make a series of moves in silence. Denali scans the display for any telltale signs that Shalius expects what's coming. He doesn't.

"We could lose everything, Denali. Everything we have worked for."

"If Intercorpex continues accumulating power unopposed, we will anyway. Raimius is a tyrant. He wants to consolidate control over us…over everything. That is to be his legacy."

"And you think that Lyris will be any different?"

"I think Lyris will be…useful," Denali says, seeing his opportunity.

"He won't play along."

"He doesn't need to, for long at least."

Denali knows that his offer is irresistible to a man like Lyris. His position as director of global exchange operations is at the top of the ladder, and he's still a young man filled with ambition. He not only thinks that he would do a better job than Raimius, he knows it in his heart. Denali plans on leveraging that.

"What about corporations and their employees?"

"Corporations exist to serve our interests. They need to be reminded of that. As for employees, what difference does it make so long as their needs are provided for?"

Denali masks his moves by sacrificing a useless pawn. Shalius thinks this is the main attack and is shifting his pieces to counter it. How wrong he is.

"I understand why you keep your plans quiet, Denali, but the others might not be so understanding."

"All will be revealed in time. Our peers must learn the value of patience."

Shalius scoffs. "Our friends value money and power, nothing more. What if your plan doesn't work?"

"It will."

"How do you know?"

Denali beams at the camera and moves his rook. "Checkmate."

Shalius stares at the board, baffled. Even though the board declares a winner, he doesn't believe his own eyes. "What the...?"

"Because, my old friend, like you, they won't see it coming until it's too late."

CHAPTER
NINETY-ONE
INTERCORPEX

ICX Headquarters
Midtown Manhattan Geographic District
New York City Municipal Corporation

In the spirit of the same commendations corporations bestow upon their deserving executives for exemplary service, Intercorpex created awards to accomplish the same goal. While many are for merit or presented to honor an employee for years of service, a couple of them reward remarkable individual actions on behalf of the exchange. The most prestigious of them is the most coveted.

"For his exemplary conduct in the face of a disastrous situation, under my authority on this eleventh day of April in the year 2088, Lyris, Director of Global Exchange Operations, is bestowed the Intercorpex Service Cross. With this prestigious honor comes the future promise of ascension into the ranks of the *gentez-minorez* following his release from exchange duties. I certainly don't think that will be any time soon."

The assembled crowd in the lobby chuckles and applauds as Raimius pulls the medal off of the velvet-lined tray. Lyris was surprised to hear he would receive such a distinguished award. Raimius harbors considerable animosity toward his executive director, so approving this honor is out of character.

"Congratulations," Raimius whispers as he hangs the hefty cross around Lyris's neck. "This is how I reward loyalty. You don't want to learn how I punish disloyalty."

The men shake hands, and he turns to the intercorporational media and audience members. There are familiar faces among the distinguished visitors seated in front of the platform. Many are patricians of the *gentez-majorez* and corporate proconsuls. Lyris's gaze stops on Denali Keating, and the patrician gives him a slight nod.

The pictures complete, Raimius moves back to the podium without another word. "It gives me great pleasure to present this next award, as it's the first time it's ever been bestowed. For his remarkable courage and valor, under my authority on this eleventh day of April in the year 2088, Zyree, Chief Inspector of Exchange Security, is awarded the Intercorpex Medal of Gallantry."

Many patricians in attendance believe Zyree deserves the medal Lyris is wearing. They aren't aware of the official internal Intercorpex account of the incident. In the interest of wrapping up the investigation, nobody asked in-depth questions or clarified disparities. Everyone wants to move on from the attack that almost destroyed the exchange. As a result, Lyris gets accolades for saving Intercorpex and Zyree only for battling Liberteum.

"You are a credit to your uniform, Zyree," Raimius says, hanging around his neck the gold medal featuring a knight jousting.

"Thank you, sir. It's an incredible honor."

"I hope I can count on you to answer the call if ever needed again."

"It's an honor and a privilege to serve, sir."

Raimius smiles and moves back to the podium. "Ladies and gentlemen, distinguished guests, and exchange employees, I present your honorees."

Lyris and Zyree get a standing ovation. Once it subsides, Raimius says a few more words before concluding the ceremony and inviting the attendees to a reception in the garden. It's the perfect place for it now that spring is arriving in New York.

A string quartet provides the music. The food, all gourmet dishes catering to patricians' tastes, is served by the best restaurants in New York. Most conversations amount to kissing up to or currying favor with the patricians. For Raimius, it's a chance to repair Intercorpex's reputation with the modern elite.

The same effort isn't being expended on America Incorporated. The relationship with their host corporation has turned frosty, if not frigid. A war of words is playing out in the corporate media, and despite numerous overtures from Chief Executive Valen to meet in person, Raimius won't agree to a summit. That's politics. Zyree has other concerns.

"*Veritatem et honorem*," Malkor says, decked out in his best dress uniform while holding a plate full of appetizers.

"*Fratres in armis*," Zyree responds with his fist over his own heart.

"I just received a special communication from Zurich."

"Is it what I think it is?"

"The lab results from forensics."

"It's about damn time."

Zyree syncs his biocomp with Malkor's, and the file gets transferred. It's more cloak and dagger than was probably necessary, but the chief inspector wanted to keep this request quiet. That includes not making it himself, which is why Malkor did it for him.

"Slick move hiding the swab on your bandage when you shook the kid's hand. Don't tell me – let me guess. There's no GSR," the junior inspector says between bites as Zyree scans the file.

"Not a speck of gunshot residue. Rykos didn't fire that gun."

Zyree's instincts were right. Rykos lied to him in that station and again in the triage area after the explosion. He didn't kill Quarren. His whole story is a lie, and executives at the White House bought it all.

"This information stays between us," Zyree says.

"Why? The kid lied. You don't think America Incorporated will care?"

"Employees will, but executives will bury it. It doesn't fit their corporate hero narrative. He's being marketed as the man who killed the dangerous leader of a terrorist organization. There's no way the truth comes out now."

"So, what are we going to do with it?" he asks. Malkor has never been a strategic thinker. He's a good man and a great inspector but never grasps the political implications of what they do.

"Nothing. I got the information I wanted and a possible connection into Liberteum."

Teman's worst fears will eventually be realized. Rykos was involved with them, somehow, which means they may contact him again. When that happens, Zyree plans to be ready.

"I'm not sure what you mean," Malkor says, shoving an oversized shrimp into his mouth.

"Don't worry about it. I'm getting out of this city for a while. I don't want to give Lyris any more opportunities to stab me in the back."

"Then watch your six," Malkor warns before stepping off in the other direction. He knows when to beat a hasty retreat.

"Congratulations, Zyree," Lyris says, admiring the medal around his neck. "I see you shaved for the occasion."

"I found my razor yesterday. Is that your way of saying 'thank you?'"

"You were lucky. That's it. Raimius may not recognize that, but I do. I would have stripped you of your title and responsibilities if I were him."

Zyree's voice stress indicator indicates that his statement is truthful. He smirks. Yeah, no kidding.

"I guess I should continue being thankful that you aren't running things."

"You never know. Someday, I might be. Until then, relish being the big hero. I hope there's never a reason for me to see you on Wall Street again."

"Or else what?" Zyree challenges.

The corner of Lyris's mouth turns up, and he brushes past him. Zyree is about to say something snarky when a VidLynk request is received, voice only. The caller identification that pops up in his peripheral vision says it's the commissioner-general of corporate security.

"*Veritatem et honorem,* Commissioner-General Jurghen."

"It's not your boss, and don't say my name. Nobody can know we're having this conversation. Get someplace quiet," Ortan demands.

"I already am. You routed the call to look like it originated in Zurich?"

"I could make it look like God himself was dropping you a VidLynk if I wanted to. This isn't over, Zyree."

"Okay, what do you have?"

"Let's call it a big piece of the puzzle." He's amused with himself. Zyree isn't.

"I'm not in the mood for games. What is it?"

"Not now. We need to speak in person. How soon can you get to Iceland?"

"I'll mop things up here and then I'm due to depart for Zurich next week."

"Good. Connect through Keflavik. Spend the night in Reykjavik. I will summon you to stop at the data center before you return to the airport for your flight to the SEU."

"All right. Is there anything you can tell me now?"

There's an extra beat of silence on the line. Zyree can almost feel Ortan leaning closer as he lowers his voice. "Have you ever heard of a black swan?"

The chief inspector immediately thinks of the bird, but that's not what Ortan is referring to. The definition pops up on his contact and he scans it.

A black swan event is a financial metaphor for a rare, unpredictable event (or series of events) that comes as a surprise, has severe consequences, and is often inappropriately rationalized after the fact with the benefit of hindsight.

"I am now. So what?"

"This is one. Just get up here."

"Seriously? That's all you can tell me? Nothing more?"

A long pause punctuates the other end of the connection. He wants desperately to say something, but balks. Whatever this is must be juicy. He's even more paranoid than usual.

"Just that you're not going to like it."

CHAPTER NINETY-TWO

REGISTRANT RYKOS

Corporate History Module 351-B-2
Dinsmore Executive Preparatory Academy
New York City Municipal Corporation

Celebrity is not something valued in the corporate world. Fame and notoriety get measured by productivity, not how well you sing or how many times you can score against an opponent in some sporting endeavor. Regardless, I've become one since my abduction.

It's strange to get words of congratulations from my peers. Registrants I've never spoken to now treat me like a lifelong friend. Girls who never once looked in my direction drool over me like I'm a dessert tray at an upscale restaurant. Even the faculty, who once held nothing but contempt for me, cozy up to their new favorite pupil.

That's a good thing since I have little chance of catching up on my modules. Not that it matters since an Ivy League education and admittance into the executive ranks of America Incorporated are now a reality. Letters arrive on my tablet every day from university presidents begging me to choose their schools. Yale, Princeton, Harvard... all of them.

I enter my Corporate History module and take a seat. I hope Balin is here today, but when the tone sounds signaling the start of instruction, he's nowhere to be found.

"Where's Balin?" I ask the registrant behind me.

"You haven't heard? He was sent to finish his studies at a security preparatory school."

"What?"

"They withdrew him from Dinsmore. I heard he's going to West Point."

I can't get my head around that. Balin is the last registrant who would be tapped for security service duty. How could that happen?

"He's going to be a BCS agent?"

"A lot changed since you were abducted." No kidding. I know my life will never be the same.

"It's great to see you back in your seat, Registrant Rykos," Instructor Shaef says with an almost annoying giddiness after he walks in.

"Thank you, sir. It's good to be back."

"I know you probably don't want to talk about your experiences, but if there is anything you can share, I'm sure your peers would love to hear it."

"Don't get abducted by terrorists," I say, earning laughter from the room.

The interrogation from the BCS was worse than my time as a hostage. I don't think I was convincing, but the narrative changed in the days following Valen's speech. Lines of questioning were dropped. In the end, they accepted my explanation of events and concluded I killed the leader of Liberteum. It's made me a corporational hero.

I know the Aristotle system is listening intently, and anything I say that conflicts with that narrative will earn me a trip downtown. Lost is the truth: Quarren was right. I was freer down there than I am up here.

"Your rescue was traumatizing, I'm sure."

"It was better than being chained to a column and beaten."

The physical recovery has been easier than my psychological healing. I'm recovering from broken ribs and a concussion. Those will heal. The tug-of-war for my mind between the ideals of Liberteum and propaganda from America Incorporated is another matter.

"What was it like being there?" one of my peers up front asks.

"Terrifying. I felt powerless, at least until the very end." All of that is true at least.

"They killed all those people. It could have been worse had your father not cleared the streets before they blew up the old station," Shaef says.

Yeah, my hero father…the man who rescued me from the tunnel and then threw me to the wolves. The BCS spent days extracting information from me. I was debriefed while at the hospital, but that was nothing compared to what I was subjected to right under his nose at One Guardian Plaza.

"I'm sorry, I'm really not allowed to discuss it further," I say, hoping to end the questioning.

"Well, I speak for the entire faculty when I tell you we're happy you're back with us unharmed," Shaef says.

I wish the same could be said for my father. Mother spent every possible moment at my side. My father has treated me like a liability. It's likely he knows the truth about the escape from the raid and hasn't said anything. He doesn't need to.

Now I understand what Quarren meant when he said I should watch what the corporation does. The official story doesn't match what happened that day. Intercorpex refutes reports that Liberteum was manipulating the exchange. America

Incorporated claims I killed the group's leader, and that the threat is mostly neutralized. Nobody has said anything about how the "kidnapping" happened in the first place. Everyone is telling half-truths or complete fabrications. If they could lie without effort about this, it stands to reason they don't tell the truth about anything.

Employees just accept without question what they're told. Everyone has lost the ability to be inquisitive or think critically. That was why Michele brought me underground after the rave. My single act of defiance convinced her I was different.

Somehow, I feel her purpose was more than that. I'm alive and back at school because that's the way Quarren wanted it. In my heart, I know that it wasn't the intended outcome. Quarren's plan, or Michele's since she's the real leader of Liberteum, had something else in store for me.

America Incorporated might think they succeeded in thwarting a dangerous group of terrorists. Intercorpex may feel like they prevailed. The patricians of the world may play their politics to advance themselves, but I wonder how many of them realize that the threat remains. Through all of this, there is one truth I can cling to: The fight for the future of humanity is only just beginning.

A NOTE FROM THE AUTHOR

America, Inc. was initially published in 2015 and explored one fundamental question: what would happen if corporations ruled the world? It was the first volume of the six that I expected to need to tell the story of the struggle between Liberteum, Intercorpex, and America Incorporated. I went in with high expectations for the saga…that were never met.

I read the reviews and listened to the feedback about the story and how it was told. In hindsight, the multiple first-person POV format didn't work. I enjoy writing characters in the first person so a reader can get a feel for their thought processes. This saga is character-driven, meaning their decisions guide the plot, not vice-versa.

The downside is that it is difficult to relay complex subject matter. The world I built is very different from the one we live in, requiring explanation. Much of that needs to be done as dialogue, and the story becomes bloated.

This rewrite sought to correct that problem. It now focuses the first person narrative on Rykos, who was always the key to the story. I sincerely hope that you found this new version compelling.

What transpires in this novel and throughout this series is not meant to be predictive. During the re-write, I was shocked about how many things have come to fruition since I first authored this in 2015. Despite offering no claims of having Nostradamus-like abilities, The America, Inc. Saga is meant to be a cautionary tale. The circumstances leading to the global calamity that plunges the world into chaos are issues we are dealing with today: substantial national debts, ineffectual leaders, massive trade imbalances, struggling currencies, volatile stock, commodities, and futures markets, and gigantic multinational corporations.

Mix that with a decaying social order, and those challenges create a perfect storm that brings an end to governing as we know it. It will be left to the readers to decide whether the corporations who assumed power in this series are ultimately benevolent or sinister. They certainly have flashes of both. Liberteum is a similar conundrum. The fact that no character or organization is strictly good or evil in these novels makes them interesting and compelling. I hope you agree.

ACKNOWLEDGMENTS

I write novels that I hope are entertaining to read and thought-provoking. I have challenged my readers to learn something from each book while getting swept up in the stories. For those who chose to spend time reading what pours out of my imagination, you will forever have my sincerest thanks. Without you, none of this is possible.

To Michele, thank you for all your love and support and for the sacrifices you make to let me dedicate myself to writing. I know it can be frustrating and annoying, and simple words can never capture the depth of my appreciation.

My father was always an inspiration in my life. My relationship with him could be contentious, but it was far better than what Rykos and Teman share. He taught me the value of balance. He worked hard to ensure the family had a roof over our heads and food on the table but still spent time with my sister and me. I lost him to cancer a few years ago. I know he is always with me every step of the way.

To my mother Nancy and my sister Kristina, you are the best family someone could ask for. Thank you for always being there for me.

The rebirth and new direction of this series need a guiding hand. Thank you to Mike Waitz at Sticks and Stones Editing for his diligent editing effort to make this story the best it could be. I look forward to working with him for the duration of this saga and beyond.

A special thanks also to JD&J Book Cover Design for the magnificent cover. I hoped to preserve the elements I liked from the original America, Inc. design and meld it with something new and improved. Dave succeeded and transformed the new cover into something extraordinary.

ABOUT THE AUTHOR

Mikael Carlson is the award-winning author of the novel *The iCandidate* and the Michael Bennit Series of political dramas. He also has written two other ongoing series: Tierra Campos Thrillers and Watchtower Thrillers. His newest series, America, Inc., is a retelling of the futuristic dystopian Black Swan Saga that serves as a cautionary tale of life in a world following a global economic collapse.

A retired veteran of the Rhode Island Army National Guard and United States Army, he deployed twice in support of military operations during the Global War on Terror. Mikael has served in the field artillery, infantry, and in support of special operations units during his career on active duty at Fort Bragg and in the Army National Guard.

A proud U.S. Army Paratrooper, he conducted over fifty airborne operations following the completion of jump school at Fort Benning in 1998. Since then, he has trained with the militaries of countless foreign nations.

Mikael earned a Master of Arts in American History in 2010 and graduated with a B.S. in International Business from Marist College in 1996.

He was raised in New Milford, Connecticut, and currently lives in nearby Danbury.